THE FIRST COLLECTION:

The Miner Books
BOOKS
1, 2 and 3

By S.E. McKenzie

ISBN-13: 1772810320

CONTENTS

The Miner:
Book 1

Rescuing
Ginger Goodwin

Chapter 1:
The Pitville Mine Disaster

In-Reach entry, Part 1, LOG #1 by Christina Watson (Accounting Assistant to Alex Coaltonstone), Sunday December 22, 2030 written around 10:00 AM:

This morning's explosion occurred at 5:20 AM, twenty minutes after the early morning shift was supposed to begin.

As soon as I heard the siren I rushed to the office. I drove through the thick fog, swerving to the right and to the left trying to dodge people as they dashed in front of my car. Some people were still in their nightwear and others were dressed in their too tight militia uniforms. Everyone seemed to be in shock, even the ones who were dressed to kill.

The people rushing about everywhere were almost invisible.

There were all kinds of people running toward and away from Mine Five.

I struggled to keep my eyes focused on the road as I drove by the red flames that were shooting out of the ventilation shaft; knowing that Ginger Goodwin, the love of my life, was trapped below in that fiery pit.

It has been five hours, and I still haven't heard anything from anyone, and whenever I phone Control Center, I feel as if I am being pushed away and it is infuriating that they won't tell me anything.

I am getting tons of email from the morning-crew. No

sooner do I finish reading one email another email arrives almost repeating what the previous one said; but no one can tell me how they are going to bring Ginger back to me.

People are saying that Ginger's quick thinking saved the morning crew but no one can tell me how they are planning to save Ginger from that fiery pit.

Ginger always stuck to his principles and look where it got him.

Ginger refused to certify this pre-morning's shift inspection and ignored the whistle-boss bot 5C as it whistled non-stop demanding that the shift begin.

Ginger also ignored James Coaltonstone as he too demanded that the shift begin without delay. So typical of Don Bell, the lead safety manager for Mine Five, to remain silent while Ginger takes all the heat.

As the assistant mine safety technician, it is up to Ginger to decide if the mine is safe, and that decision has to be an independent one.

I heard that James Coaltonstone snarled at everyone while they were waiting at the mine entrance, showing his rotting teeth and calling Ginger anally retentive.

Ginger was 1,200 feet underground in Mine Five as he stood by his principles and refused to let the shift start until in his heart he believed that the mine was safe.

And then at 5:20 A.M. the mine blew up.

After the explosion the miners were loaded onto the buses and were driven to the miners' cafeteria that is located in the same administrative building where I work. The ten mile distance between the mine and the administration building is supposed to facilitate discipline but I think the distance just emphasizes the divide between us and the bosses.

I have been sitting here all morning feeling stunned.

End of In-Reach entry, Part 1, LOG #1 by Christina Watson (Accounting Assistant to Alex Coaltonstone).

Chapter 2:
A Boom for Pitville

Sunday December 22nd, 2030 around 12: 00 PM, Mayor Stern's Office:

"This informal emergency meeting is now in session. I am not sure where to start, so much has happened," Mayor Stern explained to James Coaltonstone, John Bell, and Don Bell and to the city clerk Susan Jones as they were all staring at their computer screens. Mayor Stern also kept his eyes locked onto his computer screen making it easier for everyone in the room to avoid eye contact.

"First things' first; we must put out the fire," John Bell, head of mine security, stressed.

"We could pump water into the mine and suppress the fire, but then the water would mix with the acid water and could leak out into surrounding aquifers and sooner or later reach Pitville's ground water," Don Bell, Ginger Goodwin's supervisor, and head of mine safety, warned.

"If the ground water becomes polluted, I could lose the next election," Mayor Stern interjected without making eye contact, "we need a plan with less risk."

"Every plan will have an element of risk," John Bell explained. "We are trying to plan our way out of a mine disaster! We need to consider the risk involved if we do nothing."

"And if we do nothing? Mayor Stern asked.

"If we do nothing then the fire grows out of control. The

3

seams could catch fire and worst case scenario the fire could reach our coal reserves under Stonely Mountain," Don Bell replied.

"We have no options. We must control the spread of the fire. We could smother the fire by sealing the mine," John Bell suggested, "but then it would be almost impossible to rescue Ginger Goodwin before he runs out of air," John Bell added as he reviewed the various reports and charts which disappeared after appearing for a short moment on his screen.

"My guess is that Goodwin has been incinerated. I know it is an awful thing to say, but that was probably the most painless way to go," James Coaltonstone scoffed, as he gazed at everyone in the room who was looking at him in disbelief.

"Are you sure, sir? It sounds excruciatingly painful to me," Susan Jones asked as she tried to hide the embarrassment she felt when gasping a little too loud.

"Danger is the most certain part of mining," James Coaltonstone declared in a matter of fact tone.

"Goodwin has always tried to micromanage the risk out of mining, and look where it got him," John Bell groaned in disgust.

"Mining cannot be risk free especially in Mine Five. Mine Five is one of the gassiest mines that I have ever worked in. Adding to the gas, Mine Five also poses serious acid water management challenges," John Bell explained.

"Our coal seams are irregular, and grow thicker, the deeper we dig. Our best coal is often found in the most unlikely places, like under old underground railway tracks, under Coalton Lake and under the sea bed," Don Bell added.

"No one could ever tell Ginger that it is nature's randomness which yields the highest returns. Goodwin seemed to think if he micro-managed the risk out of the whole mining operation, all would be well. I must repeat, look where he is now," John Bell asserted as he struggled to hold back all of his mixed emotions.

"We don't know where Goodwin is right now, John," Don Bell reminded his twin brother.

"I didn't mean literally, Don," John Bell replied defensively.

"Ginger's heart was in the right place, but a man can't let

his mind follow his heart, not in the mining business, anyway," James Coaltonstone stated.

"Are we declaring Ginger Goodwin officially dead, then? In my notes I have him in the past tense, which would be incorrect if he is still alive," Susan Jones said.

"We don't have the authority to declare anyone dead," Mayor Stern replied.

"That is true. All we are doing is speculating. Unless Goodwin was able to foresee the pending explosion and was able to create a safety zone between himself and the explosion, Goodwin would be dead," John Bell explained without making eye contact.

"That Goodwin would have micromanaged me out of every penny that I have, chasing after that pipe dream of his. Look at Stonely Mountain; we have some of the Minese working there, we tunnel upwards instead of downwards, acid water drains out of there naturally. The Minese miners are better at contract work than this lot in Mine Five. The Minese work hard, take risks, and manage to bring me containers filled with coal and very little rock," James Coaltonstone acknowledged.

"Of course what goes on in Stonely Mountain must remain off the record," Mayor Stern added.

"Those outliers of coal are going to bring us a better future; and those little Minese don't need so much air anyway, they have smaller lungs," Alex Coaltonstone said with a snort.

"Off the record; this morning's explosion in Mine Five has become quite the economic boom for us. All these people from out of town are buying almost everything our merchants have in stock. Many of our city merchants are restocking using Mainland's Speed Express Drone Service since the highways are blocked," Mayor Stern said as he looked up from his key board to see who was actually listening to him as he spoke.

"I can only imagine how much we will be collecting in hotel room tax at the end of the day," Mayor Stern added as he walked toward the west-side window in his office.

"All kinds of people are making a bit of extra cash by renting their driveways for parking and renting their back yards as Camp sites. Not that this is camping weather, mind you," Mayor Stern noted.

"I suppose being hot headed will make camping in this weather, easier for that lot," James Coaltonstone said as he joined Mayor Stern.

"The message from Control Center is that at least three boreholes must be drilled so that air samples can be taken to determine if it is safe to send a crew of human rescue workers into the mine," John Bell said as he tried to redirect the meeting's focus.

"I have authorized the release of three surveillance robots. They are going into the mine through the main shaft in 'Section C' at 14:00 hours. If all goes well those in charge of Control Center will receive a live video feed which should give us some indication how our assets have held up," Coaltonstone said as he opened his cigar case, which he always stored on the left side of his coat pocket.

John Bell and Mayor Stern stood up and walked toward the west-side window, joining James Coaltonstone.

"Just look at all those people standing out there in the wind and cold fog," Mayor Stern scoffed as he pointed at the crowd with disdain.

"What do all those people expect to accomplish?" John Bell asked as he noted to himself that about 30% of the crowd were wearing surgical masks. "Don't they realize that Goodwin most likely met a fiery death, which would have been one of the less painful ways to go?" John Bell added knowing perfectly well it would be a terrible way to die. John Bell returned to his chair, and began keying a message into his com-phone.

"What do they think goes on in mines. Where do they think the electricity which powers all those gadgets that those riff raff are carrying, is generated from? And some of those troublemakers are wearing masks in public and are breaking the law while disturbing our way of life," James Coaltonstone said in disgust.

"I suppose we should let them keep the surgical masks for the moment, though we do have every right and authority to remove them," Mayor Stern said agreeably as he turned to face James Coaltonstone.

"Where do those people think we are living, La-La Land? Do they really think Ginger will rise from the dead? What do they think mining is all about? Sure G.O.D. has all kinds of regulations that take all kinds of experts to figure out, but nothing can guarantee safety when working in a coal mine. Try explaining that to the anal-retentive Goodwin, who knew nothing about my reality," James Coaltonstone said as he got up from his chair and joined the two men who were looking out of the window while half listening to what James Coaltonstone had to say.

"Sir, you have referred to Mr. Goodwin in the present and in the past, in the same sentence," Susan Jones said sounding anxious and confused.

"Write it in the way you think best, Susan," Mayor Stern said instructively.

"I suppose we should use the past tense for what Mr. Goodwin has done, and the present tense when describing where he is, until we have further information," Don Bell advised.

"It is not just Goodwin we should be worrying about. Our future is at risk too, my coal is at risk, and my assets are at risk and the whole Coalton Valley is at risk," Coaltonstone seethed.

"Yes quite right. Where would this town be without your coal and your assets?" Mayor Stern said, as he tried as hard as he could to compliment James Coaltonstone's thoughts.

"My coal made this town a payroll town, and will continue to make this town a payroll town. Without my coal, there would be no Pitville and there would be no Coalton Valley," James Coaltonstone said as he walked toward the west-side window.

"And without coal, this town could become a ghost town overnight just as fast as Coalton did," John Bell added.

"So assuming Goodwin is alive, a very big 'IF', he would most likely be in 'Section E', lounging in the rescue chamber eating food, reading the literature, and wondering if the clock was set at the right time. That food was meant for a crew of one hundred and sixty so Goodwin won't be going hungry," James Coaltonstone said.

"A testament to your generosity, Sir," Susan Jones said hoping that Ginger had found refuge in Safety Chamber E'.

"The air supply will only last for ninety-six hours and Goodwin has been trapped in Pit Five for over seven hours, already," Don Bell added.

"If we hope to save Ginger, we must hurry then," Susan

Jones reasoned.

"If Goodwin did manage to escape the explosion, which is a very big 'IF", he will be scarred for life and will be totally miserable and probably better off dead," John Bell said.

"I agree. If that Goodwin managed to survive the explosion he will be a mess. Better off that Goodwin is out of his misery," James Coaltonstone said trying hard not to imagine being in a similar predicament.

"We don't know what condition Mr. Goodwin is in, and we should do our best to rescue him," Susan Jones said as she quickly bowed her head to avoid eye contact.

"Your job, Susan, is to take notes," Mayor Stern said as he shook his finger.

"Yes sir," Susan Jones said, obediently.

"We must all remember, the event in Mine Five is technically not a mine disaster since only one person is trapped down there, not five," James Coaltonstone remarked, thankful that he memorized the Government's Official Directors' criteria, declaring what was and what was not, an official mine disaster.

"We don't know if the fire and gas levels are contained," Don Bell stressed as he looked at his twin brother who nodded in agreement.

John Bell looked up from his computer screen. "Yes, the one person who is trapped down there, in all probability, is either dead or almost dead or most likely wishes that he were dead."

"And don't forget that once the Government's Official Directors determine if we are eligible for funding, then they must determine if we qualify, before any recovery funding is issued," Don Bell asserted.

"I suppose then we will not be qualifying for any disaster relief. Ginger is probably dead and our fire is probably contained, and in a few days we can put all this behind us," James Coaltonstone said, sounding less confident than usual.

"As far as I know, James is right, G.O.D. won't be funding our efforts without a big fight, which means that we would have to hire a legal team which will cost big bucks," Mayor Stern said looking disgusted.

"I hate to say it, but we would have been better off

financially if the whole crew had been trapped in the pit, instead of just Goodwin," Alex Coaltonstone said as Susan Jones gasped again, as she continued taking notes, hoping that no one noticed.

"It is true. If five or more men had been trapped in Mine Five we would be dealing with an entirely different kind of event, it would be deemed as a real mine disaster," Don Bell added.

"Isn't that what I was implying?" Alex Coaltonstone asked.

"Yes, but I wanted to clarify the reasoning so that Susan's notes could be of greater benefit to future generations, who survive us," Don Bell said as Alex was trying to figure out if Don was being serious or being sarcastic.

"Thank you for your consideration," Susan Jones said as she made a note that the mine explosion would not be considered a mine disaster under the Government's Official Directors' rules.

"Let us hope that the fire stays contained and doesn't spread to the coal seam. G.O.D. might suggest that we seal the mine, or we could suggest to G.O.D. that we should seal the mine and that we request exemption from any applicables," James Coaltonstone said.

"I agree. We are pretty certain that Ginger is dead. If Goodwin has been incinerated, we will never find him. I suggest that we apply for a permit to seal the mine," John Bell agreed.

At a later date, once the crowds have dispersed, we can salvage and move the mine's assets." James Coaltonstone added.

"How can you seal the mine with Ginger Goodwin possibly still alive down there?" Susan Jones asked James Coaltonstone.

"How can you possibly take notes while you are always talking?" Mayor Stern asked, as he glared at Susan with a clear intention to intimidate.

"Yes sir, I am sorry sir," Susan Jones said without much conviction.

"The point is that Goodwin is not alive and was probably incinerated around seven hours ago. We need to seal the mine and save what is left of my assets," James Coaltonstone said pounding his fist on the table, knocking over the flower vase.

"Of course you are right, James." Mayor Stern said glaring at Susan. "James, you should request that your actual proposal to seal the mine, be sealed as well," Mayor Stern said, beginning to worry that his popularity would decline, if he endorsed the sealing of Mine Five with a real live hero still inside.

"I totally agree. Asking for consideration within a context of confidentiality is not uncommon these days," John Bell said, agreeing with the concept wholeheartedly.

"Requesting permission to seal the mine with Ginger Goodwin still trapped inside will most likely cost me the next election," Mayor Stern said grumbling slightly.

"Could it be possible that Goodwin is still alive?" Don Bell asked as he tried to ignore his twin's head shaking as if to say 'don't ask'.

"Are you disagreeing with me, John? Is that why you are shaking your head?" Mayor Stern asked in his practiced smooth voice, as he noticed John's head shaking to the right, then to the left.

"No sir," John Bell replied.

"You think having the mine sealed with Goodwin inside will cost me the election?" Mayor Stern asked, sounding very concerned.

"No sir that is not what I mean," John said as he glared at Don.

"I mean that the Government's Official Directors could demand that the entire mine be sealed, and G.O.D. would be morally correct to do so. And we, as a team, could protest and say if there is a chance that Mr. Goodwin is alive, we should utilize every resource at our disposal, to find a way to rescue him. Then we could look like the good guys and gain public sympathy, which you might desperately need sir, during the next election," John Bell said.

"Are you saying that I am in need of public sympathy, John? You are starting to sound like your brother Don. Are you sure, that you two didn't switch name tags? Mayor Stern asked suspecting that Don did not vote for him during the last election.

"It is so hard to tell you two apart," Mayor Stern added as he grabbed a second chance to soften his tone.

"I said the wrong word, sir, I was going to say empathy, and instead I said sympathy, it was a slip of the tongue, nothing more sir," John Bell said, hating to grovel so openly.

"I am sure that my brother was just pointing out the

obvious. Ginger appears to have gained sympathy from the public, at the moment, and we need to convince the public that we are the good guys," Don Bell said.

"Well we are the good guys," Coaltonstone laughed.

"The difference between us and those people standing around the security fence out there, is very simple" James Coaltonstone said as he walked back to his chair, "we make our future but those people wait for others to give them a chance at a future."

"It is always the same suspects willing to waste their time waiting for a miracle," Mayor Stern said sounding annoyed.

"I agree with you, totally, Mr. Stern," Alex Coaltonstone said. "Why should we stand around waiting for a miracle, letting time age us, while giving us nothing in return?"

"You know what we must do. We must shape the moments that we have and make the best of time, before time becomes history. We recognize opportunity as a rare and beautiful thing and we must seize every opportunity that we can, before anyone else can," James Coaltonstone said as Annette Sloane giggled uncomfortably as she walked into the room with the lunch trays.

"Quite right, James, and all those people are going to have to eat soon. They will need lodging." Mayor Stern said as he covered his salad with salad dressing.

"Let those people believe in their dreams so they can continue to spend their money in Pitville. Once their money runs out, they will just get cold and go home on their own," Mayor Stern said as James Coaltonstone nodded in agreement.

"I think we should publically support Police Chief Cuff in her 'zero tolerance for camping on public sidewalks' policy," Annette Sloane head of public relations for Mayor Stern's office advised.

"Yes, we must maintain public order, especially if we have to bring out the body," Mayor Stern added.

"We can't recover a body that has been incinerated," John Bell stated as a matter of fact.

"Do you really think Ginger was incinerated?" Susan Jones asked.

"What did I say about just taking notes?" Mayor Stern tried to ask Susan in a whisper, but was too cross, and his question to

Susan sounded a lot more like a grunt.

"As Mr. Stern's public relations advisor, I advise against publicizing that assumption," Annette Sloane replied.

"I suppose at some point, we will have to explain to the public, that Goodwin will never come out of that pit," James Coaltonstone said as he tapped his cigar ashes into the ashtray that was only brought out when he came to visit Mayor Stern's office.

"This is the biggest boom that we have ever had," Mayor Stern said as he tried to change the subject.

"You can say that again," Susan Jones said.

"We will have to schedule a press conference. It will be difficult to know what to say," Annette Sloane warned still maintaining her frozen smile.

"Sealing the mine is best," James Coaltonstone declared as he raised himself with difficulty from his chair to look out of the window again.

"As the city public relations' advisor, I advise that we do not mention sealing the mine at all," Annette Sloane replied looking concerned.

Though it was only noon, the sky was dark with black smoke, and the thought of a future filled with endless form filing depressed James Coaltonstone tremendously.

"It is really hard to know what to do first," James Coaltonstone said sounding very defeated. "If we do the wrong thing we could set the coal seam on fire. As far as we know, methane gas, coal dust and scattered coal is most likely fuelling the fire as we speak," James Coaltonstone said silently wishing that he could thump the fire out with his bare hands.

"Don't forget oxygen," Don Bell said, realizing that he may have upstaged his boss.

"And oxygen of course is the greatest fuel of all," James Coaltonstone said, giving Don Bell a glance of who James might really be beyond his tough exterior.

"Well we have come a long way since our last meeting when we were discussing the murder case linked to mine shaft extortion in Buzzard Creek We still have no suspects in that case," Mayor Stern said as he started to eat his salad.

"I don't know who ordered this goat food," James said,

"this lunch is not improving this horrible day."

"I think it was Anita," Mayor Stern said remembering that he had approved the lunch menu himself. "The food is not that bad. We said we only had time for a light lunch, and you know how many times Doctor Knight has said that we both need to shed some weight and this salad is as light as it gets," Mayor Stern said as he tried to sound cheerful.

"The salad is very good," Susan Jones said with more conviction than she had felt for anything all day.

"Christina has been in touch with the bank and they will postpone our loan payments for ninety days," James Coaltonstone said wondering what life would be like ninety days from now.

"Excellent," Mayor Stern said agreeably as he wiped the crumbs from one of his maps with his napkin.

"Christina has asked most of our suppliers to grant us similar terms, ninety days, interest free, so we have some extra time to make ends meet. We will not be shipping any newly extracted coal for a while, so we must keep our cash resources as liquid as possible." James said hoping he was sounding like a man who was still in control of his coal production.

"That girl is a keeper," Mayor Stern said.

"She sure is. I don't know what Christina sees in that anal retentive Goodwin," James Coaltonstone said, sounding annoyed.

"I am sure that there isn't much to see," Mayor Stern said as he continued.

"He is very organized and neat." Susan Jones said as she could feel all three men glare at her.

"Moving on with our agenda, we have been managing most of these little predicaments as they come up reasonably well," John Bell said, looking at his comphone, wondering if the email he just received was an actual death threat.

"Yes quite right. If we could handle the bridge re-alignment predicament, I am sure we can handle this minor explosion. Do you remember how the locals were so glad to see the bridge painted they soon forgot about those pesky re-alignment issues that they were so wound up about, months before. This situation can be managed the same way," Mayor Stone said as he began to eat his lettuce dipping it in a generous amount of salad dressing.

"That is why we keep this information under seal," John

Bell said.

"I agree totally. Today's problems are far too complicated for the ordinary person to understand, anyway," Alex Coaltonstone added.

"Yes the ordinary man in the street becomes too emotional when a little earth shifting occurs," James Coaltonstone said.

"Goodwin contributed to this hysteria by referring to the issue as a surface subsidence problem," John Campbell said.

"Even though a few rabble rousers will never be convinced that Pitville is safe, it is statistically a fact that sinkholes just don't happen in Pitville," Alex Coaltonstone said.

"I suppose it is true, Alex, that some people are at their happiest when they can go around screaming that the sky is falling. Such people don't belong in Pitville or any borough of the Coalton Valley.

Just because the odd building shifts a little, doesn't mean the entire town of Pitville is going to sink into the tunnels beneath it, any day soon," John Campbell said.

"The naysayers are in the minority, most people love living in Pitville. We have problems, and we solve them. We were able to solve our little alignment issues and paint the Pitville Bridge at the same time. The bridge looks brand new," Mayor Stern said, as he watched James Coaltonstone push away his half-eaten salad.

"However, small property owners are still complaining that there has been some noticeable change in some of their buildings' foundations along with cracks in the drywall. Some of these property owners are wondering if their homes and businesses are actually safe. They fear that their houses and business structures could collapse sometime in the near future," Susan Jones said as Mayor Stern sighed.

Mayor Stern never liked conflict and he wasn't sure if it was the longwall mining to blame or thieves robbing pillars from abandoned mines in the middle of the night. Whatever the cause, it was an unpleasant plight that the people of Pitville would have to tolerate valiantly.

"I am certain that precautions are being taken so that the longwall mining is being done in such a way that changes in surface height will be very limited. On the other hand if this subsidence issue is due to illegal miners stealing pillars from abandoned mines, then that is a police matter and Police Chief Cuff must be notified right away," Mayor Stern said.

"Why must Pitville tax payers waste their limited funds on controlling those illegals, anyway?" John Bell asked. "It is outrageous that those illegals are allowed to cause such trouble for law abiding citizens."

"The faster we get the blessed coal out to market, the better it will be for all of us, Coaltonstone said believing that coal solved most problems, and the few problems coal created were manageable and predictable.

"Quite right, coal is a blessing for all of us," Mayor Stern said to Coaltonstone.

"Very rarely does a modern building fall into an old mine. If such an incident did occur, it would happen to an old, heavy building. The type of building Ginger Goodwin would buy," Mayor Stern said as another matter of fact.

"My guess is that a group of illegals took one of the last remaining pillars from an abandoned mine. Once the mine collapsed, a portion of my coal must have combusted, spontaneously. I do not believe for a minute that this morning's unfortunate explosion had anything to do with our policies or methods. I certainly do not believe that our longwall mining methods are causing the Earth to shift," Coaltonstone said.

Mayor Stern looked unfordable as he began to speak; he tried to choose his words carefully "There could have been all kinds of reasons for this morning's explosion. No one can prevent or foresee when lightning is about to strike pockets of built up methane gas. All the mines which have been abandoned should be sealed and gated to prevent easy access. That is what the law is telling the owners to do, anyway. My guess is that 80% of the owners of abandoned mines on Tut Island have inherited these mines and can't afford to comply to G.O.D.'s demands, or even pay the fees that are charged to owners when they are trying to comply."

"Since when do the illegals comply with any regulation? And how can I compete? They murder their competitors when it suits them, and everything they do is undocumented. Their existence is undocumented and their mines are undocumented and

I suppose at times even their births and deaths go undocumented," Coaltonstone said, looking disgusted.

"I understand the predicament completely. I actually saw a shaft that must have been removed illegally from an abandoned mine, being sold at auction on the Internet," Mayor Stern said as he looked over his notes again.

"We are still answering complaints that buildings sometimes feel like they are shaking when a truck transporting coal drives by. There are also complaints that clouds of coal dust are also flying from trucks," Susan Jones added.

"File those issues at the bottom of the pile. We won't be moving coal any time soon. It will be a while until all is fixed, down in Mine Five," James Coaltonstone said.

"Agreed, and by then the most sensible of the chronic complainers may be glad to see the truck traffic go by taking your coal to market again. Of course transporting coal by truck is a lot safer than transporting oil by train. At least our town is still in one piece," Mayor Stern said proudly while James Coaltonstone kept nodding his head in agreement.

"I guess that problem solved itself. We won't be transporting coal for a while, possibly a long while," John Bell agreed.

"I have to remind Christina to phone our friends in freight and tell them that we have to cancel all shipping until further notice," Coaltonstone said as considered the consequences if Mine Five was permanently closed.

"I found another complaint from Ginger Goodwin, about the garbage dump again," Susan Jones noted.

"Actually Ginger Goodwin has filed several complaints over the years about the garbage dump issue," Mayor Stern complained, "Goodwin wants to let council and everyone know that he thinks it is very dangerous to have our garbage dump situated on top of an exposed coal seam. He wrote that he has seen men burning truckloads of garbage in open pits, right on top of the coal seam," Mayor Stern said, sounding very exasperated.

"The municipality owns the land under the dump and has permitted dumping and burning there for over two hundred years," John Bell said.

"It is a Coalton tradition, to dump garbage and coal ash in that location, Don Bell said agreeing with his twin brother.

"Buzzard Creek's main source of employment is created through that dump. The hobos enjoy scavenging in the dump, and it is a place where neighbors of the lower sort, enjoy passing the breeze," Alex Coaltonstone noted.

"The Coalton Valley dumpsite has been located behind Buzzard Creek for over two hundred years, where would we move those mountains of garbage and coal ashes to?" Mayor Stern asked.

"Should I file this complaint at the bottom of the pile, sir?" Susan Jones asked.

"Yes, Susan, that sounds like a good idea," Mayor Stern said agreeably.

"Yes, I agree too. At present, Goodwin is the only one concerned about burning trash at the dump, less said the better," Annette Sloane advised.

"Quite right and that piece of property has always been a dump for as long as records have been kept. I drove by our city garbage dump yesterday afternoon and I noticed that the men were busy burning our garbage and shovelling our coal ashes and I found no need to disrupt their work. I don't care if that garbage dump stays in that location for another hundred years. I will give it my blessing," Mayor Stern said.

"Sir, you aren't authorized to make a policy to last a hundred years, you are only elected for four," Susan Jones said.

"In a hundred years we will all be dead," Don Bell said.

"Yes, life is so very short; we don't have time to worry about any coal seam under the dump until that coal seam becomes documented. And as James said, the task of mapping mines and coal seams is not under our jurisdiction. Open burning in that location has been common practice before you and I were born, it is tradition," Mayor Stern added.

"Why don't you send a memo to the Buzzard Creek Dump's administration team, informing them that a certificate of permission to burn trash on their facility is not necessary? Accentuate the importance of burning our garbage fast before G.O.D. begins demanding exorbitant fees while supplying time guzzling paper work for us to complete," Coaltonstone instructed in a roundabout way.

"Yes, brilliant idea, James," Mayor Stern said.

"The next issue we must address; is that our friends and associates in the Big Seven Group, are having their hiring practices scrutinized again," Susan Jones explained.

"My God these people never quit," James Coaltonstone said feeling attacked personally.

"The complaint alleges that the Big Seven Coal Group is mostly hiring foreign workers from Mina," the mayor said before he was interrupted by John Bell.

"Oh that is about that work experience program where we are showing foreign students how to extract a sample of 100k tonnes of coal, from the Stonely Mountain Seam," explained John Bell.

"Oh," Mayor Stern replied as he filed the complaint at the bottom of the pile.

"Now that Mine Five is shut down we won't be hiring anyone for a while," James Coaltonstone said.

"I do think we should communicate the positive impact our commitment to fair hiring practices has had on Coalton Valley," Alex Coaltonstone suggested.

"Quite right, when we write our press release we must adjust our mission statement to include out intentions of continuing to hire locals whenever possible," Don Bell said agreeably.

"Shouldn't we remind the locals that without Coaltonstone Coal and the Big Seven Coal Group, there would be no Coalton Valley?" John Bell added.

"Quite right and all these naysayers are sure going to feel it now that your Mine Five operation has closed down earlier than expected. Once the miners have no other source of income, they will be begging us to return to the good old days," Mayor Stern predicted.

"Susan could you please write a press release, praising the Big Seven Coal Group's contribution to the economic growth in Pitville?" Annette Sloane asked.

"Yes, Mam," Susan Jones replied.

"Since we will be closing Mine Five sooner than expected, about four hundred people will be out of work. After a few months, they will be begging us to start removing the mountain tops from the entire Beartut Range," James Coaltonstone said as he extinguished his cigar with unnecessary force.

"I don't know how I am going to win the next election with all this talk of roads shifting, water aquifer pollution, and health problems related to breathing coal dust, coal ash and cigar smoke," Mayor Stern noted.

"Someone is complaining about cigar smoke? Who is complaining about cigar smoke? Is it that Goodwin again? The mines are my property and I should be able to smoke anywhere I want and any time I want," James Coaltonstone said as he was about to light another cigar and decided that he should wait until after lunch.

"I suggest that we consider how we will sell the idea that we must seal and foam the mine so that we can prevent the entire Stonely Coal Seam from igniting," James said. "It is my civic duty to do what I can to save my assets. All those miners and contractors depend on my assets to make a living."

"Yes, it certainly is," Mayor Stern said, agreeing pleasantly.

"My brother gave me his word that the doorway system would be used in ways that were permissible. Don told me that he would never allow the removal of mining equipment during mining operations. There was no legitimate reason to prop open doors, especially when sparks might be flying," John Bell said as he watched Susan Jones bending over as she turned on the fan before she blew her nose.

"We don't know what started this explosion. I know it was not our fault. I mean we have addressed the growing problem of pillar robberies in the abandoned mines, but that is not our problem, unless it is our pillars which are being robbed," James Coaltonstone said sounding uncomfortable.

"Goodwin has been hounding me and every other government office to fund a mapping project to document undocumented mines. The government's position has always been to encourage informal exploration, and once illegal activity occurs, and evidence is brought forth, then and only then will representatives of G.O.D. step in and intervene," Mayor Stern said taking down notes for himself.

"Quite right, that Goodwin is a fool. When is mapping undocumented mines a task assigned to a mayor of a small municipality? Mapping all the mines that are sharing veins which stop abruptly due to faults in the geology can be a time consuming and expensive process and I don't think you have the authority to even request funding to engage in such a task," James Coaltonstone said agreeing full heartedly.

"It seems me that it pays to operate a mine the way the illegals do. Every time I turn around I am paying fees just to request a permit to do everyday tasks," James Coaltonstone complained.

"Goodwin has written several proposals requesting that the municipality relocate the Pitville garbage dump because at the moment, the dump is located on top of a coal seam," Mayor Stern said.

"Sir I think you have already read that memo, and the bottom of the pile has become the top of the pile," Susan Jones explained.

"Let us get back to our emergency planning," James Coaltonstone said as he turned a page in his notebook.

"We can find a way to continue our operations even if we have to permanently close Mine Five. We can write off the loss, and still have the Beartut Mountain Range to mine. Can't you just see all those black diamonds shinning on the conveyor belt?" James Coaltonstone asked.

"If I am reading some of those signs people out there are carrying correctly, it seems that there is a sector of the population, right outside this window, who are blaming us for this morning's mishap," John Bell said. "We must stay vigilante while we protect the home front."

"I suppose all those people out there don't care that this morning's explosion has made me a victim too. I have a huge capital investment in Mine Five. A portion of my assets were scheduled to be transported to the Stonely Mountain portal at the beginning of the New Year. And the continuous miner was scheduled to be under Eagle Nest Beach by noon Monday. We need to construct gate roads under the beach to prepare for Mine Seven," James Coaltonstone said as he lit his cigar, took a long puff and coughed while managing to blow smoke rings.

"You know, Mr. Coaltonstone, those cigars appear to be killing you?" Susan Jones commented impulsively.

"What did I say about talking?"

"I am sorry Mr. Stern," Susan replied.

"Whose side are you on anyway, Susan?" James Coaltonstone asked, "I know all about your brother, Sam. Don't think I am clueless about what goes on behind my back," James Coaltonstone said, as he continued making smoke rings to emphasize not only his point but his power to flaunt the rules which kept mostly everyone else below him, not just down but terrified.

"You said that all of those pesky outsider busy bodies would sign any form that we send them as long as you agreed and that you held no reservations once my decisions were made," James Coaltonstone reminded Mayor Stern.

"Without coal, this valley will just become another derelict island district. We are better off just closing the town down than letting the riff raff take over. Without coal this whole Island would become a welfare state or worse, a haven for illegal miners," Mayor Stern predicted.

If those busy bodies continue to demand the impossible from me, or people like me, the greater the chance that coal mining will be driven underground," James Coaltonstone said as he chuckled to himself at the poignant irony mining brought to everyday life.

"Underworld coal mining will make the war on drugs look like a Peace Corp initiative, John Bell said.

"You know what I am, Ted? I am a practical man. The tragic events which happened in Buzzard Creek this summer could be just the tip of the iceberg," James Coaltonstone said.

"We don't want mining driven underground without any regulation or initiative to operate within sensible guidelines. If we leave mining to the ruthless we could land up with a seam fire which could spread and force the evacuation of Coalton, Pitville and even Buzzard Creek," Mayor Stern warned as he looked at his watch.

"I have always been a man of my word, we had an agreement which I honored to the best of my ability," James

Coaltonstone said impatiently. "I am also a man whose time is ten times more valuable than most of the people who are living in this valley. And where would this valley be without me and my coal?" James Coaltonstone asked.

"Coalton Valley would be just one more derelict island tourist trap," John Bell said with disgust.

"I sent my son out to get us some real food. He should be back by now. I don't know why he takes so long to do things. I am more than twice his age and I can still do everything faster," James Coaltonstone said as he took his cell phone out of his pocket and dialed Bobby's cell phone number.

"Bobby where are you?" James Coaltonstone asked.

"I have the food, Dad. I stopped for gas, and there is a serious problem. Bert's gas is hot. Bert was telling me he thinks there is a fire underground that is warming his underground gas tanks. Bert dropped a thermometer on a string into the tank and he said that the temperature is over 170 degrees Fahrenheit," Bobby said sounding scared.

"Ask Bobby if he has my mickey of whiskey?" Mayor Stern whispered to James Coaltonstone.

"Do you have Ted's whiskey, Bobby?" James Coaltonstone asked, stalling for a bit of time.

"Yes, I do. What is Bert supposed to do? Bert is afraid that his gas tanks may blow up?" Bobby asked.

"You should phone Bert back and make sure that he gets all the gas out of that holding tank. Tell him that is an order from the mayor's office," James Coaltonstone instructed.

"And make sure Bert does not use his cell phone when he contacts us, it would be better to use a pay phone if he can find one," Mayor Stern suggested.

"I think they took the last pay phone out of the Pitville. That was the pay phone in the library, I think. There were too many complaints that those riffraff hobos were using the phone to beg for help, and they were talking too loud and disturbing others using the library, especially the librarians," John Bell said.

"What about all the other gas stations? Shouldn't they do something too?" Bobby Coaltonstone asked.

"Just wait. We deal with putting one fire out at a time. Tell

Bert that he has to move the gas from that underground tank, now. And when he contacts us he must use a pay phone or a phone that cannot be traced back to him or us. Or better yet, tell him to not contact us, we will contact him. We have no time to discuss this now Bobby. We have to tread lightly. We can't cause panic, but we have to make sure that all of the gas stations in the valley monitor the temperature of the gas in their underground holding tanks," James Coaltonstone instructed.

"We should send a memo to the Pitville Chamber of Commerce, but we must be careful not to cause panic," Mayor Stern added.

"I say we should put this issue at the bottom of the pile too," John Bell suggested.

"We have to figure out what to do about Goodwin. There are tens of thousands of people out there waiting for some good news. We have to figure out how to insulate ourselves against financial injury. We have to postpone the economic collapse of Coalton Valley. Once we announce that we cannot reopen the mine panic runs will begin, no doubt. As if we don't have enough to worry about as it is. Now we have to worry about all the gas stations in Pitville, may be holding hot gas in their underground holding tanks," Coaltonstone said while pacing in front of Mayor Stern's west-side window.

"I am just turning into the city parking lot now, Dad. I am bringing the food up. I have extra ketchup like you asked for," Bobby Coaltonstone added.

"Bobby I thought you were pulled over. You know you are not supposed to talk on the cell phone and drive at the same time," James Coaltonstone sounded exasperated and wondered why his son showed such little respect for rules and regulations.

As Bobby entered the door he was carrying bags of hamburgers and French fries and milkshakes.

"Let's eat," James Coaltonstone suggested.

"Thank you for getting a bottle of my favourite whiskey, Bobby," Mayor Stern said as he placed the mickey in his jacket pocket as Susan Jones raised her eyebrows.

"Let's eat and enjoy life while we can," Mayor Stern said as he poured ketchup on his French fries.

"I would toast to that sentiment, if you would offer me a

drink of that whiskey Ted," James Coaltonstone said as he pushed his cup, towards Ted.

"Shall I note that this meeting is closed, sir?"

"Yes, and let me look over your notes before you submit them to the Government's Official Directors," James Coaltonstone instructed.

"Yes sir," Susan Jones replied.

Chapter 3:
Never forget

In-Reach entry, LOG #2 written by Christina Watson, (Accounting Assistant to Alex Coaltonstone) Sunday December 22, 2030 written around 1:00 PM:

Ginger was one of the rare people who actually did something to make the world a better place for others. I still haven't heard anything from Control Center.

I am still getting email and Skype messages asking me if I believe that Ginger had been incinerated. I can't believe that they are still asking me that. I know I had a vision this morning that Ginger found was heading toward the Chamber in Section E, before the explosion occurred.

I am trying to imagine Ginger's routine before the explosion happened. Ginger takes the shaft elevator and descends into 'Section C'. Ginger usually takes the rail car to 'Section A and checks the water pumps. Ginger checks to make sure that everything is working to code. Once his inspection is complete, Ginger types his reports and after logging in to the Eye-Bot Network, he sends the reports to Control Center in the administration building.

After this morning's explosion, there will be no power supply to keep those pumps running.

The machinery which pumps the acid-water out of Section A would be off line if not broken beyond repair, so only God knows how much acid water has already accumulated down there since the explosion. Those water pumps have to keep pumping out water, or the orangy acid water just takes over and burns the skin and erodes metal and must be escaping into the surrounding ground and aquifers. Sooner or later this acid water will effect our ground water which moves in different directions. I feel so guilty bringing Ginger Junior into such a cruel and toxic world.

Getting back to Ginger's routine. Once Ginger finished checking the pumps in 'Section A', he would take the rail car back to 'Section B' where pillar retrieval has been underway for a few days now and where Coaltonstone's very expensive long wall machinery is located. Then Ginger takes the rail car back into 'Section C' and he checks on the ventilation problem which has been increasing in severity especially during the last few days. 'Sections A to C' are located in the lower thick anthracite coal seam. Then by the time Ginger gets to 'Section E' the fault in the Earth changes direction and the ventilation seems to get better.

During the morning pre-shift safety inspection, Ginger takes samples and checks equipment to make sure that all of the equipment is in good working order including the equipment in the rescue chamber in 'Section E'.

Then Ginger writes reports.

The last log Ginger sent described coal dust so thick it was hurting his eyes. That log was sent to Control Center a few minutes before the explosion went off at 5:20 AM and must have been sent after he skyped me about the gas monitors on the coal shearing machine being turned off.

Most of the miners and contractors from Mine Five are waiting for news in the Miners' Cafeteria. Some went home and were given a pass on their way out, so they could get back into the building without a problem. Most of us are planning to stay put until we hear news that Ginger is still alive and that the rescue is under way. That is what I want to hear, anyway.

We all know that it will be a miracle if Ginger comes out of that pit alive.

I am glad that Dr. Knight asked me to participate in her 'In-Reach Project', I still haven't been told the results of the pregnancy test, Dr. Knight took yesterday afternoon.

I just came back from looking out of the window. I just

THE MINER Book 1: Rescuing Ginger Goodwin

hate this waiting I have no clues to what is really going on? .No one is telling me anything. I am going to email George Smoothman and see if he knows anything.

James Coaltonstone dropped into my office a few minutes ago and gave me my paycheck and Christmas bonus. Thank God for that. James also gave me a cheese platter and a nice card. That was very nice of him, but I wish he would stop brushing up against me every time he comes into my office. Anyway old James Coaltonstone told me to check the ticker price for our company shares once every hour, starting tomorrow morning. He authorized me to buy as many shares as it takes to keep our share price stable. He didn't even mention any concerns for Ginger Goodwin. Alex is so much like his dad it is scary.

Most of Pitville has, I wouldn't say developed but sprawled, around Mine Five in the same way Mina Town sprawled around Mine Four. Mina Town was disassembled decades ago.

Ironically the highest valued properties are the ones closest to the mine portals and of course those buildings are now placed at the highest risk. Many of the houses close to Mine Five are owned by miners even though the property underneath is owned by Coaltonstone Mines and the Big Seven Coal Group.

Most of us who worked for Coaltonstone joined the pay as you work program. Coaltonstone and his cronies at the bank came up with the idea at the time it sounded great since the miners felt as if they owned their own homes. Now that Mine Five is only words from being called a disaster area, who knows what will happen to those dream homes.

We have had about two or three hours of daylight, since the explosion, but the black smoke is still lurking overhead and spreading God knows what, into the air. The fog or smog, or whatever they are calling it, smells like burnt toast but much worse.

12:30 AM:
I just discovered a Skype message Ginger sent to my personal account this morning. The message was sent about ten minutes before this morning's explosion occurred. The message said that when Ginger arrived to do his safety check, which he does every morning, before the crew is allowed to descend into the

mine, the methane monitor on the coal shearing machine had been turned off. I wonder who turned off the monitor on the coal shearing machine. This is what I mean; it is so hard to trust people around here because they take such risks, as if money was more important than life and limb.

The coal shearing machine, if it still exists, is in desperate need of repair. The water sprayers were not working properly so little fires would be extinguished manually before they grew out of control.

During the last 47 days, the little fires were occurring almost on a daily basis. The carbide teeth had been broken for longer than 47 day, but as the teeth grew worse, sparks began flying unpredictably, igniting small pockets of methane gas lurking nearby.

That is why Ginger installed the monitor on the coal shearing machine in the first place, because James Coaltonstone maintained that it was too expensive to fix it. This was similar to what happened with the whistle-boss bot.

Mathew and Ginger reported that the bot appeared to have a malfunction, because it would start whistling randomly and continue whistling nonstop while hovering around a miner's head who would be working with heavy and dangerous machinery.

I am not sure what to do with Ginger's last skype message that he sent me. I really don't trust any of the Bells or the Coaltonstones right now and I don't think Ginger did either.

Air-buses are landing in the air park behind the administration building.

There are all kinds of people walking into the rescue center, which is just a giant tent, but I don't see anyone walking out.

Anne who works for food services in the mine's administration building told me that she and her staff are serving tons of sandwiches and gallons of coffee to the many volunteers who have agreed to join the rescue effort. I suppose the team members are waiting for instructions from Control Center which operates from the executive lounge. I suppose it is located on the top floor of the administration building so the executives can have a great view of the people outside without being seen. The people are crowding the Pitville streets and surrounding the security fence.

I suppose all these people are hoping to give Ginger a hero's welcome, once he has been freed from Mine Five. The security fence is becoming less visible due to all the flowers, teddy bears and cards piling up in front of it.

I just came back from looking out of the window again.

At least I am not alone.

There must be over ten thousand people standing outside, in the cold, waiting for news about the rescue, and as far as I know, there isn't any.

There are all kinds of photographers climbing up and down ladders while fussing with their cameras and cams. The bravest of them, are allowing their cams to hang from the top of the security fence. Up to now, they have nothing to photograph.

Beautiful Dianne Black and her handsome cameraman Jackson Green have just arrived, looking out of place but so glamorous. If Ginger could only see them now; we would both have a good laugh. A few photographers are taking Dianne and Jackson's picture and they are waving to everyone. Those two are so famous and beautiful.

And then there are the people I don't see.

And no one can see me, as far as I know.

I am going back and forth, writing into the thumb drive Doctor Knight assigned to me and looking out of the window to see if anything new is happening. And every time I look out of the window I just see more people arriving carrying signs in support of Ginger Goodwin, but I can't see any action coming from the rescue tent.

Lily told me that the Bells and the Coaltonstones are taking the position that the internal operations in Mine Five had nothing to do with Sunday morning's explosion. They believe that some external event or force caused the explosion.

The official working theories are based on several assumptions being made relating to external forces.

One theory is that Sunday morning's explosion was caused by spontaneous combustion, which could have been the result of either a small earthquake or an illegal mine. Another working theory is that lightning caused a spark, igniting gas and coal dust nearby. I am going to email George Smoothman again.

If Ginger is never to be rescued, we should rally for some

kind of memorial to remember him by. We should never forget what a friend we had in him. How he was willing to talk to everyone regardless where they happened to fit on the social ladder. The memorial should be grand and situated in a peaceful place. We will need to find a place where we can bring flowers on special days like his birthday.

I have to take a break and look out of the window again. I am feeling claustrophobic and I am freaking myself out.

End of In-Reach entry, LOG #2 by Christina Watson (Accounting Assistant to Alex Coaltonstone).

Chapter 4:
One Name Tag Left Hanging

Joint In-Reach LOG #1 by George A. Smoothman and Jay T. Paylor for Sunday December 22, 2030. Around 1:00 PM written in the Miners' Cafeteria:

George A. Smoothman:
I am the foreman. I often find myself in positions where I am dammed if I do, and dammed if I don't. I am the one that gets blamed when anything goes wrong because I sign the logbooks before and after each shift.

Doctor Knight asked us if we would like to participate in this 'In-Reach' project as partners. And George and I thought this would be a good idea, so we are going to write this "In-Reach" journal together.

Jay T. Paylor:
I am the assistant foreman. I get blamed for stuff too, but not as much as George does. It is unbelievable that we were able to escape. We have a lot to thank Ginger for.

George A. Smoothman:
Thank God for Ginger. I have never felt this appreciative of being alive before. I felt frozen and sweaty at the same time that is how scared I was.

Jay T. Paylor:
I know. As James Coaltonstone was trying to intimidate us so that he could hear us like sheep, we would have been descending right into a pending explosion, if it hadn't been for Ginger, God knows what would have happened to us.

George A. Smoothman:
I just hope with some luck Ginger was able to reach one of the functioning rescue chambers and found refuge from the toxic smoke.

Jay T. Paylor:
Agreed! If Ginger is able to reach one of the rescue chambers, assuming that it is still functioning, he will have about ninety-six hours of clean air, food and water. There will be batteries for his light and a sanitation system.

George A. Smoothman:
Hopefully whatever is going on down there is not too much for Ginger to handle. Ginger was telling me that he was starting to believe that the earth had a mind of its own.

Jay T. Paylor:
Do you really think there is a god or do you think it is all about that chapel business which is used to convince us that it is God's will to live in this filth and poverty, working like dogs, being treated like dogs, and being told to fetch and sit, as if we were dogs?

George A. Smoothman:
Well why can't we just thank Ginger for doing the right thing?

Jay T. Paylor:
Because Ginger is down in the Pit, the way we could have been. Ginger may have been burnt alive and we could have been too. Who knows?

George A. Smoothman:
That is why we need a miracle.

Jay T. Paylor:
Or some process which is engineered to work miracles.

Just before the explosion, Ginger refused to sign off on the safety check until he was satisfied that the mine was safe, delaying the morning shift from starting by twenty minutes. So like sheep, we were getting ready to descend into the shaft for the morning shift then boom. Everything shook. The Whistle-Boss Bot 5C stopped whistling, and then I heard the siren wail four times. And we just ran for it.

George A. Smoothman:
We ran out in an orderly way though. As we ran for the buses we could see flames, and for once the buses picked us up without any delay, and we could see the flames shooting out of the ventilation shaft. I was so scared.

Jay T. Paylor:
The explosion was unbelievable.

George A. Smoothman:
Those contractors sure changed their tune fast about Ginger. First they were calling him all kinds of demeaning things, now they are thanking God for creating such a man who listened to his own drummer, and interrupted us marching into that pending fiery pit.

Jay T. Paylor:
We all underestimated Ginger and his ability to use data to go beyond the randomness of chaos and concern for making money.

George A. Smoothman:
Ginger was able to open a door to a new destiny for all of us in a way. Cause leaving things to our devices we would have descended as Coaltonstone was about to command us to do.

Jay T. Paylor:
That is right. As we grabbed our name tags before we ran for the busses as fast as we could, we could not help but feel how sad it was to leave Ginger's name tag all alone, in the dark.

George A. Smoothman:
Then we were driven back to the administration building.

Jay T. Paylor:
And no one spoke. Some of us were shaking in our seats. And here we are in the Miners' Cafeteria still in shock eating free macaroni and cheese and feeling like our lives have been put on hold before we fall into abyss of unemployment.

We may have no job now, we probably won't get a Christmas bonus, and our lives as we used to know them have been changed maybe forever.

George A. Smoothman:
And adding injury to insult, this disaster is not officially a disaster because only one person, Ginger Goodwin, is trapped in the mine, not five. I think the word disaster in this case is being used in a political sense. This explosion is a disaster for us. Pitville surrounds Mine Five, because Mine Five made Pitville a payroll town.

Jay T. Paylor:
I think there is more funding for recovery when five or more miners are missing because then the explosion is officially called a disaster.

George A. Smoothman:
And we wonder how these disasters happen. These policies almost encourage a disaster instead of a solution.

Jay T. Paylor:
I bet you anything that they will try to seal the mine and try to avoid paying the costs involved to rescue Ginger. Look what the mine did to Christina. The mine coerced her to settle after Mathew

was killed. 'Boss-Bots R Us' have been fighting her in court for nine and a half years. They didn't even offer to settle with her. That is what happens when a person refuses to be coerced by the power clique. They have the recourses to tie us up in court until we go bankrupt or go crazy.

Dr. Knight reminded us not to use language that we would not want our kids to read or remember us by but I don't know any other word to explain how company policies screw us.

George A. Smoothman:

Sometimes people really think that because we do physical work, we are mindless and have no sense of decency as if we were the ones who were trying to push my crew into a broken mine, which was about to blow up.

Jay T. Paylor:

We should be celebrating that we are alive today. I don't believe that Ginger is dead. I just feel that he is alive. I think if the official line is to assume that Ginger is dead so they justify leaving him down there in the pit to die. It is like enabling a self-fulfilling prophecy, which I think, is totally unethical.

George A. Smoothman:

I agree. Even though you are sounding just like Christina, I agree with her too. Christina skyped me this morning, and said the very same thing. She actually went further and told me in confidence that she thought that it was possible that she thought she saw remotely Ginger fleeing with two new and very tall bots heading toward Section E, while she was lying in bed.

Jay T. Paylor:

If anyone else said such a thing I would have thought that they were losing their mind, but Christina is usually so level headed, I don't think she is making it up. There are people who do have moments of second sight.

George A. Smoothman:

As soon as we speak our minds we get cut down. We need to stick together as a mining community, and try not to cut each other down.

Jay T. Paylor:
I agree with you totally George. What I found out when reading about second sight was often people who get second sight visions, are experiencing extreme stress.

George A. Smoothman:
Well, we all fit that category.

Jay T. Paylor:
Yes. But to have second sight you normally have to be intuitive in the first place, or at least have some kind of intuitive training.

George A. Smoothman:
Christina has lived in Coalton Valley all her life, the same Coalton Valley that we know. Our side of Coalton Valley has become a place where people work when and where they can find it, and almost everyone is willing to work in a broken mine, including us. Then we all get sick and die.

Jay T. Paylor:
That is exactly how it is. Life is short especially if you are a miner in Pitville. When we speak our minds to show that we aren't mindless then Coaltonstone and the Government Official Directors call us agitators for speaking our minds. We just can't win, can we George?

George A. Smoothman:
No, winning in Pitville is really hard to do. I know.
We were going to play soccer together on Christmas Eve, which is also the eve of Ginger's birthday but the game is cancelled.

Jay T. Paylor:
Ginger was a great soccer player.

George A. Smoothman:
Yeah, we had second thoughts about canceling the game, but in the end most of us don't feel like playing soccer.

Jay T. Paylor:
Well, we have our memories and our lives to remind us of Ginger. Because if it wasn't for Ginger, we could have all down there, the whole morning a crew of one hundred and sixty, could have been lost in the Pit, the way Ginger is now.

George A. Smoothman:
Please don't say that word incinerated. I find that it is very creepy.

Jay T. Paylor:
Well I am speaking my thoughts, the way we were instructed to do. We were told to imagine free space around our heads, with no boss-bots flying around us, blowing that awful whistle nonstop. We have to feel free before we are able to think freely, I think.

George A. Smoothman:
Yes you are right. Like we said before, Doctor Knight told us that we should join the 'In-Reach' project so that we could sort out our feelings and open our minds and possibly even control our thoughts so we can stay out of trouble. But look at how much trouble the mine authorities, especially the Bells and the Coaltonstones have caused us. It is like there are two kinds of people.

Jay T. Paylor:
Yes, us who work for the mine, and them who run the mine.

George A. Smoothman:
Exactly, the way the Bells and Coaltonstones run things, it is really amazing the mine didn't blow up before now.

Jay T. Paylor:
Then there was the issue related to weighing the coal we produce each shift.

George A. Smoothman:
Since the depression of 2029, the mine brought in a new method of paying us. The Weigh-Boss bot weighs all the coal that the shift extracts at the end of each shift and we get paid by ton. We all know how much the coal in the containers should weigh, so the Weigh-Boss bot must be short changing us, especially during the last few months. That was one of the main reasons why the crew was cutting corners during the last couple of months; so we could extract more coal and meet our quota, and qualify for the Christmas bonus.

Jay T. Paylor:
Everything is against us.

George A. Smoothman:
Isn't that the truth? We have never turned other people's lives upside down the way the Bells and Coaltonstones have turned our lives upside down. I bet you anything that Coaltonstone is going to hold back our pay and make us grovel.

Jay T. Paylor:
This is what kills me. Talk about causing trouble for people. This disaster was caused by pushing coal production ahead of everything else, especially ahead of us. We don't count for anything. They can't even supply a simple tag locator program where in the scheme of things the cost would be so miniscule compared to the rest of the mine's budget, it is insulting.

I think it is pretty hypocritical, that we have to keep our heads down, and not bother or inconvenience anyone while they cause such heartache for us. Talk about flaunting rules. The Big Seven Coal Group can flaunt rules and cause serious trouble for regular people like us who are getting poorer as the Bells and Coaltonstones get richer.

Anyway, George and I work in the mine as partners and we understand each other's pain, but most people don't.

George A. Smoothman:
Technically I should have more pain that Jay because I have to take most of the blame due to my senior position as foreman. Imagine the pain that Christina must be feeling. She lost Mathew, now Ginger.

Jay T. Paylor:
The 'In-Reach Project' has been designed so that victims, finding themselves in a natural disaster or a mine disaster which from my point of view is a man-made disaster and much different than a natural disaster, can lighten their load by putting their thoughts down on electronic paper. It is hard to know, what thought to put down first, so this will be a team effort.

George A. Smoothman:
I agree with Jay this journal will be a team effort. I also agree that mine disasters are man-made disasters therefore they are preventable. I think war and mine disasters are always horrible for the loser. And we miners are always treated like losers around here.

Around here, we are always defined in relation to property and the amount of paper and plastic we have in our pockets.

I suppose, once a person feels materially superior to another person, it is easier to lose empathy for them. I think the loss of empathy could be the corrupting force, which can corrupt most of us.

Jay T. Paylor:
Except for Ginger, of course!

George A. Smoothman:
Agreed, except for Ginger!
I can't see how anyone could be friends with James Coaltonstone without finding himself with a super powerful frenemy as soon as their backs were turned.

Jay T. Paylor:
What do you mean by frenemy George?

George A. Smoothman:
You know. He could be your friend when it suits him, and once he finds that your interests may conflict with his, he could turn on you, as enemies often do.

Jay T. Paylor:
Isn't that the definition of a true friend? One who stands by you, and will let you win, even at his expense.

George A. Smoothman:
I suppose it is, and it is also what Ginger did for us. James Coaltonstone would kick down his first born son, if that meant profit for him.

Jay T. Paylor:
That is exactly what I meant by frenemy. Ginger is down there in the mine, but we could have all been down there.
Ginger must have been reading some very high counts on one of his own personal devices, and then he may have decided to use his authority to prohibit mine entry until he was able to find some answers and then something must have interrupted what he was trying to do.

George A. Smoothman:
Of course something interrupted what Ginger was trying to do, the explosion. Hopefully when he saw the numbers as they were rising, he scurried over to the cart and made his way into 'Section E, hopefully without creating any sparks.

Jay T. Paylor:
Didn't Christina say that Ginger skyped her, right before the explosion, warning her that the methane monitor, on the coal shearing machine, had been turned off.
Who would turn the methane monitor off the coal shearing machine?

George A. Smoothman:
Not someone on our side, obviously.

Jay T. Paylor:
Hopefully Ginger was able to reach the rescue chamber in 'Section E since it is the chamber which would have been the furthest away from the fire in the ventilation shaft and that is where he would have the best chance to survive.

George A. Smoothman:
Isn't that what I just said?

Jay T. Paylor:
Yes, you did. And I was just validating your thoughts. Ginger will only have four days of air supply if he reached the safety chamber.

George A. Smoothman:
The situation is so horrible and it makes me so mad because most likely this explosion was preventable.
Who would turn the methane monitor off the coal shearing machine and place us miners and the mine at such risk?

Jay T. Paylor:
An idiot I suppose.

George A. Smoothman:
The best case scenario for Ginger would be reaching chamber E. and he is now sitting there with nothing to do except count the minutes as they go by hoping that he will be rescued before his air supply runs out.

Jay T. Paylor:
Don't forget the pile of literature we left in all the safety chambers. He will have lots to read.

George A. Smoothman:
Yeah, he will probably run out of air before he is able to read all that stuff we left in there.

Jay T. Paylor:
I suppose it will be a special form of agony to wonder when your last breath of air will be.

George A. Smoothman:
Yeah, sort of like having your last meal, I suppose might be easier being dead. We have our future to worry about, though I am thankful that I do have a future, I really wish that life was not so hard. It is not clear where we stand, and you know what happened to Christina, they have been fighting her for nine and a half years, with no concern for how wrong it is to exhaust someone emotionally and financially like that.

Jay T. Paylor:
I suppose Coaltonstone and 'Boss-Bots R Us' believe that their moral obligation is to their assets.

George A. Smoothman:
Yea, Jay, you are probably right. What do you think we should do, now that we have a long life in front of us, thanks to Ginger? I suppose we might go hungry and stay penniless for a while. Regardless of any moral right, James Coaltonstone has the legal right, under the new profit-sharing clause in our contracts, to not pay us when Mine Five is inoperable, and when there isn't any alternative work that Coaltonstone Mines can offer us, Pitville will crash the same way Coalton crashed.

Jay T. Paylor:
We have so many things to worry about; it is hard to know what to worry about first.

George A. Smoothman:
James Coaltonstone was furious this morning when he made the announcement over the loud speaker that the shift must begin at 5:30 or we would all have part of our pay deducted.

Jay T. Paylor:
That is right. Coaltonstone was complaining about losing

money for the first twenty minutes of the shift, then boom.

George A. Smoothman:
We just grabbed our name tags and ran out of there as fast as we could without knocking each other over.

It was almost like James Coaltonstone believed that Ginger was creating work stoppage just for the sake of creating work stoppage. It didn't seem to dawn on Coaltonstone that Ginger was trying to figure out how broken, Coaltonstone's broken down mine was, and whether it was too dangerous to sign the morning shift's safety compliance certificate.

Jay T. Paylor:
And thankfully Ginger didn't let James Coaltonstone push him around.

George A. Smoothman:
And due to Ginger's quick thinking he saved our lives by prohibiting us from entering the mine. Coaltonstone doesn't seem to realize that there are things that have far greater value than just money.

Jay T. Paylor:
You mean there is a greater power than money?

George A. Smoothman:
Yes. It is self-evident that an explosion is a greater power than money. It takes over everything and we would have been blamed for it, not Coaltonstone. That is the way all the rules work, in his favor not ours.

But explosions work differently they are egalitarian. They shook all of us up, even old Coaltonstone.

Jay T. Paylor:
I agree though. It was really something, almost funny if it hadn't been so tragic.

George A. Smoothman:
Laughing at this is hard to do, when our entire lives have

been turned upside down.

I will always remember the look on Coaltonstone's face during the explosion.

Jay T. Paylor:

One moment he was yelling at us, next moment he was running for the buses just like we were. When the explosion happened I thought the shaft was going to break apart but you can just imagine what Coaltonstone must have been thinking.

I just wonder what it would have been like for Ginger. We were around twelve hundred feet above the mine and thank God we were able to escape. My God, I am still shaking.

George A. Smoothman:

I would say we have to thank Ginger. If it had been up to Coaltonstone, we would be down there too. He was almost ready to order us to ignore Ginger's authority, to prohibit the shift from starting when he felt it was unsafe. I just hope Ginger was able to reach the safety chamber in 'Section E'. They don't know whether Ginger is dead or where he is in the mine. The screens went dark, nothing works down there. His phone doesn't work. Of course they don't have the Wi-Fi Radio-frequency identification locator tags anymore.

Jay T. Paylor:

Right, the only tag hanging in the shaft now is Ginger's metal dog tag.

George A. Smoothman:

Those two way locator tags would have really helped Ginger right now. I mean how do they expect to rescue Ginger, if they can't locate him? Talk about causing trouble for people, look at all the trouble that they have caused for Ginger and for all of us.

Jay T. Paylor:

What about that telemagnetic radio, I thought that was supposed to work under any condition. I don't think that is set up either.

George A. Smoothman:
That is a good point. Is anyone monitoring those telemagnetic radios to see if Ginger is trying to communicate to the surface?

Jay T. Paylor:
I find this whole situation very agitating. They call us agitators but they never give any thought to how they treat us. The mine saves a few nickels and dimes and look at what it costs Ginger and us?

James Coaltonstone didn't seem to care that Ginger had been risking his life and health just to take air samples so that there would be less of a chance of making a false reading, than if the samples had been taken remotely.

George A. Smoothman:
We all knew that the mine was an accident waiting to happen. We needed to meet our quotas, so we could continue to pay for the lives that we have.

Jay T. Paylor:
I agree. Working for James Coaltonstone for fifteen years has been brutal. It is bad enough that we had to submit and comply with his will instead of ours; we are just a pay check away from being a slave.

George A. Smoothman:
The only people, who could not see the dangerous conditions building up in the mine's corners, were the bosses who spend all day working and living behind computer screens.

Jay T. Paylor:
We don't just comply to the bosses' will, but to their willful blindness as well.

George A. Smoothman:
Since when do the bosses ever step out from behind their computer screens? They seem to think living a two dimensional existence, behind computer screens, is the same as living life in the

physical world. Seeing reality through computer screens may be preferable for the bosses, but it places us miners and contractors in constant danger. Delaying an appropriate response, which impacts mine safety, could mean the difference between life and death for anyone of us.

Jay T. Paylor:
And in this case it was Ginger who took the hit. As far as I can see, the mine managers who manage behind a screen are being deceived if they think that they are viewing a true reflection of reality. The two dimensional world didn't deceive Ginger though, did it?

George A. Smoothman:
Thank God for that. It is a real mistake to make assumptions based on physical impressions. I mean it is really important to keep the data in context and to make sure that the content reflects conditions where it matters, like corners in the mine, or even areas on machines. Data, which is diluted, can do more harm than good.

Jay T. Paylor:
Exactly, and the problem with boss-bots is that they seem to dilute most of the data which they process.

George A. Smoothman:
And besides diluting the data, the data is taken out of context, especially when we are being processed by those horrible payroll-boss bots, which are continually connected to the Bot Eye Network. It is very creepy how these machines watch us while we work. It makes it hard to concentrate at times since the payroll bots have such a dominating presence in the mine.

Jay T. Paylor:
The boss-bots are technically in charge, they are powerful because they can have such an impact on reality, but machines are artificial, which could be interpreted as not being real.
I am alive. I have a wife and a kid. I should not have to

bow down to a machine, especially one which had a major role in causing Mathew's death. Christina has been fighting with 'Boss-Bots R Us' since 2021.

George A. Smoothman:
I know what you mean. When I get blamed for environmental issues, which are way out of my control, my first reaction is feeling angry, then I feel helpless, a mere mortal. I am blamed just because I am the foreman, and a human foreman at that, but I am not a boss, I am just a scape goat.

How can you really make a bot-boss responsible when it makes an error? Poor Christina has been fighting in court with 'Boss-Bots R Us' for over nine years, and her pro-bono lawyer is almost bankrupt. I am not sure if she can win.

Jay T. Paylor:
By the time the courts are through with her case, Christina's Pro Bono lawyers will probably have either died from exhaustion or have gone bankrupt.

George A. Smoothman:
Well that is the system for you; it only works for the 1% on bad days.

Jay T. Paylor:
If the Coaltonstones and the Bells could replace us with robots, you know it would have been done, fifteen years ago.

George A. Smoothman:
Well the system is very unfair. James Coaltonstone gets all the profits and we get all the blame.

I could actually be forced to work as a slave laborer up in the arctic and Coaltonstone is off the hook. If something very bad happened and I didn't prevent it from happening, it would be legally all my fault.

I have to sign-in to start the shift and sign-out at the end of the shift and today there was no shift. And I suppose no pay.

I have to report risks that may have a great impact on my crew, while payroll-boss bot Five is flying around my head.

Jay T. Paylor:

Yeah. Ginger was about the only one in management who made our work life a lot easier psychologically partly because he humanized our work conditions. I am not sure if we are supposed to refer to Ginger in the past or present. Ginger always said that those boss-bots had no place in the mine until they were fitted with some form of safety mechanism, where a human in the mine can actual turn it off, when it is causing a negative impact on the work environment.

George A. Smoothman:

I saw Christina run into the bathroom earlier today holding a paper towel to her mouth. My wife did that during the first days of her morning sickness.

Jay T. Paylor:

Do you think?

George A. Smoothman:

I am afraid to think. We are miners, we use our sixth sense when necessary, but being too aware of the pit falls slows us down, then we don't make our quota.

Jay T. Paylor:

George, are you saying you are because you don't think? How frightening is that?

George A. Smoothman:

Not as frightening as the third industrial revolution being run by boss-bots.

Jay T. Paylor:

Yeah you are sure right about that. It feels so different not having that whistle-boss bot whistling at us day and night.

George A. Smoothman:

Yeah, Christina was wondering if the Payroll-Boss Bot 5C had been destroyed since it has been missing all day. I think those boss-bots took the glory away from us, because their lights were so bright and their metal so shiny, they always looked more polished than we could ever look, while working as miners.

Jay T. Paylor:
Speak for yourself, George.

George A. Smoothman:
You know what I mean. We all know that actualizing the third industrial revolution depends on us because we are not just the producers; we drive the economic engine by extracting the coal which fuels it. I suppose it is Coaltonstone's money which funds our work activities so we can extract the coal which fuels the world's economic powers. And Ginger is made of the same stuff. We will survive this, because we have no other choice.

Ok Ginger is a data miner, but he was still part of the coal mining process.

Jay T. Paylor:
Of course he did George; he saved our lives, so we might one day, mine again.

George A. Smoothman:
I hate it when you talk about Ginger as if he existed in the past.

Jay T. Paylor:
I am sorry.

George A. Smoothman:
So am I.
And if anyone can survive this, it will be a miner regardless of what he mines.

So when Ginger wrote his safety reports, I gained a reference written by a certified safety technician. I appreciated that so much, because most of us miners suspect that the boss-bots memories are wiped clean after a serious accident, similar to Mathew's. The boss-bots involved in Mathew's accident must have had their memories we formatted, automatically through software transmitted through the Eye-Bot's network.

Ginger always logged his memories in his safety inspector's log book.

He never power tripped on us. He acted like a miner's friend, you know. He seemed to care and understand us in a way no one else in administration ever seemed to do, except Christina of course.

Ginger seemed to empathize with us, as if he had been a miner in a past life.

And he was such a good soccer player.

I am having trouble too with not knowing whether to refer to Ginger as a person who used to exist or one who still does.

Jay T. Paylor:
I vote we assume that is still alive. I think this 'In-Reach' project. Is ten times better than attending group hug meetings; neither of us are great fans of hugging.

George A. Smoothman:
Speak for yourself. I like hugs sometimes. I hug my kids, I hug my wife, and of course I hug our trees when no one is looking.

Jay T. Paylor:
I guess you are right. If Ginger appeared right now, I would run to him and hug him, then we could play soccer tomorrow as planned. I can't believe how life changes so fast without a warning.

George A. Smoothman:
Yeah, I would run up to him and give him a hug. But he is not here. He is down in the mine, possibly dead, or dying or in pain, instead of us.

Jay T. Paylor:
Or he may be okay and found refuge.

George A. Smoothman:
I hope so.

Jay T. Paylor:

I don't know who to blame first. I suppose managing mining ventilation effectively was always in conflict with managing costs related to coal production.

George A. Smoothman:

James Coaltonstone was always finding ways to adjust the interpretation of regulations to make it look like management was complying. Fear keeps most people silent. Even his sons are afraid of him.

Ginger would always speak up though when he believed something unethical or even illegal was taking place.

If an inspector showed up and management was found to not be in compliance with regulations, Coaltonstone would just bite the bullet and pay the fine for not complying.

Jay T. Paylor:

Mine Five has been in production for over fifteen years, and during this last year Ginger was concerned that there was little disclosure related to the safety risks workers and contractors inside the mine were taking.

It is not just what we know that is going to keep us safe. It is what we don't know and need to know.

George A. Smoothman:

The way it is now, coal production comes first regardless of safety.

The ventilation shaft was one of the first places where fire raged on, I suppose the combination of oxygen and other gases. Imagine if Ginger had tried using that shaft to exit the mine.

Just because the ventilation shaft had been certified as a second emergency exit does not mean that it should have been.

Jay T. Paylor:

Right, there could be hundreds or even thousands of tunnels beneath Coalton Valley as far as we know. Mapping tunnels during previous mining operations was never a priority to anyone. It seemed people like to keep such things private if they can.

George A. Smoothman:
I just can't believe that James Coaltonstone isn't bribing some government official to turn a blind eye.

How could Coaltonstone be allowed to use such a haphazard method of ventilating the mine if he wasn't paying someone to look the other way?

Since the mine was supposed to close by June 30th of next year, I guess the Government's Official Directors have been allowing the hodgepodge doorway and fan system being used as a ventilation system. There was a clause in the agreement that the independent contractors and the miners did not prop the doors open when moving heavy equipment. Of course all Ginger could do was write reports when his instructions were being ignored.

Jay T. Paylor:
How else did they expect the equipment to be moved if they didn't prop open the doors? That ventilation system designed by Bobby Coaltonstone was a death trap waiting to happen.

George A. Smoothman:
Equipment was supposed to be moved in-between shifts, but the in-between times were never long enough. Ginger kept filing reports, which protected us to a certain degree, since we could be blamed if our crew got hurt under our watch. I don't think I could survive digging for diamonds in the Arctic as a slave laborer.

Jay T. Paylor:
It is basically a death sentence for most people.

George A. Smoothman:
I know. And slave labour works for the 1% and the Government's Official Directors' office. Don't forget the lead threat was the problem with the ventilation system's ability to function adequately.

Jay T. Paylor:
What a way to die.

George A. Smoothman:
And Bobby's ventilation system was a death trap just waiting to happen.

Jay T. Paylor:
Didn't I just say that?

George A. Smoothman:
I know. You can't say enough about what was wrong with that ventilation system.
I really wish someone had shared the dust audits with the PPZ before the explosion happened this morning. I really wish we had done something.

Jay T. Paylor:
Don't you think Ginger would have been better off right now if we had sent those reports to PPZ or to someone who could have really made a difference?

George A. Smoothman:
While Ginger is stuck in the pit possibly dead or seriously injured, he may be thinking what we are thinking. I really wish that I had complained to someone when his reports were being ignored.

Jay T. Paylor:
Well if Ginger is dead he won't be thinking about anything, will he?

George A. Smoothman:
You know what I meant.

Jay T. Paylor:
The only ones who ever blow the whistle around here are the whistle-boss bots.

George A. Smoothman:
Well boss-bots don't have to worry about human things, like feeding themselves and their families. Boss-bots are only part of a two dimensional world enabling the 1% to live and manage their assets, including us, behind screens. I hope some of the boss-bots got caught up in the explosion and were blown up, especially the payroll-boss bot five and the payroll-boss bot five. I say good riddance to those two.

Chapter 5:
Beginnings

Journal Entry, LOG #1, written by Dr. Ashley Knight MD (Pitville Medical Center) reference to medical notes for patients Andrew (Ginger) Goodwin and others for Sunday, December 22nd, 2030 around 2:00 PM:

This has been a very rough day.

Like everyone else, I heard the explosion and felt the tremors around 5:20 AM.

Usually when employees or contractors have been hurt, trapped or killed in one of the mines, family is called.

Ginger Goodwin was born December 25th 1998 and is employed as Mine Five's assistant safety manager at Coaltonstone Mines. He has been trapped in that mine now for about nine hours.

According to Mr. Goodwin's birth records, he was placed in a nursing home for babies when he was a new born. During his first two years his address was a nursing home run by the local hospital which is no longer in operation.

The older couple, which was listed as Mr. Goodwin's legal guardians, were the parents of the mother who died in child birth. The child's father is actually the son of the maternal grandfather's cousin. The whole affair was very messy.

There were also notes from the nursing home that were written by the head nurse, thirty years ago. The mother was the daughter of a well-known coal baron and the father was a son of another famous coal baron who was a cousin of the maternal grandfather.

Ginger's mother was around nineteen years old at the time and Ginger's father was around thirty.

The second note is a very similar description of what transpired as the previous note.

There is so much mystery the story which shaped Ginger Goodwin. The nurse was concerned about baby Ginger's health and wrote the note anonymously.

Even though these two coal barons were cousins, they have been refusing to speak to each other directly ever since Ginger's birth and when necessary they speak to each other through lawyers.

So all of this information is sealed but was duplicated for medical reasons, just in case baby Ginger suffered complications sometime in his future due to the genetically "close" family ties.

Mr. Goodwin was adopted at two years old and he always referred to his adoptive parents as his true parents. Sadly both Mr. and Mrs. Goodwin were killed driving on the Tut Island highway. Strangely, Christina Watson's parents were also killed driving on the Tut Island highway, a year later.

As a physician practicing in Pitville I face terrible dilemmas as a daily occurrence but I have never woken up to such an awful situation as I did this morning.

I don't know if Ginger was incinerated. What I do know is that Ginger Goodwin is a survivor and certainly does not have an obsessive-compulsive disorder.

Mr. Goodwin never mentions his background most likely because he is not aware of it. On the surface his family situation seems to not even interest him. Mr. Goodwin may be ignoring the family issue since no one can change the past, and from his point of view he possibly feels no one in his biological family wanted him.

Before this morning's explosion these personal issues did not seem pressing or important.

There were several people in this town who wanted to label Ginger as having an obsessive-compulsive disorder so that they could dismiss Ginger's reports and concerns, which did not change the true physical dangers that Ginger was documenting so meticulously.

Mr. Goodwin was pushing for dust auditing capacity to be programmed into user-friendly data bots, so that a dust audit could be processed every twenty minutes. Instead of taking Mr. Goodwin's ideas seriously there were many people who tried to silence him or ostracize him. If they had only listened to him, the explosion might have been prevented.

I also heard through Christina Watson that Ginger skyped her personal account at around 5:10 AM, with a message and a picture showing that the methane gas monitor, on the coal shearing machine, had been turned off. Then minutes later Ginger sent another message to the administration building that the coal dust was so thick, his eyes were stinging. And minutes later the explosion occurred, changing life in Pitville, as we know it.

Ginger always said that his data mining was just as important as coal mining. Ginger believed that data mining was the first step in any quality control program. In order to improve working conditions in the mine for both miners and contractors, knowledge gained from data mining is power, just like in medicine. On the other hand sometimes too much knowledge becomes burdensome.

I was planning to tell Christina that I received her pregnancy test results yesterday, and that they came back positive. It just doesn't feel right to tell her right now. Christina is in a terrible emotional condition and the thought of raising two children alone, is not something I want to burden her with at this very minute.

Ginger encouraged Christina to hold 'Boss-Bots R Us' accountable through the courts, no matter how long it took. In principle Ginger is right, no one likes the way those mechanical beasts mark people for life; but what if her pro-bono lawyer goes bankrupt? Both Muni and Christina could land up as slave laborers in the Arctic for years, if not decades.

I think the court proceeding have been hard on both Ginger and Christina. The miners have the legal right to humane treatment regardless if their boss is human or a robot. If Christina wins her case against 'Boss-Bots R Us', a precedent will be set, and hopefully boss-bot related accidents may be prevented in the future, and personal records will not mark a person for life. I hate to guess what could happen to both Muni and Christina if they lose.

Ginger's data could show whether Coaltonstone Mines have been complying with regulations or not. Any data that Ginger may have sent just before the explosion occurred, in my opinion, should be protected as soon as possible by an external authority and even by the Government Official Directors.

During the last few months, Ginger tried to ignore the negativity that was meant to intimidate him. As risk taking became the norm Ginger was losing the battle.

Just like Mathew Watson, Ginger felt anxious when there were too many boss-bots flying around his head. You can't blame him; I mean who wants to be marked for life by a mechanical beast? I certainly don't want to be. Mathew Watson was especially afraid of the Payroll-Boss Bot 5C since it was programmed to take photographs of Mine Five employees randomly. The rule of the mine was to smile for the camera, in case the PR department wanted to use any of these pictures to show the general public on Pitville Island, how happy they were, working in Mine Five. After the picture was taken, the payroll-boss bot would send the pictures to the Eye-Bot Network, and the employee would have to regain his rhythm and focus before he could fully concentrate on his work while realizing that he had been marked for life, by the mechanical beast.

As I wrote before, many of my patients feel especially anxious around Payroll-Boss Bot 5C. This mechanical beast is programmed to fly around employees' heads, making them feel that it is breathing down their necks. How this inhumane treatment is supposed to increase productivity, is anyone's guess. Many of my patients complain of feeling anxious every time that boss-bot flies around their heads. They fear for their personal safety and they fear for their future.

Ginger Goodwin continued to work on his data charts so that he could tweak his ability to forecast future risk. Ginger was trying to devise a method where he could predict the time when accidents, due to faulty equipment, had the greatest chance of occurring within a reasonable margin of error, so that miners and contractors could avoid working in the mine, until the problem was corrected. I have no idea how you can predict what one miner will do especially when the coal is being weighed on scales that may be programmed to be lighter than the coal actually weighs.

Ginger's theories depended on everyone playing fair and acting reasonably, including the Earth. I can see how someone can predict what a population of a thousand might do, a lot easier than predicting what a group of one hundred and sixty might do, especially if they were under pressure to meet a quota regardless if the scales were faulty by design.

And if Ginger's charts were able to predict when an explosion could be expected based on conditions such as air quality, he could prevent, in theory, random deaths related to gas explosions. Ginger stressed however that he could not predict the unpredictable behaviour from unauthorized mining nearby. Who could predict that? This activity is not documented in any way. Neither are most of those workers.

Not that Mr. Goodwin thought that he could actually prevent an explosion, but he realized that he could prevent the miners from being inside the pit during the time of an explosion.

I guess that is exactly what he did do.

Ginger Goodwin heroically prevented the whole morning shift from entering the pit because he was concerned about something. I hope he was able to take the cart to 'Section E'.

For some reason there has been no communication with Ginger since the accident. I have been told that the tele-magnetic radios theoretically should work under any condition.

Ginger knew his numbers were correct, but the Coaltonstones did not give him the power to turn things around so that he could do his best to prevent this morning's explosion. It seems that Ginger Goodwin was given the power to record data related numbers, but he was not given enough power to make a difference. This morning I suppose Ginger just took the power to make a difference. I sense that Ginger has a very strong, sophisticated chi, and sometimes I wonder if he was here, on this earth maybe even this valley, one lifetime before. He seems to know things before they happen, or before they have been learned.

Christina is actually listed in Ginger's medical file as his next of kin.

At this time I have advised all my patients to keep a personal journal of feelings and events and possible solutions they are considering.

This self-empowerment is actually the theme and purpose of my 'In-Reach Project'. I hope when necessary, this project might even free their chi and give them the strength to overcome whatever is in their way.

On today's rounds I collected one thumb-drive from Christina Watson and one thumb-drive from George Smoothman and Jay Paylor who are sharing the same journal.

I consider myself a practitioner of evidence based medicine. I am also aware of the unexplained power that gives some people strength to act in a super human way when in danger, while others in a similar position just crumble. I believe that it is possible that the power, which gives someone in an emergency super-human strength, can also give person strength to take a giant leap onto a new path, at will. The power to change one's destiny lies in the path that one takes, either by choice or by design. I believe this super strength is the power of one's chi.

I know a lot of people were making unfair assumptions that that Ginger had an obsessive-compulsive disorder. Ginger was often treated as if he had something wrong with him. It is just too bad that they didn't listen to what he was trying to say; maybe if they had listened, this morning's explosion would have been prevented. Ginger wrote all those reports because he was doing his job. It had nothing to do with having OCD.

Sometimes I think I was crazy for allowing Mayor Stern to talk me into moving to Pitville which was beginning to sprawl around Mine Five, without much of a city plan, let alone design. Before the mine opened, this town was nothing more than a small village and most of the population was either on welfare, retired or was employed in the tourist industry of sport fishing in the summer and skiing in the winter.

I am sure the mine would have opened with or without me, but at the time I was told that the mine had insisted that the town have a medical clinic with at least two full time family doctors who would be on call. So I joined Dr. Daniel Smith's clinic, and have been working with him ever since.

Ginger Goodwin has one unusual concern. He is often haunted by vivid dreams which seem so real, that when he awakes from them, he spends days feeling hunted. Yes hunted, not haunted. His terrible nightmares are similar to the content of a horror movie and he often dreams the same dream regularly.

Mr. Goodwin has assured me that he does not watch horror movies and has no idea where these dreams come from or why they are so similar and repetitive. I believe these dreams could be part of a trauma he experienced in a past life.

One dream in particularly, Goodwin has regularly, begins with him running through the bush, arguing with someone, then he hears a gun shot, and ends with him being carried through the bush as maggots are eating his face.

Working in Mine Five can cause all kinds of ailments from skin irritation, irritated eyes, and lung diseases but it is very unusual to experience such vivid and horrific nightmares as Ginger experiences. I believe it is Ginger's chi trying to communicate to him. There could be something else that is causing these nightmares, but I believe at times, a person's soul, if it is very old, tries to communicate to a person's conscious mind, usually in their sleep.

I have examined patients with all kinds of ailments, which I believe, have a direct correlation with working in Mine Five and living relatively close to the pit. I see patients with foot problems, hearing loss and all kinds of lung ailments. I agree with Mr. Goodwin, that conditions either need improving, or Mine Five needs to be condemned.

During the past couple of weeks the severity and frequency of lung ailments, eye irritations and feelings of constipation have increased dramatically. I don't agree that employees and contractors should accept lung disease as an occupational hazard. These people are strong, brave and rather stubborn.

As I read Jay and George's and Christina's, journal entries their honesty and willingness to share their most inner thoughts means that they are opening up to my 'In-Reach' Project.

I certainly hope that I am doing the right thing. Such openness I believe could reveal the secrets of one's chi but there are also risks of course and this is why my project is sometimes considered controversial and even dangerous.

I know a mind can be fragile, but these people, as I said before, are strong, brave and though at times stubborn, I believe will not break easily.

Is it right to experiment with a person's mind. Well I certainly hope that is not what I am doing.

Anthracite coal is rapidly replacing oil as the fuel to power various militaries and industrialized machines. And many miners believe what they are doing is their patriotic duty which includes ignoring their occupational illnesses.

It is hard these days to know if we are in a war or almost in a war or preventing a war.

I just don't feel that Mr. Goodwin is dead. Until I see the actual evidence that he is dead I am assuming that he is alive.

Mr. Goodwin has given me permission to make decisions if he cannot do so for himself. The list of items he would like me to take care of are enclosed in this sealed envelope that I am not sure if I should open now or wait until it is certain that Ginger Goodwin is dead.

I have decided to wait.

I certainly hope that the teams of rescue robots are put into action soon, even if the robots are only able to retrieve Mr. Goodwin's body. I recommend that they do not seal this mine without retrieving Mr. Goodwin's body.

This is one of the most dramatic situations that I have ever had to face during my career in Pitville. Authorities should be treading lightly but they don't. Bosses seem to promote polarizing words such as calling the public a mob, or individuals agitators, since these people really are the people. I mean that is who they are, local people, and many are my patients and I fear for their safety.

I fear social unrest, rioting, injury and even death could be the end result of this already tragic situation. Many of the people standing out there on the street complete with miner's light and candle are my patients, and of course I cannot treat them all at once if they all get injured.

Thank God Reverend Martin Coaltonstone is leading the crowd in prayer and song; he is such a calming influence.

Mr. Goodwin once told me that he believed in super-naturalism, and I am not quite sure what he meant by that. When I asked Mr. Goodwin to explain, he told me that he believed that the earth was a giant breathing life form and when we are being called to the wild, it could be the same magnetic force which some believe, guide wildlife. Even though the Earth seems solid, it is actually very porous, dynamic and often mysterious.

It is common knowledge, in this day and age, that heat can make the Earth soak water up like a sponge, creating cavities which at some time in the future could lead to massive sinking holes and possibly even quicksand.

Mr. Goodwin also said that he believed in the power of physical renewal, and that stem cells in the blood, had a very important role in regulating and expanding a person's biological life, so that time does not have to run out as fast as we are led to believe.

Ginger also believed that we could develop into a different type of human that exists today, in the early twenty-first century.

During my stay in Pitville I have grown to believe that the only common ground is the ground we stand on and one day we will be buried in. And if that ground, sinks beneath our feet when we least expect it to, well I just hope that never happens.

End of In-Reach entry, LOG #1 by Dr. Ashley Knight MD (Pitville Medical Center).

Chapter 6:
Robot confusion

In-Reach entry, LOG #3, written by Christina Watson (Accounting Assistant to Alex Coaltonstone) written around 2:00 PM:

Lily just skyped me again; this time she told that that Don Bell said that he was certain that Ginger thought the guard-bots waiting in Don's office were the data bots that Ginger had been promised years ago.

Don Bell told James Coaltonstone that he thought that Ginger may have thought that the new guard-bots were meant for the mine's safety department. The new robot guards had been sitting in Don Bell's office waiting for processing. Since Ginger had been requesting robust robots which were friendlier to humans for years, the mix up was understandable.

Any reasonable person could understand how this mix up could have easily happened.

I don't know anyone who recollects a time when safety was put before coal production in this mine, even though explosions and accidents cut into profits and lower productivity, in the long run.

Most members in the mining community are often torn, since everyone knows a serious accident like this morning's will be a serious setback for the whole process of coal production.

On the other hand, it is hard to believe that if corners are not cut, extracting coal, from otherwise almost depleted resources seam, could not be economical.

Lily said that James Coaltonstone had been planning to arm those guard-bots and possibly use them as replacements to avoid paying the human cadet's overtime.

John Bell told Lily that Alex Coaltonstone believes that arming guard-bots will be even more cost effective, than his ventilation designs used in Mine Five have been. So how scary is that?

These new guard-bots could be killing machines, and my Ginger, is all alone with two of them, in Mine Five.

Lily said that she believed that the new bots were meant to be weapons not helpers. Lily wasn't certain if the guard-bots were going to be used as weapons to control the crowds outside the security perimeter, or if they were going to be used as weapons against the miners. Anyway Lily said that Don Bell stuck up for Ginger as best as he could.

That is good. Hooray for Don.

Don Bell told Lily that these new guard-bots might help Ginger keep his spirits up since they are also programmed to sing and play uplifting songs whenever the bots sense that their human counterparts are in distress, especially when trapped and immobile.

Maybe it is a good thing that Ginger has these two state-of-the-art guard-bots with him. Hopefully they were also able to warn Ginger that the air quality was becoming toxic so that he had some time to respond and to seek safety, as far as humanly possible, from the mine's death zone.

Lily said that Don Bell said the same thing. If the guard-bots are with Ginger they could give him some cover, protection and some hope of being rescued.

Don Bell is a pretty good person. I think he cares about our safety, but he also spends a lot of his time working with his brother, John in security, which probably is how the mix up happened. It is hard to know when Don is working for our mine's safety department or when he is working for the security department.

I can see how Ginger may have assumed that the guard-bots were meant for his department. I mean Don had the bots in his office for days, and Ginger had been asking Don to purchase more robust and user friendly robots ever since Mathew was killed.

In fact Ginger wanted the criterion, of being human friendly, included in the settlement between the boss-bot manufacturer and myself. He wanted all boss-bots designed to be respectful and compatible with human needs and temperament.

I can't imagine boss-bots being built to be user friendly. I thought their main purpose was to terrify the crew into submission, so the crew would extract coal as fast as possible, oblivious to the dangers cutting corners may cause them, down the road.

I can definitely see how Ginger just assumed that the new bots were meant to replace the old boss-bots which were so demeaning, and in Mathew's case, deadly, to work with. It makes a lot of sense to have boss-bots that look more humanoid in shape, instead of looking comparable to a satellite dish floating around the sparsely lit mine.

I don't know why the telemagnetic communication center isn't set up yet.

The telemagnetic radio is supposed to work under all kinds of conditions.

If Ginger was able to reach the rescue chamber, he will only have eighty-seven hours before his air supply runs out.

I still can't figure out why Ginger sent that message about the gas monitor being turned off, to my personal Skype account. I suppose Ginger didn't trust the work accounts anymore.

End of In-Reach entry, LOG #3 by Christina Watson (Accounting Assistant to Alex Coaltonstone).

Chapter 7:
A Family Secret

Journal Entry, LOG #1, written by Dr. Daniel Smith MD (Pitville Medical Center) for Sunday, December 22nd, 2030 written around 2:30 PM:

As I look out of my office window, I see a scene which reminds me of a pre-war zone. There must be more armed men behind that security fence than there are at the military academy.

I can see why these 'In-Reach' journals can work. Sometimes the over exposure to negativity can leave a person in a permanent state of agitation.

It is almost like a person could get trapped in a feedback loop of negativity.

Looking from the outside, that security fence defines the division between the owners of the mine and everyone else I suppose. From the inside the divisions are a lot more complicated.

The whole approach of power division in this town is very antagonistic partly because it feels so unjust. The mine operators haven't even tried to communicate to the public yet. It is the public who are paying for the military personnel standing behind that security fence over there.

I suppose it is true that who we are, will be defined through our relationship to production, or what we produce. It seems to me that our relationship to production is more important to our social standing than our relationship to other humans. It is very sad. And maybe as the gap and alienation between humans increases, things at least as they appear to be, will just grow sadder.

Ginger, with his whole life in front of him, and a baby on the way, is alone, disconnected from all of us lucky enough to be on the surface. In this day and age this suffering was preventable and yet we still tolerate it. The suffering hurts more because it was so preventable.

It may not be a certainty what caused the early morning explosion, but what is certain is that James Coaltonstone chose the most cost effective ventilation system that he could get certified. The fact that James Coaltonstone hired his son to be the chief ventilation engineer is also suspect, though I do realize that Bobby is certified, but Bobby is not really able to think or act independently from his father, James Coaltonstone.

It has been a really rough day.

It is hard not knowing whether Ginger is still alive or not.

I have little faith in government outsiders. These outsiders do not really have that much experience in operating around methane gas and hot rocks and they are also the ones who are certifying ventilation systems rather liberally.

As I drove to work this morning, I could see red flames and black smoke shooting out of Mine Five's ventilation shaft.

Unbelievably, that ventilation shaft, because it had a 1,200 foot built-in ladder, had been certified as a second emergency exit.

Despite the fact that the ventilation shaft was actually a fire trap, the 1,200 foot climb was a problem in itself during optimum conditions, let alone during an emergency.

On the bright side, earlier this afternoon, the air-buses which brought in hundreds of cadets left, making room for, another air-bus. This time the air-bus arrived with a flash mob of mostly ladies from various church choirs accompanying the men from various coal miners' choirs. They all came out of the air-bus singing "We Shall Overcome" very passionately. Having singers leading the crowd in holiday songs and old time spirituals, I think was a very good idea. My guess is that Sam Jones, who is technically the secret union representative for our area, organized it.

Hope, without a specific goal or plan, at the best of times is a rather flimsy sentiment which sooner or later betrays most of us who are not directly related to the power clique.

I realize many of the young people do not remember when Coalton Valley was beautiful and had plenty of salmon; let alone care about the Coalton Valley Glacier shrinking almost before our eyes. Of course blaming the political power structure from the past and the unexplained energy force from below will never bring the salmon population back to the valley. At least the generations from the past had the foresight to keep the waterways open to the public to use for navigation and recreation. Once private parties took ownership of the rivers, public trust began to erode. Coalton Valley used to be a world class tourist destination, but not anymore. Will Coalton Valley become the next Pompeii? I certainly hope not.

All the beauty, or what is left of it, is kept alive behind fences and barriers, creating two worlds; the beautiful one only accessible to the few and the other one we would rather not see.

There is nothing worse than when the power clique clings. Their powers as emotional vampires seem to have no end. The power clique, are able to pull the treasures buried deep inside the Earth, by pushing Coaltonians into a mind numbing trap which will sooner or later not just drain the population but the very earth itself; and what will be left? Empty cavities filled with acid water? Certainly not gold; that precious metal was depleted over a century ago.

I will always miss the days of my childhood when this land had a strong foundation. Now most of the land above the pits, must depend on the pillars to hold it up, and without those pillars, the land cannot maintain its strength.

Over the years, the pillars beneath many properties were stolen, letting the land above sink into a black hole, often when Pitvillians were sleeping in their beds.

And if that wasn't bad enough, tailings and residue often found their way into Coalton Valley's ground water.

As I wrote earlier, I am writing this journal partly because I am obligated to, and I won't write lies.

I am the doctor who brought Ginger into this world I don't think it is fair to assume that he is dead without giving the rescue effort a chance to succeed. He was born on Christmas day and we were short staffed. It seemed from the minute he was born he was being pushed around. Ginger's biological mother Marie-Rose

Diamond died that day, so I had to write out a birth certificate and a death certificate. I thought I would never witness a sadder Christmas than the one I had during 1998.

Once the Government's Official Directors declare that it is legal to seal the mine, rioting could follow.

At the very beginning Ginger had a rough start, but in many ways he is a stronger person for it. We need more men in Pitville with a bit of spine.

I never thought it was a good idea for an asthmatic to be working around coal dust. Coal dust is hard on everyone's lungs and even more so for an asthmatic.

I don't know what is wrong with that James Coaltonstone. The way he lords his power over people as if he were the only one involved in the process of producing coal in this valley.

The people who almost die in coal mines, or who witness environmental damage or the miners who work under continuous surveillance of boss-bots that are sometimes malfunctioning, soon become hardened to their conditions, and even accepting of them.

Money is not in great supply since so much money is being spent on the "prevention of war" effort.

The Power Cliques depend on the negative conditions. If the miners had a surplus of income, they would have more choices, which is the last thing that the members of the Power Clique want them to have.

Ginger really did try to consider everyone who was working in Mine Five. He understood that the employees and contractors were involved in the production of the most valuable coal on the planet and that their rights as human workers could easily be ignored during the rush to get this coal to market after the production process has been completed. To add to everything else, I just feel terrible about what has happened to Ginger. I was actually on the team when Ginger was delivered, and sadly I have been hiding his family background information from him ever since.

If Ginger doesn't get out of that hell pit alive, he will have died not knowing who he really was.

Of course I can't blame myself. The liabilities involved have stopped me from telling Ginger about his true background.

Now, at this very moment, I have never felt so torn in all my life.

Due to my involvement with Ginger's actual birth, I have never felt comfortable being Ginger's doctor. From the very beginning I did not believe that it was right to be so secretive about Ginger's origins. Knowing the truth about Ginger always made me feel that I was living a lie by withholding information from him. I know I am not the only one lying, but that does not make me feel any better. I know it is a lie, sealed by the great power of the Government's Official Directors. Nevertheless a lie is still a lie.

Ginger always tried to make the mines safe and I hate to say it, but I am afraid he may have lost the battle. My rational side believes that nothing can be done now. Ginger's situation is hopeless.

With all that said, I have a little voice inside me which is telling me that Ginger is alive, and was successful in finding refuge in Section E. The air supply in the rescue chamber will be depleted the morning after Christmas day, so there is little time to waste.

If Ginger were able to access 'Section E' then he would have had the opportunity to transmit a message from the telemagnetic radio, which would be installed in each rescue chamber.

The telemagnetic radios have the ability to transmit a text message over a range of around two thousand feet and for voice; the distance is a little bit less.

Ginger is only twelve hundred feet underground, so I don't understand why there isn't someone setting up and manning a telemagnetic communicator station. It is almost like Ginger is being ignored on purpose while his time and air run out.

I don't see any sign of building a communicator station on the surface.

I am wondering if the underground power source which powers the invisible fences which surround the mine and other properties are interfering with the telemagnetic radio signals that Ginger may be trying to send up to the surface.

I have seen many end results of what the locals call the 'Curse of the Black Diamonds'. I have seen how the greed of a few, which is verging close to madness at this point, is allowed to dominate all factors of public and community life, causing misfortune for ordinary people.

There are many miners who have physical ailments, which could be easily managed, but they are afraid of adding extra costs to their employer's expense sheet. They do not speak up and they allow the ailments to cause them serious discomfort while altering their enjoyment of life.

And then there are the miners who are working in the flame pits who don't even know who their employer is and they are paid in cash. Talk about madness.

End of In-Reach entry, LOG #1, written by Dr. Daniel Smith MD (Pitville Medical Center).

Chapter 8:
Nothing Is Being Done

In-Reach entry, LOG #4, written by Christina Watson Sunday, December 22nd, 2030 written around 2:45 PM:

I see that the air-buses, which brought all, the cadets into the mine parameters, are now flying away. I guess the air-buses are going back to the base.

I think most people, myself included would be very thankful, if we were told that something was being done to rescue Ginger.

And after Ginger is rescued, the authorities can investigate the causes, which led to Sunday morning's explosion. Nothing else really matters to me except Ginger returning to the surface.

Of course knowing the cause of the explosion is important too, but I think we already know that everything we say will be called hearsay, and whatever evidence is found will be talked around by some thousand dollar an hour law firm.

We all know what the risks were, and how the risks were increasing as the ventilation system became less effective.

Lily said that Mayor Stern told Don, that the Big Seven want to make the boundaries very clear to the public. If the public crosses the boundaries, and steps onto private property, immediate action will be taken to push the crowd back into the section of property which is public. That would be the time when Mayor Stern might read the riot act and announce a curfew.

It sounds to me like old James Coaltonstone is trying to provoke the crowd so that they can respond to a negative with a negative.

Ginger would hate all this. He always wanted peaceful interaction. And it would really upset him because this is all happening at Christmas time, his favorite time of the year, not just because his birthday falls on December 25th, but because he always thought everyone seemed nicer to each other during the holiday season.

Public safety and fair play are always interpreted differently depending on what side of the security fence you happen to be standing behind.

I am not sure what the difference is between a state of emergency and martial law but they both sound horribly unfriendly and harsh to me. Not a situation that I would think would be compatible with the holiday spirit of skiing in the still untouched Beartut Mountain Range, which is always so popular this time of year.

I really wish I knew what they are actually doing to help Ginger.

I emailed Lily again and she said she had no idea what they are actually doing to help Ginger. She said she didn't think for practical purposes there is a difference between a state of emergency and martial law.

Since we are on the private property side of the fence it is hard to know if we are actually being protected or being held prisoner. Lily thinks I am joking.

She said that the quality of life will be restricted and confined within tighter boundaries and if we leave the building we will need to keep our ID cards handy so that we will be allowed back into the administration building. The mine workers will need a pass which will be issued by security as they leave, so they can get back into the building.

Lily said that she thought it might be easier and safer just to stay in the building even if our movements are being controlled than to walk out into the crowd.

I phoned Mathew's mother (Maria Watson) and she said that she has been very happy taking care of Junior and she was planning to take Junior flyking on Christmas Eve before all this happened so I could spend some alone time with Ginger on Christmas Eve. Actually Maria said she really enjoys being Grandma but only wished that Mathew could be here to enjoy Junior too.

Maria always said that Junior reminded her of Mathew when he was the same age as Junior is now.

I am sure glad I am not being watched by the Eye-Bot today. During ordinary workdays, everything we do is calculated so that we produce as much as possible every day. I really don't believe that the Eye-Bot and the "In-Reach" project are compatible. I mean I am writing this, and I am told that as long as I am enrolled in the "In-reach" project, due to the circumstances, the Eye-Bot is set into resting mode. I am not sure how true that is.

The Eye-Bot Network reminds me of the old Spy-Bot Network, which closed down about fifteen years ago when it had been discovered, that the Government's Official Directors and their representatives had been spying on the general public for years.

The spy-bots used to fly all over the downtown streets of Pitville, about fifteen years ago, when Mine Five first opened and Mine Four was beginning to close. When Uncle Ned was alive, he used to tell me about the Coal Wars in Coalton, which at the time was a new borough beginning to sprawl around the economic activity generated by Mine Two. Mine Five gradually replaced Mine Two, and Minatown which grew around the economic activities generated from Mine Two was disassembled and disappeared along with most of the borough of Coalton.

Pitville gradually replaced Coalton as the economic hub of Coalton Valley as Pitville began to prosper from the economic activities generated by Mine Five; Coalton and Minatown became ghost towns.

Often miners would just disassemble their houses once a mine closed and move it to the area where the next mine opened, creating a new borough of miners practically overnight while leaving behind a ghost town.

The miners of the Coalton Valley also supported a thriving agriculture sector and a merging and lucrative banking industry. As technology advanced, the little spy-bots soon developed into boss-bots, and flew around together like a pack of flies but looking more like flying dishes with blinking blue, red and green lights.

Rumor has it that those spy-bots had sensors, and those sensors were passed on to the boss-bots. With that kind of technology, the boss-bots were able to profile a person's state of mind, and categorize the human based solely on a ten minute assessment.

It was never clear to me though, how the boss-bots differentiated between the person's state of mind resulting from having a boss-bot flying around their head, assessing them, or resulting from a more abstract science based on such things as social economic status or expectations of future social-economic status based on the person's social connections. Social structure was everything in Coalton Valley. The faster you were able to disassemble and rebuild your house, the brighter your future prospects could become.

It is hard to feel positive and hopeful when there are so many armed and faceless people, mostly men, marching below my office window. I know it is all about perspective. Lily said the cadets are stationed below our office windows to protect us and to protect mine assets, but their presence makes me feel like a prisoner.

I just hope no one is provoked. With all these negative vibes that are so hard not to feel, we are all on the edge, and some of us could fall off that ledge.

The boss-bots are notorious for flying around a person's head. I haven't seen any of them outside today. Maybe all the localized ones were destroyed when Mine Five exploded. Any one of the bots annoying vibes could lead to a human reaction. Reaction we all try to avoid.

Living with regret is even worse than living with these boss-bots. Once marked by the mechanical beast, one has a negative record lasting for the rest of one's life.

Many Coaltonians have been forced to return to nature, becoming closer to a pre-civilized man, almost ape like without the strength.

Boss-bots can cause incredible physical turbulence too, not just emotional. Their wind turbulence can be so intense, a grown man, if he isn't hanging on to a lamp post, could be blown right into oncoming traffic.

Ginger did not believe in violence because he didn't think violence worked for people like us, it just gave the Power Clique an excuse to use the might of the military, which was always at their disposal, against us.

End of In-Reach entry, LOG #4, written by Christina Watson (Accounting Assistant to Alex Coaltonstone).

Chapter 9:
A Grisly Find by Mine Four Entrance

**Volunteer Worker Eleven Log Entry #1 written by
Jason Bell on Sunday December 22nd, 2030: around 3:00 PM.**

**Beginning personal log report #001
Written by volunteer #11**:

I am identified as Volunteer Worker Eleven, but I have
been working alone for about four hours and something awful just
happened. As my drill suddenly broke I could feel the earth
between Mine Five and Mine Four shake.

I was in the process of drilling borehole COALT-11-C into
the floor of Mine Four, which is about six hundred feet above
Mine Five, and six hundred feet below the surface.

The new drill bits were delivered to this site around 10 AM,
and one of the drill bits hit rock, broke, about fifteen minutes ago,
about the same time as that Earth Tremor.

Now, I am sitting on a rock, a few hundred feet away from
the mine entrance, waiting to receive new orders from Control
Center.

Before the drilling mishap I was thinking a lot about
Ginger, hoping that he was able to reach a rescue chamber
somewhere in Mine Five. I suppose I just spaced out. Hopefully,
assuming Ginger found a rescue chamber, and is able to sit out the
explosions, he will only have about 86 hours of air supply left.

The drill holes that I was drilling were supposed to speed
up the rescue effort. Time is so critical.

I was told at the beginning of my shift this morning that the other volunteers will be joining me when they are able.

Drilling boreholes during a rescue is never easy volunteer work, and I can understand why I was the only one who actually showed up for this morning's shift, prepared to do the drilling.

When a life is saved, the rewards are indescribable, which motivates me to do this work.

I really want to make a difference. That is why I was drilling borehole COALT-11-C into the floor of Mine Four, which is technically the ceiling of Mine Five. Once my drilling is complete, I will send an air sample to Control Center for analysis. Once my air sample is received, Control Center will determine if it is safe to send in a human rescue team, possibly backed up by rescue robots.

Drilling into Mine Five through Mine Four creates a six-hundred feet short cut. So we are that much closer to rescuing Ginger Goodwin than we would be if we were drilling from our surface location, near the corn field, on the Evans' family farm.

The plan was, once borehole COALT-11-C was drilled, we were going to send in a camera on a line, to explore below. Before the explosion, I could have sworn that I heard banging. The noise could have just been wishful thinking, or just bats planning their exodus, after my intrusion.

There has been heated discussion, back and forth on the phone, concerning Ginger's fate, if the mine is sealed. If it is too dangerous to launch a rescue under present conditions, I don't think the Coaltonstones or G.O.D. will have much of a choice.

End of personal log report#001 for volunteer #11.

After Jason listened to his log twice, Jason took another minute to think about the situation and wrote an addendum.

Beginning personal log addendum for
Report #001 written by volunteer #11:

I am not sure if the drill bit that broke a few minutes ago, contributed to this sudden earthquake which may have triggered a simultaneous explosion in Mine Five, just below the area where my work station was located. I really don't know what happened

S.E. McKENZIE

first. Everything happened so quickly. I left the broken equipment and just made a dash for it.

Since Mine Four is above Mine Five, it is possible that my drilling did cause sparks in the mine below, igniting a pocket of methane gas. Who knows what happened? I sure don't. If the right combination of air, methane gas occurs and a spark from something, the end result would be very explosive, so no wonder no one really wanted to do this volunteer job.

As soon as I heard the loud explosion below I took the elevator up to the surface, and I have been sitting on this rock outside the shaft entrance ever since. I am now waiting for someone from Control Center to call me.

The geology in this area has numerous faults, which can cause coal seams to go into different directions. It is common knowledge that not all tunnels have been documented since not all mining from the past has been fully documented.

This sudden explosion this afternoon could really throw a monkey wrench into Ginger Goodwin's rescue and I am the one to blame. I feel just awful. I was trying so hard to help, and it seems that I have just made matters worse and I guess right now he would have about three and half days of air supply left if he found refuge in one of the rescue chamber.

End of addendum for personal log report#001
Written by volunteer #11:

As Jason continued to wonder if he had caused the second explosion in Mine Five he soon became oblivious to his surroundings.

The more Jason thought about it, the more Jason worried that it was his drilling through the floor of Mine Four that sparked the explosion in Mine Five. He was also worried, that if he did get blamed for causing the second explosion, he and all the Bells could become a target of retaliation.

Jason knew how politics actually worked in Pitville, instead of all Pitvilians working together, groups with conflicting interests, seemed to work against each other.

Jason was just doing the volunteer job that he had been told to do. Jason was donating his time to make the world a better place; instead, he may have lessened Ginger's chances of being rescued from Mine Five.

The worst case scenario would be a coal seam fire. Jason was beginning to feel overwhelmed. As he continued to sit on the rock Jason hoped that he wasn't going to be the one blamed for this set back.

Jason hoped that everyone, well everyone of importance, would realize that whatever happened in Mine Five due to his drilling was not his fault. He was just following orders and was donating his time and if the entire coal seam was not mapped correctly how was he supposed to make the correct decision? Anyway, it was up to Control Center to make decisions, not Jason.

Jason felt incredibly tired. The weight of his operator's suit and oxygen tank were getting unbearable. He wished his opinions held just as much weight as he removed his gear. Jason had no idea when someone from Control Center was going to phone him, but he hoped it would be soon since he was exhausted and wanted to go home. The work was hard and thankless.

Jason tried to think of something else to think about. He started to think about how freaky it was to see all those bats appear from nowhere, right before the explosion, as if they had a sixth sense and knew that there was very little time left to exit the mine shaft. He thought it was the most amazing thing that he had ever seen. The exodus of bats reminded Jason of his old feelings that life was going by without him.

Jason felt awful. It was bad enough that his good intentions may have led to sparking a second explosion and could have even set the Stonely Coal Seam on fire, but it was a certainty that his actions also disturbed a congregation of bats that were living in Mine Four.

These days it was usually the bat that was often the unwitting air tester in a coal mine, the new canary.

As Jason turned around he could feel his heart almost jump out of his chest. Behind a boulder he could see four dead and badly charred bodies covered in dirt. He had no idea where they came from, though they appeared to be small enough to be Minese, and Jason knew that this location used to be the old Mina town site, which had been dismantled and moved to another location, a few decades ago. These bodies were either dumped at this location or just died on the spot, and sadly left to rot.

As Jason was trying to remain calm and functional, he was about to phone his Uncle John, who was head of security and he would know what to do, he could see Dianne Black and Jackson walking towards him.

After finding a way to sneak around security Dianne was now juggling the tasks of carrying her shoes in one hand, her microphone in the other hand and recovering from the shock of seeing a swarm of bats fly by.

"Where did all those bats come from?" Dianne asked Jackson as he was trying to keep his balance, while holding the camera equipment and carefully walking over the rocks.

"I don't know," Jackson said.

"Maybe they came from over there," Jackson added as he pointed to the entrance of Mine Four.

"What a spooky day. It is foggy and bats appear from nowhere. Now we have to report that the authorities are seriously considering foaming and sealing 'Sections A, B and C' including all the boreholes and shafts in Mine Five as an attempt to extinguish the fire before it ignites the Stonely Coal Seam, if it hasn't already," Dianne said feeling cold and exhausted.

"I wonder if we will ever find that communication center which is supposed to be set up to receive Ginger's telemagnetic radio transmissions," Dianne asked Jackson.

"Are you sure that the communication center actually exists?" Jackson asked, feeling just as tired and cold as Dianne was feeling, but was too manly to admit it.

"I don't know. This whole place is creepy. Maybe we should just park ourselves in front of that opening. If we spend any more time looking for the communication center we will be late broadcasting," Dianne instructed.

Dianne found walking on the cold rocks painful. As she cursed Steve for telling her to travel light, Dianne wished that she had brought a few pairs of her sensible shoes with her. Guys were allowed to wear sensible shoes why not her? Dianne began to stoically point in the direction she thought would lead to the best background which would frame her afternoon broadcast.

Jackson followed Diane's directions, as he looked around admiring the beautiful Beartut mountain range.

Dianne quickly glanced around and then decided that the back drop of Mine Four would make a backdrop for her broadcast. She gave a hand signal to Jackson and Jackson put all the equipment down, thankful that a rival broadcaster hadn't laid claim to the site first.

Without looking back, Dianne carefully put her shoes on her feet, checked her hair and then smiled at her reflection while inspecting her face.

As Jackson was holding the camera and checking his zoom lens, he noticed a man sitting on a rock nearby. Jackson zoomed-in closer so that he could see Jason's name tag and mentally memorized Jason's name.

"That man is just another Bell, just another gatekeeper," Jackson thought to himself.

"Welcome viewers. Today our source has revealed to us that officials are considering foaming and sealing Mine Five, with Ginger Goodwin still trapped inside.

Steve was standing by at the PPZ headquarters.

Jackson turned on the camera and the light shone brightly illuminating the exposed bodies behind Dianne, making the partially scorched and rotting human remains visible for the entire world to see.

Once Jackson realized that Dianne was standing in front of two dead men that were only partly hidden by a boulder he also realized that smoke was coming out of a crack in the ground.

Steve who was sitting in his office back at PPZ headquarters, watched as Jackson struggled to focus his lens on the human remains as his hands shook.

Dianne with microphone in hand was beginning her live broadcast.

Dianne performed the first toss of her wavy blonde hair while greeting the audience.

"Good afternoon viewers. I am Dianne Black, with the PPZ bringing to you another live update from the Pitville Mine Disaster of 2030, brought to you by the municipality of Sunrise Beach, where friends meet and sometimes stay.

As you can see, we are standing in front of the entrance of Mine Four, where rescuers were hoping to drill a new borehole so that the process of accessing Mine Five and the mission to rescue Ginger Goodwin could be accelerated.

We hope and pray that Ginger Goodwin, Mine Five's assistant safety officer will be found alive.

I would say that we need a Christmas miracle right now," Dianne said as she stopped for a moment and looked at Jackson, and then she realized that Jackson was actually staring at something behind her and his face appeared frozen.

As Dianne turned around she realized that Jackson was staring at partially scorched and decomposing human remains as smoke was coming out of a crack in the ground. Dianne screamed and began to hyperventilate, startling Steve, Jackson and Jason.

Jackson felt numb as he tightened his grip to keep his camera steady while trying to maintain his focus on the grisly scene. Then Jackson focused on Dianne. He had never seen Dianne look so natural and beautiful before.

Jason who had been oblivious to Dianne and Jackson's presence until now, had no idea what he was supposed to do or say, but he knew that he should say and do something, since he was the man in charge. He was a Bell.

Since the volunteer job description said nothing about guarding human remains or investigating the cause of smoke coming out of a crack in the ground; Jason decided to remain oblivious to his fear that he may be responsible for the Stonely Coal Seam being on fire.

As Dianne regained her composure she surprised herself by walking toward Jason and asked him a sensible question just the same way any other hardened news broadcaster was able to do.

"I see that your name is Jason Bell. My name is Dianne Black from the PPZ. What can you tell us about that? Dianne asked as she pointed to the human remains with one hand as she shoved the microphone closer to Jason's face with the other.

"This is not my responsibility. I know nothing about this. I cannot be blamed for not knowing anything, because I was not told anything so I have nothing I can tell you," Jason said realizing that he was sounding whiny and ridiculous.

"I am a volunteer, and our group will be assessing the area. We were hoping that we could accelerate the rescue mission by drilling through Mine Four, to access Mine Five. And I have nothing more to say about that either," Jason said, hoping to have brought closure to this conversation with Dianne Black.

"Has anyone notified the police concerning that?" Dianne said, not wanting to say what it actually was. Pointing at the remains was only slightly more comfortable.

Dianne was trying to remain calm even though she felt that she was going to hyperventilate any minute, again.

"Actually Mam, all these matters are being investigated by the authorities and cannot be discussed openly with the public at this time. This mine is private property and I could have you arrested and charged with trespassing. And that is the only comment I am prepared to make," Jason said as he pushed the microphone away from his face with one hand and the camera away with the other.

Dianne touched Jason's shoulder, and he turned to face her, realizing that he had never been this close to such a beautiful woman before, or such a famous one.

Jason realized that he sounded too defensive especially considering that the conversation could have been broadcasted live for the whole planet to see. Jason knew he wouldn't have sounded so frazzled if he had been told what to do in the first place.

Not knowing what else to do, Jason decided to do what his uncle John would do in a similar situation, he would show these two paparazzi, who was in charge, and control the perimeter with force if needed.

Jason wished that he had softened his approach, but it was too late. His response would most likely go viral any minute.

The last person Jason really wanted to be following in his footsteps was his Uncle John. Nevertheless his uncle John was the head of security and Jason wanted to be respected as an authority figure too.

"I am not sure how you were able to get past security today, but I could be the one blamed for the breach," Jason said with a pause, which was practically a whimper.

"I mean there could be more dead people in there," Jason said while pointing toward the shaft of Mine Four.

"I am very sorry that you had to see this. But when these mines are taken over by the criminal element, this kind of unpleasantness is bound to happen. These people are no better than animals. They are not civilized like we are. They mine illegally, they live on other people's private property and they often steal things to survive. Like the coal they are taking from mines that do not belong to them. I am not authorized to even say that. So you didn't hear that from me," Jason said, realizing that Jackson's camera was still rolling.

"This is not my fault. I know nothing more about this. I don't think my Uncle John who is head of security had any idea that there would be dead bodies so close to the opening of this mine when he volunteered me to do this job," Jason said again realizing he was beginning to sound like a professional apologist.

"Conditions are worse in Buzzard Creek. The big fear there is catching typhus from homeless illegals. Those lice carrying illegals work in those flame pits so they can sell coal at cut-throat prices," Jason said.

"I am actually waiting for my Uncle John to phone back. The conditions in Mine Four could be super unsanitary, a perfect environment for a cholera epidemic. Often illegals become opium addicts and even though opium dens haven't actually been found in the Minese camps, it is just a matter of time that Uncle John will find them.

It is just too dangerous for civilized miners to work with illegals. Civilized miners are protected by the Government's Official Directors. Civilized miners have grown accustomed to decent work conditions," Jason said realizing that he was possibly saying way too much.

"I am sure it is possible that the illegals' opium addictions give these Minese miners the strength to slave down there wearing oxygen masks and tanks," Jason said.

"And that is all I am going to say," Jason added.

"You know you two are trespassing, right now. This is private property," Jason said.

"Off the record I don't blame you at all for your response. Many of the volunteers have given up and have gone home to celebrate Christmas with their families. They left me all alone to face this horrible situation. I think they all hate me," Jason said.

"That camera is off, right?" Jason asked Jackson who looked sheepish.

"You have to take a break sometime," Dianne said to Jason.

"No I don't. I am like my Uncle John and Uncle Don," Jason said as he looked at Jackson and realized that everything he had said, and everything that could be seen had been recorded, and most likely was or would be broadcasted live. Jason thought that this day could not get any worse.

"I work until the job is finished. You are not recording this are you? I am obviously not authorized to give you a statement," Jason said, knowing this would be the story and photo session of a lifetime for both Dianne and Jackson.

Jason knew that this story could define Jason for life, which would make this day the worse day of Jason's own life.

Jason felt conflicted. He didn't want to be the one stepping in Dianne's way. Dianne should be the first to broadcast the story, especially if disclosing this story meant that she was disclosing the story of the century for Coalton Valley? "Jason knew that fate had already been sealed for this pile of bones and possibly for him too. Fate most likely was also sealed for Ginger Goodwin.

"I am just a volunteer. I am trying to find a way to help Mr. Goodwin," Jason said as he sat back on the rock. Jason put his head into the palms of his hands and began to laugh hysterically.

Dianne and Jackson look at each other and then Dianne started to shake, her heart started to race, and she thought she was about to die, as she started to hyperventilate again.

"Back to you Steve," Jackson said.

"Thank you Dianne for this news breaking story. PPZ is again the first network to bring to you live the latest developments in the Ginger Goodwin Rescue. Now, for the weather," Steve said as he took control of the screen.

Once the weather had been reported, Steve turned on another switch and programmed music began to play again.

As Steve reviewed the broadcast he zoomed-in to determine if he was really seeing smoke making its way out of the crack in the ground. Steve thought to himself that the next big news story might be that smoke. Something is happening underground and it is not just the illegal miners getting killed.

"You guys better move from there, quickly but calmly," Steve said to Jackson through Jackson's earpiece.

Jackson realized that this had been the action that he had waited for most of his life to film.

Jackson just hoped that Steve didn't break any law by broadcasting real news into people's homes without being sanitized first. The practice was usually frowned upon, but Jackson didn't think it was actually illegal.

"Are you ok, Di? We have to get out of here or at least move to a spot that is safer. I think that hole is getting bigger and the smoke is getting thicker. I mean this is a great scene. We have it. It has been sent. Let's go. You were great," Jackson said without even saying goodbye to Jason.

Chapter 10:
Is It Right Or Is It Wrong?

Journal Entry LOG #1 (Camera operator for PPZ)
written by Jackson Green on Sunday, December 22nd, 2030
written around 3:45 PM:

We are at the Pitville Medical Clinic. I am here to support Dianne and to get a doctor's note, which is required, by the head office for tax purposes.

We were given thumb-drives to use to report our thoughts and feelings.

When Doctor Knight gave me a thumb drive so that I could participate in the 'In-Reach' project, the phone rang and she left the room in a hurry, leaving the box of thumb drives on the table.

So I have plugged the thumb drive into my comphone and took out my folding keyboard. I don't like the idea of losing my objectivity or giving strangers evidence of my inner true feelings. Not that I have anything to hide, but I don't think it is anyone's business what I am thinking.

You know I am just a product of so called civilization. I guess more correctly the decline of it. Everything is breaking down. We have very little left that is new. We recycle everything. And once civilization is gone, hopefully our instincts will help us survive, not hinder us.

I suppose, as the gap between people widens, the reptilian brain will no longer be free to roam. The military will be out in force similar to what we are seeing at the Mine Five fiasco.

I know deep down inside me, lays an animal force, a combination of a lion and a wolf, I suppose a hybrid of some sort. If I revealed my inner beast, or let it control my actions, there is no doubt that the powers to be, especially in this town, would declare me insane. Nevertheless, I still believe in my homing instincts. My homing instincts never let me down. Whenever I am stumped, I let my homing instincts kick in. I even have iron crystals transplanted in my nose, so that I can make a strong connection, with the Earth's magnetism, and be prepared for the hard times ahead.

We all need our fronts. I think our fronts give us dignity and style.

I just keep staring at that box of thumb-drives.

I think once Dianne realized that she had let herself go, while broadcasting live on international television, I think Di just panicked. I don't know why, Di is at her most beautiful, when she is being herself.

After the broadcast, Dianne was really shaken up. Steve recommended that I take Dianne to see Doctor Knight who is one of the most sought after trauma therapists in the free world, some say even on the planet.

Once we arrived at the Pitville Clinic, we sat in the waiting room, and Dianne hid her face behind a magazine.

Doctor Knight insisted that we both see her.

Doctor Knight is wonderful. She is so passionate about her 'In-reach Project'.

Anyway, here I am sitting here writing into this thumb-drive.

Dr. Knight suggested that I start with the way I felt when I was filming the dead men behind the boulder. How I felt around death.

I don't think that those men completely died. Part of them, possibly the message in their DNA, lives in the creatures which may have eaten part of them, and then the humans who may have eaten the creatures, and then those memories will be passed through time, through the mass collection of DNA.

In my line of work I have to stay objective. I suppose the whole purpose of objectivity is that you can dismiss your own feelings as well as other people's feelings.

I see life as a project just half filmed, just half-done.

At one point we are all forced to leave the planet for the next generation to continue where we left off.

I have to feel objective about death and about news in general or I would unravel just the way Dianne did. Dianne reviewed our broadcast. I told her that she didn't look awful. Dianne looked beautiful. It is physically impossible for Dianne to not look beautiful. She did not look that bad. It was a natural broadcast, and it was a rare moment to see Dianne appearing to be real. There is no shame in that. It wasn't my fault that the broadcast went viral either. I was just doing my job. And I think I did a very good job.

Dianne is one of the most beautiful women in the world that is not just my opinion, it is a worldwide opinion. Dianne is always on top of the ten most beautiful women in the world lists. No one says they pay attention to those lists, but I bet they look at the pictures when no one is looking.

Dianne never looked horrible. She looked even more stunning in my opinion when she was being herself.

I usually align my shots with the sky. I am not really that experienced shooting in the confining space of mine shafts. Though I think the analogy is typical of the times in Pitville. Everything seems confined, restrictive and sad.

Dianne is in the other room I think she is still freaking out.

I suppose Dr. Knight is with her now.

I am writing this while Dr. Knight is trying to calm her.

Dianne was really shaken up. And I don't know what caused her the most traumas, the fact that she saw those dead bodies unexpectedly, without proper preparation or the fact she realized that she had let herself be unguarded on a live international broadcast.

I was in shock too. I guess that is why I kept filming even after Steve gave us the "Weather Cue". Seeing those half decayed bodies was a shock because it was the last thing that I was expected, so I was not on my guard the way I always am in war zones. The difference between the cosmopolitan culture which I am used to, and this Pitville monoculture, is also is sort of jolting. You feel like the culture is trying to shape you into something that fits into all this harshness, mud, and dirt. It all jumps out at me when I am behind the camera.

We drove past the crowds. The armed men were still marching around the perimeter of the fence.

I don't know how great all this self-revelation is. Everything scares me, especially myself. I know I am the man in the team at PPZ, and Dianne is the boss.

I shouldn't feel scared but I do. When I am around Dianne I know I shouldn't feel helpless, but I do.

I am just as much a newsman as anyone. I don't regret keeping the mike and camera on because the moment was real. A real person experiencing death is a story in itself.

I wish I could make it up to Dianne somehow. But why should I wish that? I was just doing my job. I made the decision that was right at the time.

Dr. Knight came in for a minute. The box of thumb drives is still on the table. The phone rang and she hurried out again.

End of Journal entry, LOG #1 (Camera operator for PPZ) written by Jackson Green.

Private Journal Entry written by Jackson Green on Sunday, December 22nd, 2030 written around 5:00 PM from Eagle Eye Inn Room 113.

It is unbelievable the amount of info I found on these thumb drives. It is amazing stuff. I have been reading most of the headings and I can get the picture without reading all the words and this is just amazing stuff.

Mathew Watson, the man who was crushed by the continuous mining machine around nine and a half years ago in Mine Five, during the time when the gate roads were being built, appears to have predicted his own death.

There are several logs written by Mathew Watson's widow, Christina Watson. She explains in great detail what was known about her husband's accident. She is also fighting with the boss-bot manufacturer in court, and has been wearing a debtor's chip for nine and a half years, in case she loses her case and is forced to pay costs. After all that time, a settlement with the boss-bot manufacture still has not been reached, which is bad enough, but if she loses her case, she could become a slave laborer in the Arctic for the rest of her life, until she pays back the bot manufacturer's legal fees and related costs. That is so inhuman.

Christina regrets having reached a settlement with the mine's owners. After the accident she felt that she needed closure and wanted to focus on bringing up her son, Mathew Watson Junior.

At the time, Christina did not realize that the mine owners would bring in the quota system, where miners are paid for tonnage of coal, instead of time worked. Christina is feeling partly responsible that she did not hold James Coaltonstone and the Big Seven Coal Group accountable when she had the chance.

The mine owners' quota policies, force the miners to work recklessly, while they extract as much coal from Mine Five as fast as they can, so they can make a living.

Christina blames herself for some of that recklessness, since if she had not settled with the mine, after Mathew's accident, she believes that the mine owners would be complying with safety procedures, if they had been held accountable for Mathew's accident. I doubt it.

I also discovered the results of Christina's pregnancy test.

I also found notes, which Doctor Knight inputted into her private log. Doctor Knight has Christina's test results but doesn't think she should tell her right now that she is pregnant, in case the stress pushes her off the edge. What a predicament to be in.

Back to Christina's husband's accident; two boss-bots; a whistle-boss bot and a payroll-boss bot were crowding Mathew while he was working with heavy mining machinery. The whistle-boss bot was whistling nonstop and was most likely malfunctioning. The payroll-boss bot was not programmed to address that kind of issue and continued to threaten Mathew with a having a bad report written up about him. Such a report would then be sent to the Eye-Bot Network while the whistle-boss bot continued to blow its whistle. Both boss-bots use a propeller-jet system which allows them to fly around the miner's head, but it also causes a lot of wind, which in itself could have pushed Mathew into the machine's radius.

Mathew got mixed up in the continuous mining machine's cables, as it was turning a curve. Mathew landed up in the radius of the continuous mining machine and was crushed to death. I can see how that could happen.

Mathew had been complaining about the Payroll-Boss Bot 5C's erratic behavior for weeks before his accident, which killed him back in June of 2021.

Ginger Goodwin had been submitting safety infraction reports concerning coal dust build up and the haphazard way that the ventilation system had been designed and maintained.

I also found some interesting posts written by James Coaltonstone, Pitville Mayor Ted Stern and Doctor Smith.

George Smoothman and Jay Paylor describe being general foremen. They have very little power to control the process of production. Nevertheless, they are being forced to take all the responsibility. George and Jay would most likely be blamed whenever something goes terribly wrong in Mine Five.

I also found a strange conflict between the signals, which are deep in the ground, and I am assuming are designed to control the invisible fences around Mine Five. Anyway, these signals could be interfering with the emergency telemagnetic radio transmissions. This radio is the only communication system Ginger Goodwin would have to reach someone on the surface who may be trying to locate him. The radios have a very limited range, about two thousand feet for text and maybe eighteen hundred feet for voice. This interference could be one reason why we haven't received any messages from Ginger Goodwin yet.

I feel that Ginger is alive too.

Sometimes doing the right thing is impossible. Especially in this case since so much that has happened was unexpected. It is part of our job to walk into the unexpected and ask questions and get evidence. Maybe we have license to do the wrong thing for the right reasons.

Dianne is usually great at commenting about conflicts, between right and wrong, bias, ethics, that kind of thing but commenting is different than actually making a difference. Some kind of action bound in strategy sometimes can change the balance of power, not just question it, but change it.

I think being behind a camera most of my career, I think I have had an opportunity to see the big picture. And it always seems, whenever there is an imbalance of power, there is also some sort of injustice which has occurred.

As observers, it is easy for us to criticize and ostracize. It isn't our lives being turned upside down.

Chapter 11:
A Terrible Loss

In-Reach Entry, Log #2, written by Doctor Ashley Knight MD (Pitville Medical Clinic), for Sunday December 22nd 2030 around 5:15 PM:

Something terrible has happened. My patient's thumb-drives from the 'In-Reach' project are gone. The box is still here, but all the thumb-drives are missing, including mine.

All my clients that are participating in my 'In-Reach' project have been reaching in, opening up and sharing and trusting me, so this could cause a real set back in their recovery.

My program can only work if my patients feel safe. Once my patients don't feel safe anymore they could shut down. The feeling of not feeling safe often triggers feeling of trauma long after the actual event occurred. My patients trust that their inner thoughts will remain private. And I have failed them.

I facilitate the unburdening of the soul, so that my patient's individual chi can be set free to strengthen them, when in need.

When thoughts become overwhelming due to traumas such as coal mine disasters and war zone activities some people are not able to stay strong until they build an internal structure, which is able to sustain inner strength.

Any time a person's situation has been so severe that the patient feels that his or her integrity has been compromised, often patients feel so powerless that their whole system breaks down, both physical and mental. My 'In-Reach' project often helps in centralizing and stabilizing the power of the chi.

Often reflecting on traumas can help a person regain their sense of personal power and integrity.

I left the box of thumb drives on the table in the Blue Room where Jackson was sitting, so that I could run to attend to Dianne Black who was hyperventilating in the Green Room again.

The primary suspect is Jackson the cameraman for PPZ, but I can't just accuse him of theft without proof. How can I get proof when the prime suspect is most likely hiding the evidence somewhere that is out of my reach?

All those confidential files are gone. I am so upset. I know it wasn't entirely my fault, and I guess my malpractice insurance could pay compensation to my patients if it comes to that.

I feel so terrible about this.

I know my security system was rudimentary, but everything in this town is breaking down. All the technology that was the state of the art fifteen years ago is getting harder and harder to fix or replace.

I just hope Jackson returns the flash drives, with no questions asked. How could he have done such a thing?

End of In-Reach entry, Log #2 by Doctor Ashley Knight MD (Pitville Medical Center).

Chapter 12:
The Waking Of The Dead Miners

In-Reach Entry, LOG #5 by Christina Watson written on Sunday December 22nd 2030 around 8:00 PM:

Things couldn't get much worse.

I know there is a lot the illegals are being blamed for, but sometimes I wonder if the first explosion was actually the illegals' fault or if someone much higher up was to blame.

Coaltonstone suspects that the illegal mining activity nearby may have caused the explosion. John Bell also says that he believes that it is possible that illegals are stealing pillars from operating mines, now. No one can be certain if that rumor is true.

In my opinion it is very possible company insiders could be retrieving pillars illegally. How does someone run down the street carrying a pillar anyway in the middle of the night?

It takes specialized equipment and knowledge of the underground gate roads as well as surface back roads to pull off a job like stealing pillars in the middle of the night. I wonder who is buying this illegal coal.

As far as I can figure out, there is a greater probability that this pillar thieving could be an inside job.

Whoever is stealing these pillars and letting the mines collapse is putting thousands of people. The third industrial revolution was meant to be a combination of a new age of enlightenment and a new age of reason. All I can see is the same old oppression. Sure the oppression has gone high tech, but the old form of ruthlessness still lingers. As the machine bosses take all responsibility from human bosses, we grew harder just to survive these new forms of dehumanization.

Junior was not doing so well this morning. He was very upset right after the explosion. Kids were phoning him and asking if Ginger had been incinerated. My God people can be cruel. Junior has been asking Maria whether our house is safe, whether I am going to be safe when I am at work and if he is going to be safe when he goes back to school after the Christmas Holidays.

Maria has been going over our disaster plan; I suppose it is really Maria's disaster plan. Maria seems to be prepared for anything, now, but I feel so shell-shocked, I don't know if I could cope with another disaster, and I am missing Ginger so much, I just don't know what to do first, so I am not doing much of anything.

Anyway, Maria went shopping for items to pack into our families' disaster preparedness kit and she said that she noticed other families doing the same. Maria described small runs occurring at the grocery store, hardware store and bank. Mathew Junior helped set up our kit, and all the related activity appeared to have a calming effect on him. Maria said that we now have enough water for all three of us to last for 72 hours, band aids and a first aid kit, dried food, radio, batteries, an old fashioned compass, face masks, whistle, duct tape, plastic tarp, our tent and sleeping bags, canned food, can opener, and many changes of underwear and socks and of course cash. Maria and Mathew Junior have also been stacking up a small pile of comic books and games.

Junior usually runs to get to the phone first. Maria is getting slower at moving around but she promised that she would try to answer the phone before Junior does. Maria said that Junior is ignoring the phone when it rings ever since the last phone call really upset him. Maria was considering ignoring the phone too but decided against it, in case someone was trying to get through to communicate any news related to rescuing Ginger or I suppose picking up what remains of him.

I suppose Junior is sorting out all kinds of feeling that he has never felt before, especially in such intensity. Once Junior realized what may have happened to Ginger, or what a lot of people in town are saying what they think happened to Ginger, his feelings of anger seem to get the best of him. Maria is continually explaining to Junior that at this time there is no proof that Ginger is not alive.

Thank God for Maria. The last thing I would have thought of today, was to go shopping and prepare an emergency kit, even though it makes a lot of sense to do have one. I am ashamed to say I didn't have one. Doing something that makes a person feel stronger and allows them to feel that they still have some influence over their destiny, probably has just as much healing potential as this journalizing for the 'In-Reach project'.

I just felt an earthquake. The power is gone. The emergency lights in my office just kicked in.

I just came back from looking out of the west-side window.

The armed cadets just formed an arms linked position, as if they are ready for an attack. I can see a red glow from the window, but it looks like it is coming from Bert's gas station not from Mine Five.

End of In-Reach entry, LOG #5 written by Christina Watson (Accounting Assistant to Alex Coaltonstone).

Chapter 13:
A Loss of Life

**In-Reach Entry, LOG #2, written by Dr. Daniel Smith for
Sunday December 22nd 2030,
Around 9:00 PM:**

What an awful day it has been today. There was another explosion this evening, which means we have suffered three explosions, all in one day. How can a town, the size of Pitville survive another day like today?

The third explosion happened suddenly at Bert's gas station. The source of the explosion is believed to be Bert's underground gas tank. The Health Authority assigned me to drive out to the site so that I could give medical service and identify the remains of the deceased. Unfortunately there wasn't anything left to identify except some human remains. DNA is destroyed in fire.

It took hours and only God knows how many gallons of water before the flames were extinguished. The experience was worse than a nightmare. Words can't really express how it really feels to be in such a predicament.

Now I am back from that ordeal and I must consider the terrible situation that Ginger must be in, assuming that he is still alive.

The rule of best practice is to write my log while it is still fresh in my mind.

Well I don't think that I will ever forget this day.

And now to top off this horrible day, Ashley told me that all of her clients' thumb-drives that were in the 'In-Reach' project's box are missing.

Of course she is being kind.

I would say that the thumb-drives must have been stolen.

Ashley was carrying the thumb-drive box and left it in the same room as Jackson the cameraman, who works with Dianne Black, was sitting. The best case scenario would be that she misplaced the flash drives, but I think that would be wishful thinking. I know she would never in a million years misplace that box any more than she would misplace a heart.

Anyway Ashley still has the box, which is why it took several hours before she noticed that the actual thumb-drives were missing.

What kind of person would do such a thing?

Ashley thinks it was Jackson Green, the cameraman from PPZ. She isn't sure how to handle the situation.

Ashley is so afraid that everyone is going to stop trusting her if this lapse in security is discovered. She is afraid that the reputation of her 'In-Reach' project will be ruined. The project is built on trust, and as a social science is trust in its infancy.

Who else could have taken the drives but Jackson? Jackson had the opportunity and the motive. The opportunity would have been the time when Ashley was attending to Dianne Black's hyperventilation problem and the motive would have been to get "inside information" so that it could be reported by his team on PPZ.

I was really skeptical of those two paparazzi to start with.

Paparazzi don't usually break down like that. I have seen that Dianne Black reporting from some of the most brutal war zones known to modern man. Usually those war correspondent types are hard as nails. Maybe it was the combination of the rugged conditions, the cold, the fog, and not being prepared when seeing death Ms. Black did mention that her anxiety level rose quite high when a bat almost flew into her hair. Dianne Black has been broadcasting from all kinds of war zones and death zones. Reporters always baffle me since I am never sure what newscast is actually real and what newscast has been so sensationalized it is more of an info-entertainment show that news.

It didn't even dawn on me that the thumb-drives of the 'In-Reach' project were at risk; considering the impact the mine disaster has had on the participants; it is hard to believe that anyone, could be so callous.

Though I have mixed feeling regarding the 'In-Reach' project, Ashley's program does give an option to those who have chosen to write about their feelings instead of talk about them,

Ironically, people chose to participate in the 'In-Reach' project since writing was more private than talking out loud during a support group. No one talks out loud to themselves; that would be seen as the first sign of insanity, and would not go unnoticed, especially in Pitville.

I do think that thought-control is necessary in this day and age. If you are able to control your own thoughts, you can avoid a lot of interference from the Power Clique who prey on those whose thoughts betray them. Once a person is down and is trying to get back up the last thing a person needs is to have their most inner thoughts stolen from them.

With that said, I still feel that I am being forced to participate in this program.

I don't think the pace of life has made me a better typist. I am still all thumbs when it comes to this sort of exercise. I am not always able to type what I mean.

I guess I will always be an awful typist in spite of all the practice I have had lately.

To start with I feel writing one's thoughts down can be compromising to say the least. And my worst fears about this program have already been realized.

Like I wrote before, I have only been participating in this 'In-Reach' project because the Health Authority ordered me to participate.

We all work for the Tut Island Health Authority so yes my most inner thoughts have been stolen too. This is exactly why I resisted writing down all of my feelings and thoughts in the first place.

And to top it off, the prime suspect is a paparazzo of all people. What a callous thing to do.

Yes I know the 'In-Reach' project saves therapists time, since they don't have to do the writing, and the project can help a client to gain control over their thoughts and emotions, in theory anyway. I do have concerns though since I can see how automatic writing, which is very subjective, could also be counterproductive and lead to confusing subjective opinion with evidence based thought.

The eight patients Ashley is most concerned about at the moment are Christina Watson, Mathew Watson Junior, Smoothman and Paylor, James and Bobby Coaltonstone and Mayor Ted Stern. I have just counted seven, I am not sure who the eighth one is, maybe it is the little one that Christina is carrying or maybe it is that lady newsman Dianne Black.

Each thumb-drive represents a client in pain reaching into themselves for answers and strength. Every single patient is suffering from some degree of trauma related anxiety, and this 'In-Reach Project' allows these people to bare their soul to a degree in ways that would not be safe in today's society. The 'In Reach Project' is designed so that Ashley can lead the clients to consider more reflective and rational responses instead of just reacting immediately to their pain. The 'In Reach Project' gives clients a chance to listen to their own thoughts while possibly rediscovering their strengths during a disaster. In the end, it is the client who is really the first responder and should have the right to effect the outcome somewhat.

I am sure that Dianne Black did get a shock when she saw the two dead men. Most people haven't seen bodies half decayed, and that was right after that idiot John Bell's even more idiotic nephew's drilling possibly sparked the second explosion during the drilling of a sub-terrain borehole in Mine Four, which was often referred to as Mine Five's second level, once housing one of the thickest known anthracite coal seams, on Tut Island.

Goodwin has been trapped in Mine Five since early Sunday morning.

I don't think that mine authorities know yet, what actually set off the first explosion let alone the second. And if they did, I doubt that their lawyers would be advising to disclose such details to the public. It is possible that drilling borehole COALT-11-C did contribute to the Sunday afternoon explosion. It is also possible that a number of other events could have caused the second explosion in Mine Five.

I mean those gassy mines are just accidents waiting to happen.

I find it difficult to believe that Dianne Black actually faked her hyperventilation episode on international TV. Everyone has limits. When we discover our limits; it is usually at the worst time possible.

Nevertheless the thumb drives are missing and Jackson is still our prime suspect, and he most likely did take advantage of our habit of leaving doors open. How does a person operate a medical clinic without leaving the doors unlocked? If we locked doors to all the rooms in our clinic, our clinic would become a jail.

It is entirely possible that Jackson just seized the moment and took the thumb drives when Ashley put them down for a moment to see if she could help the nurse help Dianne Black with the immense task of composing herself.

The real victims though in this theft, are Ashley and her patients. I am a victim too, I suppose. We all wrote our thoughts down on those thumb-drives. Now our most inner thoughts appear to have been stolen by a Paparazzo of all people.

I know James Coaltonstone wanted to make sure that Smoothman and Paylor didn't stir up other employees and contractors when they are socializing in the cafeteria which is why it was suggested that they enroll in the 'In-Reach Project'.

As far as I can see, James Coaltonstone is able to agitate people without any help from anyone.

The sad thing is, it would have been Smoothman who could have been blamed for his crew being hurt or killed during the early morning explosion, and Coaltonstone and his cronies would have been let off the hook. Smoothman is the foreman and the one who is legally responsible for his crew from the time he logs in at the beginning of the morning shift to the time he logs out at the end of the shift. It is Smoothman who must report any losses and injuries. It wouldn't be the first time a foreman became the fall guy during a mine disaster.

If James Coaltonstone had only once considered the workers and contractors and the risks these people take every day to produce coal, he might have tried to do something to de-escalate tensions between the employees and the boss-bots.

Of course James Coaltonstone is always inside that security fence and doesn't really see out that much. If he could only see how awful it looks from this side of the fence. Actually it looks a bit better, with all those flowers and teddy bears piling up around it.

I don't think Christina Watson ever got over losing her husband in that horrific accident back in June of 2021. She has been involved in a legal battle with the boss-bot manufacturer ever since. I know that Christina needed closure and she needed to keep her job, and she knows no other place than Pitville, but I always wonder what would have happened if Christina had refused to settle with the mine, and took Coaltonstone and the Big Seven Coal Group to court. The cost in money and time, to whoever agreed to represent Christina against Coaltonstone and the Big Seven would have been prohibitive I suppose.

Before the accident Mathew was often sick with worry and he was one of the first patients who participated in the 'In-Reach' project his logs were also stolen.

Mathew was certain that one day he was going to land up in a serious accident, because if those bots fly around a person's head, it is very difficult to concentrate on operating heavy equipment.

It appeared to Mathew's colleagues that the whistle-boss bot five had a malfunction and began to whistle nonstop while turning blue and flew toward Mathew, pushing him into the wrong place at the wrong time. As Mathew became tangled in the mining machinery's cables, he was trapped inside the continuous mining machine's radius and was crushed almost instantly.

Even before his fatal accident, Mathew had a terrible working relationship with that Whistle- Boss Bot 5C. I don't know if it had something to do with the Wi-Fi tag hanging on Mathew's neck. At the time those two way locator tags were mandatory for miners to wear. It was obvious that whistle-boss bot five was programmed in such a way that it could not respond to unpredictable situations in an intelligent or common sense manner.

Mathew said he had dreams that a whistle-boss bot was whistling in his ear at a pitch that sounded similar to nails being scratched on a black board. Mathew felt that the whistle-boss bot five got in the way when he was working with the heavy equipment down in the mine and was posing a serious threat to his safety and Ginger would write up a safety infraction report whenever Ginger witnessed the malfunction. We all know what happens to those reports that Ginger writes. The reports are never taken seriously.

The equipment down in Mine Five seemed to be breaking down all the time. I don't know how many repair requests Goodwin had submitted during the last forty-seven days. The coal shearing machine, was never fixed and Ginger resorted to installing a methane gas monitor onto the machine, so that if gases reached a dangerously high level, the monitor could close down the coal shearing machine, while generating a report of its own.

I heard from Ashley that some unknown person had shut down the methane monitor on the coal shearing machine. Ginger had discovered the situation and reported it to Christina through her personal Skype account, only minutes before this morning's explosion occurred.

During the last forty-seven days, Ginger reported all kinds of near misses, attributed to the ventilation system, designed by Bobby Coaltonstone. Cutting corners in this mine, was the last thing any sensible mine manager would be doing in such a gassy mine. Mine explosions are very costly to all concerned.

I also observed that there is a great divide between bosses and miners, in Mine Five. The executives don't eat or speak to the miners; they don't even use the same elevator or lavatory. And talk about tensions. They talk to each other through lawyers while everything said between the two parties is documented in a file archived on the Eye-Bot Network somewhere. It is a totally impersonal and polarized situation, which is a shame, since the miners may know a lot more about the true nature of the mine than the Bells and the Coaltonstones.

It seems that because Mine Five is scheduled to be closing down at the end of June of next year, the owners are becoming too relaxed when flaunting safety regulations.

The ventilation has always been the greatest concern in Mine Five.

Ventilation has been an important issue in the long fight for miners' rights for years. The Coaltonstones take intimidating miners and contractors to the next level.

During the last forty-seven days, coal dust had been so thick that miners and contractors, working in the mine, were suffering from severe eye irritation, violent coughing and itchy feet.

Ashley has advised Ginger several times that such a working environment was very dangerous for an asthmatic.

Ginger was the only one who actually tried to improve working conditions in Mine Five. It was against Ginger's nature to conform to bad policies related to mine safety, because in the end, the costs to prevent a disaster are far less than the amounts spent recovering from one.

Ginger is one of the most dedicated mine safety professionals that I have ever met. He could have sent in the bots to measure air quality and dust spread and all of those other measurements that he takes during a pre-shift safety inspection, but he didn't trust them.

Ginger suspected that the remote measuring process was providing diluted and inaccurate low readings, leading to a false sense of security regarding air quality.

Instead Ginger descended into the pit, using old fashioned techniques, which the old timers believed were less prone to error.

I am not that surprised that the methane monitor on the coal shearing machine had been turned off.. I suppose that is what Ginger was doing this morning before the explosion; he was trying to make sense of it all.

The area surrounding Coalton Valley has twelve known coal seams, within a twenty-five square mile radius. And there must be hundreds if not thousands of mines all over the island that are undocumented.

And then there is the growing problem of gangs of bandits robbing the pillars from abandoned mines. Those pillars were left in the abandoned mines to hold the surface in place. There are many slopes and shafts that are dug with very rudimentary machinery, so those pillar thieves can gain access to the tunnels, secretly in the middle of the night, when honest Pitvilians are sleeping.

There seems to be all kinds of confusion at the moment.

Ginger needs someone to help him quickly if not valiantly, and pigs will be flying before that happens around here. I have been praying a lot, but I think I need to keep my eyes open.

And those armed cadets marching around the security fence in complete riot gear, raising tensions like you wouldn't believe, is just going to make matters worse.

Sadly most of the machinery produced during the golden age, which was only about fifteen years ago, is just hanging on by a thread, right now. I don't even know if we have the materials to even replace simple machines like phones and cars and even those pesky drones and boss-bots that seem to hover over everyone like busybodies. I can't say I will miss those boss-bots and spy-flies when they become inoperable.

11:00 PM:

If Ginger is expecting to get out of that mine alive he better have a plan. These idiots seem to only be making everything worse.

It is possible that Ginger did survive the explosions. It is also possible that Ginger was able to inflate the portable seals, and then was able to reach the rescue chamber in 'Section E'. Then the next concern would be that Ginger would be out of air in about eighty hours.

Once Ginger is in the rescue chamber, he will have enough emergency equipment to help him survive but the air supply is only going to last for four days. The asthma is another big concern. Knowing Ginger he might have one or two emergency puffers with him at most. He may not have his regular medications with him and this could become a serious problem.

I don't understand why the rescue team's focus is not set on 'Section E'. There is supposed to be an emergency telemagnetic radio station beside every rescue chamber. Section E' is considered to have the best location since the walls are higher than in 'Sections A, B and C'. Section E would be situated at the greatest distance from the explosion site.

The telemagnetic communicator is supposed to receive and send text messages within a range of about two thousand feet, but someone has to be ready to receive these messages.

There is talk of sealing all the boreholes and shafts in Mine Five so that any existing fires could be smothered.

As I said before, I have no idea why the rescue efforts are focusing on 'Section A, B and C'. If this is supposed to be a rescue mission and not a recovery mission, 'Section E' should be the point of focus.

Monday, December 23rd, 2 AM:

I have been having my eyes closed in prayer for a while, but I wish I could do something more tangible, to help Ginger.

End of In-Reach entry, LOG #2 by Dr. Daniel Smith MD (Pitville Medical Center).

Chapter 14:
Deep Coal

Monday December 23rd, 2030, around 8:00 AM:

"Good morning. This is Steve Jones for the PPZ. We are on our second day, observing the events after the Pitville Mine disaster, which occurred early Sunday morning. Mr. Goodwin has been trapped in Mine Five on the southern outskirts of Pitville since early Sunday morning. At the very time that we were expecting to report the reading of the riot act, we at PPZ were presented with a pleasant surprise. We at PPZ have exclusive rights to an immense document leak, by a whistleblower going under the name 'Deep Coal'," Steve Jones announced from his makeshift broadcast room at Eagle Eye Inn.

"According to our mysterious whistleblower, Deep Coal, Mr. Goodwin had filed forty-nine reports during the last forty-seven days, concerning safety violations and infractions. Deep Coal has given PPZ a data package, which includes all forty-nine reports. Twenty-one of those reports were rated as critical due to the highly dangerous methane gas measurements in certain areas of the mine. Twenty-eight reports are classified as moderate concerns. Amongst the list of moderate concerns is the Pitville garbage-dump, which is actually situated on an exposed coal seam. As if the methane gas, which would be a by-product of the garbage being dumped, would not be a big enough risk in its own merit, open burning is also taking place at the Pitville dump. The land which is owned by the municipality of Pitville is one of the Big Seven Coal Group's many leaseholds.

I suppose it is just a matter of opinion, but in my opinion any form of open burning on top of an exposed coal seam should be not only classified as a higher risk than just a moderate concern, but such activity should be forbidden. It is unbelievable that in this day and age, open burning is being allowed on top of a coal seam. Coaltonstone Coal Mines, a subsidiary of the Big Seven Coal Group which operates Mine Five, denies any wrong doing.

Nevertheless, attention is being focused on a hodgepodge of doorways and underground fans, which have been in use as the Mine Five's primary ventilation system since 2015.

Over the years this ventilation system passed government inspections but insiders have told PPZ that it is most likely partly to blame for the early Sunday morning explosion.

To make matters worse, one of the coal shearing machines was in disrepair. As the coal shearing machine's exposed carbide teeth scraped against rock, sparks would spread randomly and at great speeds. Miners and contractors had to put out small fires with fire extinguishers. Sometimes the men extinguished the flames by urinating on them.

According to insiders whose identities we cannot reveal, the situation in Mine Five was an explosion just waiting to happen.

Even a small explosion could put the ventilation system in Mine Five at risk since the fans were installed underground therefore vulnerable to power outages, and without working fans, the mine's ventilation system would become inoperable.

Our insider also told PPZ, that Mr. Goodwin had installed a methane gas monitor on the coal shearing machine, which was in disrepair, so that if the methane gas levels reached measurements, which were not permissible, the coal shearing machine would shut itself down.

Our insider, Deep Coal has informed PPZ, that the methane gas monitor was turned off, which most likely led to Mr. Goodwin extending his pre-shift safety inspection by twenty minutes. We at PPZ have timed images to back up this claim.

Mr. Goodwin's quick thinking is believed to have saved the morning crew of one hundred and sixty from descending into Mine

Five, minutes before the underground explosion occurred, which left Mr. Goodwin trapped in Mine Five since early Sunday morning.

If Mr. Goodwin was able to find refuge in the rescue chamber found in 'Section E' he will only have about three days of air supply left," Steve took a breath and continued.

"We at PPZ are also discovering that Mine Five management had been accusing Mr. Goodwin of having an obsessive-compulsive disorder and refused to take any of his reports seriously. Insiders have told PPZ, this negative psychology, often referred to as mind war, between Mr. Goodwin and Mine Five's managerial hierarchy. The negative psychology was often used against employees and contractors whenever there was a conflict between coal production and personal safety.

If Mr. Goodwin's reports had been taken seriously and acted upon, and the ventilation problems corrected, possibly Sunday's explosion could have been avoided," Steve announced as he looked into the computer screen and after reading the report to himself a second time, he wondered why these reports were not leaked to PPZ sooner.

As noted earlier, Mine Five insiders, who were too afraid to reveal their identities, believe that Ginger Goodwin might actually be alive and could have found refuge in the rescue chamber in 'Section E'. If this is true, once Mr. Goodwin's three days of air supply is depleted, his life will once again be in danger.

Concerned observers have noted that even though there are signs of activity in areas above 'Sections A, B and C', there is no rescue related activity above 'Section E', where our 'moles' believe Ginger would have the greatest chance of survival. As previously noted, Ginger's supporters are hoping for a speedy rescue as they surround the security fence in peaceful protest. Supporters are linking arms and holding candles while singing Silent Night.

Even though Mine Five has a telemagnetic communication center inside each rescue chamber, there appears to be no one inside the range of transmission who is actually monitoring the equipment.

The emergency telemagnetic radio runs on very low power. This radio does not present a risk of setting off sparks. At present there isn't any sign of a communication center being constructed.

Insiders have informed us at PPZ, that there may be a conflict between underground signals used to control invisible fencing around the perimeter of the mine and the telemagnetic radio transmissions.

The magnetic signals which control the fence may be interfering with any effort Mr. Goodwin might be making to transmit a voice or text message to the surface.

If Mr. Goodwin is trying to communicate to the outside world, the outside world is not hearing him.

The three surveillance robots which were sent into the mine on Sunday around 2 PM are believed to have been submerged in orangy acid water which is flooding 'Section A' of Mine Five. This acid water is highly corrosive and must be continually pumped out with special machinery.

The three surveillance robots managed to take some photographs, before they became inoperable show, that in 'Section B', the pillar retrieval process was underway. Photographs also show severe damage to equipment. Photographic evidence indicates that at least three pillars were blown to pieces causing a portion of the mine's roof to collapse.

There are differing opinions concerning who should be paying for the rescue and salvage missions.

The Big Seven Coal Group believes that it is the responsibility of their insurance carrier to pay for any rescue or salvage effort. The insurance company argues that they are not required to cover incidents, which are a direct result of illegal or rogue mining or an act of God. The Big Seven's insurance carrier claims that it is up to the tax payer to pay the costs if Sunday morning's explosion was due to illegal mining activity or due to an act of God.

This is Steve Jones for the PPZ giving you the latest in news, weather and sports, broadcasting live from the Pitville Mining disaster of 2030. Now, back to you Dianne," Steve said as he handed over the broadcasting duties to Dianne who was somewhere inside the parameter of the mine's security zone.

"Good morning and thank you for joining me. This is Dianne Black reporting live from the Pitville Mining Disaster of 2030. It has been twenty-seven hours since Sunday morning's explosion, deep inside Mine Five and Steve has given us a thorough report, thank you Steve," Dianne Black said, wondering why Deep Coal hadn't come forward, forty-seven days ago. Maybe if he had, the Pitville Mine Disaster of 2030 could have been avoided.

Before I begin my interview with John Bell, head of security for Coaltonstone Mines, I would like to thank all of my concerned viewers for the lovely flowers, cards and chocolates. I also would like to say that I was shocked to see what we all saw at the opening of Mine Four. But why were we shocked? I for one have visited some of the most brutal war zones of the century, so why did I find myself so unguarded and so shocked, when I found myself so close to human remains? Partly it was the fumes, but partly it was the worms and maggots that sent me into shock. But why did I have such a subjective reaction to such a natural process? Was it because I have only been exposed to clean kills? I have learned something new about myself.

We should not fear human frailty and error, but we should fear our inhumanity to man and our ability to justify our cruelty, due to that fear.

Our fear often drives us to avoid risk taking, and while avoiding risks we also avoid moving forward into the unknown.

Since our tax money is supporting the New World Order, which has many departments designing weapons which can actually vaporize human beings from the face of the Earth, we will soon be living in a world where we won't have to see remains of the discarded, undocumented and destitute. But will that mean that we have made ourselves a better world? I fear not.

I believe it is my role, as a reporter of observations, to ask the poignant questions, so we can discover if our right to freedom and happiness is still being respected. After the Mine Five explosion, it is hard to believe that freedom and happiness can ever return to this Coalton Valley, situated on the East Coast of Tut Island," Dianne said as she crumbled up the script she was supposed to read, and threw it into the garbage can, nearby.

"Good Morning, Mr. Bell. Welcome to our broadcast," Dianne said as she greeted John Bell to the show pleasantly.

"John Bell is the head of security for Mine Five. Don Bell's brother, John Bell, is the lead safety manager for Mine Five, and is Ginger Goodwin's boss. Don Bell also assists in security matters. Don Bell will be interviewed at a later date, which will be announced once the date and time have been confirmed.

"Good morning John, welcome to my show," Dianne said wishing that she had been interviewing his brother instead.

"Good morning Dianne. Thank you for having me," John Bell replied.

"What can you tell us this morning about the progress being made to free Ginger Goodwin from Mine Five?" Dianne said.

"Steve has explained to your viewers that we programmed three surveillance robots to enter the mine though the shaft entrance situated in 'Section C', on Sunday afternoon at around 2:00 PM. The robots entered the mine successfully. They were able to take gas readings and photographs. Unfortunately, as they turned north they entered 'Section A' where they encountered around 500,000 gallons of acid water. The surveillance robots drove through the acid water, and all three of them are now inoperable," John Bell explained.

"Why couldn't the three robots have been re-directed remotely?" Dianne Black asked.

"Our signals could not reach the robots in time. We are guessing that the source of the acid water is coming from an abandoned mine located beyond Mine Five's property boundary. If this acid water is not managed it could soak into our local aquifers," John Bell warned.

"The water pumping equipment which was pumping out acid water before we lost power, during yesterday's early morning explosion. Our pumps are made of special alloys and are insanely expensive. We are unable to determine at this time, if Mine Five will be re-opening in the near future.

Our intention is to regroup and rebuild and carry on from where we left off, as soon as we can," John Bell, said. "The surveillance robots were sent into the mine to map everything they saw, including pillars and rubble, and we did get a partial view of the mine which will be very useful in our future rescue and salvage missions," John Bell explained.

"Didn't I read, recently, that Pitville suffered a tremendous amount of acid rain last year, during growing season?" Dianne asked.

"Yes. That is correct. The acid rain was blamed for damaging crops during last year's growing season," John Bell said.

"Were there any other tasks which the three surveillance robots were expected to undertake during yesterday afternoon's failed mission?" Dianne asked.

"I do not call yesterday's mission a total failure. Yes, our three surveillance robots were programmed to find evidence of illegal entry. The robots were able to send us photographs, which showed extensive damage to our assets.

"One more question; what about Ginger Goodwin? Did the surveillance robots find any sign of human activity while they were still functioning?" Dianne asked.

"No, unfortunately they did not. We were hoping that the robots would be able to locate Ginger Goodwin, since locating Mr. Goodwin is the first crucial step in our rescue plan. If we do not know where Mr. Goodwin is, we cannot rescue him" John Bell replied.

"Thank you, John Bell head of security for Mine Five, which is a subsidiary of the Big Seven Coal Group, and owner of Mine Five," Dianne said as she shook John Bell's hand.

"Sadly, we have another tragedy to report. About twelve hours ago, there was a terrible explosion at Bert's Gas station, which killed Bert Clarke. Bert Clarke inherited the gas station from his father Bert Senior, about ten years ago. Bert and Sons Gas station had been serving Coalton Valley for over fifteen years. Bert's gas station was one of the few gas stations still serving Coalton Valley and was a popular pit stop for many of the locals. Bert Clarke and this family have always played an active and important role in this close knit community of Pitville, nestled on the East Coast of Tut Island. Bert Clarke will be missed. Almost everyone knows someone from the Clarke family and this terrible tragedy is the third explosion, which Pitville endured yesterday, Sunday, December 22nd.

According to our inside sources, it is alleged that this third explosion may have been just as preventable as the two earlier explosions in Mine Five might have been. The Government's Official Directors have stressed that a complete and thorough investigation must be launched before any conclusions can be made at this time," Dianne said as she was reading her script in disbelief.

"With us today is the doctor who was at the scene to identify Bert Clarke's remains and to certify Mr. Clarke's death certificate. Welcome to our show, Doctor Smith and thank you for sharing your expert opinion with us today," Dianne Black said as she shook the doctor's hand.

"Dr. Smith, could you tell us what you were able to observe twelve hours ago at the scene of this horrible explosion?"

"Good Morning Dianne. Actually I could not write out a death certificate for Mr. Clarke, because there wasn't any DNA left which I could use to identify him," Daniel Smith said.

"My God," Dianne Black replied.

"Yes, the whole situation was very disturbing. Fire destroys DNA. I mean all that I could identify was a bit of human remains as being human. A country doctor cannot issue a presumptive death certificate based on circumstantial evidence when there isn't an identifiable body to be found," Dr. Daniel Smith explained.

"It must have been a terrible experience, to not find Mr. Clarke anywhere," Dianne said sympathetically.

"It was a terrible, and much worse for Mr. Clarke's family. The explosion was so unexpected. The heat was very intense, and it appeared that Mr. Clarke had been instantly incinerated," Dr. Smith said.

"Oh my God," Dianne asked.

"We are assuming that Bert Clarke is dead, since we know that he was at the gas station at the time of the explosion. Possibly there will be court proceedings related to this case and then one of the Government' Official Directors could issue a presumptive death certificate," Dr. Smith said.

"This must be terrible for Mr. Clarke's family," Dianne said.

"He will be missed; you know I was the doctor who delivered Bert about three decades ago?" Dr. Smith answered.

"No I didn't know that. I am so sorry that we are running out of time. Thank you again, Dr. Smith," Dianne said while closing the interview.

"Now, for more news relating to this morning's earthquake, which occurred around 5:00 AM, this morning. Many Pitville residents reported that the earth beneath them shook, but no injuries were reported. Our inside mole is alleging that an abandoned mine nearby may have had its pillars stolen; causing the mine to cave-in, resulting in this morning's tremors and possibly spontaneous combustion occurred.

Strangely this morning's earthquake occurred around the same time as yesterday's explosion and mild earthquake occurred.

Now for our feature story; the only man still trapped in Mine Five, Ginger Goodwin, is considered to be a hero by many, after his quick thinking saved the morning crew from descending into a pending explosion. As you can see Steve, there are tens of thousands of people who have taken the time, during this Christmas week, to travel to Pitville, and pay tribute to Ginger Goodwin, a miner's friend and everyone's hero. The line of people is said to be a mile long.

As we know, throughout the ages, the good die young. Ginger Goodwin at 31 years old should have a life of hopes and dreams to live, and since early yesterday morning he has been trapped in Mine Five. If Ginger is not rescued soon, he will run out of air and die alone, in what is considered one of the gassiest mines on Tut Island, if not the world.

During our early morning broadcast, our mole informed PPZ that the Big Seven Coal Group's insurance carriers are refusing to fund Ginger Goodwin's rescue. We also have inside information that G.O.D. is also refusing to fund Ginger's rescue. So the question we are posing is who will be funding Ginger Goodwin's rescue?

If the recent explosions were due to illegal mining in nearby mines, the costs to salvage the remaining assets should be passed on to the Government's Official Directors' office, which is usually referred to as G.O.D.'s office. G.O.D. is claiming that the

Big Seven's insurance carriers are responsible for cost recovery, related to Sunday mornings' explosions in Mine Five.

Insiders on both sides of this conflict have been revealing concerns that illegal pillar retrieving is becoming a lucrative business in the Coalton Valley area.

Undocumented mine bosses generally hire illegal miners, some are Minese immigrants who are believed to be tunneling to Tut Island from the Bering Strait; other illegals are hardened escapees from mining prison camps scattered throughout the Arctic.

In summary, undocumented mines generally use undocumented workers and do not pay fees or even taxes, let alone minimum wage. Back to you, Steve," Dianne said, as she quickly put on her puffy jacket which increased her warmth factor by 15 degrees even though she risked looking six pounds heavier by doing so.

"Thank you Dianne," Steve responded even though Dianne was no longer visible to the public who were watching the Pitville Mine disaster in growing numbers as each hour rolled by and Pitville's troubles continued to unfold.

"Are we off the air now, Ms. Black?" Daniel Smith asked.

"Yes we are, Doctor Smith," Dianne said as she cuddled her warm jacket.

"Good. I have an urgent matter to discuss with your cameraman, and I must discuss this matter with him privately, man to man," Dr. Smith said as he looked at Jackson. Jackson was standing in front of Dianne and holding onto his camera as tight as he could. The way things were heading, one never knew when a disaster was going to strike Pitville, and Jackson wanted his camera to remain in one piece, when the next disaster strikes. Jackson wondered why anyone would want to live in such a horrible one-industry town, which seemed to be cursed.

Dianne had no idea why Doctor Smith would need to talk to her cameraman, but Jackson did. Jackson also knew that the root of a man's character was his sense of duty.

Jackson realized that the only way that he could avoid a confrontation was by simply walking away and ignoring Doctor Smith. Jackson believed that it was imperative that he continued with his plan.

Chapter 15:
Paying For Results

Monday December 23rd, 2030, around 10:00 AM.

"So are we having another informal back room meeting?" Mayor Stern asked James Coaltonstone.

"It is your office so you can call this meeting whatever you like," James Coaltonstone replied.

"I thought the drilling crews would be more organized today." Mayor Stern commented.

"I know I did too and I should have known better. If I paid everyone in this valley for their good intentions I would go broke," James Coaltonstone said with a snort.

"I know what you are saying. When I am at the office, at city hall, everyone is watching me and criticizing me but no one seems to be adding anything of real value, the way you do. You are always contributing resources and new ideas to our town. You are a pillar on which our community is able to build upon," Mayor Ted Stern said hoping that he did not sound too pretentious.

"I pay for results," James Coaltonstone said, "Otherwise I would go broke."

"Not everyone is able to produce results the way you can James. All those people walking around city hall, looking constipated, watching me as if their lifestyles depended on my success. Sometimes these strangers get so close to me, I can feel them breathing down my neck. And still I feel invisible, they are only watching a shadow of me but they don't actually see who I really am. They hear me but they don't really seem to be listening to me or they wouldn't get so many tasks mixed up the way they often do," Mayor Stern said almost whispering.

"I know exactly what you mean. I think the experts call this a mutual feeling of alienation," James Coaltonstone said.

"The difference between hearing, listening, watching and seeing is the intensity of engagement. I mean as long as people get their pay and are able to put food on their table, and if they are lucky enough to have a little bit left over so they can drink themselves into a stupor, what else do they need or care about? Coal makes all this gracious living possible for all of us to exist together. Coal brings all of us to Pitville. Fifteen years ago the lack of coal made us close up the Coalton mine and the town became derelict practically overnight. Without coal; our city would become a village. We both know how fast one industry towns can disappear," Mayor Stern said as he looked out of the east-side window of his office.

"My God don't those cadets ever stop marching around the perimeter of the security fence. Just watching those kids makes me nervous," Mayor Stern said realizing how quickly this tense situation could grow out of control.

"Yes they do get breaks. They are on duty for four hours then they can relax in the barracks behind the administration building or sleep for about 8 hours. And the next shift replaces them for the next four hours, and then a third group will replace the second group," James Coaltonstone said.

"I have received a generous grant from the Ministry of Industry to provide opportunities for all those cadets so they can apply their skills and assist industry at the same time. Though, I am still required to pay the cadets' overtime, so far that has not been necessary," James Coaltonstone said, feeling very pleased with himself that he was able to negotiate such a bargain.

"If I said it once, I can say it a thousand times your little data miner has caused quite the boom for this town. The longer he is down there, the better off we will be," Mayor Stern said as he laughed at the irony of it all.

"Maybe when the city re-adjusts and paves Anthracite Row you could rename it after Ginger Goodwin. I mean you would only need to rename that skid row part of town after Ginger if he doesn't come out of the mine alive which I suppose is a certainty," James Coaltonstone added.

"There must be over ten thousand people out there, and I don't know if we can pass a curfew. Reading the Riot Act and enforcing it would look heavy handed since this crowd has been very well behaved so far," Mayor Stern noted and he began to cross off items on a list he had made hours ago, in his favorite black book that was turning gray. All those people are going to need food, lodging and drinks. They are going to have to buy those things here if they plan to stay here. I have never seen so many people all at once in town before.

Yes, I believe that we don't even get these crowds for the Christmas parade any more. That Goodwin has been more value dead than alive. Our city merchants could make a mint out of this. And then there is the accommodation tax on all of our hotel rooms. That will increase revenue for the city possibly by tenfold," Mayor Stern said.

"Quite right, I bet those losers were so upset that they forgot to pack their toothbrushes. They are going to need everything, and then we will send them on their way once they run out of money. Don't they realize how inconvenient this entire situation has been for us? I am the owner of the property that those out-of-towners have been staring at since yesterday morning and they make me more nervous just looking at them," James Coaltonstone replied.

"I think we will have to get G.O.D. to order the mine sealed. And if the crowds start misbehaving I will be ready to read the riot act and enforce a curfew in no time flat. First let these people spend all their money here before we run them out of town," Mayor Stern said to James Coaltonstone who was nodding in agreement.

"Quite right," James Coaltonstone said.

Chapter 16:
Tension Mounts In The Miners' Cafeteria

Monday December 23rd, 2030,around 5 PM.

"Welcome viewers to our exclusive coverage, broadcasting live from the Pitville Mine Disaster of 2030. I am Dianne Black for the PPZ bringing to you another live up to date coverage straight from the lively and anxious Coaltonstone's Miners' cafeteria often nicknamed the 'Number Two Café'.

Viewers, as you can see, a Christmas candle has been lit and set at every table.

This evening we will be tying up all the loose ends resulting from the tragic disaster which has united this small, close knit community of Pitville," Dianne said as she realized that the people in the cafeteria must have been feeling as miserable as they look. The word lively was not really a fitting description to describe the atmosphere, nevertheless it was a mine disaster and two days before Christmas, and news stories had to have sensation, to keep the general public interested.

"The beautiful borough of Pitville is situated in the center of Tut Island, often referred to as the center of coal country," Dianne continued as she looked around the cafeteria, smiling at everyone who just stared back at her with a look which made it clear, that she was definitely an outsider.

"Ginger Goodwin has been trapped in Mine Five for almost thirty-six hours. People from all over the world have stepped out from their usual walk in life to join the growing global movement to support Ginger Goodwin.

As the hours tick by, Mr. Goodwin's air supply decreases.

Ginger Goodwin, in his capacity as assistant safety officer for Coaltonstone's Mine Five, which is a subsidiary of the Big Seven Coal Group, and the primary employer in Pitville, extended the morning pre-shift safety inspection by twenty minutes at 5:00 AM yesterday morning. This time extension which Goodwin obtained by refusing to certify the pre morning shift inspection, prevented a crew of one hundred and sixty from descending into Mine Five, minutes before yesterday morning's explosion occurred, leaving Ginger Goodwin trapped inside Mine Five alone.

Many of Ginger Goodwin's supporters believe that Ginger Goodwin's quick thinking saved the entire morning crew of one hundred and sixty lives.

If Ginger was able to survive the two explosions which occurred yesterday, and was able to escape from the mine's most toxic zones; he will most likely have found refuge in the rescue chamber located in 'Section E'. Rescue chambers are usually stocked with 96 hours of air supply meaning that Ginger will only have around sixty hours of air supply left."

As Dianne completed her commentary she turned towards George and Jay.

"Joining us today are the two foremen who are in charge of the morning crew which Ginger Goodwin stopped from descending into yesterday morning's pending explosion. These hard working men escaped with their lives, due to Ginger Goodwin's quick thinking and perseverance just minutes before the explosion occurred leaving Mr. Goodwin trapped 1,200 feet below the surface, deep inside Mine Five.

Besides working with Ginger, George and Jay play soccer with Ginger Goodwin regularly every Tuesday evening. Welcome George Smoothman and Jay Paylor to our show.

"Mr. Smoothman, you and your colleagues have been waiting here in this cafeteria for thirty-six hours, what are you hoping for?" Dianne asked as she placed the microphone in front of George Smoothman's face

"Actually Dianne," Jay Paylor said as he moved Dianne's hand holding the microphone towards his face.

"We miners call our cafeteria, the Miners' Cafeteria. It is those guys on the top floor who call our cafeteria, the number two café, and we miners find the term derogatory. This is a good time to show solidarity for all miners across the globe who are being put at risk day after day by greedy mine owners. We have the technology to design internal controls so that the mine environment can be adjusted to accommodate threats related to gas and other environmental dangers as they change at the molecular level but cannot be seen by the human eye.

Instead of using modern technology to cheat us at the scales when weighing our coal output, technology could be used to put out fires before they start. Instead, we are locked out and we are being forced to wait for these fires to grow beyond the raging point while Ginger Goodwin remains trapped 1,200 feet below. That is what Ginger was trying to do, he was introducing a technology which could control or at least measure the threatening elements from inside the mine as conditions change." Jay Paylor explained.

"I am so very sorry but you lost me," Dianne said, flushing a little and looking wide eyed at Jay Paylor.

"Do you mind repeating the question, Dianne?" George Smoothman requested.

"Mr. Smoothman, you and your colleagues have been waiting here in this cafeteria for thirty-six hours, what are you hoping for?" Dianne asked as she placed the microphone in front of George Smoothman's face.

"We want the rescue to begin before Ginger runs out of air," Jay Paylor said as he moved the microphone back to his face.

"Yes, that is right Dianne. We are hoping that the rescue mission, once it begins, is able to locate and rescue our friend and colleague Ginger Goodwin. We are sleeping on mattresses which the Red Cross has provided mattresses for us. We are hanging out in the cafeteria, trying to keep our hope up. We canceled the Christmas Eve soccer game which was supposed to be tomorrow; it won't be the same without Ginger," George Smoothman said.

"We are waiting together, as a support unit. Not only have we lost our good friend Ginger Goodwin, we may have lost our Christmas bonuses and our jobs. When times are hard we miners need to stick together. We really need each other's support right now, since we have no idea what the future has in store for any of us," Jay Paylor said sounding as gloomy as he felt.

"We miners are used to hard times, but times like these could be easier if Control Center would communicate with us," George Smoothman said.

"You mean the executive lounge?" Jay Paylor asked.

"Yes, they are calling that floor Control Center. Anyway, we are planning to stick it out with other good people from Pitville. We are just ordinary people facing an extraordinary situation. We are torn between what we need and what we are hoping for, and often those lines are blurred. At the very time that we need clarity, our future and Ginger's future are up in the air," George Smoothman said feeling just as gloomy as Paylor sounded.

"Most of us are waiting for our pay packets and hoping Ginger will be freed from the mine before his air supply runs out. Though we could say this is one of the worst Christmases we have ever had, if we are able to see Ginger again, it will one of the best Christmases, ever. I suppose that at the moment it is the worst of times and the best of times. And that defines a miner's life in Pitville," Jay Paylor interjected.

"Actually that defines the book 'A Tale Of Two Cities' Jay," George Smoothman said.

"Exactly George, that defines Pitville, a tale of two cities," Jay Paylor said.

"The cafeteria served us macaroni and cheese which was very good," George Smoothman added.

"Yes, and what do you think the commanders up in the executive lounge are eating?" Jay Paylor asked.

"I suppose it is none of our business. My son and wife have been staying with me in the Miners' Cafeteria, and we are just here supporting each other. We have been washing up in the washroom in the back and we have been taking care of each other the best we know how. Under these terrible circumstances we can only do the best we can do, and we all like macaroni and cheese," George explained.

"Thank you, George Smoothman and Jay Paylor for your contribution to our show. It is greatly appreciated."

"Now for our early evening recap.

"A combination of foggy skies and dangerous gas readings from inside the mine are delaying authorities in their efforts to rescue Ginger Goodwin who may have reached the rescue chamber in 'Section E', and will only have an air supply of about sixty hours left. Today mine authorities who did not want to be identified in fear of reprisal, are saying that at present, it is too dangerous to enter the mine, and the mine should be sealed.

Company insiders tell us that only G.O.D. has the legal right to make a life and death decision, since government officials are expected to have opinions independent from the Big Seven Coal Group. We at PPZ are told by a reliable source that every political party on Tut Island relies heavily on campaign funding from Big Coal.

Government authorities appear to be agreeing with mine authorities that the situation in Mine Five is far too dangerous for humans to enter and the mine should be sealed.

"So what else is new?" Jay Paylor said into the microphone making Dianne lose her train of thought for a small moment.

"For those of you who have just tuned into our broadcast, I will describe the local scenery to you; since it is too foggy to see it. You are imagining clear skies, make sure that you block out the black cloud of toxic smoke which is lurking overhead, due to yesterday's explosions. Just imagine looking toward the west and you will see the beautiful Beartut Mountain range, which hosts a world class skiing and snowboarding resort, and usually is a very popular destination for young families, during the Christmas holidays.

It has only been recently that the Government's Official Directors have given themselves permission to allow a mining concern. to lease part of the Beartut Mountain Range, which has been owned by G.O.D. for over a century.

During the depression of 2029, the government sold a 100 year lease which includes but is not limited to approximately 1.5 million acres of property to the group known as the Big Seven Coal Group which also owns Coaltonstone Mines. This property includes the Beartut Mountain Range's mineral rights, Even though the Big Seven Coal Group have mining rights to the wealth under the ground, environmental groups on a global scale believe that the real wealth of Tut Island lies above ground. The beauty of Beartut Mountain Range is second to none and has been a popular holiday destination for generations.

The Tut Ski Hill is technically no longer leasing part of the same mountain range from the Tut Island Government but is leasing it from the Big Seven Coal Group.

In other news related to the Coalton Valley. Many mines in this region, especially the ones which have been abandoned or were never formally mapped or registered with the Government's Official Directors, are easy pickings for the illegal coal cartel. These ruthless masters of the underworld coal industry employ undocumented miners and are often willing to go to extreme lengths to satisfy the growing demand for anthracite coal.

Registering a mine is a costly process, a process which undocumented miners are able to avoid.

Municipal and regional jurisdictions earn royalties once the mineral wealth is extracted. If a disaster occurred to a municipality, for example a city like Pitville, then the next level of government would take control and enjoy the benefits from the mineral royalties before the source of wealth was depleted and no longer economical to harvest. The bureaucratic process can be long, expensive and tedious but so was the great depression of 2029.

At the present time Mine Five is one of the few legally operated mines left in the Coalton Valley.

As I look out of this west-side window, I can see tens of thousands of people waiting on the public side of the security gate, which surrounds Coaltonstone Mines. Many of these people have travelled great distances so they could join the tens of thousands who are standing here in support of Ginger Goodwin who has been trapped in Mine Five for about thirty-six hours.

All of these people who have travelled from so many different places have one thing in common; they are hoping for a positive outcome for Ginger Goodwin.

What do we know about Ginger Goodwin?

Ginger Goodwin was the lead student organizer of the Great Student Strike of 2015.

Ginger Goodwin won a scholarship to study mine management and safety after he entered a contest, which was open to all Coalton High School students during Coalton's hay day. The contest was a race in designing a safety mechanism, robot, harness or a process to enhance mine safety. The rights to this device are now owned by the Big Seven Coal Group. In exchange for those rights Goodwin was given a scholarship to study at the Tut Island University which has campuses situated in various locations on Tut Island.

I would like to bring attention to the sometimes somber and sometimes festive atmosphere found outside this window. I will now open this window and please ignore the wind and fowl smelling air," Dianne instructed as she opened the window, the wind blew inside the cafeteria with a ferocity which shocked many of the people sitting at the tables. The Christmas candles that were enforcing a holiday feel to the Miners' Cafeteria were suddenly extinguished by the unwelcomed breeze.

"Through our lens courtesy of the PPZ, you will see that there are air-buses arriving, bringing more people to join in as the Coal Miners' Choir leads in the singing of Christmas carols and other upbeat songs as we wait for the rescuing of Ginger Goodwin to begin.

Mr. Goodwin's boss Don Bell, lead manager of mine safety for Mine Five, has joined us in the miners' cafeteria.

"Good Evening Mr. Bell," Dianne said pleasantly.

"Good evening Dianne," Don Bell replied trying not to stoop.

"I know that there is a lot of hope out there that Ginger is surviving and is persevering," Dianne said.

"Ginger Goodwin is very knowledgeable and has always been a great asset to my department. Mr. Goodwin knows how the safety equipment works, how the ventilation system works, he knows how he might be able to avoid the impact of the explosion when possible. If there is a way to survive, Ginger Goodwin will find it," Don Bell said.

"As you know, any comment that I have, is purely my own opinion based on years of experience as a safety manager working beside my assistant, Ginger Goodwin. This is the first time that I can recall that an actual safety officer was the only one trapped in one of our mines or any mine as far as that goes. I know everyone is doing their best during this very difficult situation," Don Bell said, knowing that in many ways his assistant's actions were heroic and beyond what he would have done himself.

"Mr. Bell, insiders are saying that Ginger Goodwin prevented the whole morning shift from being trapped in the mine, is that true?"

"Yes Dianne, I believe that Ginger Goodwin did save the morning crew when he extended his early Sunday morning inspection by twenty minutes yesterday morning.

In my opinion Ginger is a real hero. As I said before, my comments are purely my own opinion. We really don't know what caused yesterday's explosions.

We don't know where Ginger is, or what condition he may be in or whether he is still alive or if he has fallen. But yes, regardless of all the questions and unknowns, it is still a fact that Ginger Goodwin is a hero. His actions may have not prevented a disaster, but he was able to prevent the morning shift from descending into one.

If Ginger is alive, we hope that he is not trapped in fallen rock and that he was able to reach the rescue chamber in 'Section E'. If Ginger is able to reach the rescue chamber in Section E, he will find food, ninety-six hours of air supply left and of course he will have sanitation facilities. We hope that Ginger was able to inflate the emergency sealing equipment which is designed to separate 'Section E' from the contaminated areas of the mine, during an emergency.

The air will be polluted especially in 'Sections A, B and C'. Some experts are saying that it will take a miracle to save Mr. Goodwin. A rescue based around technology is a lot more complicated, of course.

"Do you know if Ginger Goodwin extended the pre-shift safety inspection because he found something that was violating the International Mine Safety Standards' Code?" Dianne asked.

"I do not know," Don Bell replied.

"Our inside sources have told us that Jason Bell is your nephew, and was in charge of drilling borehole COALT-11-C, in

Mine Four, so that access to Mine Five could be accelerated, is it true that Jason Bell is your nephew?" Dianne asked.

"Yes, Jason Bell is my nephew," Don Bell said.

"Our inside sources have also told us that Jason's drilling of borehole COALT-11-C may have been responsible for setting off the second explosion in Mine Five. Do you have anything to say in your nephew's defense?" Dianne asked.

"As I said before, explosions can happen for all kinds of reasons. At this time we must determine how we conduct ourselves, so that everyone stays safe during the rescue and salvage mission," Don Bell said

"And when will the rescue mission begin?"

"I don't know," Don Bell replied to Dianne's unscripted question.

"One more question. We have been told by our reliable source that there is an emergency tele-magnetic radio, which uses low power and is situated in 'Section E'. We have also been told that this emergency radio can be used to transmit voice and text messages, through the rock, and up to the surface without any risk of creating sparks which could ignite gas. We are also told that these magnetic waves could be blocked by signals, which are being used to transmit invisible fencing around the security parameter surrounding Mine Five and other properties. Can you clarify this situation for us, Mr. Bell?" Dianne asked.

"No, I am sorry I cannot," Don Bell said feeling troubled.

"Our reliable source also told us that the rescue is being delayed because the Coaltonstone Mines' insurance carrier is refusing to fund the rescue. Can you comment on this matter please?" Dianne asked.

"No, I am sorry, I cannot. Good day and Merry Christmas," Don Bell said realizing his response must have sounded pretty shallow if not outright condescending.

"I hate to leave all this up in the air. So if Ginger Goodwin can feel our vibrations, from deep within the ground, Ginger, we want you back with us. And all these people standing on the other side of the fence are also praying for a miracle," Dianne interjected as she stuck her head out of the window.

"Ok, on your mark, one, two, three, go," Dianne exclaimed as she cued the tens of thousands of people waiting for this very moment on the other side of the fence.

"Ginger, we care," The crowd shouted in unison.

"My God this is such bull shit. If all the Coaltonstones and all the Bells hadn't ignored Goodwin's reports, possibly no one would be trapped down there right now. We would all be enjoying the holidays and our bonus packets, and we would still have our jobs," Jay Paylor said as he spoke into the microphone as fast as he could, with George Smoothman nodding his head frantically in agreement, before Dianne pulled the microphone away.

"This is Dianne Black, with the PPZ, live from the Miners' Cafeteria, often called the 'Number Two Café'.

"Like I said before, this cafeteria is never called the 'Number Two Café' by miners, just by the executives who usually are dining on the top floor of this building, not the bottom floor. The rest of us always call the Miners' Cafeteria by its real name," Jay Paylor said as he pulled the microphone to his face before Dianne pulled it back again.

"Thank you Jay Paylor and George Smoothman for contributing to our show; back to you Steve."

"Thank you Dianne. For those just joining our newscast, we are in the 36th hour of the Ginger Goodwin rescue vigil. Now, a word from our sponsors; the Big Seven Coal Group," Steve announced before he flipped the switch.

"We care about Pitville. We care for the beautiful Beartut mountain range. We at Big Seven Coal Group, care for our neighbours, our employees and the environment. We care about Ginger Goodwin. We are assessing the situation carefully. As one of the major employers on Tut Island, we take great pride in our operations and the impact they have on Tut Island economies."

"What bull," Sam shouted as he threw his paper cup at the very old television set?

"Our vision is forward looking. We take our responsibility to the community of Pitville very seriously. Our coal mines, which are located on Tut Island, are maintained by technicians and contractors who have up to date training and state of the art machinery. We own and lease some of the most advanced mining machinery in the business."

"Thank you Big Seven Coal Group. Now for a recap," Dianne announced.

"Ginger Goodwin has been trapped in Mine Five since early Sunday morning.

Ginger Goodwin is believed to be the only one trapped in the mine therefore technically this ordeal is not considered a disaster because there are less than five people trapped in the mine," Dianne Black said in disbelief.

"This evening we have with us in the miners' cafeteria, Father David Bell from the Presbyterian Church," Dianne placed the microphone close to Pastor Bell's face.

"For Mr. Goodwin time is crucial. Do you believe that God can hear crowd sourced prayer?" Dianne asked realizing that the question was rather loaded.

"Thank you Dianne. Pastor Bell said with a bit of a chuckle

"I am not usually called Father Bell. As pastor I am usually called Reverend Bell. It is wonderful how so many faiths have been brought here together at this challenging time. Yes I do. I believe God hears our prayers and we must have faith in those things that we cannot see.

We do hope that this ordeal has a purpose and is not just merely an accident, which it could very well be.

I suppose it is part of our faith that we believe that God is listening to our prayers whether we are in a crowd or alone. Prayers are not always answered the way we would like them to be answered, sometimes it seems that our prayers are being ignored, sometimes we are even tempted to doubt God's existence, but I also believe anything is possible. Just look around us and you can see the miracle of life everywhere. I see God's beauty in Beartut Mountain Range, and I see God's beauty even in Pitville,"

"Thank you Pastor Bell," Dianne Black said as she picked out John Bell, head of security, from the people who had agreed to speak on camera.

"We have with us this evening John Bell head of security for Coaltonstone Mines, which is a subsidiary of the Big Seven Coal Group and the owner of Mine Five," Dianne said as she introduced John Bell to the world she wonder how a man who was identical to another could appear so much harder and callous and possibly even be cruel, unlike his brother Don whose body seemed so gentle.

"Good even Mr. Bell, and what do you think life in Pitville centers around?"

"Life in Pitville centers on coal. Coal, not only made this town, coal made this Island. Without the benefits of coal, we would no longer be a payroll town, we would become a ghost town similar to Coalton.

Today, our machinery is able to extract coal, at greater quantities and at faster speeds, than ever before. We have a highly regulated mining industry where bureaucrats are often standing in our way, so that we cannot maximize production.

When we are allowed to work at full capacity, our equipment is able to produce around 30,000 tons of coal a day," John Bell said.

"So, Mr. Bell do you believe that life in Pitville centers on coal and not God?" Dianne asked as a gasp of mass surprise echoed throughout the miners' cafeteria.

"No, I did not say that. I said that without coal we could not remain a payroll town and in time the town would be abandoned. Mr. Goodwin has the training to collect data and manage this data in such a way that risk can be foreseen scientifically. We all hoped that negative outcomes could be prevented. But no one can prevent or foresee when lightning is about to strike pockets of built up methane gas. Though I would not call lightning igniting methane gas an act of God, insurance companies might," John Bell said as a loud collective gasp echoed behind him.

"You heard Steve's news broadcast, earlier today, concerning all the reports Deep Coal entrusted to us? All forty-nine reports appeared to have been ignored by Coaltonstone Mines," Dianne said as Jackson tried to zoom in on the faces of a group of miners who were sitting at a table, playing cards.

"Whoever that Deep Coal person happens to be," is anyone's guess but he or she has revealed data which is owned by Coaltonstone Mines and the Big Seven Coal Group's shareholders. When any information which is meant for internal use only, is taken out of context, conclusions can be reached which are misleading. Our legal advisors have told us to not discuss this matter any further since it is still being investigated by the appropriate authorities," John Bell insisted as Dianne Black took control of the microphone.

"So you do admit that these reports do exist and that those reports compiled by Ginger Goodwin were being ignored?" Dianne asked.

"No, I did not say that," John Bell said.

"So now you are saying that those reports do not exist?" Dianne asked.

"No, I am not saying that either," John Bell insisted.

"Thank you John Bell, for taking time out of your busy day as head of security for Coaltonstone Mines, to talk with us, and our viewers from all over the world," Dianne said.

"Over to you Bill," Dianne added.

"Thank you Dianne. Now for another word from our sponsor, Sinking Hole car burial services located two kilometers west of Coalton. We are famous worldwide for having one of the largest burial sites for obsolete automobiles. Give your car the respect it deserves, with a dignified burial."

"Thank you Bill. Now back to our continual coverage of the Pitville Mine disaster of 2030, where Ginger Goodwin has been trapped deep inside Mine Five since 5:20 AM, Sunday, December 22nd.

At the present time, we are told that the mission to rescue Ginger Goodwin has been delayed due to another small earthquake which happened early this morning, measuring 4.5 on the Richter scale.

Three aftershocks measuring 3.1, 2.2 and 2.3 were also recorded.

Before this week, this region's last recorded earthquake occurred around seventy years ago which destroyed the chimney of the local library, and contributed to the death of one Miss Simpson who had been on a ladder while placing a returned book onto a top shelf.

During the second explosion, which occurred in the afternoon on December 22nd, is believed to have caused a portion of the roof in Mine Five's 'Sections B and C' to collapse, which some experts believe also triggered a small earthquake measuring around 2.2 on the Richter scale.

Complicating the rescue efforts to free Mr. Goodwin from Mine Five was the submerging of three surveillance robots in about 500,000 gallons of acid water flooding 'Section A' in Mine Five.

Support for Ginger Goodwin is gaining in organizational momentum as Global work stoppages in coal mines are being staged all over the world.

Ironically the miners of Pitville gave up their right to strike as part of their contract when agreeing to work for Coaltonstone Mines, a subsidiary of the Big Seven Coal Group and owner of Mine Five.

This global general strike is also supported by the students of Coalton High. During 2015, as a student from the same school, Ginger Goodwin led a similar strike to draw attention to unfair hiring practices on the opening day of Mine Five in Pitville as Coalton's economy was left to crash after the closing of Mine Three," this is Dianne Black for the PPZ, back to you Steve."

As Dianne and Jackson left the Miners Cafeteria, the miners and their families, many shedding tears, as they watched Dianne's short presentation of the student strike of 2015. The presentation was meant to fill in the time but many recognized themselves and their friends and families, fifteen years ago while Coalton was still a livable place to be.

"Haven't we aged?" George Smoothman joked.

"You have aged quite a bit George; I am about the same, as I was," Jay Paylor replied, as he grabbed some of the tissues from the box which had been set in the middle of each table, and threw them at George.

"Now that feels better," Jay said, as he tried to focus on the archived news clip being shown.

The miners worked eight-hour shifts and there were usually three shifts a day. Very rarely were there this many miners in the cafeteria at the same time.

More people were expected to arrive including retired miners. "Things haven't changed much. This explosion shouldn't have happened. Everything that we were striking against, as students happened anyway," Jay Paylor said.

"Ginger brought us together back then; Ginger is bringing us together, again," Kevin said as he wiped his glasses. It was rare to see Kevin with clean glasses.

"Now they are showing us on TV as we are sitting here. And look at us; we look worse than in real life. We all look ten pounds fatter, stupider and dirtier than we really are," Jay Paylor complained as his chest tighten he cough helplessly into a napkin that he pulled out from his coat pocket. Jay pulled out his green puffer from another pocket and inhaled. "I don't hate my life, because it is the only one I have, and if I had a choice, I would choose no other," Jay spluttered as he tucked his inhaler in his pocket. The other miners stared at him while trying to follow his logic.

"It is hard not knowing whether Ginger is alive or dead. But if they don't get to him soon, he will be dead, even if he isn't dead now. Ginger only has sixty hours of air supply left," Marlene complained as she cupped her hand around the candle she was holding. Look at that, two more air-bus loads of people have just arrived, and they are wearing their miners' lamps.

"I think though Ginger was an idealist and a dreamer and if we still had a union and a gas committee on that union, perhaps Ginger would have been more appreciated," Sam speculated.

"What do you mean, 'was'?" George Smoothman questioned Sam with a tone which sounded more defeated than confrontational.

"Until we know that Ginger is dead, we must assume that he is alive. The sentiment will keep us motivated to push for Ginger's rescue. We can't let old James Coaltonstone convince us that it is ok to bury Ginger alive to save the Big Seven Coal Group money. Ginger was also a doer. He did something practical to make a difference regardless if there was an official gas committee or not, Ginger knew what could be managed, if effort was focused, either collectively or singularly, to the end. Ginger was above getting involved in the lateral violence which goes on from time to time which keeps us divided and angry with each other. We can't forget that Ginger found a way to bypass all that negativity which is used to divide us," George Smoothman stated.

"More people are arriving. I am seeing people I haven't seen for years," Kevin observed as he cleaned his glasses again.

"When was the last time you had a new pair of glasses Kev?" George Smoothman asked.

"I don't remember," Kevin replied.

"Why don't we march into the executive lounge the way we marched out of our high school building during the great student strike, fifteen years ago, and demand our pay packets, or at least ask for them politely?" Sam Jones asked

"Because we don't want to land up on a leased convict chain gang, stuck in the arctic wearing thin soled shoes; that is why we have to stay in control of ourselves," Jay Paylor said shaking his finger to emphasize his point.

Chapter 17:
The Executive Lounge

Monday December 23, 2030, around 7 PM:

The Coaltonstone Coal Mine's executive cafeteria was full. Executives and their spouses were sitting at tables sporting white tablecloths. Flowers in vases, which were placed in the middle of each table a few hours ago, were quickly losing their beauty, as the wilting process had begun.

Though today was only Monday, Don Bell wondered what life would be like at the end of the week. Friday was his favorite day because it usually was a day of closure. He tolerated Mondays for he had no other choice. He enjoyed casual Fridays since the atmosphere was less stuffy than the other days of the week. Don also enjoyed the selection of fish that was always part of Friday's menu.

There was very little hope that today would be a day Don would want to remember any more than yesterday had been. Don speculated that Sunday, December 22nd during the year of 2030, would not be the worst day of Don Bell's life, there would be worse days to come.

At times Don feared fate more than he feared death.

Don found working on security with his brother, even if it was false security, easier to tolerate than working with Bobby Coaltonstone when the various safety issues, usually related to the ventilation design, was in Bobby Coaltonstone's control even though Don could be blamed for the outcome.

Don never believed for a moment that any intelligent person expected Mine Five to be safe. It was one of the gassiest mines on Tut Island.

It was just a basic fact of life that there were many issues in the world that were just too expensive to change. The world could solve world hunger too, but it just was not cost effective to do so. Of course raging war in the long run was much cheaper and much more profitable if you had the right family connections, than feeding all the people in the world, who would only reproduce, making the world even more crowded than it already was.

Don Bell visually scanned the room and wondered how so many people could be so relaxed as if the mine disaster never happened.

The executive dining room smelled lovely and a world apart from Pitville. The lobster that was being served to executives made the late supper seem very grand compared to the macaroni and cheese being served in the Miners' cafeteria.

Christmas day was only two days away. The Christmas tree in the corner of the executive lounge made the room look festive and unlike the miners' cafeteria, there was still a holiday mood in the air.

Don Bell understood that DNA and evidence, along with everything else, was usually destroyed during a powerful explosion. The only person who knew what actually happened moments before the explosion would be Ginger. Don realized that everyone except Ginger missed warning signs. There were people in this very room who might feel that their prospects would be better if Ginger had died in Mine Five. With Ginger out of the way the cause for the explosion would most likely remain hearsay, speculation or just a mystery.

Creating wealth always took risks. The greater the wealth, the greater the risks taken, and this logic was certainly true with coal mining.

Don believed that mining in itself was not oppressive. In fact coal was a symbol of commerce and was the fuel which won wars and enhanced social mobility.

Accidents do happen, and looking back is always easier than looking forward.

Don liked Ginger Goodwin. He never saw a man who cared as much about mine safety as Goodwin did, and that was a good thing, but Goodwin did not need to be in the mine to do his pre-morning shift inspection but chose to his inspection the most effective way that he could.

In many ways it didn't make sense that Goodwin was Deep Coal. He never appeared to be that manipulative or sneaky. Goodwin also never appeared to fear retribution when telling the truth Ginger just appeared to assume that the truth would be self-evident and would make future events more predictable and less chaotic. Ginger always appeared to believe that there was a freedom related to truth and was beyond just being right or wrong, the truth could create a better place to be. Truth could even manage risk so that mine disasters could be prevented.

Whoever Deep coal may be, he would have to have some of the characteristics traitors usually possess. Goodwin wasn't like that, he wasn't betraying anyone, if anything, he was just trying to liberate his colleagues.

Don Bell guessed that no one, not even the paparazzi from the PPZ cared about Ginger's reports. The reports were only being used to increase ratings and sensationalism for the PPZ. Even though it w a common held opinion that Ginger was acting out his obsessive-compulsive disorder, and shouldn't be taken seriously at all, let alone exploited, Don was wondering if he really understood the content of the reports. Of course he couldn't raise his doubts out loud, but maybe he had not comprehended the significance of Ginger's reports and just went along with everyone else who was assuming that he was acting obsessively and compulsively.

Don wondered if PPZ just knew about the reports and did not actually have physical possession of them.

Don Bell did not blame himself for the explosions. Danger and explosions were just part of the nature of mining and actually added some excitement to life in Pitville.

It didn't make sense to Don that Deep Coal appeared from nowhere, the day after the two explosions occurred in Mine Five. Don knew Ginger well enough to know that if Goodwin were going to blow the whistle, he would have done so during the last forty-seven days. As a shareholder, Goodwin could lose out financially by leaking internal records and documents to external forces. As an employee, Goodwin would also lose his job. It just did not make sense that Goodwin was Deep Coal. But who could Deep Coal be?

Don did not want to accuse the wrong person for being Deep Coal. Goodwin would be suffering enough already even if he did manage to make it to 'Section E' and found refuge in the rescue chamber, which was a big 'if'.

"Why doesn't someone ask this Deep Coal fellow where would Pitville be without coal?" James Coaltonstone asked as he looked over Ginger's reports, the same reports that were allegedly leaked by Deep Coal to PPZ.

"Whoever this Deep Coal is, he is an enemy of Coaltonstone Mines, an enemy of Coalton Valley, an enemy of the Big Seven Coal Group and an enemy of the rights of man," James Coaltonstone declared as an uncomfortable silence filled the room.

"And certainly a security risk. Where would we be without coal?" John Bell asked as James Coaltonstone placed the company documents down and dipped a french fry into hot gravy as his wife Jane frowned disapprovingly.

"I always read Goodwin's safety reports but he can't possibly expect us to redesign our ventilation system when we are planning to close Mine Five by June 30th of next year. It is just not practical. And I find it hard to believe that anyone who wrote that many reports in forty-seven days doesn't have some sort of an obsessive-compulsive disorder," James Coaltonstone scoffed.

"I was reading Goodwin's last log before the explosion, and he could have easily have written the same log without putting himself in danger. Why should we pay for his rescue when he had no business being down there in the first place? He had every opportunity to undertake his inspections remotely. In my opinion, Goodwin put himself in danger," John Bell maintained.

"A few months ago, the defunct Miners Union of Tut Island found evidence that our data taken remotely from Mine Five, was misleading, since air found in different areas of the mine, had been mixed together. Goodwin may have been verifying that the data used in his research was a fair representation of the actual air quality in Mine Five by making separate measurements in areas where pockets of gas often accumulated," Don Bell explained until Coaltonstone interrupted him, rudely.

"Look at all these logs." James Coaltonstone began to rant in an exasperated tone.

"How much do you want to bet, Goodwin was standing right in the coal dust as he wrote about the requirement of spreading a generous amount of rock dust within forty feet of the working faces of the mine, and that this requirement had been violated."

"That appears to be his second last log," Don Bell speculated while trying to sound agreeable but couldn't hide his feeling of exasperation.

"Thank God for small mercies," James Coaltonstone scoffed, if I know Goodwin, I bet he was measuring the rock dust spread a third or fourth time to make sure the first measurement was correct. The day we opened the mine we met all safety and environmental standards imposed upon us at that time," James Coaltonstone said reassuringly as he struggled to break the lobster shell before he moved his plate to Delilah who did the task for him.

"The problem with Goodwin was his determination to use science to control fate. I bet you anything that Goodwin was data mining right before the explosion happened, and now he is probably dead. How much data does anyone need on an ongoing operation?" Bobby Coaltonstone asked anyone who was listening.

"We are mining coal not data. I am the lead manager of operations here, and I know from experience that there is not one shareholder who would encourage wasteful spending. I bet you anything that Goodwin is enabling that criminal Deep Coal, giving those paparazzi more opportunity to magnify and exaggerate every single spec of coal dust in our mines and tunnels. Where will my tormentors check next for coal dust?

"I know that those doctors at the Pitville Medical Clinic are filing reports related to coal dust irritating coal miners' body parts, sir," Don Bell noted.

"I don't think this has anything to do with what we are discussing, Don," John Bell remarked.

"You don't think that health has anything to do with safety?" Don Bell asked his brother who was rolling his eyes mockingly.

"I was about to say, that we don't have to worry about rescuing someone who has been incinerated because he happened to be in the wrong place at the wrong time. Goodwin could have taken all the measurements his little heart desired above ground like all the other safety technicians hired on the Island do," James Coaltonstone said condescendingly, barely controlling his exasperation he was feeling toward Don Bell.

"After seeing those surveillance images that we received Sunday afternoon; I have little doubt that Ginger survived the explosion which occurred earlier in the day," Alex Coaltonstone said as he tried to avoid eye contact.

"I have a question for Don Bell. Could he stand up please?" James Coaltonstone asked as he lifted his head from the pile of reports that were sitting in a neat pile beside an empty dinner plate. As James Coaltonstone looked around the room for Don Bell he remembered that he was sitting right beside him. Don Bell was standing as he cleared his throat.

"What do you make of PPZ's claim that they have Goodwin's forty-nine reports that he submitted to us over the last forty-seven days prior to Sunday's first explosion?" James Coaltonstone asked.

"I don't know what to think without more evidence, Sir. I would hope that PPZ is bluffing and they just heard how many reports Ginger submitted during the last forty-seven days. I do agree with you sir, anyone who writes that many reports could very likely have an obsessive-compulsive disorder. I mean Goodwin is the only assistant that I have ever had, who has written so many reports. I really believe that Mr. Goodwin had some kind of mental health issue and but I seriously doubt that he would have sent PPZ all of his reports, after the accident. How could he? I do not have any evidence to prove Goodwin's guilt and he does not have to prove his innocence, since it is presumed that he is innocent until proven guilty," Don Bell replied.

"Where is John Bell, stand up please, and tell all of us in this room if you agree with our look alike," James Coaltonstone commanded.

"I agree. The PPZ hasn't shown anyone the actual reports that they claim to have in their possession but I believe with

Goodwin's mental health issues, he could be capable of anything. I agree that it is very possible that PPZ is bluffing and it is also possible that Goodwin did send someone copies of his reports, but I agree with Don, Deep Coal is most likely not Ginger Goodwin, but someone close to him. I would advise that we ignore PPZ's report about our reports, and write a report of our own. And if Goodwin sent those reports he has breached his contract with Coaltonstone Mines, and if he is not dead when we find him, we should fire him," John Bell said.

"Who else would do such a thing?" James Coaltonstone asked.

"I don't know sir," Don Bell said.

"I am asking your brother, John, he is the head of our security, and I say if this is not a breach of our security, I don't know what is," Coaltonstone said in a rage.

"I am sorry sir," Don Bell said

"These reports are our internal property and outsiders have no right to these documents," James Coaltonstone continued to rage, as he crossed off an item from a long list that he had written in his red notebook with such force, the point of his ball point pen went right through the paper, to his annoyance.

"Since we do not know who if anyone is actually leaking our reports we need to be communicating the old fashioned way with hand written notes that can be burned to ashes in a fire. All we know is that PPZ is aware of Goodwin's reports but I know one thing, our use of technology makes us vulnerable to leakage," John Bell said as he retrieved a brand new red pen from his jacket pocket and gave it to James Coaltonstone.

"Yes, quite right. I suppose it is possible that PPZ could be bluffing, but it is also equally possible that they aren't. I suppose we need to see the evidence to know for sure, and until then we will communicate to each other the old fashioned way. We will do all our communication with pens, and when they run out or break, we will use pencils," James Coaltonstone said feeling in control once again.

"I second that motion, sir," John Bell offered.

"I suggest from now on that we make two logs, one for good reports that we can share with the public and one for internal reports which would only be meant as internal controls and one way communications between ourselves. All memos must be shared in a way that is less traceable until we find out who our whistleblower is. He will be a man living behind a mask. Deep Coal appeared out of the blue, a day after the explosion, so our whistleblower could be anyone of us.

"Isn't that what we already do? Make inside memos and outside memos." Alex Coaltonstone asked.

"Yes, but we need to make sure that each page is officially stamped. We must take a stand and stay vigilante while we protect our internal records from preying eyes. Our intellectual capital must not be stolen, if it is, we are placed at a disadvantage. We must make it clear that if any member of the public receives a copy of our official internal communications in error, it must be destroyed and the error must be reported back to us without delay," James Coaltonstone said, then smiled as the people who were listening to him, gave him a standing ovation, cueing the rest of the audience to clap in unison.

And all of our informal memos must be written and distributed by hand," James Coaltonstone said as the clapping ended suddenly.

"Do you really think people will actually follow those instructions?" Alex Coaltonstone asked.

"No, but if they are caught with our records which clearly show our company stamp on each page, then we will have a legal framework already set up, so when or if we take action or threaten to take action, all documents will be identifiable. So if a member of the public is caught in possession of any new internal documents we can frame the argument around why do you have these documents instead of arguing about content. The crime here is not what we are communicating, but how others are trespassing against us," Coaltonstone declared.

"What will we say to that Dianne Black if she asks whether we have a conflict of interest between our financial bottom line and the safety of our employees and the environment?" Don Bell asked James Coaltonstone.

"Do not discuss anything related to Goodwin or our internal mining operations with Dianne Black or anyone from the PPZ," James Coaltonstone replied.

"Will we be accused of being unethical by not fully disclosing the good with the bad?" Alex Coaltonstone asked, as Anita Jones noticed James Coaltonstone's face beginning to turn a bright red and wondered if he had forgotten to take his blood pressure medication.

Anita wrote a short note and passed it to James Coaltonstone, who after reading it, nodded graciously, took out a small bottle of Diltiazem from his pocket, popped one of the pills into his mouth, then proceeded to light a cigar.

An alarm wailed as the sprinkler above James Coaltonstone's head sprinkled water vigorously all around leaving James Coaltonstone's cigar to smolder in his mouth. There was a mad rush to move all the paperwork to a dryer table.

"No smoking of any sort is permitted in this vicinity, municipal bylaw number 10k2,"The automated female voice bellowed into the room of straight-faced executives, as wives and cronies struggled not to laugh. Delilah sneezed and Don Bell handed her his handkerchief from his jacket pocket and winked as her cheeks turned crimson.

"Who turned that sprinkler system on after I ordered it to be turned off?" James Coaltonstone asked as he threw his soggy cigar on the floor.

"The fire inspector did sir," she said, hiding behind the handkerchief Don had loaned her.

"Is everyone in this Valley afraid of a few sparks? I remember the days when men acted like men and used their own water to extinguish sparks when working in the mine. They also had the sense to smoke a cigar without setting their own building on fire, unless there was a purpose in doing so. Yes in those days men had purpose, and purpose defined the man. I blame Goodwin," James Coaltonstone raged loudly as he hit the table with his favorite coffee mug with just enough force to make his point without breaking it.

"That man is a disaster wherever he goes. If any man could get hit by lightning more than once in a lifetime it would be Goodwin. If Goodwin was even hit by lightning once he would most likely remain standing in the same spot, logging in a freshly written report about the risk of being hit by lightning and then he would be increasing his own chances of getting hit by lightning again. That Goodwin would send out a stop work order to God if he could," James Coaltonstone ranted as he took out a bottle of antacid. Coaltonstone made a face as he took a long swig.

"At least Goodwin made an accurate log, which gives us valuable knowledge when we are taking risks below." Don Bell added in Ginger's defense.

"Neither you nor Goodwin have any need to work below in the pit. We pay those miners to do their work, and they don't expect us as operators of this mine to control fate. We let God do that," James Coaltonstone said as he stood up and stretched his aching legs.

"Is there going to be a problem with insurance covering the rescue operation? According to PPZ, their moles have informed them that we have a problem, and they announced this rumor as a fact on their continuous coverage relating to our rescue and salvage efforts." John Bell said wondering what the correct response should be.

"Just ignore it; most people will have forgotten what Dianne Black said in a few days," James Coaltonstone said.

"What kills me about those Paparazzi is they use all those gadgets needing all this electricity, and where do they think, electricity is generated from?" John Bell asked.

"Exactly John, they use electricity as if it were water. What do those people at PPZ think we have down there in our pits, an antiseptic board room?" James Coaltonstone asked.

"No, Sir, we have coal," Don Bell answered.

"That is right. Our coal is black and dirty and precious," James Coaltonstone said

"Whoever is sending PPZ our internal documents should be horse wiped. It is totally unproductive to magnify everyday events, which occur in an underground coal mine as if it were a crime to not be able to guarantee safety," John Bell ranted.

"Imagine that I am paying Goodwin to write forty-nine reports over a forty-seven day period. Goodwin writes report after report about coal dust buildup in a coal mine and Dr. Knight is trying to convince me that Goodwin does not have an obsessive-compulsive disorder," James Coaltonstone said.

"As soon as you fork out money to solve one problem, Sir, Goodwin manages to find another problem," John Bell said, James Coaltonstone's logic.

"I have no idea how anyone in the mining industry can determine what a generous amount of rock dusting means. Success is often due to inspiration and taking chances. To see the opportunity in the coal dust instead of the risk, gives us power, and the masses electricity," James Coaltonstone said, with conviction.

"When there is too much regulation, the illegals gain advantages over us," John Bell said.

"Exactly, such a regulation makes just as much sense as declaring mines to have a permanent ventilation system. These words "generous" and "permanent" are not practical words in mining and have no business being used in this business. Our doorway ventilation system has been approved since it was being used before this impractical regulation was put into place. Obviously we can't ask for permission every time we need to prop the doorway open to move our industrial sized equipment around, that is why we use our underground fans, then they tell us we shouldn't be using underground fans. Those pansies in government have no idea what kind of sacrifices we make to continue to run a successful operation so that we can produce coal to generate electricity to fuel our industries at home and our peace efforts abroad.

Why would anyone be surprised that we need to open the doors and sometimes prop them open when moving heavy equipment?" James asked

James asked as he rang the bell, which was in front of his now empty plate. A waiter appeared with a cake tray. Another waiter removed the empty plate.

Old James Coaltonstone continued with his train of thought.

"Don, I want to be very clear that this is not just about your assistant being trapped in Mine Five with two of my guard-bots being converted into data-bots and messing up my plans. I know you must be aware that my money is also trapped down in the mine too. That pit, is just a pit from hell if it doesn't make money for us. That fire down there in the pit is actually burning my money. The sooner that mine is sealed the better, for all concerned." James Coaltonstone said.

"I have told you often enough, that the longwall mining machinery costs us millions of dollars in capital and operating expenses. And we pay the price because that machinery down there can retrieve thirty thousand tons of coal every day. As you must be aware, when that machinery is sitting idle, it becomes dead weight.

When any mine is idle for any reason, it is costing us a bundle not only to finance an idle machine trapped in a hellish pit but also to guard the equipment from scavengers and illegals. And my brand new guard-bots, which were bought so that we could economize, are possibly worthless now since they too are lost somewhere in Mine Five.

Do you know how much it could cost me if I have to pay those cadets overtime?

I receive grants from the Ministry of Industry to offer opportunities to these young men, and these grants are very generous, but they do not cover overtime costs. I will have to pay for those costs out of my operating budget, if they should arise.

Those cadets have been outside my administration building since December 22nd, doing military exercises. Anyway they will cost me a bundle if I have to pay them overtime." James Coaltonstone said as he began to break out in a wet sweat.

Delilah Brown, James Coaltonstone's senior secretary, was quietly taking notes but raised her eyebrows for a moment.

"As I said before, I truly believe that the explosion was caused by either lightening hitting undocumented methane well or possibly a pillar from an undocumented mine was stolen, forcing a mine nearby to collapse, causing the surrounding coal to spontaneously combust." Coaltonstone said as he waved his hands to emphasize his point.

So technically if the first explosion had been an act of God, there will be no insurance coverage and no investigation." James Coaltonstone said as he swiveled around to look at the numerous screens that were situated behind him. Ginger's last report was on one screen. Another screen showed a slide show of photographs sent by the surveillance robots during their journey from 'Section

C' and moving north to 'Section A' before they were submerged in acid water and became inoperable.

"Were there reports of lightning around 5:20 am on December 22nd? Don Bell asked.

"I don't remember hearing or reading any reports of lightning on Sunday morning." Don Bell added.

"There could have been. I wish I could see some progress on those screens. It is frustrating just to be sitting around not being able to produce coal. It is boring and it is costing me too much money to stay idle. I wonder how long it will be until we can restore power to the mine." James Coaltonstone said.

"We can't restore power until we do some air quality tests. We do not want to set off any more explosions by striking off any more sparks. Officially we do not know what set off Sunday's second explosion. We do know if a power source creates sparks, and with the right amount of oxygen and gas, we could set off an inferno in Mine Five," Don Bell said.

I think it was risky to send in those robots, considering we did not get any more information than if we had just set up fiber cables to monitor air quality in the mine.

"How do we know that those rescue bots didn't contribute to the second explosion? My nephew Jason is blaming himself for starting the second explosion and he is taking it very hard. He thinks that his drilling was the only possible cause for the explosion," Don Bell said, as he looked around the room hoping that he did not show the disgust that he was feeling

"We shouldn't restore ventilation to Mine Five until we have assessed all the risks. If we start circulating air in Mine Five, when conditions are so volatile, we could cause a third underground explosion and possibly even set the coal seam on fire. We would be better off if we seal the mine and starve the fire of oxygen. Without air, the underground fires will just burn out," Don Bell said.

"I agree, we do not want any more explosions in Mine Five. Another explosion will make us appear to be repeat offenders and we could get our ventilation plan evoked, which would be very costly and make it more difficult to recover from this set back. We need to re-establish trust between ourselves, the public and external authorities so we do not have to spend tons of money on producing a new ventilation plan and system, which would be so costly it would not be worth reopening the mine," Bobby Coaltonstone said.

"Possibly that is a good thing then, that the backup power didn't kick in. Only God knows what damage a non-permissible lamp may cause down there right now." James Coaltonstone said as one waiter tied a bib around James Coaltonstone's neck as another waiter brought a plate of lobsters and placed the plate beside a tomato and cucumber salad. The genetically modified tomato was a strange shade of purple. James Coaltonstone pushed the salad aside and immersed himself in the task of trying to crack open the lobster so that he could begin to eat its sweet meat before another crisis occurred. Coal mining is just the same as eating lobster," Coaltonstone said, "it is a struggle, but the reward is worth every effort."

Don glanced over Alex's shoulder and eyed the ticker price for COALT stock which was still being recommended as a "buy" by market analysts despite everything else, coal was still king.

"Neither Sunday's mine explosion nor Deep coal's meddling appear to have had a negative pull on our COALT stock. After market closing bell today, our stock had actually gained a dollar. Thank G.O.D. for that. If there is a fear in the market that the supply of coal will decrease then it makes sense that the value of our stock is gaining in value," Alex Coaltonstone explained sounding pleased.

"Hopefully the trend remains in our favor and no one triggers panic selling," Bobby Coaltonstone cautioned.

"Christina Watson is supposed to be watching out for that," Alex Coaltonstone said.

"Talking about Christina that reminds me," James Coaltonstone said.

"Waiter will you please send some of that wonderful lobster to Christina's office and make sure that you include a few of these wonderful pieces of cake." James Coaltonstone added.

"The villain here is not our profit or methods," Dave McGuire one of the many accountants at Coaltonstone Mines said, "the villain here is the nature of mining," It is dangerous work, regardless of how much money we spend on technology and training,

"At the end of the day, mining is dangerous and we accept the risks as should our employees so that they can keep food on their tables and profits in our pockets," Josh Coaltonstone head of marketing added as an uncomfortable laughter filled the room.

"If we could only find a way to program the two guard-bots that were supposed to be with Goodwin before the explosion, we might find a way to communicate with him." Don Bell suggested.

"Those robots were not supposed to be with Goodwin, Goodwin took those robots because they were standing in your office and he assumed that they were meant for his department. I am very upset that those robots have been wasted." James Coaltonstone said, whispering to Don Bell.

"Sir, I think it will all work out in the end," Don Bell said trying to reassure himself as much as he was trying to reassure James Coaltonstone.

"Attention, I have an announcement to make," James Coaltonstone disclosed.

"We, my colleagues and I, have been scheduled to meet important officials from the Minese Government sometime this week, so that we can continue to work out an arrangement between ourselves concerning the M.T.C. Railway. As you all know, I am the major shareholder for the M.T.C. Railway, and underneath our new proposed railway line, is coal. So we are promising to share our know-how and goodwill as we co-operate in this joint venture. The task will be immense, and so will the profits. The task of building a state of the art railway line which will ship our coal from Pitville all the way to the other side of the Bering Strait. This project will create opportunities for our people within majestic proportions. I have been given rights to the land and to the resources below the strait, on the Minese side of the Strait and on the Tut Island side of the Strait. This project is our future, and we are estimating that it could take five years, to fit all the necessary modules underneath the Strait. In return we have exclusive access to the mineral wealth underground. And while we install this state of the art railway line we will be extracting our new source of coal," James Coaltonstone explained as everyone stood up and clapped loudly.

"Yesterday afternoon we sent three of our surveillance robots down into Mine Five," James Coaltonstone said to more applause.

"Now young John Bell, our man who heads security for us, will share and address certain issues relating to logistics during yesterday afternoon's challenging exploration. Ladies and Gentlemen I present to you John Bell," Coaltonstone announced as he sat down and took a long drink from his glass goblet, while the people in the room continued to applaud politely.

"Thank you, Sir," John Bell said as he rose to his feet.

"Earlier this afternoon, the three surveillance robots were able to determine that the temperature in 'Sections A, B, and C' was around 40 degrees Celsius, which would be around 104 degrees Fahrenheit. The air quality is not yet safe for humans to enter those sections of the mine, since the methane gas count is still very high. The three surveillance robots sent us photographs which show that much but not all of our mining equipment was blown apart during the explosion. Pillars in 'Section B' were blown apart during the explosion. We also have photographs showing portions of the roof in 'Sections B' having caved in. The mine is definitely a disaster. The surveillance robots transmitted this data from 'Sections B and C' before the rescue robots became inoperable. We need to set up a receiving station within range of 'Section E' so that we can receive messages from Ginger if he is still alive," John Bell said.

"No, do we need to waste valuable resources searching for a man who has been incinerated?" James Coaltonstone said.

"How do we know that Goodwin has been incinerated?" Bobby Coaltonstone asked his father who did not answer but scowled at Bobby until he bowed his head.

"Is it true that the underground signals, which control our invisible fencing, could be interfering with the emergency radio in 'Section E'? That radio should be working. Why can't we turn the invisible fence off for now? We still have the barb wire fence, and the electricity is still running through it," Don Bell inquired.

"No, we must leave those fences on, no matter what." John Bell and James Coaltonstone said at the same time.

"And we don't need to worry about building a communication center when the only person in the mine is dead," James Coaltonstone added.

"Can we go back to the issue related to boss-bots working together? Don Bell asked.

"I don't know if boss-bots can or should be working together as one unit. Maybe if they were programmed to network into the Eye-Bot Network, instead of being departmentalized and out of touch with each other's departments, integration could solve the very problems which departmentalizing our roles often creates." Don Bell said.

"You realize that the main reason why the bots are departmentalized is because if any of the data-bots were captured or stolen by one of our many competitors including the ruthless members of the coal cartel, we would only have a portion of our data and not all of it stolen or misused. The same strategy applies to laptops. The accounting department only has accounting data. The logistics department only has data which applies to logistics." James Coaltonstone explained.

"And tell us again, whose idea was it to program the whistle-boss bots with the payroll-boss bots with the data-boss bots?" James Coaltonstone asked.

"It was Goodwin's idea, sir. He was hoping to mine the data so that we could predict the probability and timing of any gas related event occurring, so we could change our strategy and policies and minimize any chance of a negative outcome." Don Bell said realizing that Ginger did not only predict would will happen if safety infractions were not corrected, Ginger also demonstrated what could have been, if only the mine had been managed with a long term perspective in mind.

"Well Goodwin did a bloody poor job of avoiding this disaster, now didn't he?" James Coaltonstone said.

Don Bell sat motionlessly as he reviewed Ginger's report from Sunday morning that was sent moments before the first explosion occurred. Don grimaced to himself as he heard others in the room arguing about the terrible predicament that the company and its shareholders were finding themselves in but were happy that they were going to benefit from the new M.T.C. Railway.

"Don Bell, could you please share your strategy update with all of us in this room?" James Coaltonstone asked as heads turned to glare at Don Bell.

"I don't have one, sir. I have been depending on the rescue team to keep me in the loop. I just assumed that they were in charge now." Don Bell said.

"Stand up Mr. Bell and tell all of us in this room what you just told me, and please add any detail you may think will widen the scope of your visionary plan." James Coaltonstone said as hit the table with his hand, making the vase tumble to the floor as it broke into several pieces.

Silence echoed through the executive lounge.

Don wished that he could stand up and scream so that the whole room could witness that he just quit his job and was now free to speak his mind, of course that was never going to happen. Don needed his job, he had a wife and two kids to support. Don took a few minutes to respond as he thought of all the reasons why he needed his job and how his job was so connected to his family ties.

"I have been waiting for the rescue team to share their plans with me, Sir." Don Bell repeated.

"Isn't that what you just said?" James Coaltonstone asked.

"Yes sir. I have been looking into other problems, which I believed were more important, since the three surveillance bots were sent out on Sunday afternoon, I have been considering other ways that we might use the technology which is at our disposal to locate and to communicate with Goodwin. We need to locate Goodwin so that we can rescue him." Don Bell said.

"How can we rescue a man who has been incinerated?" James Coaltonstone asked.

"There is a chance that Goodwin is alive. We are actually hoping that the guard-bots, which were accidentally converted into data-bots, are with Ginger Goodwin. These new bots have the capacity to determine when a dangerous situation is about to occur, and they also have the ability to make this analysis much faster than a human is able to do, even Goodwin. It is possible that the converted guard-bots were able to predict the explosion before it happened, giving Ginger enough time to reach 'Section E'. The converted guard-bots could actually increase the odds that Ginger survived the explosion," Don Bell explained.

"Assuming that Goodwin found refuge in the rescue chamber and assuming that he is in 'Section E', we could seal 'Sections A, B and C' and smother the fire until it burns out and before the fire ignites the Stonely Coal Seam if it hasn't already. The risks are unknown if we start pumping out the acid water from 'Section A' at this time since the machinery could cause another spark. Sealing 'Section A' along with 'Sections B and C' might be the best option that we have at the moment." Don Bell said as he looked over his notes, making sure that he didn't miss any important detail.

"If Ginger is either in 'Sections A, B or C', the prognosis will be very poor, meaning we would not be on a rescue mission but on a recovery mission." John Bell said as Don Bell nodded in agreement, "But if Ginger is in Section E, there is a very good chance that Ginger is still alive," John Bell said as he hoped he was helping his brother clarify their plan.

Chapter 18:
Land Deals

**Email message to George Smoothman
(Foreman for the morning crew),
Written from Christina Watson's office.**

CONFIDENTIAL

December 23, 2030:

Hi George:

I was thinking about all the thousands of mines all over the Island. So many of these mines, at one time yielded ultra-high grade anthracite, almost a century or two ago. Still, there are scavengers who manage to pull a pillar or two out of those mines when no one is looking. How do they do it without anyone ever getting caught?

I heard that our G.O.D. and Mina's G.O.D. are going to do land deals with James Coaltonstone. In return he is going to build a railway from here to the Bering Strait, and the plan is to burrow under the Bering Strait, build a tunnel for a railway which will bridge two continents together. The train will be called the peace train with the expectation that the new economic opportunities will either bring world peace, or super-duper conflicts.

What do you think?

In reality we all seem to be living in a house of cards.

We have been such fools. We were living life so innocently, getting excited about Christmas, and thinking everything was fine, as if we were little kids. And though I love Ginger, I didn't entirely believe how dangerous it was in the pit, until early Sunday morning, when Mine Five blew up.

Maybe we have been fools to plan our lives assuming that there would be no shifting of the infrastructure, the buildings we work in and live in. When I hear of someone's house falling into a sinkhole, it is always someone else's problem. I never dare to wonder if my house will be the next house to crumble!

Most of us used to laugh at the "Black Diamond Curse". Now look at us.

The Big Seven Coal Group and their associates, that we call the Power Clique, technically own the rights to most of the coal under our homes, schools and hospitals and of course will own the rights over the railway.

Ginger never thought in those terms. He didn't see things in terms of "us" and "them".

I don't mean to torture you, George, I hope everything works out.

Your Friend,

Christina Watson.

Chapter 19:
Junior Gets a Flyke

Tuesday December 24, 2030, around 8:00 AM.
Location: the Watson's living room.

Mathew Junior sat by the Christmas tree and looked at the big box which had his name on it. It was from Santa which meant that it was from his mother, Ginger, and his grandmother.

Junior ate his breakfast in the living room while he watched the web.

His grandmother, realizing that this Christmas Eve was going to be sad and lonely, allowed Junior to open one present.

Christina stayed overnight at her office again and appeared to be in a daze when Maria spoke to her on the phone. Christina said that she was hoping that Ginger would be carried out of the mine any minute now so they could celebrate his birthday and Christmas together. Of course the minutes turned into hours then into days.

So after much thought, Maria gave the ok and Junior quickly tore open the biggest box under the tree. Junior saw exactly what he wanted. Inside the big box was a flyke, the newest must have item on the market.

Junior's eyes lit up.

"I know that Ginger wanted to help you assemble the flyke in the garage, but I am sure you can do it yourself. The instructions are in the box," Maria said encouragingly.

"It is beautiful," Junior said.

"I feel bad having fun when Ginger might be dead, and my mother is struggling. I feel like I should be in mourning.

"Ginger would want you to move forward into the future, since that is what successful living is all about," Maria said.

"Your mother is trying to make it possible for you to have a decent future, and so did your father. Never feel guilty about having a good life. We all want that for you. Once you assemble your flyke, you can try it out and I may take mine out, and join you later. Maybe we will see some eagles today," Maria said hoping that she was saying the right thing.

"Grandma, what are all these feathers for?" Mathew Junior asked. "There are so many of them, and they come in different sizes.

"You put them on your flyke after you assemble it, and you will be able to fly with the eagles without freaking them out," Maria said, smiling for the first time since the mine disaster.

Chapter 20:
A New Red Gate

Tuesday December 24, 2030, around 10 AM.
Location: near Mine Four Portal.

Last Sunday afternoon wasn't the first time Dianne Black had seen death on the job, but this was the first time she had been so ill prepared. Dianne had been sent to some of the most brutal wars during the early 21st century as an eye witness and news correspondent and had been thoroughly prepared.

Dianne believed that news shouldn't be just choreographed responses to horrible events. Adding a real human reaction when seeing a horrible event could serve to wake the public up to the very real intense feeling of horror when confronted by such a scene, especially when it is completely unexpected. When viewed as a sanitized news event on the TV screen often helps to desensitize the public to violence and tragedy.

The Goodwin rescue assignment was meant to be more of a marathon story. Dianne was very good at marathon stories. Dianne could keep audiences glued to the screen as long as she found entertaining people to interview and remembered to toss her wavy gold hair at the right moment.

"Good Morning. Thank you for tuning into our live broadcast from the Pitville Mine Disaster of 2030. This is a sad Christmas Eve for many in Pitville. Ginger Goodwin has been trapped inside Mine Five since 5:20 AM Sunday morning," Dianne announced.

If the mine were ordered to be sealed, G.O.D. would declare a state of emergency in the Coalton Valley, so that the gates could automatically block roads. Under such conditions, only the people with current identification proving residency would be allowed to enter the gates. The gates would be guarded by the volunteer militia.

Even though this crowd was one of the best behaved crowds that Dianne had ever come across during her ten years of investigative reporting, Dianne knew the crowd, which was nearly a mile long, and outnumbered the actual Pitville residents by at least 8,000, could be enraged at a moment's notice, if future events did not lead to a positive outcome.

"Insiders, who wish to remain anonymous, believe that the Government's Official Directors and the mine owners have already decided to seal Mine Five and will be refusing to accept any responsibility or blame for any negative outcome their decision could lead to.

Opinion polls show, that the public believe that Ginger Goodwin is alive and is being denied his human rights relating to being rescued.

It seems that most efforts are being centered around 'Sections A, B and C' deep inside Mine Five even though Ginger Goodwin, is believed to be in 'Section E'.

Now for a recap of our live broadcast from the Pitville Mine Disaster of 2030. On Sunday afternoon, around 2 PM, three surveillance robots descended through the main shaft into 'Section C'. As they turned north and navigated toward 'Section A', all three bots became inoperable after they drove through an estimated five hundred thousand gallons of acid water which has been leaking into 'Section A' since Sunday morning.

Our inside source has informed us, that along the way to 'Section A'; the surveillance robots did manage to transmit air quality, air temperature and other data to the Control Center. Our inside sources tell us that the robots took photographs of the rubble, the pillars, the machinery and whatever they could see. The robots transmitted the data and photographs through the telemagnetic radios, which are located in 'Sections A, B and C'.

The data and photographs have not been made available to us at PPZ or to the general public.

Observers have commented that this effort appeared to have been planned with very little foresight. One insider compared this botched surveillance effort to burnt toast." Dianne finished her live commentary and motioned Jackson to follow her.

Dianne eyed the men behind the security fence as they eyed her back. She wished that she could see Jason and interview him again.

After returning to Mine Four entrance, and still no sight of Jason, Dianne was disappointed to see that a new red gate had been installed, most likely overnight.

"My God they put that gate up fast." Dianne said to Jackson.

"Is that my cue to roll?" Jackson asked, not knowing what to do if Jason did not show up.

"Do what we always do. We will improvise," Dianne said to Jackson as she looked in the mirror. Dianne was obligated, due to the contract she signed with PPZ, to maintain her look, no matter what.

Dianne began her broadcast free styling with her fingers crossed.

"At this very moment, we can reveal that one of the most grisly finds in Coalton Valley history was discovered shortly before our 3 PM Sunday afternoon broadcast. The remains were found directly behind us, in this location.

After the bodies were genetically tested at the local lab, we have determined that the remains most likely belonged to two Minese males who were possibly murdered. Authorities suspect that there might be a mass grave of human remains hidden somewhere in Mine Four. Mine Four was once known for its thick anthracite coal seams, was now behind this red gate which was locked. This gate appeared to have been installed very quickly after Sunday afternoon's discovery of human remains since the red paint had not been painted evenly or professionally.

Many people standing around these cold streets of Pitville are wondering when Ginger Goodwin's rescue will begin.

The man you see walking toward us is one of the many volunteers that have called this site home for the last three days.

Dianne felt great relief when she saw Jason walking toward her.

Jason waved, looking haggard and worn but his rugged good looks could still be seen in the long shot.

"Today we have with us Jason Bell, one of the many volunteers involved in the rescue. The discovery of human remains at this site is just one of the many disturbing incidents, occurring in this mining town during the last three days." Dianne said as Jason began to explain.

"As you may know Dianne, I volunteer for the Global Rescue Initiative for miners, GRIM for Short. The human remains appear to have belonged to two Minese men even though their identity is not yet known. At this time no one has claimed the bodies and the investigation is still ongoing," Jason said, not feeling as confident as he was trying to appear.

"Why do you think those men were left near Mine Four's opening, to rot?" Dianne asked as she quickly moved the microphone in front of Jason's face so that his voice would be audible.

"I really do not know," Jason replied.

"Do you know if this matter will be investigated soon?" Dianne asked.

"I am certain that this matter is under investigation as we speak," Jason replied. "I have been entrusted to protect the dignity of these remains, while the rest of the rescue crew continue to plan and design a rescue operation to free Ginger Goodwin from Mine Five," Jason explained.

"And how has that been progressing?" Dianne asked.

"I was drilling a test borehole, known as borehole COALT-11-C, that we could determine that the environment would be compatible with a rescue mission," Jason explained.

"Can you tell us the outcome that you were hoping for?" Dianne asked.

"Yes, I certainly can. We were hoping for positive results so that we could proceed with our preparations for the rescue mission, which would include sending down a camera, and we were hoping to repair the ventilation system and send in clean air into Mine Five, and possibly start pumping out the accumulation of acid water from section A," Jason said as he was starting to feel relaxed and off guard.

"So what is getting in the way?" Dianne Black asked expecting a precise answer.

"I don't think you can fight Mother Nature and win. I think we can make nature adapt to our needs, but I think nature can rebound quite ferociously. There are natural laws that we humans just cannot break or we will die. Fires need three elements fuel, heat, and oxygen. If one of these elements is missing the fire cannot exist. It is very likely that we may seal the mine, if it is found that it is not safe for humans to enter," Jason explained.

"It sounds as if there are two conflicting problems," Dianne noted.

"Yes, but we at GRIM prefer to manage these two problems as part of the solution, so that conflicts can be harmonized," Jason replied.

"It sounds like you have borrowed some lines from the Big Seven's PR office and are possibly sweeping more dirt under the rug, to accompany all that coal dust," Dianne said, sounding disgusted.

"What you just said, Dianne does not sound like a question, so I will clarify; as long as we believe Mr. Goodwin is alive we will try to postpone sealing the mine. At the same time, as we postpone sealing the mine, the fire will have more time to burn and spread, making it even less likely, that Mr. Goodwin will be found alive," Jason explained.

"Many insiders, miners and contractors who escaped with their lives, during Sunday morning's explosion, believe that if Ginger is alive, he will most likely have found shelter in the rescue chamber found in 'Section E'. And you are seriously considering sealing 'Sections A, B and C' so that you can get the fire and flooding under control, it will be more likely that Ginger will run out of air and suffocate," Dianne said, sounding more confident than ever than Jason was sounding.

"Do you think Ginger Goodwin is going to survive down there with all of these fires and explosions going on, without much warning?" Jason asked.

"I believe it is possible if Ginger found shelter and is a comfortable distance away from the death zone in the mine," Dianne replied.

Realizing that it was much easier asking difficult questions than answering them; Dianne decided to ask a loaded question, this time.

"Don't you think that Ginger Goodwin deserves a fair chance? I believe that he is a hero. Ginger Goodwin prevented the whole morning crew from descending into Mine Five, minutes before the first explosion occurred, Sunday morning?" Dianne retorted.

"I think we on the rescue crew are doing our best. As I said before, we are hoping that Mr. Goodwin was able to reach the rescue chamber in 'Section E'. We believe that 'Section B' is where the first explosion originated, and we have concerns that acid water leaking from an undocumented mine is flooding 'Section A' of Mine Five. If anyone knows the layout of the mines, and knows where all the safety equipment will be, it is Ginger Goodwin," Jason said, thankful that he took the time to memorize his lines so thoroughly.

"Is it true, that Mine Four, which is partly above Mine Five, but no longer a working mine, is missing 'pillar 2c? And is it possible that this missing pillar may have been stolen; triggering a cave-in, leading to the Earth tremering, contributing to last Sunday morning's explosion?" Dianne asked.

"I am not familiar with any evidence supporting such a hypothesis, Dianne," Jason said thankful that his voice did not betray his inner turmoil.

"Insiders, who have requested their names to not be revealed, believe that this cave-in could have been a contributing factor to the series of earthquakes that have been occurring since Sunday morning. It is not clear how this series of earthquakes or aftershocks will be contributing to Ginger Goodwin's rescue operation, could you clarify for us, Mr. Bell?" Dianne asked.

"As far as I know, one group of experts believes, off the record, that the series of earthquakes are causing the explosions and another group of experts believes that the explosions are causing the series of earthquakes," Jason replied.

"What matters to all those people standing out in the streets of Pitville, waiting in the cold, is that we find a way to rescue Ginger Goodwin, before his air supply runs out. Once Ginger is returned to the surface, we can give him the hero's welcome that he deserves. Ginger Goodwin should not be forgotten." Dianne said, as she punctuated her statement with a quick toss of her golden brown hair.

"Going back to the human remains found on Sunday afternoon at the entrance of Mine Four, which is technically part of the second level of Mine Five. We have circumstantial evidence supporting that Mine Four may have been used as a mass grave. Mine Four could have been a place where members of the illegal Coal Cartel, dumped their bodies of their enemies and bodies of miners who were too to work," Jason hypothesized.

"How awful," Dianne exclaimed.

"Dianne, during the great depression of 2029, as you know the movement and mingling of races, genders and social classes was restricted," Jason said, knowing that if he turned the focus to the known human rights violations of the past and the badly kept secrets of the Minese Exclusion League, the broadcast would run out of time.

"Yes, I also realize what we don't know is more important than what we do know," Dianne scoffed, trying to not sound apologetic for asking tough questions.

"Yes, you are right Dianne. Experts are speculating that these remains could be remains of illegal miners who may have either been hiding from extreme members of the 'Minese Exclusion League', which gained its greatest support during 2016 and up to 2023, or were hiding from other illegals, primarily the Coal Cartel bosses," Jason began to explain.

"Is it possible that these victims were hiding from a third party?" Dianne asked.

"Of course, anything is possible," Jason responded wondering what Dianne was going to ask next.

"It seems as if you are referring to a lot of 'ifs'. What concrete news can you actually share with my viewers today? Dianne enquired as she moved the microphone closer to Jason's face, so that his voice could be heard clearly.

"As you know, Dianne, the Coal Cartel is now believed to be operating secretly and more viciously than ever before, so of course there is a lot we do not know. A third explanation might be that these men could be illegals brought into our country to mine until they die," Jason explained.

"Do authorities know how these illegals were able to enter Tut Island in the first place?" Dianne asked.

"Illegals could have been brought into our country undocumented and could have been forced to work in abandoned or undocumented mines illegally by enforcers, and could, have died paying off their debt. The Exclusion League makes this problem worse by isolating and preventing these people from freely mingling in public places and mainstream society," Jason said, catching his breath.

"There is a rumor floating that more human remains will be found. Do you agree with that sentiment, Mr. Bell?" Dianne asked.

"Though I am not at liberty to disclose too much information at this time," Jason began.

"Trust me, you won't ever be found guilty of that sin," Dianne said, interrupting Jason's train of thought, leaving him struggling for coherency during this live broadcast.

"I was about to say, that we, at GRIM, suspect that there are even more men buried in a mass grave possibly inside Mine Four. We are also hypothesizing that when men in this type of situation go missing, barely anyone notices. If a man goes missing, rarely will any of his colleagues report him missing, in fear of being sent back to Mina," Jason explained, trying to maintain a neutral sounding tone.

"How can we allow undocumented people to be treated so badly? This whole situation sounds so barbaric?" Dianne asked. "I mean, I do hear the rumors, like everyone else does, but how can this be still happening in the 21st century?" Dianne asked again knowing there was an answer, but it wasn't one anyone wanted to hear.

"The Coal Cartel will shock most civilized people with their brutal ways, that is for sure," Jason said, trying to redirect blame for this tragic situation.

"So getting back to Ginger Goodwin's rescue how is that going? Dianne asked, realizing as she spoke, that she sounded exasperated.

"Ginger Goodwin is a hero and needs help right now. These people are already dead and beyond our help." Jason said as he looked at Dianne.

"So how is the rescue mission coming along then? I haven't been given one shred of evidence that the rescue mission has even started," Dianne said, realizing that her time for this segment would soon be running out.

"Without documentation the remains of the missing would remain nameless and faceless but these men did exist and must matter to someone." Jason said. "And of course rescuing Mr. Goodwin is our first concern at the moment." Jason added.

"Is it possible that these people were smuggled into the mines and lived and worked behind invisible fences without being seen or without seeing daylight?" Dianne asked, knowing that Jason would be way over his head if he tried to speculate such a thing.

"The 21st century exclusion leagues are believed to be modeled against similar exclusion leagues that existed in the early part of the 20th century primarily active in the West Coast of North America." Jason said.

"Today, multinational rescue operations are waiting, with ambulances nearby preparing for the rescue of Ginger Goodwin to begin." Dianne announced, starting to feel completely exhausted.

"For those in our audience who are just joining our broadcast, here is another recap. After discovering bodies of two men, partially buried in Mine Four, possibly murdered, or excluded from society until they starved, the rescue plan will be adapting to this discovery out of respect of the dead.

Instead of drilling into Mine Four to gain access to Mine Five as previously planned, rescue workers will be drilling into Mine Six to gain access to Mine Five's south end.

Mine Four, including the tunnels under Coalton Lake, are now being treated as a crime scene." Jason explained.

"The main portal which descends into Mine Six runs parallel to 'Section E' in Mine Five. Plans to seal 'Sections A, B and C' which are also part of Mine Five will not hamper rescue attempts as long as Ginger Goodwin has found refuge in Section E" Jason said.

"The best plan would be to drill into Section 6 E, and to install an escape capsule. This is the preferred plan by theorists, but it is also the most expensive plan." Jason added.

If Ginger Goodwin was unable to escape from 'Sections A, B or C during the explosions, it is very likely, that Ginger Goodwin was incinerated, there would be no need for recovery mission, let alone a rescue mission," Jason said.

Realizing that time was running out, Dianne began to announce the weather conditions for Pitville, but was interrupted abruptly as Steve announced news of another earthquake.

"We interrupt this program with a news breaking report that another mild earthquake, measuring 3.3 on the Richter scale occurred about twenty minutes ago. This is another in a series of earthquakes which have been occurring since Sunday morning. It is not clear how these earthquakes and aftershocks will effect the Ginger Goodwin rescue operation. If Mr. Goodwin is in the rescue chamber in 'Section E', he will have about forty-three hours of air supply left.

There are tens of thousands of people assembling along the road to Coaltonstone Mine. The Pitville Youth Choir has joined the Coal Miners' Choir, and accompanied by Coalton High's Instrumental band, in leading the crowd in a sing along where the favorite song appears to be Silent Night. I can hear the singing as I sit in my makeshift broadcast room at Eagle Eye Inn, back to you Dianne," Steve said as he flipped the switch.

"Another recap, we at PPZ have been given reports on a regular basis insinuating that Mine Five management were allowing a higher than permissible amount of methane gas to circulate in the air, especially when large mining equipment was being moved around," Dianne began to report.

"Actually I object to that analysis," Jason said.

"We do not have concrete evidence to show that Mr. Goodwin's theory was nothing more than an outcome of an obsessive compulsive problem," Jason added.

"I realize that it is mine policy to deny these allegations even though Mr. Goodwin's data appears sound," Dianne responded.

"The data which you refer to is technically stolen and could easily be taken out of context," Jason said in the mine's defence.

"Yes, Jason, we know that company representatives have always denied the credibility of Mr. Goodwin's reports," Dianne said as she looked at Jackson who was making a hand signal, possibly for Steve, if he was watching to cut the conversation short.

"Many experts, who work beyond Mine Five's boundaries, believe that the Pitville Mine Disaster is the direct result of ignoring Mr. Goodwin's data reports. Even though mine officials, who requested anonymity, called Mr. Goodwin's reports fear mongering and rabble rousing, Mr. Goodwin was able to send data to Control Center, minutes before the Sunday morning's first explosion, revealing that the methane monitor on the coal shearing machine had been turned off. This last report was included with all the other reports, which our mysterious whistleblower, Deep Coal, sent us.

'How did that man, Deep Coal send you those reports?" Jason asked, grabbing Diane's hand holding the mike, and moving it toward his face. 'How did that man send you those reports?" Jason asked again, sounding shaken up but also realizing that he was no match for Dianne Black.

"How do you know that Deep Coal is a man?" Dianne asked while avoiding Jason's question she successfully pushed his hand away and regained control of the microphone.

"Insiders from the now defunct Tut Island Mine Workers' Union are refusing to speculate who this whistleblower is. We at PPZ were sent reports alleging that coal dust was not being managed up to world class standards. Insiders are telling us that coal dust, in Mine Five, was being swept under the proverbial carpet, back to you Steve." Dianne said as she signaled Jackson to stop filming.

Chapter 21:
Bad News

Tuesday December 24, 2030, around 11:00 AM.
Location: the public side of the security fence.

"Good morning Tut Island, this is another PPZ broadcast sponsored by the municipality of Sunrise Beach. This is Dianne Black reporting on another chaotic day, with very little new information available to us.

Our inside source, who has asked to not have their name revealed, informed PPZ that Sunday's explosion at Bert's gas station, the third explosion occurring in Pitville on Sunday, was possibly due to an underground coal seam fire. And this coal seam fire may have started at the Pitville garbage dump, which is actually situated on an exposed portion of Stonely Coal Seam according to our source.

Insiders who have requested that names remain private, suggest that the planning that went into situating the garbage dump in such a location shows that those people, maybe a hundred or two hundred years ago, did not consider future generations or life after their death. The question is, did the majority of the people during that era, have the power to make decisions to benefit the public good, including future generations. Did a small elite group organize all of their activity around one main purpose which was to mine coal the fastest way possible?

Our moles have told PPZ that the petrol held in underground tanks at Bert's gas station had reached temperatures of over 170 degrees Fahrenheit hours before the Sunday evening explosion. Our condolences go out to Mr. Clarke's family and friends. This must be a very difficult time for all of you who knew and loved Bert Clarke.

On to other events, related to the Pitville Mine disaster of 2030. There have been reports of smoke sightings coming out of cracks in sidewalks and roads.

G.O.D. has warned residents to stay clear of those places and to report any new smoke sightings when they occur so that local authorities can attend to these fires before they engulf the beautiful Coalton Valley.

Now a recap of the highlights related to Ginger Goodwin rescue mission. Ginger Goodwin has been trapped in Mine Five since early Sunday morning. There is concern that the lines used for gas drainage, inside the mine, may have been damaged during the first explosion, which occurred early Sunday morning at 5:20 AM.

If the damage to the gas lines occurred during the first explosion, then we have a new hypothetical explanation to why the methane gas accumulated in the mine so quickly, causing a second explosion during the drilling of borehole COALT-11-C on Sunday afternoon around 3:00 PM.

The broken gas line is bad news for Ginger Goodwin. Unless Ginger Goodwin has found his way to the rescue chamber in 'Section E', authorities believe that Ginger Goodwin would have not survived the second explosion, and have decided that they must seal the mine so that the process of smothering the fire inside the mine can begin without delay.

Authorities have issued a press release announcing that there will be crews working around the clock, so that they can complete the process of sealing 'Sections A, B and C'. These plans also include the sealing of all the boreholes and shafts in Mine Five.

At this time experts have determined that it is not safe for humans to enter the mine, especially sections A, B and C.

It is also being speculated, that when a borehole was drilled into 'Section C', Sunday afternoon, the same day of the first explosion, the intention was to release the gas from within the mine, lurking near the ceiling of Mine Five. Instead of meeting the intended objective, the new source of oxygen, combined with the fuel and heat, created the perfect environment for an explosion to occur; therefore borehole COALT-11-C was one of the first boreholes to be sealed.

'Section E' has not been accessed by camera to determine if Ginger Goodwin is actually in there. No explanation has been offered but our inside source tells us that government and mine authorities are assuming that Ginger Goodwin is now dead.

Our investigative reporters from PPZ have spoken to experts who disagree and say that Ginger Goodwin does have a good chance of survival if he was able to inflate the inflatable seals so that 'Section E' was sealed off from the rest of the mine. If Ginger was able to access the rescue chamber in 'Section E', Ginger would have had a good chance to survive the explosions.

Our inside source has informed us that if the borehole in the rescue chamber were uncapped, cameras could be sent into it, and it could be determined if there was any human activity going on in that location. It is as if 'Section E' is being ignored while all energies are being focused on the preparations needed before the sealing and foaming of 'Sections A, B and C' can begin.

It is still not certain what actually caused the first explosion on Sunday morning, let alone the second explosion on Sunday afternoon and the third one on Sunday evening at Bert's and Sons Gas Station.

It is believed Ginger Goodwin was trying to prove scientifically that there was a dangerous situation building up due to worsening problems with ventilation combined with equipment needing repairs, and possibly illegal pillar retrieving from neighboring mines which could have caused cave-ins.

Undocumented mining is notorious for not using adequate ventilation.

Lawyers for the Big Seven Coal Group strongly deny corporate responsibility for the two mine explosions on Sunday and deny any connection to the explosion at Bert and Sons Gas station, which occurred Sunday evening.

And above ground there are all kinds of accusations from angry employees and contractors who are now waiting in the

Miners cafeteria which is located in the Coaltonstone Mines' administration building about ten miles from Mine Five.

Our insiders have told PPZ, that Coaltonstone Mine employees and contractors need a miracle this Christmas Eve since the Grinch from the Big Seven Group, stole their Christmas, along with their pay and bonus packets which have been placed on hold for the time being, by mine authorities.

The causes for recent explosions in Pitville remain a mystery. Some experts have speculated that lightning could have provided the sparks needed to ignite pockets of methane gas lurking underground. Other experts describe such speculating as self-serving, and the real cause for the recent explosions will be found in the forty-nine reports, which Ginger Goodwin had submitted to mine management, over a period of forty-seven days.

We at PPZ wonder how coal dust and methane gas were able to accumulate to such dangerous levels, if proper procedures were being followed. Why were forty-nine reports, which Ginger Goodwin wrote over a period of forty-seven days ignored? Why was the methane gas monitor on the coal shearing machine, which was allegedly in disrepair, turned off? Who would do such a thing?

Again there are accusations that the accumulations of methane, gas deep inside Mine Five, were due to the hodgepodge set up of ventilating doors and fans that were installed inside the mine, that officials say were certified but possibly shouldn't have been.

PPZ has discovered that Mine Five employees accepted deteriorating working conditions, including inadequate coal dust management that failed to meet code, so they would not lose their jobs.

Medical records show that many miners went to the Pitville Clinic to access relief from chronic cough, itchy eyes and itchy feet. These are common ailments that affect mine workers when coal dust levels are too high.

Rescuers and investigators are not expected to begin their work in Mine Five until repairs are made to the ventilation system and when all fires have been extinguished. The mine must pass safety inspections before human rescue teams will be allowed to enter.

All working mines on Tut Island are required to have rescue chambers located every 2,000 feet throughout the mine even though years before the depression of 2029, these rescue chambers were required to be 1,000 feet apart." Dianne paused and could see Steve's gesturing to accelerate her commentary because time was running out.

"Until Mr. Goodwin is rescued from Mine Five, his supporters will continue to believe that the process of maximizing profits will be a higher priority to the Mine Five owners than the lives of mine employees," Dianne said as she took a breath before smiling into the camera.

"In another development, illegal mining is being blamed for a strange and terrifying phenomenon, which is often referred to as 'sinking holes', due to spaces underground growing too big to hold the surface, bringing down the ground above, into a deep hole beneath. The frequency of sinkholes is believed to be due to human activities, such as mining, drilling and heavy traffic stressing the already weakened Earth. Illegal mining is considered to be the straw that is breaking the proverbial camel's back for the borough of Pitville, a small close knit mining community, situated in the center of Tut Island," Dianne said as she wondered if hope spent in Pitville was better spent elsewhere.

"Now here is Steve Jones with the weather brought to you by the municipality of Sunrise Beach and its Chamber of Commerce where good friends meet and sometimes stay."

Chapter 22:
Back to the 'Number Two Café'

Tuesday December 24, 2030, around 12:30 PM.
Location: The Miners' Cafeteria.

"Not much of a Christmas Eve. We don't even know if we are going to get paid for the time we are stuck here doing nothing," George Smoothman said to everyone still sitting at the table.

"We could call an unofficial union meeting except Ginger could never be an official member of our unofficial union since he was one of our bosses," Jay Paylor said.

"Goodwin told me that he wanted an accurate log. He didn't want to report a diluted reading. Goodwin didn't trust the bot-bosses any more than we do," Sam Jones said.

"The human bosses can't feel empathy for us because they look down on us so much. These bot-bosses have no capacity for empathy, so all they can do is respond within the internal boundaries which have been programmed by someone that we have never met," George Smoothman said.

"In the same way that our coal is weighed by a weigh-boss bot, programmed by more vain men that never see us, or speak to us, or have no concern about us," Jay Paylor said.

"Men our age should be looking forward to our future. Instead we are always watching our backs. If any one of those boss-bots' are programmed to tighten the boundaries, regulating us, so that the owners gain even more advantages over us. I don't know what our unofficial union can do to help its membership,"

Sam Jones noted with some bitterness trapped in his voice.

"At least we had Ginger to look out for us. Now we are dammed if we do and dammed if we don't. If the mine re-opens conditions could get a lot worse, now that Ginger is gone. Once those boss-bots are given full reign, and are still being programmed by heartless and faceless me, another accident like Mathew's could happen to any one of us," Jay Paylor said, feeling rather unnerved.

"The Coaltonstones and the Bells only care about their 30,000 ton a day production quota," George Smoothman said.

"And you better believe that the Bells and Coaltonstones will be getting their Christmas bonuses," Jay Paylor added.

"And we all know who could have been blamed for this disaster," George Smoothman said.

"Partly me, and mostly you," Jay Paylor said.

"Exactly, if it weren't for Ginger, we from the morning crew would have been in the same predicament as Ginger is in now. And if we managed to be rescued, George and I would have been welcomed back to the surface with threats of a lifelong sentence in the Arctic working in the mines as slave laborers. We are the ones who have to sign-on and sign-off whenever a shift begins or ends. It is Ginger though who does the morning pre-shift safety inspections, so we can refer to those reports when making our own," George Smoothman said.

"If you think conditions are tough down here, it must be murder up in the Arctic, mining for diamonds, not very far from the front of the cold war," Sam Jones speculated.

"We could include those guys in our unofficial union too I suppose," Jay Paylor said.

"Agree, so we know that Ginger went down into the mine because he had a hunch that the methane readings were inaccurate. It is being announced on PPZ that the methane monitor on the coal shearing machine was actually turned off. No wonder there was an explosion down there on Sunday morning. And who is to supervise the going ons down there. Those boss-bots can't think for themselves or correct random errors within themselves," George Smoothman said.

"The Coaltonstones and the Bells will do anything to save a buck and to accelerate production and those boss-bots just do what they are programmed to do. Boss-bots have no conscience or ability to empathize with us," Allan Brown said, remembering the boss-bots behavior moments before Mathew Watson was killed back in the summer of 2021.

Allan Brown had been mining in Mine Five since the day the mine opened, fifteen years ago. Allan was there when Mathew Watson's accident took place. Allan knew more than anyone how the boss-bots seemed to be oblivious to human suffering especially at the time when such awareness was needed the most.

"Talk about lack of empathy, they can't even acknowledge when a person has spoken, no matter what the situation is," Sam Jones said.

"The whole process is so frustrating," Kevin blurted out. "When a mindless and soulless machine acts like a superior and can't even think or respond properly, it always feels so dehumanizing, mindless and silly. And I blame management. Of course Ginger is one of the good ones. Boy did he add value for us. He saved our lives," Kevin said knowing that words could not express the regret he felt, leaving Ginger in the mine to die.

"Being blamed for the ventilation problem was a going concern for Ginger.

Ginger was always afraid that he was going to be blamed along with George and Jay, if he did not find a way to prevent the explosion, which he couldn't do. All he could do was predict the probability of an explosion occurring, but he couldn't prevent one, if the Coaltonstones refused to follow basic safety regulations, there was not much Ginger could do." Sam Jones said.

"Like us, Ginger gets the blame as soon as he signs the dust audits or any kind of audit that he signs off on," George Smoothman explained.

"Ginger believed that the boss-bots were not being programmed to follow required procedures let alone programmed to have any human aspirations to empathize with us at all. In fact Ginger found the bot-bosses scary looking at times, especially the payroll boss-bot which sometimes turns blue. Ginger thought that the payroll boss-bot belonged in the administration building, not in the actual mine because it was so distracting and most likely did contribute to Mathew Watson's deadly accident. Ginger believed that any bot flying around a miner's head was a safety hazard and should not be tolerated and of course I agree," Jay Paylor added.

Now Ginger is alone, I sure hope that that he has enough batteries to keep his headlamp working. It would be horrible to be in such a dark place with no light at all," Dan Finch added.

"I would guess that there are plenty of batteries in the rescue chamber if Ginger was able to make it that far. It seems that Ginger Goodwin sees the risks that he takes, and is able to plan for them. Ginger has always been driven to see beyond his own limitations," Sam Jones stated as a matter of fact.

"Maybe because he is so short, he is driven to work harder," Dan Finch wondered.

"If he is still alive he would be in quite a state," Brenda Brown said, thankful it wasn't her husband in Ginger's place. "I believe that Ginger prevented my husband from entering the pending explosion last Sunday morning and that he is a real hero."

"Ginger saved our unofficial brotherhood from a horrible death. Ginger should be remembered as a man who was able to turn fate around for one hundred and sixty crew members and their descendants." Dan Finch agreed as he swept away the crumbs on the reports that he had placed beside his plate.

"Ginger never wins battles he just seems to wait them out, while gathering some kind of energy to spring up at the very moment the forces against him seem at their weakest. There are so many problems, one after another. I mean if I weren't a drinking man, I would break down and cry," Sam Jones said as he took a flask from his coat pocket and poured the liquid with the missing label, into his own coffee mug and then Dan's.

"Merry Christmas Dan does anyone else want a shot?" Sam Jones asked.

"Thank you," Dan replied.

Several cups were passed down the table as Sam Jones poured a little bit of Christmas cheer in each cup.

"Well we are strong and brave and have each other and a flask to share when times get super tough." Dan Finch said.

"And watching it all happen on TV just makes it worse. Those people who run TV always make people like us look fatter, dirtier, and scruffier. "Sam Jones said as he took a swig of his drink and then popped a mint in his mouth.

"To Christmas of 2030 whatever it may bring us." Dan Finch and Sam Jones said in unison.

"To the unofficial brotherhood of miners, may we stay united," Dan Finch said as he raised his mug in the air.

"To Ginger, the man who found a way to save us from a fiery death," Sam Jones declared while raising his cup too.

"My God I feel so guilty. One small guilty pleasure when we have no idea what is happening to Ginger. Death would be better than suffering horribly," Sam Jones said taking another sip of his drink and then popped a mint into his mouth to hide the smell.

"I think we should walk up to the executive lounge and demand our pay packets, and have a sit-in to protest old James Coaltonstone's greedy ways.

Dan Finch held up his mug, "I will toast to that," he said.

Sam Jones raised his mug and replied; "count me in!"

Chapter 23:
Jason Is Being Blamed For Everything

Tuesday December 24, 2030, around 1 PM.
Location: near Mine Four Portal.

Jason was thankful that he had the foresight to bring two phones with him today. In his left hand his Uncle John was screaming at him for failing in his duty to discretely guard the grave site and causing embarrassment to the family name. In his right hand, Jason's Uncle Don was telling Jason that turned the fate of undocumented workers into a mockery and caused the deceased and their families whoever they may be, a lot of grief.

In his left hand, Jason's Uncle John blamed him for letting PPZ make an unauthorized broadcast on Coaltonstone Mines' private property. Even though it all seemed to just happen, broadcasting the finding of human remains without proper authorization was downright wrong, and made Coaltonstone Mines look bad and even creepy.

Jason had no idea what to say. His father, Pastor David Bell relied on faith, so he found that his uncles' advise was often more worldly and practical than his father's. He took thankless job because he had experience drilling boreholes. He also drilled wells once in a while. Jason always felt when drilling that there was an element of chance that defied explanation. When he drilled boreholes he was able to document the drilling process accurately enough in the log he was required to maintain, but often there was something about drilling that left Jason in awe. He could feel something down there as if energy of some sort was responding to his drilling, and that energy felt alive.

Anything of significance happens quickly during a rescue operation. Jason found it easier to avoid listening to his uncles and replied with a weak 'I am sorry' any time he thought appropriate.

Realizing how loud his brother's voice sounded on Jason's other phone, Don Bell tried to soften his voice, but it was too late. Both uncles had sounded equally loud and harsh and appeared to be equally upset because Jason's public speculations had not just gone viral once, which was bad enough, but they had gone viral twice, once on Sunday afternoon, and once this morning.

The outcome of these viral broadcasts could be described as public outrage. At Coaltonstone Mines; phones of every shape and size had been ringing nonstop for the last three days. It seemed that the entire citizenry of Pitville were terrified of the possibility of illegal immigrant miners living below Pitville while stealing pillars and causing mayhem. The public wanted to know what was being done to put a stop to such activities.

Reverend Bell agreed with his younger brothers, John and Don, that it would have been wiser if Jason had remained silent.

It was all his fault that the story was even in the news to start with.

The red fence was up and the crime scene or burial site or whatever the mine had become was now secured. Nothing else could be done and everyone of importance wanted to celebrate the holidays in peace.

"Please memorize the script that I sent you." John Bell said as he hung up the phone leaving Jason feeling as if he let down his and the two men that had been left near the Mine Four entrance to rot. Whose fault was that? Not his.

John Bell had been head of security for Coaltonstone Mines for ten years. He had heard rumors of illegals operating on Tut Island, but this was the first time that he actually had hard evidence that illegals were operating in one of the closed mines that he was technically in charge of keeping secure.

John Bell needed a strategy, an explanation to feed the press, and he needed a very good one. When John delegated the job to Jason this morning, he had no idea that Jason was going to just tell the truth, the way he saw it to be. Jason had no reason to believe that he was supposed to limit how much information he was going to share with the public. Jason just assumed that the truth meant the whole truth.

John Bell emphasized to Jason, next time that he was discussing mine business with any representative of the PPZ, he should be more careful. An explanation given can be slightly speculative but must never be incriminating.

Jason wondered why he did such volunteer work in the first place and why were his uncles and his father advising him after the fact. Whenever Jason volunteered he seemed to always find himself in the middle of a situation every other volunteer had the good sense to avoid.

There was nothing that he could do now about the last two broadcasts. When the remains were discovered he was in shock just as much as Dianne Black was. Almost anything can go viral these days.

Jason told himself that he made his own decision and he was being true to himself. And that was all that mattered besides feeling that he was blamed for the second explosion, which occurred Sunday afternoon.

Jason didn't know if he could face a future of being defined by the events that had happened during the last three days. If only he could find a way to distance himself from the last three days. He could be frozen in time as a memory for the critical mass to scorn. How will he prepare for his future, if no one of significance would let him forget the events related to the past three days? And even if no one remembered his name, they would all remember his face. Jason knew that he just happened to be in the wrong place at the wrong time and now the events of the last three days will probably shape relationships between people he has not yet met, in a negative way for the rest of his life. What could he do about that now? Not much.

Jason couldn't remember a time when he had been more depressed than this Christmas Eve. He imagined a life living alone, poor and as an outcast. No one will ever want to love him or hire him or even give him a volunteer job to do, ever again, not even his Uncle John or his Uncle Don. And his father, Reverend Bell, might stop praying for him.

Jason climbed a tree, and took an 'E' String that he had concealed around his waist, and tied it around his neck. Jason was too afraid to jump, so he just sat there, vulnerable but not giving up hope just yet. 'E' was Jason's favorite note.

Chapter 24:
Rising Tensions On Christmas Eve

Tuesday December 24, 2030, around 2 PM.
Location: near Mine Six Portal:

"Good Morning to all those who are tuning into our afternoon broadcast, this is Dianne Black reporting live from the Pitville Mine Disaster of 2030. This afternoon's broadcast is being brought to you from the Mine Six Portal, owned by Coaltonstone Mines which is a subsidiary of the Big Seven Coal Group. We are standing near the shaft of Mine Six where work is expected to begin shortly, assuming that there are not any more interruptions." Dianne explained.

"Once a connecting shaft is built from Mine Six to Mine Five, and ventilation is restored to industry standards, an escape carriage will be installed, so that Ginger Goodwin can be carried up to the surface. Ginger though has to be found first before he can be rescued and insiders are afraid that Ginger will run out of air before he is found," Dianne said hoping that this plan would have a better outcome than the previous plan which led to Jason Bell's suicide. Dianne was going to add a few more details to her broadcast but Steve Jones interrupted her as he announced a news breaking story was about to be broadcasted.

Steve began to read the Coaltonstone press release out loud. "About twenty minutes ago, a third explosion occurred in Mine Five, which is the fourth explosion in Pitville since Sunday morning. There are many theories to the cause of the third mine explosion but all explanations are being considered purely speculative. It is understood that the authorities will be accelerating the process of sealing 'Sections A, B and C'; since it is now determined that these sections of Mine Five are very unstable and too dangerous for a rescue crew to enter at this time. Government and mine officials doubt that Goodwin survived this last explosion if he had been in the vicinity of 'Sections A, B and C'," Steve announced.

"On the other hand, Mr. Goodwin's supporters and other experts in the field believe that if Mr. Goodwin was already to find refuge in the rescue chamber located in 'Section E' he would avoided the effects from the third mine explosion" Steve explained.

"Back to you Dianne," Steve said flipping a switch to return Dianne to her broadcast.

"If Ginger Goodwin was able to reach the rescue chamber in 'Section E' he will have enough air supply to last for another thirty-nine hours. The rescue chamber is an artificial environment designed to maintain life until a rescue can be executed. These are a lot of 'ifs', but it sounds quite reasonable to me that Ginger does have a chance of beating the odds which are against him. Ginger could be very much alive, as long as he was able to reach rescue chamber in 'Section E'.

Tensions are rising between officials and the public and no wonder. This whole story has so many "ifs" and today is Christmas Eve, which makes the situation even sadder and tenser. The decision makers, the people who are sitting in Control Center situated in the executive's lounge, are deciding whether to seal the entire mine, pushing any efforts relating to rescuing Ginger Goodwin onto a back burner, despite their pretentious efforts making it appear, otherwise.

Now for a recap, live from the Pitville Mining disaster of 2030.

Ginger Goodwin's supporters and rescue professionals, who did not want to be identified, believe that there is a realistic chance that Ginger Goodwin was able to survive all three mine explosions.

On the other hand, mine and government officials appear to be saying chances that Ginger Goodwin is still alive are very slim, and in order to put out the fires while minimizing damage to equipment and remaining coal, the mine must be sealed including all the boreholes and shafts in Mine Five. And retrieving Ginger's body will be too risky for a rescue crew to undertake so officials regret that Ginger will rest in peace deep inside Mine Five.

Mine officials have told PPZ that every employee and contractor on site is provided with a self-rescue device, which is designed for miners who need clean air to breathe and protection from carbon monoxide poisoning.

The ability to escape the effects of a mine disaster and maintain health and strength so that a miner has the best chance to reach the safest rescue chamber available is a combination of luck and planning. The million dollar question is "did Ginger Goodwin have the right combination of factors going for him so that he was able to beat the odds and able to survive?" If Ginger Goodwin did survive, and is somewhere in the mine, the first thing authorities must do before they can rescue him, is to locate him.

Ginger's supporters are wondering if official pessimism could jinx the end outcome for Ginger Goodwin. It is entirely possible that the authorities' negative expectations could lead to self-fulfilling prophecies. In short, if nothing is ventured nothing is gained.

Ginger's supporters believe that if the authorities assume that Ginger is dead, then placing their full attention on preparing the mine to be sealed could be justified. The authorities will be using their considerable power of pessimism to deny a positive outcome for Ginger Goodwin during his time of need, on this very foggy Christmas Eve.

There is further news related to the Pitville Mine Disaster of 2030; that the process of drilling borehole COALT-11-C may not have led to the second explosion in Mine Five, this past Sunday afternoon. Insiders believe that sparks could have been generated from other sources and the matter is under investigation at this time.

Even though it is believed drilling borehole COALT-11-C may have caused the sparks which may have ignited methane pockets lurking around the roof of Mine Five, insiders believe that other causes are just as highly probable if not more so. The explosion may have caused a portion of the roof in 'Sections B and C' to collapse setting of another small earthquake measuring around 2.2 on the Richter scale, Sunday afternoon.

This small earthquake is believed to have uncovered a shallow grave hidden near the entrance of Mine Four.

Jason Bell, the man who was drilling borehole COALT-11-C, had the best of intentions, when he was operating a special drill able to drill a borehole length of around 65 feet per day. He was also the man who discovered the two partially charred and decomposing bodies believed to be connected to the dangerous and highly illegal business of grabbing underground mine pillars that are often left in place to support the roof of non-operating mines and the surface ground above it.

With great sadness I have to report that Jason Bell was found hanging from a tree near the entrance to Mine Four, about forty-five minutes ago. Pitville medics retrieved Jason Bell's body. The Bells are requesting that their privacy be respected. Our sympathies go out to the Bell family on this Christmas Eve and funeral services will be remaining private.

Tensions in Pitville are increasing. Many ordinary people that I have spoken to today, and did not want to be quoted publicly, are demanding that Mr. Goodwin's life be prioritized over any other concerns. There are people in the industry who also believe that the technology is available to communicate to Mr. Goodwin and once Ginger Goodwin's conditions are better understood, best practice related to his rescue can be planned and executed.

Other news related to the Pitville Mine Disaster of 2030, robots have discovered a mass burial site deep inside Mine Four. The Minese Consulate has allocated a hall as a temporary morgue, so that the remains of the deceased can be processed and when possible, reunited with next of kin.

"Patience is requested from everyone at this time. We hope that the dignity that was not shown to these invisible miners while alive will be shown to them today," was the only comment the spokesman from the Minese consulate would give to our PPZ representatives as he refused to comment further.

This is Dianne Black for the PPZ, back to you Steve."

Chapter 25:
Running Out Of Time

Tuesday, December 24th 2030, around 3:00 PM.
Location: Miners' Cafeteria.

"Good afternoon, to all those who are tuning into our afternoon broadcast, I am Dianne Black, for the PPZ broadcasting live from the Pitville Mine Disaster of 2030.

I have with me this afternoon, four of Ginger Goodwin's colleagues.

Welcome to our show, Sam, Kevin, George, and Jay, and thank you for agreeing to share with us, some of your memories with us tonight. George and Jay, it is nice to see you again.

"It is really nice to see you again, Dianne," Jay Paylor said, as he gave Dianne a bear hug, while George, Kevin and Sam Jones, continued to look on.

"I am glad you are so glad to see me again Jay, Dianne said.

"Now Kevin, how would you sum up the situation from your point of view?" Dianne asked Kevin as she placed the microphone in front of Kevin's face.

"Ginger Goodwin knew everything about that mine, and all those tunnels that were never on the map, Ginger knew where all those tunnels were. He had them all mapped out in his head. It was just like Ginger trying to find a way to make the mine as safe as it is described in a book of regulations. How realistic is that?" Kevin asked.

"Is it honorable to find a way to stop coal dust from being swept under the rug so to speak when no one can guarantee that a coal mine is safe from moment to moment?" Sam asked.

"Don't you think that in modern times science should be used to minimize risks and stay ahead of disasters? Don't you think that is exactly what Ginger was trying to do? Wasn't he collecting data and charting it in the hope that one day he could design effective boundaries to contain and control risk taking when mining?" Dianne asked.

"Mining is dangerous and often unhealthy work. We accept those conditions, because we are bred into the life style. Ginger knew all the rules and regulations and was collecting evidence to show that one day we could find a better way. Isn't that what Ginger was trying to do?" Jay asked.

"We are all asking all these questions when sometimes there is no right answer. It is all about timing. Sooner or later that coal dust will be exploding under someone's feet and I try to make sure those feet aren't mine. That is the fate of the coal miner. This week it happened to be Ginger being in the wrong place at the wrong time. We all know the risks. So what is the point of all this science? Being in the wrong place at the wrong time is more about fate and bad luck," Kevin interjected fighting back the anger he could hear in his voice.

"I know Ginger took his job seriously and wanted to observe the actual logistics of operations to improve mine safety and improve the mine's safety record, but we need our jobs, what are we going to do now that the mine is closed earlier than scheduled? George asked.

"I think it is Dianne that is supposed to be asking the questions," Jay said, winking at Dianne.

"Well, maybe someone should find out the answers to our questions, for a change," Sam Jones suggested.

"I just don't see how you can totally prevent methane gas from exploding," Kevin said.

"I know Goodwin saved our lives when he delayed our descent into the mine by twenty minutes. I know there are many unanswered questions and so little time to waste. Time is not on Ginger's side. There will be plenty of time to investigate what happened later. I hope that they make rescuing Ginger the priority. If Ginger is in the rescue chamber in 'Section E' he will only have thirty-eight hours of air supply left," George said before Dianne apologized that she had run out of time.

Jay responded that maybe Ginger had run out of time too.

Chapter 26:
Miners March

Wednesday December 25th, 2030 around 8 AM.

As the Minese miners marched from their secret tunnel into broad daylight, they could see that the armed riot police were standing on the highest level of the Coalton Valley Parkway, complete with black body armor, black helmets and long guns which could shoot ten rubber bullets per minute.

All the visible miners from Mina were wearing mining helmets and headlamps. Some were wearing protective gear, which was designed for either hockey or football but not armed warfare.

As thousands of citizen miners from Tut Island and beyond were marching down the highway toward Pitville, they were joined by the invisible miners from Mina.

It soon became obvious that the harsh conditions had made the Minese miners the most hardened miners in the march.

The march stopped at the Coalton Valley Parkway where there were many ramps, which went into different directions. There were lines of riot police looking over the rails. This was the perfect place to create chaos.

The trucks carrying hundreds of old tires stopped on the Coalton Valley Parkway. Men quickly removed the tires from the trucks and rolled them into the middle of the Tut Island Highway as motorists stared for a moment then hurried on their way, armed police officers blew their whistles as loud as they could knowing that they were being ignored.

Another group of men started to unpack the crates of gasoline and proceeded to pour gasoline onto the tires that were now in the middle of the highway.

Another man, complete with miner's flag which was wrapped several times around his face, leaving only his eyes showing, grabbed a long flame stick and yelled something either in a foreign language or with such a thick accent that he might as well have been speaking in a foreign language.

Once gasoline-soaked cloths were tied to ends of sticks young men ignited the sticks and threw them into the bundle of tires, setting them on fire, and then not knowing what else to do, they sat by the road looking bored. Another group of young men were carrying long metal tubes which could shoot tiny rockets made out of fire crackers, they sat beside the men who were watching the tires burn.

Other groups of young men continued to march towards Pitville.

Chapter 27:
Drilling More Boreholes

Wednesday December 25th, 2030 around 9 AM.
Location: inside Mine Six.

Justin Bell wished that he had done more for Jason while he was alive. He wished that he hadn't left him alone on Christmas Eve.

The work orders came from rescue operation's Control Center not from Jason. Jason was just following orders. Jason didn't make any decisions relating to drilling position. If Sunday afternoon's explosion was caused by Jason's drilling, it would have not been Jason's fault. Jason was a good driller, and he was very conscientious.

Jason had asked Justin, before he committed suicide if he thought a boss-bot had designed the job order relating to the drilling of borehole COALT-11-C. Both Jason and Justin believed that boss-bots were taking over everything, were impossible to relate to, and soon would replace almost every human job on Earth. Justin noticed that the worst part of interacting with a boss-bot was that it could make a man feel silly and dehumanized.

Justin wished that he had spent more time with his brother. He blamed himself for leaving Jason alone to brood, especially it being Christmas Eve and everything.

What a horrible Christmas it turned out to be, for everyone.

Justin wondered why Jason had to do something so

permanent. He wondered what went through a person's mind before taking such a drastic action. Justin speculated that suicide was just an escape; an irreversible escape to nowhere.

Justin thought to himself for a few minutes, and wondered if it really was an escape to nowhere or whether what was left of his brother was actually somewhere. His father thought that Jason was somewhere of course, and so did Reverend Martin Coaltonstone. Jason's funeral service was up in the air and there was actual talk of just burying Jason and maybe having a memorial service in a couple of months. Justin's father could not preside over the funeral, and having Martin Coaltonstone preside would feel awkward.

Situations could turn out to be very emotional over the Christmas holidays, but to give up so quickly and to ruin your whole life with such an irreversible over reaction as suicide was cowardly, Jason thought.

Now with Justin's younger brother gone, there was a huge hole left in his life. The drilling was hard work and he thought that there should be more support for the drillers but of course there are only so many people available who can do this kind of work.

Drilling boreholes was risky and thankless.

The plan was still in the works to access Mine Five through another upper level which would be Mine Six. Work would include a 700 foot vertical extension to the shaft and a short horizontal shaft to connect the two levels. There was transportation carriage already installed.

While Jason had been drilling borehole COALT-11-C before he committed suicide, Justin had been drilling borehole COALT-12-E which was expected to reach 'Section E' in about ten to fifteen days, then an elevator would have to be installed since Ginger, if alive would be in no shape to be climbing a 700 foot ladder. The drilling was averaging 65 feet a day, similar to Jason's production speed, and it was estimated that the area close to the rescue chamber was 1,200 feet below the surface.

Justin didn't think Ginger was still alive or anywhere near 'Section E'. Justin would just continue to follow orders the way Jason would continue to follow orders.

Justin accepted that Ginger may have been good at some

managerial tasks but it would be a miracle if Ginger had survived all three underground explosions. Ginger looked like such a wimpy guy at the best of times and Justin who appeared to be a lot stronger than Ginger could not imagine surviving such an ordeal, or knowing what to do to survive while waiting to be rescued.

All boreholes and shafts were sealed in Mine Five, except the capped shaft 5-E which led to the inside of the rescue chamber located in Section E'. This portal was supposed to be sealed too, but someone from high up with a lot of clout had filed a restraining order on James Coaltonstone and the Big Seven Coal Group and stopped the sealing of shaft 5-E.

Borehole COALT-11-C was the first borehole that was sealed. It was typical of Jason to have such bad luck. Imagine doing all that hard work for nothing in return, except contempt.

Chapter 28:
Plans To Remove Mountain Tops

Wednesday, December 25th 2030, around 10:00PM:

"Merry Christmas to all those who are tuning into our noon broadcast, this is Dianne Black for the PPZ bringing to you another live up to date coverage of the ongoing Pitville Mine Disaster of 2030 and what we hope to be the rescue of Ginger Goodwin.

"With me today is one of Ginger Goodwin's longtime friends, whose identity we must keep secret, therefore this person's voice will be muffled, and this person will be covered with a special cloak, manufactured by PPZ, just for occasions such as these. Our mystery guest just happened to have a spare key to Mr. Goodwin's home." Dianne announced, making Christina cringe realizing that it wouldn't take a genius to figure out who had a spare key to Ginger's loft.

"To our viewers who are just tuning into our round the clock coverage, a warm welcome. Very little has changed since our last update. Ginger Goodwin is still trapped deep inside Mine Five, located on the southern outskirts of Pitville and south of Coalton on beautiful Tut Island.

If Mr. Goodwin was able to reach the rescue chamber in 'Section E' around 5 am, on Sunday, the 22nd, he will now have around seventeen hours of air supply left. If he is not rescued soon, or if his air supply is not replaced soon, Ginger will die." Dianne said.

"Mystery guest, can you recap for us?" Dianne asked

"I certainly can." Christina replied.

The three towns, Pitville, Coalton and Sunrise Beach, are all part and parcel of Coalton Valley.

During the last forty-seven days, Ginger Goodwin had filed 49 reports hoping that safety concerns, primarily related to the ventilation system and a coal shearing machine, which was in disrepair, could be corrected. It is believed that on Sunday morning, during the pre-shift safety inspection, Ginger found that a methane monitor, which he had installed earlier that week, had been turned off.

Representatives for the Big Seven Coal Group deny this allegation of course.

Then there is the issue of finding what is believed to be a mass grave in Mine Four.

And top that off, there is the issue of open burning at the dump which is situated on an exposed coal seam.

And on Sunday Evening Bert's and Sons Gas Station blew up.

There was the suicide of Don and John Bell's nephew, who believed that he had caused the second explosion in Mine Five while he was drilling borehole COALT-11-C, on Sunday afternoon.

There was the discovery of a broken gas line which experts believe could have also contributed to the second explosion, which happened Sunday afternoon in Mine Five.

Then there was the loss of three rescue robots in 500,000 gallons of water in 'Section A' of Mine Five. This mishap occurred on Sunday afternoon around the same time that the second explosion in Mine Five happened.

Then around 1:20 PM, on Tuesday, Christmas Eve, a third explosion occurred in Mine Five, and I believe by then commentators were too worn out to speculate any further to what may have caused that explosion. The cause is officially unknown. The end result was an announcement that Mine Five was to be sealed, with Ginger Goodwin still trapped inside, though public authorities believe that Ginger could not survive the third mine explosion and might have been incinerated. His supporters believe that Ginger could survive. If anyone knows Ginger, they know that if he could, he would find a way to survive just to beat the odds. He was just that way," Christina said, wondering if she had said all there was to say.

"And what do all these events mean to you, does it change the way you see to role of coal, in a modern society?" Dianne asked as Jackson shook his head.

"All of these events this week indicate to me that there could be some truth in the curse of the Black Diamonds. If Pitville isn't cursed, it might as well be, since misfortune, injury and death are turning this town into a hell hole," Christina said without remorse.

"Do the events of this week remind you of any place in particular?" Dianne Black asked, while Jackson continued to shake his head

"Hell. It feels like hell. There is the issue of smoke coming out of the sidewalks. And in Hell, we are told, has a lot of fire and smoke, maybe Pitville is turning into Hell," Christina said.

"Was there anything else that you would like to add to your recap?" Dianne Black asked.

"As long as the Big Seven are willing to pay the fines, the government allows us all to take these risks. We accept these risks which lead to all this bad luck, injury and death, so that we can keep our jobs even though the mine is supposed to close at the end of June, next year," Christina said.

"So how do you think you could change the way things work in Pitville," Dianne asked.

"As far as I can see, things are not working very well in Pitville. Maybe the only chance of changing the state of the current disorder is if the owners were forced to spend an eight-hour shift with the miners in the mine. Maybe safety in the mine would matter to them then. I mean at this moment, Ginger has about seventeen hours of air supply left, assuming that he is in the rescue chamber in 'Section E' and what is James Coaltonstone doing?" Christina asked.

"Do you think Ginger has a chance of being rescued while alive?" Dianne asked.

"It seems to me that the Big Seven Group will find it easier just to seal the mine, regardless if Ginger is alive or not. It is so barbaric, and we have become so used to this madness, we don't even question it anymore," Christina said.

"I think the priority should be rescuing Ginger," Dianne said.

"I agree of course, but I am starting to wonder if it is too late. I would hope that a thorough inquiry will be done some time in the future, but I want authorities to focus their collective energy on rescuing Ginger now, before Ginger runs out of air," Christina said.

"Coaltonstone Mines do produce a product, which has helped advance the industrialized world. But we as employees are the producers of this product and we have been manipulated to accept below standard work conditions so that we can produce coal as inexpensively as possible. This practice does place us in the center of the third industrial revolution, and for that distinction, we in Pitville can be proud," Christina said.

"Do you think, considering the know-how the Big Seven has in coal mining, could they be doing a better job in trying to rescue Ginger?" Dianne asked.

"I certainly do. I believe it will be the coal industry which will lead us to connect two continents, which have historically been in conflict.

We will construct the MTC Railway to tunnel under the Bering Strait. Connecting the two continents will not only become an engineering miracle, it will set the foundation for the fourth industrial revolution. This new railway will increase our mobility between continents, and change the way we do business. Why can't those people rescue Ginger, and bring him back to the surface?" Christina asked realizing that she had to be careful to not reveal who she was.

"That is a very good question," Dianne replied.

"I know James Coaltonstone always asks where would we be without coal. I know coal will fuel the fourth industrial revolution and as the arctic ice melts away, a new source of wealth will be within our reach."

"When the Arctic ice melts all kinds of new problems and very dangerous problems could develop," Dianne replied.

"Yes. The metallic tyranny may twist minds so we neglect to manage the risks which we are able to control. All I care about right now is Ginger. Ginger isn't a 'nobody'. Ginger is a hero. We can talk about how we will adapt as the Arctic ice melts another day, but today we need to find a way to free Ginger from the confines of Mine Five. He is all alone down there assuming that he is still alive; he will be alive because he fought to stay alive. We should find a way to honor Ginger's ability to harness enough hope in his heart so that he was able to live the dream of putting people before profits. And we must use the power of hope to find a way to bring Ginger back to the surface."

"So what would be the right approach be?"

"We need to believe that there is a way to locate Ginger, and once we locate him we will be able to rescue him. As I said before, the most important thing to do right now is to rescue Ginger. After we rescue Ginger, compliance issues can be discussed. There will always be dilemmas when extracting coal from the earth. I don't think it is possible to guarantee a 100% safe work place in a coal mine." Christina said.

"So are you saying it was not Ginger's job to pursue management until they corrected all the hazards?" Dianne asked, as she noticed Jackson stomping his left foot while shaking his head.

"Of course I am not saying that. What I mean is we all agreed to not take job action as part of our job contract, but we were coerced to agree to such terms. I believe that Coaltonstone Mines will be successful in finding new sources of high quality anthracite coal. The power generated by finding new sources of energy to power the grid will create new paths for society to follow. New discoveries will new paths which we can take into the future. When Coaltonstone and the Big Seven Coal Group complete the construction of the MTC Railway line, a new power clique will be created which will only exploit the people who can't fight back. Most people will say the truth when they are wearing masks, but not Ginger. And if they had listened to Ginger, the outcome could have been very different." Christina said, hoping Dianne would catch her drift.

"What is the answer, from your point of view?" Dianne asked.

"I don't think this is about answering a question. It is about building a foundation so that the optimum outcome can be situated.

A good outcome is a physical situation which should benefit more than just the '1%'. We need to create a special place beyond defining sides as good and bad. This ideal situation could happen in a garden or a coal mine. Most people prefer to be in places where they have choices. Being grateful for employment doesn't mean that anyone should give up their personal privacy while the mine bureaucracy has no transparency at all. No one likes a payroll-boss bot flying around one's head day after day while using its sensors to determine if your mind is on work or on something else. Many of us believe the use of these boss-bots creates a safety hazard that would not be tolerated by less oppressed people." Christina added.

"We need to get Ginger out of Mine Five before he runs out of air. I want Ginger to be rescued. Blaming someone for the explosion will not bring Ginger back to the surface. I know that the public, including all those people standing outside in the cold, want an enquiry. Hopefully this enquiry will lead to improvements in process and quality control." Christina said, reminding herself that her inner self, the one who is hiding her own identity, wanted to quit her job a long time ago but never did.

"Why didn't we go on strike on December 21st 2030, when we knew conditions were getting so dangerous at the mine? Were we coerced into accepting substandard work conditions?

I think an inquiry may discover than many of us believed that we had no choice but to go to work, since we had very few other options. Many of us are raising kids, and with inflation the way it is now, the last thing on our minds last Saturday, the day before the first explosion was to go on strike.

But now, all I think about is 'if I could have convinced Ginger to stay home from work on the day of the explosion. But if Ginger hadn't been in the mine and didn't prevent the morning crew from descending into the pending explosion, the whole crew, one hundred and sixty men, could have been down there instead of just one person.

If we had gone on strike the day before the explosions, James Coaltonstone would have just brought in replacements. And we had no idea the mine was going to blow up, the day after winter solstice. And we certainly had no idea that Ginger's data was able to predict what was going to happen. Most of us don't understand

Ginger's data. I suppose as conditions worsened the predictability of a pending explosion increased.

We were too busy to think much about it. Everything is so expensive. We are trying to make ends meet, and the last thing on most people's minds was Ginger's data. It was easier to dismiss him and to assume that he did have some form of an obsessive-compulsive disorder. Reminiscing always feels great to the critics, but can often feel like torture to the victims.

It is easy to say 'if I knew this, we could have done that'. The problem is no one knew that the explosions were going to happen.

Now Ginger is trapped in Mine Five on Christmas day and it doesn't get much worse than that. The bosses have sealed the mine, with Ginger still inside, and they are trying to convince us that he is dead. Sure we have to accept their decision but we don't have to internalize their logic or forget Ginger. Sure, the bosses are talking about naming 'Anthracite Row' after Ginger Goodwin, to make up for the loss of his life, but who are they kidding? How could the bosses ever believe that having a miners' ghetto lane renamed after Ginger be enough? I say, name the Coalton Valley Parkway after Ginger, not some muddy laneway known only to locals, and even we distance ourselves from that road. I mean Ginger had his whole life to look forward to," Christina stopped as she fought back tears. Christina wondered if she had said too much. Dianne had assured her that her identity was concealed, but in a small town such as Pitville, it doesn't take many clues to figure out the identity of a person Dianne Black would take time to even talk to.

"This is so interesting." Dianne said realizing that Christina was beginning to feel self-conscious and uncomfortable.

"Do you have any photographs of Ginger Goodwin, from old high school yearbooks?" Dianne asked.

"I am sure Ginger wouldn't mind if we went into his room. I think he has our old year books in the top drawer." Christina said.

"And won't Ginger be thrilled to know that you are expecting?" Dianne said while startling Christina.

"How the hell does she know when I don't know for sure? Did she just announce that I was pregnant to the world before I even got my test results back? I thought our confidentiality agreement meant that my identity was supposed to be protected." Christina wondered to herself but did not share her thoughts while Dianne looked through Ginger's top drawer before Christina could figure out what to say or do to stop her.

"What is this?" Dianne asked as she continued to rummish through Ginger's top drawer before Christina could stop her. Jackson continued to film.

"Oh my God!" exclaimed Dianne, "these look like plans to remove our Coalton Valley's mountaintops. It looks like Coaltonstone Mines have permission to remove the top off the Beartut Mountain Range." Dianne said to Christina as she waved the plans in front of the camera.

These plans show that James Coaltonstone's intentions have not been fully disclosed to the public, which is a huge understatement."

"Figures," Christina replied.

"If James Coaltonstone plans to remove the top from the beautiful Beartut Range so that the thin coal seam can be harvested, Coalton Valley will be transformed into a very different place. It is hard to imagine what it would be like. Just look how long and thin that coal seam is."

"Why am I not surprised?" Christina asked wishing that she had a better reply, but she was too tired to feel anything.

"I see that someone wrote notes to the effect that the anthracite coal is estimated to be worth hundreds of millions of dollars in direct and indirect spinoffs." Dianne noted.

"Well a billion dollars is a thousand million so who knows how much mountain tops are worth in dollars. I am sure we will miss the mountain tops once they are gone and how will we replace them?" Christina asked.

"Mountain tops can't be replaced. We all know that. Mina will buy the anthracite coal so it can continue to generate affordable electricity to sustain its economic growth. I suppose the question should be, how much is a mountain top worth?" Dianne asked as she looked straight into the camera.

"The only positive thing I can say about this project; it might mean safer work conditions for the miners, since the work would be above ground. The obvious drawback would be the irreversible damage to the mountains," Christina said as she wondered why making a living was always so complicated.

"I see that there are plans to landscape, to cover up the scars, after the mountain top removal process is complete. I suppose, window dressing if you will is better than nothing," Dianne said, not entirely convinced.

"Of course the landscape will never be the same, after the mountain tops are removed but what can we do about it? James Coaltonstone will just hire replacements if the local miners refuse to do the work. This was the same problem we had in Mine Five. There were no practical options." Christina said.

"If we protest physically, the mine owners will use those cadets who are probably still marching around the administration building, to put us back into our collective submissive places." Christina said, hoping her voice was being adequately disguised.

The moment was interrupted by a Barry Manilow ring tone ringing from Dianne's purse nearby.

It was agreed between the PPZ crew that Dianne's number would only be phoned when there was a new break in a current news story.

"Excuse me world, I have to answer my phone and it better be a very important call." Dianne said as she retrieved the phone from her purse, while Jackson steadied the camera to focus for a moment on Dianne's beautiful silhouette.

"Oh my God" Dianne said. "They found Ginger. He is alive. They finally got the telemagnetic radio to work. PPZ's own equipment was the first to make the connection with Ginger. He is ok. PPZ's state of the art equipment was found a frequency that was able to bypass the noise coming from the signals in the ground which control the invisible fences surrounding Mine Five and other Big Seven properties."

Chapter 29:
Sunrise Beach

Wednesday December 25th, 2030 around 12:00 PM:

Lance Diamond, the principle owner of the famous Black Rock Mines and member of the Big Seven Coal Group was the Mayor of Sunrise Beach, Mike Stone's favorite companion. They descended from the air-bus arm in arm. From a distance it was not clear who was supporting whom.

The Mayor from Sunrise Beach was carrying a bullhorn which looked exactly like the bullhorn that Mayor Stern had been carrying around but never used since the crowd was being so well behaved.

Despite all the hardships the people in Pitville were enduring on Christmas day, they were finally hearing what they were hoping to hear since Sunday morning's explosion, four days ago. Ginger was alive and apparently not hurt, not injured and not disfigured.

Now that Ginger was found he still had to be rescued. Some of the crowd stayed and some of the crowd began to disperse, not knowing what else they could do.

Mike Stone knew that his mission in life, especially as mayor, was to create a livable town, where most people could have jobs and a good quality of life. Mike Stone never wanted to live in a town like Pitville again.

"Ladies and gentlemen," Mike Stone said over his bullhorn. "There is a lot more to Tut Island than just Pitville. In fact our social structure in Sunrise Beach doesn't even include exclusion leagues which watch people as they walk about deciding what to buy or where to eat or even where they should go to the bathroom. We just know people respond negatively when power cliques dominate. Sure we can question the Power Clique's self-serving and time consuming assumptions, but we can't forget the motive which seems to be insulating Pitville while creating a vulture culture which accepts man's inhumanity to man in exchange for the almighty dollar.

As gatekeepers, the Power Clique did a fine job of marginalizing and excluding outsiders who would never be accepted by the Clique of Coalton Valley. All those excluded people could only hope for jobs that took care of the Clique's dirty work while men and women risked their lives and collective health for next to nothing in return.

There seems to be little room for innovation in Pitville. Not true in Sunrise Beach, innovation created our town, we have decentralized our Power Grid.

If you feel that you have been treated unfairly in Coalton Valley why don't you take a free ride in our heated air-bus, and of course refreshments will be served. Take a free ride back to Sunrise Beach with us and have a real Christmas. Sunrise Beach is not even on the Tut Island Highway, so we will get there in one piece without getting tied up with the protest activities which may still be blocking traffic on the Coalton Valley Parkway.

I have brought bags of Sunrise Beach money. Just reach into the bag and try your luck, this is how we keep our local economy working, and how we keep people housed, fed, looking desirable and happy. Money is just an exchange. The lack of it should not destroy whole towns or turn civilized men and women into hungry beasts.

We have modern people that can serve you with a smile and they don't make you wait in line while you have to ask them to correct their mistakes or accept being short changed.

Many of our Sunrise Beach businesses accept a mixture of Sunrise Beach dollars and North American Dollars in exchange for goods and services.

Our people are able to multi-task, when it comes to multicurrency; they understand how accepting a fair mix of local and North American currency can keep the cash flow moving so that goods and services can be distributed more fairly. All of our banks in Sunrise Beach offer accounts in both checking and savings in Sunrise Beach currency, and North American currency. Currency is different than discounts because currency gives people more independent personal choices which include having a private roof over one's head.

We are a luckier town than Pitville and Coalton because we consciously try to create positive vibes, not negative ones. We just don't have 'In God We Trust' written on one side of our currency, we also have 'In Humanity we Trust' written on the other side," Mayor Stone continued to explain.

"So our town did not become frozen in time and draconian during the great depression of 2029 the way Pitville appears to have become.

We are a happy and friendly town and have never used riot police on guests or on residents. If people need something we give them Sunrise Beach money. The merchant or landlord can use this money to even pay part of their municipal taxes. Gaps between people are not so wide in Sunrise Beach since we all manage to find common ground somehow. We trust each other because we don't let each other die, destitute outside a convenience store the way people sometimes die in Coalton with only one legal tender in their pocket.

We are a progressive town and pride ourselves in being friendly and courteous to guests. Don't stand around here and become provoked by the stares of the riot police on Christmas day, of all days. Don't go hungry either.

We heard your beautiful singing.

"Air-bus seats are available for anyone who would like to join us to celebrate Christmas in our friendly town of Sunrise Beach." The Mayor of Sunrise Beach was talking clearly and smoothly until he began to choke on what appeared to be cigar smoke nearby.

"What the hell are you doing coming into my town and inviting all these people to your town before they spend all of their money in my town?" Mayor Stern asked sounding very annoyed as James Coaltonstone stood by nodding in support.

"Just look at this town. It is the Pits. A huge black cloud full of toxic fumes is lurking over our heads while we speak. This is no place to spend the holiday season," Mayor Stone said.

"My town is better; it is cleaner, prettier and it is not on the verge of civil war either," Mayor Stone added.

"If I were the mayor of Pitville I would be thinking of declaring a state of emergency too, then I would consider all the stakeholders, not just the ones who are regular contributors to my campaign fund," Mayor Stone said.

"What are you insinuating, Stone?" Mayor Stern asked.

"Never mind all this, we do know that Mr. Goodwin is alive. That is cause for celebration. We know it may take about ten to fifteen days to get him out of Mine Five. This will not be a job that should be rushed. We know if we allow our most knowledgeable engineers to do their best, Ginger might have a good chance of being rescued and still remain in one piece," Mayor Stone said.

"Are you insinuating that our engineers are not as good as your engineers?" James Coaltonstone asked sounding very offended.

"No, I am just saying that the best engineers would have never allowed this disaster to happen in the first place," Mike Stone said.

"If I were mayor of this town I would respect the efforts that everyday people are making to the Pitville way of life. Pitville is a very interesting and a viable community when everything is working right and when people are relaxed enough to greet each other pleasantly. But lately you must admit the town appears to be curs, Mayor Mike Stone said.

"We are just having a lot of bad luck lately that is all," Mayor Stern said defensively.

"There is the scuffle out on the outskirts of town, that has to be managed or it will just get worse, and could even turn into a war between the haves and have nots. I took a jetcopter ride above the riot earlier today, and there are issues, which need to be addressed in a kind way. Aggression feeds aggression so when everyone is assumed to be adversaries, chaos is about the only possible outcome," Mayor Stone warned.

"Coal made this town a payroll town, without coal there would be no Pitville." Mayor Stern said defensively.

"This is a mining town and once the single source of good paying jobs is shut down the scavengers will take over, what do you have left? Broken people living in a wasteland and a vulture culture?" Mayor Stone asked.

"Pitville is a payroll town," Mayor Stern said.

"At what cost? You don't know when a building is going to cave-in because you can't control the people who are robbing mines of their pillars which are supposed to be holding up the surface which hosts the foundations of your buildings." Mayor Stone replied.

We have over thirty hotels in our vicinity. All of our hotels have a three to five star rating. And we are not raising the hospitality tax so that we can pay cadets from the Tut Island Military Academy to march around the richest building in town while frightening our guests. We are actually giving away Sunrise Beach dollars so that people can enjoy our town. We believe in planning for the long term," Mayor Stone said as Lance Diamond discreetly took Coaltonstone by the sleeve.

"And what was your plan? Were you really going to leave Ginger to die in that mine with the borehole to the rescue chamber capped indefinitely until the air supply ran out?" Lance Diamond asked James Coaltonstone.

"We did the best we could. Having your mine blow up is quite the shock you know," James Coaltonstone replied.

"It seems to me that you were deliberately avoiding the expense to rescue Ginger Goodwin who has been your loyal assistant safety manager for ten years," Lance Diamond said in disgust.

"Didn't you care that the telemagnetic radio couldn't work as long as you kept the fences under your control while neglecting to build a communication center by the shaft entrance in Mine Five so that Ginger's transmissions could be received? And what are all those fences for anyway?" Lance Diamond asked James Coaltonstone.

"Those fences are important, that is all I can say about that right now," James Coaltonstone said in reply.

"Don't you realize that Ginger is your son? No son or

grandson should be left down there in the mine, but especially not ours. We have the power to change everything, so we must," Lance Diamond said before James Coaltonstone was able to think of what to say in response, Lance Diamond walked away.

"My God, look at the smoke coming out of the cracks of this sidewalk," Mayor Stone said as he kicked the cracks with his shoe.

"What is going on down there?" Mike Stone asked again.

"It is a little worrisome, isn't it?" Mayor Stern admitted.

"I could swear that smoke was coming out of the cracks of the Coalton Valley Parkway this morning, though at the time I thought the smoke was coming from the rowdy protest I flew over. What is going on under the ground, here?" Mike Stone asked again.

Chapter 30:
In Search For A Plan

Wednesday December 25th, 2030, around 12:30 PM.
Location: Pitville Airpark.

As he climbed into one of his city's jetcopters, the mayor of Sunrise Beach, Mike Stone, wasn't sure how he could bring peace to Coalton Valley. Even though he was a man of invention; Mayor Stone doubted his ability to bring peace in such troubling times.

Nevertheless, Mayor Stone summoned another three jetcopters to follow him and ordered them to be filled with Christmas dinners, extra bread, cheese and things like that.

While Lance Diamond was trying to find a way to free his grandson from the ramifications of the Pitville Mine Disaster of 2030, Mayor Stone was content making a Herculean effort to create goodwill amongst angry men. He knew this mission would make good use of the four jetcopters at his disposal and if nothing else he would be able to create a counter wind and shake things up a bit.

The mayor had decision-making power and since the jetcopters were at his disposal this Christmas day, how could he refuse to act.

Mike Stone realized that the jetcopters could function as food trucks at a pinch while the counter wind was just an added bonus that would only be noticed when people's hats were blown from their heads, or a lighter person was swept off his feet.

And this was one of those times the promise of experiencing the power of thrust was hard to resist, since it made Mayor Stone feel young and powerful again.

The people of Sunrise Beach found love their food trucks so why would these rioters feel any different. Since the blockades were disrupting traffic flow on the Tut Island Highway, the four jetcopters would serve as substitutes for food trucks.

As Mayor Stone held on to his bullhorn with both hands as the jetcopter descended onto one of the many ramps on the Coalton Valley Parkway.

"Hold on to your hats and to a nearby a solid object if possible, for I bring to you good tidings and a bit of a jet blast this fine Christmas day." Mike Stone warned over the jetcopters loud speaker. Those on the ground were too busy antagonizing each other to pay any notice until the jet blast blew many of them over while others stopped rioting so they could chase after their hats.

Mayor Stone hoped that the Goodwill that he was about to bring could make a difference and end the riot without bloodshed.

Meanwhile, Lance Diamond was in search of a copy of the rescue plan. Lance was hoping to find clear-cut plans designed by experts in mine rescues and up to date technology. After spending a couple of hours trying to find a blueprint outlining the rescue mission's plans, Lance realized that there probably wasn't a plan and no one was willing to admit it.

Lance Diamond learned a long time ago, that most people are better at talking than doing. Over the years, Lance had witnessed so many ideas failing to take place because there was no plan of design in place to actually turn these ideas into physical reality. Since it was just human nature to prefer to forget one's ideas than to admit defeat, this was not an option for Lance Diamond.

A workable plan needs to be framed and designed so that the intended outcome could be actualized. A plan could grow and change shape, and have a path or two added to it when necessary and when all was said and done, a plan had a purpose.

And Lance Diamond's purpose was to free his grandson from Mine Five. That was his only purpose for now.

Chapter 31:
Riot On Coalton Valley Parkway

Wednesday December 25th, 2030, around 12:45 PM:

Location: Coalton Valley Parkway.

"And Sunrise Beach dollars is a means of exchange between people living in Sunrise Beach, not just a means to control and exploit, but a means of exchange." Mayor Stone explained to chief of police, Officer Florence Cuff.

The rioters could see that money was falling all around them. They looked up into the sky and saw Mike Stone throwing the mixed currency into the crowd even though Police Chief Florence Cuff advised against it.

After emptying two of the five bags he had to give away, Mayor Stone took his bullhorn and wished everyone a merry Christmas, from the friendly people residing in Sunrise Beach.

"And we certainly don't let people starve or go homeless, or call the destitute hobos to justify our cruelty and indifference towards them. Why should all the currencies on the planet be centralized? What was the third industrial revolution all about if it wasn't about decentralization of the power structure and about increasing ordinary people's power factor in the economic equation?" Mike Stone declared as he spoke into his bullhorn.

"Power to the 99%," the crowd responded back.

"Was dehumanizing the destitute and unemployed as if they did not belong anywhere justified or even necessary?"

"No," the crowd responded back.

"We give everyone a chance to earn Sunrise Beach currency. Sunrise currency is a means of exchange, which is inclusive, and allows the holder of such currency access to our markets and society. Our community draws our power from our decentralized renewable energy grid" Mayor Stone continued to explain to Officer Cuff who was standing on the Coalton Valley Parkway, looking stunned, for she had never heard of such concepts before, and she wondered if they were legal.

"Decentralize the power grid and free the people from the tyranny of the 1%," the crowd shouted back.

"In Sunrise Beach, we don't exclude people just because they can't find work. We give them a chance to fit in anyway. We don't treat the dispossessed and the homeless like criminals and mindless; we give them opportunities to live like every day people.

We don't just talk about the third industrial revolution, we make it work and we make horizontal integration work too. Competitiveness between neighbors and co-workers is not so fierce when people are not so desperate. We have shortened the vertical ladder, which has to be climbed in order to succeed. So as long as we don't have a system based on the adversarial process, most of us are able to share and see our common ground." Mayor Stone said as he continued to throw a combination of North American and Sunrise Beach Dollars into the riot from one of the many ramps which were part of the Coalton Valley Parkway system. Police Chief Cuff stared in disbelief still not sure if Mayor Stone was behaving lawfully.

"Since people in Sunrise Beach began to accept Sunrise Beach dollars during the great depression of 2029 as a means of exchange, the city was able to avoid the despair the great depression caused in so many cities." Mayor Stone continued to explain, not just to Police Chief Cuff but to the crowd of rioters who had stopped rioting so they could collect the money falling all around them.

"A combination of Sunrise Beach dollars along with the legal tender for North America was a perfect combination for the market of Sunrise Beach which prospered.

While other towns grew poorer, Sunrise Beach grew

wealthier during the depression of 2029, because we had a plan which integrated vertically. Since Sunrise Beach dollars could only be spent in Sunrise Beach much of the wealth was kept in town so that the local government and local businesses were able to form partnerships. We no longer took sides; we moved forward and shaped our future, as a brotherhood and sisterhood of man. As social problems related to the inequitable allocation of money almost disappeared. Our time could be invested in growing food and improving the decentralized power grid to increase efficiency. Greenhouse towers some as high as twenty stories were built. So the hungry 20's were not so hungry for Sunrise Beach residents." Mike Stone hoped he had explained all the important elements to the foundation his town, which was the closest thing he knew to a Utopian model a city, could be built upon.

"We are sick of being hungry," the crowd chanted.

"Sunrise Beach became a self-sufficient city, a Utopia of sorts. Not quite a utopia but at least the sidewalks and roads were not smoldering at the seams." Mayor Stone explained to the crowd as Police Chief Cuff who was still looking stunned.

Many of the young men had stopped rioting just long enough to hear about a dream or at least to see if the police chief was going to arrest Mike Stone.

"We are all familiar with times when there were food shortages. The depression of 2029 was not kind but we were able to actualize the real third industrial revolution and Sunrise Beach became a Land of Plenty because we were self-sufficient. We grew food in blocks of twenty story green houses, we built with a combination of Sunrise Beach dollars and North American dollars where climate was controlled, energy to power the greenhouse towers was decentralized and renewable, we worked not just for the few but for the many. Since our way of life was so economical, everything kept working out well for us," Mike Stone continued.

So against the advice of Chief of Police Florence Cuff, Mayor Stone continued to wish everyone merry Christmas and continued to throw bags of Sunrise Beach currency into the crowd with some North American dollars mixed in.

"Stop everyone, that old man is throwing money from the bridge again, he must be crazy." One of the young men carrying an aluminum tube said to another as they and several others looked up into the sky.

"He sure sounds crazy, but if the food is real, I think we better eat, I haven't eaten in days, and I am feeling weak, and I think that is exactly how they want us to feel," another young man said who was sitting beside the burning tires.

"We need to make this Christmas merrier than any other Christmas has ever been before, because today is the stepping stone into a better future. It is not about taking sides. It is about taking steps to make a better future for ourselves and our descendants. Miracles do happen. Ginger Goodwin has been found. It could take up to fifteen days to get him out of Mine Five, but it is a wonderful thing that he is alive and well." Mike Stone said.

"Sir, I am not sure if what you are doing is legal?" Police Chief Florence Cuff said.

"Of course it is legal. We are out of Pitville city limits, thank God, everything we are sharing with these hungry people, we own," Mike Stone said.

"Now let us carry on," Mike Stone said, we have brought all kinds of food with us and that you can buy with the currency that you are collecting from the ground and most important of all, we brought our Goodwill," Mike stone said.

"Now is that currency legal?" Police Chief Florence Cuff asked again as she looked at it closely. "It certainly is in our store, we have a small selection of donuts, if you would like one, just use this currency and we will give you one, or even two. Well we will give you as many donuts as you want," Mike Stone said.

"I can't stop to have a donut break at the moment; I am in a middle of a riot," Police Chief Florence Cuff snapped.

"Of course you are welcome to buy a donut with our currency when you are ready to take a break. This currency has my face printed on every bill. Admittedly the picture was taken a few years ago now, but as long as the people in Sunrise Beach accept the currency, it is legal. Money is just a means of exchange. Our currency keeps our local economy liquid and moving, even the source of federal currency dries up. If you haven't noticed, the centralized economies are moving so slow, they are crashing which leads to needless human suffering. All kinds of national currencies are devaluing at alarming rates. My currency gives the excluded a chance to be included."

"You didn't answer my question though Mr. Stone is your currency legal?" Police Chief Cuff asked again.

"Yes it is, and today we are using Sunrise Beach Currency to grant good tidings to all during the holiday season and into the New Year," Mike Stone said.

And this riot is blocking the highway, so we came to you in our jetcopters, believing in goodwill for all, which means no more rioting. Rioting is not civilized and it certainly is a fire hazard," Mike Stone said.

"Sir, what you are doing is very dangerous. You are not wearing riot gear and rubber gloves which are the appropriate attire to wear when you are mixing with very volatile, dangerous and undesirable people," Police Chief Florence Cuff warned.

"Of course I am not wearing riot gear and I am certainly not wearing rubber gloves. And who says these people are undesirable? In Sunrise Beach, we do not promote the adversarial culture, where one side is considered righteous and wins and the other side is considered undesirable and loses out on the finer things of living. We built many of Sunrise Beach's assets during the depression so fast because we had everyone working together as a team. We survive and thrive because we know true community has never been about taking sides. Community is about working together and moving forward into the future. We do not have the time to work against each other. Sunrise Beach is a town, which is moving forward, not backward, and we are creating a future worth living for everyone. We are building a future together, a future to share and believe in, and as I said before, today is always the stepping stone into a better tomorrow." The crowd clapped and cheered loudly and then quickly found places to sit so they could eat their Christmas dinner which had been placed neatly on paper plates, in peace.

"Mr. Stone, you never answer my question. Are you sure this is all legal?" Florence Cuff asked again as she watched Mike Stone throw another mixed bag of currency over the highest railing on the Coalton Valley Parkway.

"Of course it is. Does Santa Claus get arrested when he gives away presents? We share this currency with honor. We want peace and it is love which will create peace for all. You are free to collect as much Sunrise Beach currency as you can, but please don't fight with each other, help each other, be kind to each other and buy things you fancy from our jetcopters. All these things are grown in our town and surrounding fields," Mike Stone said.

"I don't see anything good coming out of rioting. What we need to do today and every day is spread and show our goodwill to all people, everywhere," Mayor Stone exclaimed, as the crowd continued to applaud, even Police Chief Florence Cuff began to clap her hands, so happy to see that the riot had ended without bloodshed.

"Today is a day for celebration," Mike Stone announced. "Today is better when we trust each other. Trust is all about goodwill toward man and this universal trust will bring peace on Earth. Today is about everyone having something nice to eat not just on Christmas day and but every day, which is the way it should be, just the way it can be. Today we will start working together instead of working against each other." Mike Stone said, and then sat down, feeling very tired but well spent.

Back in Pitville Lance Diamond was on the phone with his favorite lawyer, Martha Mason.

"I waited too long to meet my only grandson. I will not let bumbling fools get in the way ever again. These people don't have a plan in the works. How did they think they were going to rescue my only grandson, without a plan? It seems to me that they were going to leave him down in the pit to die." Lance Diamond told Martha Mason.

Then Lance went for a walk down the street and found James Coaltonstone looking at the ground in disbelief as smoke was coming out of the sidewalk.

"My court order is going to prevent you from sealing the borehole leading to the rescue chamber in 'Section E'. So at this time I am thanking God for small mercies that we got here just in time," Lance Diamond said.

"We will see," James Coaltonstone responded.

"Would you have really entombed my grandson, and your son?" Lance Diamond asked James.

"No normal person would have survived that explosion,"

James Coaltonstone said.

"Did you really make the telemagnetic communicator inoperable by continuing to use the same frequency to control the signals which keep all of your invisible fences around the mines wired up? Why do you need so many invisible fences wired up anyway? Lance Diamond asked.

"That is none of your business," James Coaltonstone responded.

"Why didn't you at least try to find out if Ginger was in the rescue chamber? Why didn't you at least uncap the borehole in Section E's rescue chamber, so that a camera could be sent down into the rescue chamber to see if Ginger was sitting in there, twiddling his thumbs? He has been in there for four days and no one thought to look in there? Is that all you cared about was protecting your equipment and what was left of your coal? Lance Diamond asked James Coaltonstone in dismay.

Instead of waiting for an answer, Lance continued.

"Despite all of those things that have gone wrong, I have been able to talk to Ginger through the telemagnetic communicator that the PPZ installed. He told me that he had been banging on the metal plate the way he had been trained to do. Once he realized that something was interfering with the telemagnetic communicator he gave up, and began to read the literature which he found in the rescue chamber," Lance Diamond said.

"Well that Goodwin pulled off a minor miracle. It was almost impossible to believe that anyone could have survived that explosion," James Coaltonstone said.

"Of course he did, Goodwin is a Diamond. For four days, whenever Ginger heard drilling he banged on the metal plate but no one stopped to listen or to answer back. Ginger kept trying to send voice and text messages that seemed to go nowhere adding mental distress to an already horrible situation for him, and at Christmas time of all times," Lance Diamond said.

"I am glad to see progress on Shaft 6-E, now we need to get Ginger out of there, as soon as possible. So as soon as we have a camera set up we can get the rescue mission on track. Ginger's asthma medications will be sent to him, plus a few little things that will make his life more comfortable while he waits for the team to work together with the considerable resources that we have at our disposal, we could celebrate Christmas together," Mike Stone said.

"It would be a cold day in hell before I spend Christmas day with you or any other Diamond, James Coaltonstone said, "I blame your daughter for Ginger."

"My Mary-Rose was the only one I who ever knew who actually trusted you with her soul. And that was her only failing, a fatal one mind you. Every December 25th for the last 32 years, I am reminded how I lost my Mary-Rose," Lance Diamond exclaimed as he jumped on James Coaltonstone with vigor seldom seen in such an old man.

As James Coaltonstone and Lance Diamond rolled in the dirt passersby stopped and stared, some were even cheering Lance on, even though they had never met him before.

"You can't blame this mine disaster on me. That Goodwin is the only assistant safety manager I know who could single handedly land up in a mine disaster while everyone else managed to escape," James Coaltonstone said.

"You can't blame this mine disaster on Ginger. Doctor Smith told me everything, or as much as he knew about the situation. He had been watching out for him all these years, and because he did not know what else he could do, he told me that I was the only person who would be your equal, and could balance the power structure in Pitville," Lance Diamond said.

"How was I supposed to know Ginger was the kid? He looks nothing like me," James Coaltonstone said still feeling overwhelmed by the situation.

"Thank God for that," Lance Diamond replied. "You have made a fine mess again haven't you;" Lance added.

"You can't blame me for this," James Coaltonstone said.

"Oh yes I can, I blame you for everything." Lance Diamond said.

"PPZ's Steve Jones has spoken to my grandson at great length. Ginger told Steve that he was able to use the inflatable seal kit to seal off 'Section E' so that its atmosphere could be protected from the toxic fumes and the hell hole that seems to be growing in 'Sections A, B and C'. Ginger told me that the ventilation shaft was useless as a second exit. The ventilation shaft caught on fire quite quickly. Ginger was also saying that during practice evacuations climbing the 1,200-foot ladder built into the ventilation shaft was traumatic for the employees. Ginger told me that Mine Five employees and contractors found climbing 1,200 feet straight up, was overwhelming, difficult and frightening during drills, and the ventilation shaft was the first thing that lit up during the explosion," Lance Diamond said.

"If my accounting department was not able to succeed in keeping costs down when costs were soaring, we may have closed the mine months ago," James Coaltonstone said."

"Of course producing coal the cheapest way possible mattered more to you, than the safety of your son, and the workers and contractors who were working in the mine. I think that was very short sighted of you. There is a lot about Mine Five that would terrify even me, and I have been around some pretty difficult situations. My grandson also told me that a functioning third exit was supposed to be built in Mine Five since the ventilation shaft in Section C was obviously not suitable as an emergency exit. Now we know how unsuitable the ventilation shaft really was as a second exit considering how fast it caught on fire," Lance Diamond said.

"Having a second escape exit is no longer required by law, so we had to do the best we could with the limited resources that we had," James Coaltonstone said defensively.

"As soon as Ginger was able to enter the rescue chamber, he was able to eat and drink and use the provisions available to him. So far 'Section E' has been holding up pretty well," Lance Diamond explained to James Coaltonstone.

"And who paid for those provisions?" James Coaltonstone asked.

"You did. But what you did was required by law," Lance Diamond explained. I am financing this operation but I will be expecting to recover my money after the law suit, if there can't be a more amicable solution reached before hand."

Dianne Black and Jackson were the first news team to arrive on the scene since Jackson and Dianne were filming the smoke coming from the sidewalk across the street.

"Aren't you two a little too old to be rolling on the ground fighting?" Dianne asked Lance Diamond and James Coaltonstone.

"Of course we aren't too old," James Coaltonstone said.

"I suppose getting back up is always the hard part. Dear Dianne, could you give me a hand? " Dianne held out her hand. Lance quickly rolled away from James Coaltonstone, jumped on to his feet and kissed it as Dianne who was caught off guard quickly put her hand inside her pocket.

Lance could see that Dianne was blushing. "My dear, you are so invigorating, but I am sure all this excitement will catch up with us tomorrow."

"My God, are you ok, sir, should I have this mad man arrested?" John Bell asked terrified that he was going to get fired as head of security.

"I tried to get here as fast as I could," John Bell said in defense as he gasped for air.

"No, it is fine we are having a little family discussion that is all. Lance is one of my many distant cousins no one knows that I have," James Coaltonstone explained. "We are trying to come to an amiable agreement."

"We might not be a traditional family but we rumble like many families do on Christmas day, maybe not as fast or as hard as we did when we were young, but we sure have a lot to be grateful for. Ginger is alive and seems to be unharmed, Christina is expecting a little one in July making me an expectant great grandfather." Lance Diamond said getting up from the ground, and dusting himself off.

"How do you know you are having a great grandson?" James Coaltonstone asked.

"Jackson from the PPZ told me." Lance said as he handed his handkerchief to James who was wiping the blood from his nose with his sleeve.

"Jackson from the PPZ told you? Well how would he know?" James Coaltonstone asked.

"I noticed Christina going in and out of the bathroom a lot during the last couple of days," John Bell said. "That is exactly what my wife used to do during the early stages of our pregnancy, so I thought that was why she was keeping to herself and not joining our discussions in the executive lounge."

"Jackson from PPZ told you? Christina never mentioned this to me, why would she mention it to a paparazzo of all people?"

James Coaltonstone sounded shocked, realizing how old he must really be. How could he be so attracted to the woman carrying his first grandson?

"I don't think Christina knows yet, though she suspects of course," Lance Diamond said.

"What? My God, you are just as nutty as you were when we were kids." James Coaltonstone said.

"But you sir are bloodier. Now enough time wasted. We must consider the best way to get Ginger out of that hell pit. As soon as the shaft 6-E becomes operational and the elevator is installed, if all goes well we will be able to bring Ginger back up to the surface in about ten to fifteen days in one piece.

Dianne Black was always ready to record any news worthy moment, regardless of how exhausted she felt.

"Welcome viewers to another live broadcast from the Pitville Mine Disaster of 2030. Lance Diamond, the majority owner of the famous Black Rock Mines and a member of the Big Seven Coal Group, will be financing Ginger Goodwin's rescue from "Section E" deep in Mine Five. Mr. Diamond has been directing the creation of a 'line of air' which will be sending compressed air down into Chamber E. It is a miracle that Ginger Goodwin has survived all three mine explosions." Dianne said in her best broadcasting voice. "Mr. Diamond would you like to add anything?"

"We will work around the clock, together," Lance Diamond promised.

"I still don't understand how you could have done this to anyone's grandson, let alone mine. He happens to be your son even if you won't recognize that fact," Lance whispered to James Coaltonstone while sounding disgusted.

"You are so lucky that privacy laws include DNA, or I would have your splattered all over the place right now," James Coaltonstone replied.

"Why you, isn't that what I should be telling you? It was your cold heartedness that drove my daughter to suicide, and it is your cold heartedness that might kill your son. I would rather die than let that happen," Lance Diamond proclaimed as Dianne Black deliberately changed her position so that she could stand between the two most famous men on Tut Island.

"I am sorry sir; did you say that Ginger Goodwin was your grandson? Dianne asked, disturbed that she almost missed such an interesting bit of information.

Jackson stood there filming the scene, wondering if there could be another place in the world as tragic as Pitville.

"Damn you paparazzi. I said 'is'. Ginger Goodwin is alive and well. Ginger Goodwin still exists therefore he is. And yes, Ginger Goodwin is my grandson. And instead of intruding in my affairs, why can't you see that Stonely Mountain top is on fire? Why aren't you out there finding out the cause, and while you are at it, get the volunteer fire department up there, instead of engaging in idle gossip. You paparazzi could cause the decline of modern civilization."

"Sir, that is not fair. You know we were instrumental in finding Ginger Goodwin," Dianne responded defensively to Lance's harsh words.

"I know and for that I am very grateful. I am just saying, and I know this from my own experience, we have to go forward and remain positive. Otherwise our negativity could bring us all down," Lance said. Our duty to ourselves and to each other is to progress forward. We shouldn't think it right to pry into other people's business especially when such prying could be harmful and contribute to the decline of our town and the decline of each other. We must make opportunities not destroy them."

"My job is to explain…"

"No, your job is to know what needs to be public and what needs to be private. We need to know if the air we are breathing while in Pitville is toxic. Mayor Stern should be submitting a request for toxic air and contamination monitoring. You could possibly encourage him to do so."

As the fire raged it threatened to change Stonely Mountain's landscape within days if not hours. Considering PPZ always billed itself to be the first network to break a story which was in the public interest, they were doing a shoddy job.

"Why don't you find the source of those flames and smoke before they are able to engulf Stonely Mountain?" Lance Diamond added.

As Dianne looked towards Stonely Mountain, she too

noticed the smoke and the flames.

"Oh my God Stonely Mountain is on fire," Dianne exclaimed as Jackson raised the red bandana that was tied to his neck, so that it covered his mouth and nose. Jackson, with his video camera in hand, zoomed-in on the beautiful mountain top's landscape as he wondered if there was ever a more toxic and tragic place than Pitville.

Chapter 32:
Creating A Link

Wednesday December 25th, 2030, around 1:00 PM.
Location: Communication Center above Mine Five.

As everyone gathered inside the waiting room which was just another tent connected to the communication center which was also a tent, everyone sat comfortably waiting their turn to speak with Ginger. Everyone included Ginger's doctors, Christina and Mathew Watson, Lance Diamond and two of his attendants; they all sat patiently waiting to take turns to speak to Ginger wishing him a happy birthday and a merry Christmas. It was hard to know whether to be happy since Ginger had been found or sad because Ginger could not be rescued yet.

Lance Diamond won the draw to go first.

"Ginger, can you hear me? I am your maternal granddaddy. If you allow me I would be honored to stand by your side, which I should have done thirty years ago, and get you through this. And for the life of me I will not let any nincompoop tear us apart ever again or leave you down in that hell pit.

As Lance Diamond put the radio closer to his ear, then he added:

"Your Daddy is James Coaltonstone."

Lance could hear a loud oh my God. Coaltonstone almost let me die here? He didn't even bother to uncap the borehole in the rescue chamber to see if I was here. I thought I was going to die down here. I thought I was going to run out of air. I thought I was never going to see the surface again. And what did that creep do to my mother?"

"There is lots of time to go over everything. Now that I have found you, I will always be here for you. I am never going to let you go or let you die down there. I will always be here for you son, as long as I live and if the Lord willing even for longer than that," Lance Diamond said.

"We have so much to catch up on, you just rest now son, and whatever you need I will try to get for you.

I have had many Christmases in my day, and this is the best one I have ever had. I have met my grandson and I am expecting a great grandson.

There wasn't a day that went by when I did not think of you. Not one day. And you have turned out to be someone that I am proud to call my grandson," Lance confessed. "Christina is the next one in line to talk to you."

"How do you know I am expecting?" Christina asked, "I haven't got my results back yet from Doctor Knight?" Christina added wondering why so many people knew about the results of this private matter before she was able to find out for herself.

"Being part of the old boys club has its advantages dear." Lance Diamond said while he gave her a gentle hug. "Now you go in there and remind Ginger that his Granddaddy is going to take care of everything while he is still able."

"Ginger can you hear me?" Christina asked as she talked through the radio.

She could hear him say yes.

"I missed you so much. The hole you left in my life was so big. It was unbelievable.

Christina could hear Ginger's reply.

"It is not nearly as big as the one I am in right now. Is it true? Are you really expecting our baby?"

"I don't know. I haven't been told the results of my pregnancy test yet. But it seems that someone has told your grandfather so it must be true. Thank God for your Granddaddy, you know he punched old Coaltonstone in the nose? Anyway, your Granddaddy is arranging everything and if anyone will be able to get you out of that hole, it will be your granddaddy. Lance Diamond is not letting anyone ignore or forget you or him. He will get you out of there. Maybe it will take a bit of time. They think around 10 to 15 days. It takes about a day to drill 65 feet very carefully. They sealed all the passageways you know. We were all frantic," Christina said.

"Doctor Knight has your asthma medication and a bunch of things even a tooth brush and toothpaste.

Do you know anything about Deep Coal? They are saying that you are Deep Coal?" Christina asked Ginger, not knowing how it could be Ginger since Deep Coal showed up only after Ginger became trapped in the mine.

Christina could hear Ginger say that he was in deep coal. Ginger also added that he thought that he could hear a group of people making noises in the mine while he was waiting to be rescued. Ginger said that he thought it might be the rescue team but the tall bots could not register any of the common technology rescue team members carry.

"Well the rumor mongers are saying it is you. They were trying to pin it on Smoothman and Paylor but they didn't have direct access to your forty-nine internal reports," Christina said.

"I really don't know what you are talking about," Christina heard Ginger say.

"I still think old Coaltonstone would have had you entombed if he had his way regardless if he is your biological father," Christina replied.

"I can't believe that creep is my father. My God, what a shocker," Christina heard Ginger say.

'I was sure they were going to seal every borehole and shaft in the mine. I was so frantic. Then your incredible Granddaddy Diamond appeared from nowhere with Doctor Smith and a team of lawyers. I just couldn't believe it, it was like a miracle. You have to come back to me. I can't imagine life without you. I am so grateful that you are alive. I realize now, that I am just not complete without you, Ginger," Christina replied.

'This is the best Christmas present ever. I spent so much time trying to not imagine the worst possible thing that could have happened to you," Christina said as she wiped her nose with her sleeve. Lance made a motion to one of his attendants, and a clean handkerchief was handed to Christina, and then the attendant discreetly returned to where he had been sitting.

Christina could hear Ginger reply.

"I know what you mean. I was fighting back my worse thoughts too. My worst fear was to never see you again without saying I love you. Without giving you the ring I have had in my pocket for months, waiting for the perfect time to give it to you, to ask you, if you would marry me. I want you to know how much I love you. Even if I can't get out of here, my love will never die." Christina could hear Ginger say.

The End

THE CONSPIRACY: The MINER BOOK 2

Chapter 1

Beginning of In-Reach entry, LOG #6:
by Christina Watson
(Accounting Assistant to Alex Coaltonstone).

December 25th 2030, around 6:00 p.m.

I am sitting here alone in my office. The waiting is torture.

Doctor Knight believes that this private journaling is very important and will help me to maintain some positivity while creating ownership of my self-identity. But she hasn't told me whether I am pregnant or not and she hasn't really told me the effect the pit atmosphere will have on Ginger's lung condition. I think he has something worse than asthma.

I was assigned a new job with a substantial raise today. James Coaltonstone dropped in my new assignment. I found out on the internet that Coaltonstone is giving the miners low interest loans so when this is all over they will owe Coaltonstone. He always finds a way to get ahead, no matter what. So my new assignment is to proof read his manuscript, "The Blessing: Black Diamonds." At first I thought he was joking and that he was going to give me updates concerning Ginger's rescue but he told me there is nothing to tell.

I can't imagine my life without Ginger. I really need him back. He has been stuck down there since Sunday and it is now Wednesday, Christmas day. It was wonderful to talk to him. The communication system worked without a hitch, thanks to Ginger's grandfather. It is easy enough to forget how much danger Ginger is still. I wish there were more people, than just Ginger's grandfather, willing to take a chance.

There are lots of people on both sides of the security fence coming and going. People are waving signs demanding that Ginger is rescued no matter the cost. Other signs being waved more aggressively are demanding the inclusion of the Exclusion League's policies. As I write, militia men and cadets are building a new wall, around the security fence between the public and Coaltonstone Mines' administration building. I feel like I am on the wrong side of the fence.

There are thousands of people standing together, some still in their mining clothes, complete with helmets and lights waiting for Ginger to ascend from Mine Five.

There are nuns, priests and pastors; I think I see a travelling rabbi too. Most of these people must be out of town since I have never seen them before except those waving vote for A.B. Peel placards. Most of them are here to support Ginger I hope.

End of In-Reach entry, LOG #6 by Christina Watson (Accounting Assistant to Alex Coaltonstone).

Chapter 2

December 25th 2030, around 6:15 p.m.

"Good Evening and welcome to Black Times. This is Dianne Black broadcasting live from Pitville Mine Disaster of 2030, on Christmas Day, which is also local hero; Ginger Goodwin's birthday. Unfortunately, Ginger Goodwin is still trapped 1,200 feet below the surface, as we speak.

Mr. Goodwin's location was discovered only after hours of PPZ's News Team's tireless investigative journalistic effort.

My moles tell me that all Coaltonstone Mine Five employees will be eligible for loan interest loans. Considering how high interests are at present, loans below market should be wonderful news for the miners. These loans will help the miners and their dependants subsist during the time the mine is closed.

At this time, we cannot stress how much, we at PPZ wish Mr. Goodwin a speedy rescue.

Ginger Goodwin's beautiful partner, Christina Watson communicated with her beau for a short time earlier this afternoon. The first explosion in Mine Five occurred at 5:20 a.m., Sunday morning, and many at PPZ are asking why didn't G.O.D.'s representatives facilitate communications with Ginger in a timelier manner?

According to Mr. Goodwin, the emergency telemagnetic radio, located in Safety Chamber in section E, has been in working order. The equipment survived the explosion which occurred in

240

Section C partly due to design, and partly due to luck, according to our moles.

Now let us see if the beautiful Christina Watson will share a few words with us. As you can see the office building housing Coaltonstone Mines is luxurious. This long hall which leads to Christina's office is decorated with the usual Christmas fair including tinsel and lights.

"Hello Christina Watson."

"My God Dianne, you scared me, I was just writing my personal journal, I wasn't expecting you, are we live?

"Yes we are! We have so much to celebrate; just one miracle after another. Ginger being found in one piece and a little one on the way. We, my viewers and I, are here with you. We know how hard this has been for you, especially with you expecting and all."

"How did you know I was pregnant? I don't even know yet. I mean I haven't talked to my doctor about my results yet."

"Well what do you want to know? It looks like you are going to have a boy and he is a healthy looking 21 week old fetus. He is adorable."

"You actually have a picture and I haven't even been told yet? How does that happen?"

"Christina, you know better to question how resourceful we are at PPZ. It is my job to know everything. We, and me in particularly, never reveal our sources. How was your visit with Pitville's hero?"

"The visit wasn't long enough. I wish they could find a way to get him out of there. I am so frightened for him, for me, for our little boy," Christina said as she struggled not to cry.

"You Know Christina, we all admire your courage, strength and sincerity."

"Thank you. I must say I am feeling overwhelmed. I have been waiting for news about Ginger and about my own condition, and I had no idea you could find out about such matters before me."

"I can't reveal my source but I can say one thing about the atmosphere on this side of the Security Fence, which is now being referred to as a wall. There is one atmosphere on the public side of the wall and another atmosphere on the private side. Right now everyone's movements are being watched by John Bell and his security staff but that is nothing new, my moles tell me."

"I was told that I would be better off not leaving the Admin Building until this horrible situation is resolved, but nothing seems to be happening. I must say that the military presence around here scares me, partly because I have never been around so people with so many guns. And they all seem to be lining up around the wall. I don't get why they are even building a wall. I guess I will just have to hang out in my office and wait."

"I just want to remind our audience that it is alleged that Ginger Goodwin wrote forty nine reports in forty seven days, complete with air quality measurements and photographs and every single report which we have in our possession, was ignored. Can you comment on this situation Christina?

"Not really. I don't know how you got hold of those documents any more than I can figure out how you got hold of my medical records. I doubt very much Ginger has anything to do with it at all. If anything I think Ginger is being set up at a time when he is the most helpless."

"So you believe that Ginger Goodwin is not Deep Coal? Tell me why."

"I never heard of Deep Coal until PPZ discovered him. I have seen no real evidence that Ginger Goodwin, my Ginger has intentionally revealed any privileged Mine information. Ginger has been trapped in Mine Five since Sunday and he needs rescuing. I and my son Mathew need Ginger alive and by our sides."

"We all respect and admire Ginger Goodwin for his selfless action which saved Mine Five's morning crew on Sunday. And according to my sources, Deep Coal is thrilled that you are expecting a little boy sometime in late May or early June."

"Everyone seems to know all about my condition except me. I don't see how I can possibly officially be pregnant before my pregnancy is confirmed by my physician."

"Now, it is I who has an important question, and I certainly do judge. Do you believe that Ginger Goodwin is Deep Coal?"

"Of course I don't believe that? How could he be? He has been trapped in that mine since early Sunday morning. It has been three days that he has been down there. No one ever heard of Deep Coal until after he was trapped. I am grateful that PPZ was able to locate Ginger, but he is still in terrible danger. Did your source reveal Ginger's lung condition to you? He has been officially diagnosed with asthma but I think he has something more than that. He is trapped 1,200 feet under the ground and no one seems to be doing anything to get him out of there."

"Are you angry Christina?"

"Of course I am angry. I wish someone would rescue Ginger before another disaster strikes. This rain is scaring me. The smoke coming out of the sidewalk terrifies me. So many terrible things are happening and they are happening all at once."

"Well the weather conditions are certainly getting worse but reporting it is not my job."

"I know. Soon we will be under another water boil advisory," Christina said. "The rain will make the acid conditions in the mine worse, as in big time."

"What I meant, Christina, was that the weather report is separate from this report."

"Well that is stupid. The weather affects the safety of the mine."

"I thought you would be grateful that PPZ found Ginger.

"Of course I am grateful. Finding Ginger is the first step, and it shouldn't have been so hard. If he had been someone more important, like James Coaltonstone, I am sure he would have been found sooner. I hate waiting for the rescue to start. Everyone is talking and no one is doing anything."

"Talk about talking, I heard that you had a visit with Ginger. How is he doing? How is his lung condition?"

"Talking to Ginger this afternoon seemed surreal. He was so trapped down there you wouldn't believe it. Everything is so confusing. The militias are all over town, either working to expand the security fence or they are just staring at whoever they please, but no one except Ginger's grandfather seems to be doing anything to help actually rescue him."

"What do you mean exactly? I am sure that the rescue teams are doing their best. You must realize Christina that this situation is very complicated."

"Well the militias seem to be more organized and active than the rescue team. They had their guns strapped to their backs and were working on different parts of the security fence and now it looks like a wall in some parts. Everywhere I look, there are armed people in militia uniforms either looking out over the wall, or working on expanding the fence into a wall."

"Christina, I am sure they know what they are doing."

"What are they doing? I have heard nothing and I wish someone would at least tell me what they are actually doing. I hope they can pull him up to the surface without a lot of delay. They are going to send things down to him to improve communications and to make him more comfortable. They are sending things down to him in a tube through the air ventilation which is too narrow and too dangerous to expand into an escape shaft."

"Have you heard anything from G.O.D.?

"No nothing." Christina replied.

"The Government's Official Directors' office hasn't returned our calls either," Dianne said as she could see Jackson mouth out the word 'CUT'.

"While we were talking, Ginger was coughing so hard that I fear if he doesn't get out of there soon the damage to his lungs could be irreversible."

"I am sure everyone is doing the best they can. I am sure he is thrilled to be expecting a little one."

"He is. I think his grandfather told him. His grandfather told me that he heard I was expecting from the Old Boys Club. I find the whole thing rather strange since I haven't even received my results yet, or talked with my family doctor concerning my condition. I am glad Ginger's grandfather is here, and I am glad Ginger's grandfather is so rich, maybe now Ginger too will be too rich to ignore.

Chapter 3

December 25th 2030, around 6:30 p.m.

"Before we begin this meeting, I would like to apologize for interrupting everyone's Christmas day celebrations and I would like to introduce to you Jethro and Bill, who will be assisting John Bell with security," Mayor Stern said while Jethro and Bill waved while trying to maintain a pleasant manner in a very unpleasant situation.

"Everyone's Christmas has been shot this year. I can't remember a worse Christmas," James Coaltonstone said.

"That lowlife bar deal has finally gone through, so Pitville is now the proud owner of the Thirsty Pit'.

"Why?' Susan Jones asked.

"Because no one else wanted to buy it, and it has been under court ordered foreclosure for some time. So the plan is to tear it down and widen the roads, and bring in more coal trucks and send out more coal," Mayor Stern explained.

"How can anyone think of celebrating Christmas while Ginger is still trapped in the pit?" Susan asked as she looked around the room.

"What else could go wrong?" Don Bell asked while staring at his com-phone

"Well, I had my car stolen when I ran into Starbucks this morning," Mayor Stern grumbled.

"How did that happen?" Don Bell asked.

"We know how it happened. We are letting these strangers from outside take control over our way of life. We need to be more vigilante, We need those lazy cadets to work faster so that wall I ordered can start protecting us by keeping those people out of our world." John Bell said as he started to add more items to his list of things he wanted to control.

"Are you joking?" Susan asked.

"Why would I be?" John replied.

"I suppose it was partly my fault. I left the car running as I rushed in to Starbucks to get a quick coffee," Mayor Stern admitted.

"We used to always leave our doors open and cars running," James Coaltonstone said.

"It is a miracle that Ginger survived the explosion. We should be very thankful that Ginger was found alive by the Minese," Susan said. "I have updated all of my notes. I was referring to Ginger Goodwin in the past tense, which would now be incorrect since he is very much alive which I suppose makes this a very miraculous Christmas." Susan glanced around the room in her usual cheerful manner. "I have a question. Why can I hear and feel heavy freight coming in and going out when all of our shipments are officially cancelled due to the explosion in Mine Five?"

"Susan, what did we say about talking?"

"I am sorry sir, but if I can't communicate, my notes won't be a true record of what is being said in our meeting."

"Susan, please," Mayor Stern said as he stared at Susan.

"Okay, what should we discuss first?" Mayor Stern asked.

"We now know that our two new enforcer bots are with Ginger, so I have hired these two new detectives sir as replacements. I also suggest that we discuss implementation of a pass system, so that anyone who is moving about will be obligated to explain themselves, that way the strangers will know that they are being watched," John Bell said as he looked at his brother who was staring at him in disbelief.

"That Ginger seems to find a way to mess up my plans. Those bots were meant to be for security not to be data banks. Those bots are the state of the art bot-drones."

"Ginger must have assumed that the bots waiting in my office were the bots that he had been requesting for years. I had them sitting in my office, since John's office space was being used for something secret," Don Bell explained.

"Don, I was having a meeting with Bill and Jethro and we were discussing the feasibility of implementing a pass system, so that we can keep track of people's comings and goings.

"Splendid," Mayor Stern and James Coaltonstone said at the same time.

"Bill and Jethro used to work for Senator Puffy, Sir.

"Oh, isn't that the Senator who is accused of double dipping?" Mayor Stern enquired.

"Yes sir he is."

"Then I would guess that Jethro and Bill are very knowledgeable in the art of surveillance techniques." James Coaltonstone stated as he took a sip from the flask which he always concealed in his jacket pocket.

"Yes Sir. That is right; they are very knowledgeable and have connections to our Government's Official Directors surveillance equipment," John Bell confirmed.

"Are they for or against this Minese Exclusion League? Mine's Seven and eight have been hiring primarily Minese. The Minese are good workers, dependable, and they demand very little as long as we are willing and able to send their bones back to their home country after seven years from the day of their death. This is why Mine Seven and Mine Eight are economically feasible to run and Mine Five is not." James Coaltonstone said as he took another sip from his flask.

"The original meeting was mostly about designing a pass system so that we can determine who is illegal and who is authorized to be living in Coalton valley. Since the pit explosion we have considering the escalating of our pass system."

"And what about Deep Coal and his sharing of internal data with the PPZ," James Coaltonstone said as eyed the detectives up and down.

"The usual suspects are being watched very closely sir," John Bell said as he looked over his notes.

"Well they better be. That Ginger Goodwin is no fool. If it is him, it will not be easy to catch him in the act," James said as he exhaled cigar smoke.

"James, once we are under a state of emergency, we will have the authority to detain anyone as we see fit, regardless if we have evidence or not," Mayor Stern said as John Bell nodded.

"Sir if I may add, I think we should be careful that we don't provoke the crowd. The threat of being placed in glass cage is known to drive the weaker minds into psychosis." Don Bell said as he glanced at Susan Jones hoping that she would back him up.

"Sir, we need to rescue Ginger first before we can arrest him," Susan said nervously.

"Susan."

"I am sorry Mr. Stern."

"First we extract Goodwin from the pit, then we arrest him, then we find the evidence. I also suggest as the militia constructs our secondary security fence we should authorize the inclusion of Walmart, Wendy's and McDonalds within its perimeters," James Coaltonstone said in one breath and smoke escaped from his nostrils.

"Yes that is a splendid idea James," Ted Stern said admiringly. "That way the outsiders with campers can continue to camp at Walmart and eat at McDonalds and Wendy's."

"Do you think we should inform our stakeholders?" Susan asked.

"Certainly, but we will do it after we declare a state of emergency and after the walls are up," James Coaltonstone and Ted Stern said at the same time.

"Our cadets must still be paid over time but daily eight hour shifts are free to us, and the academy will be paying the cadets with credit earned toward their credentials," John Bell explained feeling exceptionally tired.

"I think it is mostly our local senator who is stirring up negative feelings against the Minese. Not all of them are here illegally." Mayor Stern said; not yet sure what side of the controversy he should be taking.

"That A.B. Peel and his Exclusion League cronies, will never get my vote. He is always stirring up local miners. All he wants is their vote; nothing more and nothing less," James Coaltonstone complained trying not to sound as agitated as he felt.

"My wife is on the Pitville Outreach Committee. She always welcomes those people. We don't believe in the 'not in our backyard' philosophy. That sort of snobbery does not come from us but it seems that the Exclusion League is growing legs." Mayor Stern said hoping to clarify his liberal standing in the community.

What will Jethro and Bill be doing?" James Coaltonstone enquired.

"Officially Jethro and Bill's duties will be secret," John Bell explained.

"They will be spying," Don said.

"Not exactly Don. We will be mixing with the riff-raff below there, and we are also looking into whether any of the illegals know about Mina's high altitude testing of nuclear testing. These tests in outer space," Bill explained.

"I thought those sort of tests were illegal now since the last few tests fried underground cables, telephone wires and street lights," Susan said while writing down notes.

"Yes, they are, and so is illegal mining. The Pitville Airbase depends on satellites and we believe it is not beyond the Minese capability to use high-altitude electromagnetic pulses, which is usually referred to EMPs, to kill our satellites. Nuclear weapons testing in space will also create a an artificial radiation belt which can kill our satellites too, even unintentionally.

"Why us? Why here? Why not stick to illegal mining and fuel their war machine that way?" Don Bell asked.

"Possibly because we have a base here, we also had what the Minese are interpreting as suspicious experimental explosions which some conspiracy theorists are attributing to the reason why

Pitville and Buzzard Creek high schools were closed down due two hundred students in one school alone getting sick."

"We know why so many students fell ill so quickly," Ted Stern said. "Our students fell ill due to a regrettable outbreak of the Norwalk virus and nothing more. There is not one shred of evidence that the recent experimental explosions have anything to do with our students becoming ill so suddenly," Ted Stern said in defense of the local base.

"And we have no proof it wasn't. We don't even have proof that is it was the Norwalk virus any more than we have proof that the sudden illness was the direct result of the experimental explosions," Susan said as she avoided eye contact.

"Changing the topic slightly; I am deeply concerned that the Minese Exclusion League is gaining legs due to all these rumors being spread about. I think we need to stay focused on the pit fire and what we can do about it so it is controlled. I am very concerned that fires that seem to have no other explanation are occurring so randomly, and I have said it before, I believe that the explosion in Mine Five was caused by lightning. I need Mine Eight to be producing dividends for my shareholders from the Old Countries. We have invested millions into that mine, and as you know we are still building tunnels to connect our newly installed railway lines and harbor fronts. We are even building a tunnel under Coaltonstone Manor. We must not let the Minese Exclusion League ruin, my, our plans," James Coaltonstone said as he looked around to make sure that everyone was listening to him.

"I would like to discuss our plans concerning the out of town militia members and our need to card those outsiders surrounding our security fence and local riff-raff who may want to agitate this sensitive situation." John Bell, head of security said as he played with his wilting lettuce.

"Do you really think that is necessary to card all those people who came here to support Ginger? Don Bell asked still feeling guilty that his assistant in his department which was responsible for mine safety was trapped in Mine Five.

"Of course not! We just need to card the ones who look suspicious," John replied while glaring at his twin.

"Remember you two, wear your nametags. Last thing we need today is somebody getting you two mixed up. You John must be clearly identifiable as head of security as you Don must be clearly identifiable as head of mine safety," James Coaltonstone said while he watched Susan take notes.

"Susan why are you taking notes. What we are discussing is supposed to be secret."

"I am sorry sir.'

"It is okay Susan as long as you take those notes and shred them this instant. We don't need to be giving Deep Coal, whoever he may be, inside information and remember we all must tip toe lightly around that security fence. Remember there are more of them than us and the parents of those cadets vote. I don't want any of them getting hurt. I would like to place a motion that we raise the hotel tax.

"I will second that motion Ted," James said.

"I will third it," John Bell added.

"Why do we always meet in the board room at the Pitville Inn whenever we are going to raise taxes?" Susan asked.

"It is tradition," Mayor Stone replied.

"I must continue with my expansion," James Coaltonstone said as he took a drink from his flask. "John Bell, please stand up and report on our enforcement strategy."

Susan stood up and walked towards the window. Mayor Stern stood up and did the same thankful for the opportunity to change the subject.

"I have never seen a Minese in anyone's backyard. They keep to themselves as far as I know."

"Susan," Mayor Stern interjected before James Coaltonstone interrupted him.

"Most of the Minese have spent the best years of their lives here. They send money home to their families. They don't ask for much. They are so hard working. And their labor has built this region just as much as anyone's have. I think this Minese Exclusion League business is deplorable and despicable."

"This view is splendid. I can see the drones and the ship carrying our supplies from here," Susan said before she was interrupted.

"Susan, please," Mayor Stern interjected.

"Drones? Are those drones going to be used to spy on all those people waiting to meet Ginger?" Don Bell asked. Don still considered himself to be the head safety manager for Mine five until notified otherwise.

"I think those Drones are meant to be protecting our shipment."

"Shipment of what?

"John, control your brother or I will have to send him somewhere dark and gloomy to count things, it is hard enough to follow this conversation as it is," James Coaltonstone ordered.

"We are in the final stages of re-negotiating our lease, with the Government's Official Directors. The city has agreed to manage the operation of Buzzard Creek Dump for the next twenty five years," Mayor Stern said. "I really do think Ginger's concerns related to the fire hazard posed by our dump's present location are grandiose, to say the least.

"My guess is that Ginger is right sir. There is smoke coming out of the sidewalk, smoke coming out of the mountain area, it is just a matter of time smoke starts to come out of Buzzard Creek Dump," Susan Jones said before James Coaltonstone slammed his big fist down on the table in a fit of rage and yelled "What?"

"Now, Susan what did we say about talking. Your role is to take notes. As mayor, I am the one who assesses value placed on anyone, anything, and any place. Am I making myself clear, Susan?" Mayor Stern asked in a condescending tone which made Don soothe with anger as he typed on his com phone.

"I am glad to see someone is sitting quietly and taking notes; good work Don," James Coaltonstone said approvingly.

"Sir what is that glow coming out of that container ship?

"My god, that ship is on fire, I think we are under attack," Mayor Stern warned as he screamed and ducked under the table where he found James Coaltonstone already under and still smoking his cigar.

Chapter 4

December 25th 2030, around 7:00 p.m.

"Good evening to all and welcome back to 'Black Times' broadcasting live from the Pitville Hotel. As you can see behind me the entire fleet of Pitville ambulances are being employed to serve the injured, which may be at least a hundred. The container ship, King Coal, was carrying flammable goods from the mainland, when this terrible tragedy occurred. At this time we do not know officially what those goods were. Some reports are describing these goods to be explosives. This matter is under investigation and authorities are not speaking to any PPZ representative. Nevertheless we have a familiar face with us this evening, Doctor Smith.

"Thank you, Dr. Smith it very good of you to join us at such short notice."

"Well I can't stay long. I have many patients to attend. Glass was shattered all the way from Pitville Hotel where Mayor Stern was in a closed meeting and was covered in glass."

"Was Mayor Stern seriously injured? Are there others were injured? It seems there isn't a day that goes by where there isn't some horrible disaster occurring in Pitville," Dianne Black noted.

"It are sure getting our share of disasters. Windows exploded all along Main Street. The injured are filling the hospital emergency room, and I have never seen anything like this before. When the ship exploded it was not too far from Pitville Harbour which is right downtown, across from the street from the Pitville Hotel."

"How many people do you estimate have been hurt by shattered glass, Doctor Smith?"

"It is too early to know. So far there must be at least a hundred people, including Mayor Stern, who are being treated for glass related injuries.

Chapter 5

December 25ᵗʰ 2030, around 7:15 p.m.

Why is it whenever that Dianne Black talks to us I feel defensive and angry?" Jay wondered out loud.

"I don't know," Kevin replied.

"You are always on the defensive."

"No I am not, George."

"Okay!"

"I know what it is. I feel she keeps projecting these stereotypes onto us. She starts us at zero as if we didn't exist before she interviewed us. When the interview is over I think of all the things I wish she had asked me that are more important than the things that she actually did ask me," Jay said.

"I agree with Jay," Sam said. "And what really gets me upset is the way Ginger is being ignored while his lung condition is worsening by his entrapment."

"Exactly! And the entrapment keeps expanding as if we were all on different sides. Even getting this free alcohol instead of free energy drinks bugs me."

Chapter 6

December 25ᵗʰ 2030, around 8:00 p.m.

Are you sure that we are going the right way?" Kevin asked as he was feeling miserable and tired. The weight of the oxygen tank had taken its toll as he crawled behind his friends. The smell was horrid, and the smoke made seeing clearly very difficult.

"Of course I am sure," Sam said. This is our mine too. This is our coal and those illegals are stealing it from us. We go in there, and take their cable hoister and any equipment that we can get. If they chase us we show them our guns and then demand their lamps, then we get out and we close over the shaft opening the way we should have done a long time ago. We are getting Ginger out and we are going to give him a hero's welcome while he is still able to breathe."

"We can do it," Kevin said. "We just have to keep up the momentum."

"You mean act faster than the Minese. There they are," George said as loud as he could while whispering.

"Are you sure that we are going the right way? Why are there so many of them?" Same asked as his voice betrayed his fear and anxiety.

"I thought these tunnels would be more primitive than these," Jay said.

"What are all these crates for?" Sam asked no one in particular.

"I don't know. The signal is coming from over there and it is really strong," George said.

"I have never been on this side of Section E before; I never knew this section was so I have never seen such a nice looking pit railway before, I wonder where it goes." Jay said.

"What do you think is in all these crates? This tunnel sure doesn't smell anything like coal to me," Sam asked.

"You boys, stand up!" Ono commanded. He was a big Minese man holding onto his super-sized gun as tightly as he could; just in case his broken English was misunderstood. "What you do snooping around here?"

"We need help," George said.

"Help to do what? You look ignorant and sloppy." Ono said.

"Who are you to call us ignorant and sloppy?" Sam replied.

"We are all miners. We should respect that. I am George Smoothman, the morning crew's foreman. We need help freeing our friend and colleague, Ginger Goodwin. He freed us now we must free him. Only person on the surface who seems to be doing his best to organize a rescue is Ginger's grandfather, everyone else is sitting around, or building a wall around the security wall."

"We down here, including the ones who have passed to the other side, know who you speak of. The man who is now called deep coal by James Coaltonstone is on our side. Ginger Goodwin put his crew before himself. We go together and then go through tunnels and use gear that is in Mine Eight. I have key to door but this must remain secret. No one must ever know."

"What do you need?" Ono asked.

"We need at least a 1,200 foot ladder and air tanks," George said.

"I have a better idea. We get the tanks and back up batteries, and a stretcher, and we carry Ginger from the Safety Chamber and use the shaft lift to bring him out to the surface in Mine Eight," Ono suggested.

"If it is that easy why didn't control room arrange the same thing? Jay asked.'

"Mine Eight is not a coal mine. It is not official and no one would dare to question James Coaltonsmore, especially if he wins the election," Ono replied.

"You really think James Coaltonstone has a chance against A.B. Peel and his Exclusion League backers?" Jay asked.

"You don't?" Ono replied.

"So is Mine 8 just a coal mine then?" George asked.

"Of course not. Mine Eight is a Hemp Plantation. What you see, stays with you. We will get Ginger out, but we must never explain how. That will be the hard part."

"Is Mine Eight guarded?"

"No one guards what doesn't exist. If Mine Eight were guarded, someone would notice.

Chapter 7

December 25ᵗʰ 2030, around 9:00 p.m.

"And why wasn't the ventilation shaft in Section E made wide enough so that it could be used as an escape shaft?" Lance Diamond asked James Coaltonstone?

"We never thought an emergency exit would be necessary. Anyway having a second escape exit wasn't required, so did our best to keep expenses down so that we could stretch the limited resources that we had," James Coaltonstone replied defensively.

"Hold on, that young doctor, Dr. Ashley Knight just sent me an email." Lance said as he turned around and opened it. James stood on his toes to look over his shoulder.

"Is it about the baby?" James asked.

"I don't know, let me read it. James, this is private."

"Email isn't that private."

'Well this one is. It is addressed to me because it is private correspondence with a physician. James. Please will you give me some privacy?

"It is very long. It seems to be about some tests that my personal physician ordered last month, back home. Oh these doctors, they never tell you what you want to hear. She is advising rest. My God, I am the only one doing anything around here. If I could I would snap my fingers and just make everyone do their job. Instead, everyone is sitting around waiting for a member from G.O.D. to tell them what to do. I must free my grandson from that hell hole that you run, and I cannot do that while resting. Just look around. Everyone is resting. No one is doing anything but resting. My grandson is 1,200 feet below the surface without a basic escape route. As Ginger's lung condition worsens, as we speak, this doctor is telling me to rest?

"Are you ill?"

"Of course not."

"Ginger will be dead soon, if we don't get him out of that hell hole."

"Let me read that letter."

"No, you can't. I deleted it."

Chapter 8

- ### December 25th 2030, around 9:30 p.m.

"To all my faithful viewers welcome back to 'Black Times.' All of us at the PPZ wish that Mayor Stern has a speedy recovery. The container ship 'King Coal' exploded just minutes before it was to dock at Pitville Harbor. There were at least a hundred people lining up in the Pitville's Emergency Rooms, needing treatment from shattered glass. More on this news breaking story as it unfolds," Dianne paused for a moment and then began reading the next page of her script.

"It is hard to believe that it has been only two days since the early morning explosion in Mine Five, which occurred 1,200 feet below Pitville, a small town situated in the beautiful Coalton Valley," Dianne Black explained as she spoke into the microphone."

"While we speak, we are walking towards the Miners' Cafeteria. There is George A. Smoothman, foreman for the morning crew sitting at the head of that table in the center of the Miner's Cafeteria. Good evening Mr. Smoothman. Do you have a few words to share with the world?"

"Good evening, Dianne, thank you for having me on your show. As the head foreman of the morning crew, I witnessed how Ginger Goodwin prevented us from walking into a pending mine Explosion early Sunday Morning by putting our safety before his own. If it wasn't for Ginger Goodwin we would all be trapped in Mine Fine or worse, instead of just him."

"Thank you, Mr. Smoothman."

"And sitting beside Mr. Smoothman is Jay T. Paylor, Assistant Foreman of the morning crew."

"Good evening Mr. Paylor, would you like to share a word with our faithful 'Pitville Mine Disaster' viewers this evening?"

"I sure do. I would like to wish everyone a Merry Christmas. As the assistant foreman, I am second in command; therefore I will delegate myself to cutting the second piece of cake and to opening the second bottle of beer even though this is actually my first. As you can see, here we are having Ginger Goodwin's birthday party and our own Christmas party all in one. We would also like to report that Ginger was wearing his birthday hat, but we can't. Here is to you Bro. I would like to wish a speedy recovery to Mayor Stern and to all of those injured in the container ship explosion, which happened just a little while ago,"

"Thank you, Mr. Paylor."

"Hold on, I am not done. If it wasn't for Ginger Goodwin, we would have been trapped down in that pit, instead of him. Ginger left the safety of his office and actually descended into the mine before we did. He was investigating why the gas monitor numbers were not being transmitted."

"Do you know why these numbers were not being transmitted, Mr. Paylor?"

"Yes, I do, because the methane monitor had been turned off by someone."

"How do you know that, Mr. Paylor?"

"Ginger sent a message to Christina, Ginger's fiancée, right after he realized that someone had turned the monitor off. I really hope that this matter gets investigated as soon as possible, and I really hope that Ginger Goodwin is rescued before something horrible happens to him. I hate to say this but I am starting to believe in the Black Diamond Curse."

"Come on Jay," George scolded.

"Thank you Mr. Smoothman and Mr. Paylor. I am Dianne Black bringing to you live coverage from the heart of the Pitville mine disaster of 2030."

"Hold on we are not done. We want to say that we don't know much about the Pitville Harbor explosion. We have been in the Miners' Cafeteria all day, which is in the basement and doesn't have any windows and the news we are given is regulated. We want to make sure that the focus stays on rescuing Ginger. We are concerned that rescuers from out of town may rely too much on the maps they are given. Many of the tunnels down below have never been mapped or documented."

"I am sorry Mr. Paylor, we are pressed for time. We need to get to the hospital and interview some of the victims of the container explosion and of course we must hear from our sponsors. I am sure that the professionals are thankful for your concern, but they know more about what is going on down there than you do."

"Right! I have only been working down there for fifteen years, so what do I know?" Jay replied sounding hurt.

"And another issue which is being ignored is all this rain. You didn't ask us what we thought about all this rain and how it could hamper rescuing Ginger while making the conditions in the mine worse and more acidic."

"You must know by now, Mr. Paylor, I am not PPZ's weather girl. I understand your concern, but this story is about the mine disaster."

"This rain could make the flooding in Mine Five more dangerous for Ginger."

"I am sorry Mr. Paylor, Dianne said before Jay grabbed the mike from Dianne.

"Hold on. I want to know something. When are they getting Ginger out of the pit?"

"You have to be patient. I heard that Coaltonstone Mines is providing you with all these refreshments free of charge. James Coaltonstone is doing his best."

"If that disaster down in the pit had been prevented we could have been celebrating with Ginger. And we would have had enough money of our own to pay for our own party," Jay said forgetting to hide the hostility he was feeling.

"I am sure that you are very tired, Mr. Paylor. The Government's Official Directors will do everything they can to assist all of Coaltonstone mines' employees."

"Did G.O.D. actually say that?" And what is James Coaltonstone actually doing to help us miners recover from our pay loss?

"As far as I know James Coaltonstone will be arranging loans for you all. Goodbye and Merry Christmas."

"And now a word from our sponsor," Steve Jones said as he watched the interaction from his PPZ control room at the Eagle Eye Inn.

Chapter 9

December 25ᵗʰ 2030, around 10:00 p.m.

"You know I feel like we are wasting our lives here," Kevin said as he sipped on his third beer.

"Aww, you just feel that way because we almost lost our lives today and everyone else is going about as if we are not in the loop anymore. Don't forget that thousands of people are congregating around the Admin building and Mine Five, waiting for Ginger to show his red head. It not like we are really alone," George said as he faced Jay.

Jay replied, "Sure we are being forgotten. Now we are out of work we are nothing. We have no function. And this loan business that James Coaltonstone is pushing on us doesn't just scare me, it makes me angry. **We don't need more debt and James Coaltonstone doesn't need more money.**"

"We are all feeling out of the loop. Wanting a way in and a way out," George said looking at Sam Jones for support."

"Who doesn't wish for a way out of Pitville?" Sam said.

"And where would we go?" Kevin asked his cousin.

"Talk about needing a way out. Just think about Ginger. He really needs a way to escape his situation. If we start feeling defeated now how is Ginger supposed to feel tomorrow and the next day? Ginger hasn't lost the battle yet and we need to be there encouraging him to remain strong and positive until we get him out of there," Jay said.

"We sure look like we have lost the battle. We have lost our bonuses; we have lost our jobs which means we have lost the entitlement to company owned homes. Ginger is still stuck down there in the pit with no one is doing anything except saying sweet nothings," Kevin replied.

"Well Ginger's grandfather is giving the Coaltonstones a run for their money," Sam said. "So changing the subject a bit; I wonder how much free beer the Coaltonstones will give us before we become pitiful alcoholics," Sam said.

"It seems that everything around here is done around us, to us, and against us. Instead of someone in the know telling us what is really going on, they leave us out of the loop, they start us at zero whenever they speak to us so we never get ahead, and whatever we say makes us appear as if we don't know what is going on," Kevin said.

"Well we don't," Sam replied.

"Yeah, I know what Kevin and Sam are saying. It is not just our lives being turned upside down that makes us angry. You have all seen my mother sitting outside rain or shine waiting for the mail ever since the Harris family's mailbox was stolen. Well, two days ago, a man came around with some contraption to measure distance, and he was measuring the property lines surrounding my mother's house. My mother said that the only thing the man said to her was you better get out of the way if you don't want your picture taken. And then he took about five pictures of her house and left, leaving my mother worried cause she had no idea what was going on. It could have been the city, it could have been the bank, it could have been someone mapping buildings on top of undocumented coal deposits though her house was the only one she noticed was having its property line measured," Sam wasn't sure what to say next so he took a sip of his beer.

"If Ginger were here you know what he would say," Kevin said while he ate two peanuts.

"Yes, he would say that we are at the bottom of this crony capitalism which only favors those in the loop and locks everyone else out.

"Yes, and if anyone hears us talking like this, we could be accused of being communists, so tone it down," Sam whispered nervously.

"Hey guys George just got a skype message from Christina," Jay said as took a closer look at the tiny print.

"Stop looking over my shoulder Jay, this could be private which means a confidential message," George responded trying to sound like he was still in charge. "I know it says confidential, but it isn't private the way some messages are and maybe we share what Christina is seeing up there. So I will read it out loud," George added.

Confidential:

Skype message to George Smoothman (Foreman of the Morning Crew) from Christina Watson (Accounting Assistant to Alex Coaltonstone).

Hi George:
I don't know what to say first. The visit with Ginger was far too short. I returned to my office, even though I could have just gone home, in theory anyway, I am being told I have to stay here. While everyone is celebrating I feel so awful that Ginger isn't rescued yet.

You won't believe this, but they are building the wall higher. Of all the things they could be doing right now, they are spending money on building a wall. The cadets and the militia are working on the wall together as if the crowd weren't standing there watching.

There are lots of new people congregating. I can see them through my window. They have the whole area lit up. The public is as close to the admin building and mine as they will be allowed to be.

The timing is so bad I think the wall is being built for no other purpose than to antagonize the public to act out a self-fulfilling prophecy. That is what it feels like anyway, George. I just sit here, watching and waiting.

The crowd of people around the security fence is growing. I can't imagine how many people there must be now. Tens of thousands I suppose.

I wish there were more rescue workers, and more machinery and drills coming in. Nothing seems to be happening. Ginger's grandfather is vowing that if one way doesn't work then another way will have to be found.

James Coaltonstone and Mayor Stern seem to be ok after the explosion at the hotel. They have small band aids stuck here and there and are mingling with the crowd passing out pizza vouchers; which seems very strange since they are probably the ones in charge of the admin relating to building the wall.

They are also passing around boxes of pizza as shifts begin and end for the cadets behind the security fence. So I hope you guys are having a bit of fun at the party. I suppose you can't really see what is going on like I can. Remember Dr. Knight told us all to stay positive.

Yours Friend Forever Christina Watson (almost Christina Goodwin)

"What do you think we should do, Jay?" Kevin asked.

"Don't know. Those illegals must have all the equipment that we need? They work against us just like everyone else does. If we have to ask permission to do something why don't they? We follow the rules and look at us now; we are jobless. The illegals are still working so they must have all kinds of equipment. I say we get into Mine 2 and descent into mine six and then tunnel into section E of Mine Five. That way we can use what is available and avoid the area that unstable in Mine Five," Jay said.

"Well if it is that simple why isn't G.O.D.'s rescue team down there already?" Kevin asked.

"Because it won't be simple. Rescues are never simple or even safe," George said.

"So what? Nothing we do is safe," Jay replied.

"How are supposed to do something when we are being cut off as we speak from the other side of the wall. We still have our passes, so we probably could get back in again. Ginger is more important anyway." Sam said.

"We could use those old tunnels that link Mine Five to Mine Eight. Once we get what we need maybe we could try. I mean those tunnels are also being used as the ventilation system for the illegals or that is what I hear anyway." Kevin said.

"It sounds dangerous." Sam said a little louder than he meant to. "My wife wants me to quit mining. She keeps telling me how much she loves me, which is a good thing, but then she adds that I am on borrowed time."

"I agree with Kev. We go into their neck of the woods, where the illegals mine, we grab all their cables and oxygen tanks and throw some fire crackers at them before we leave. That is the only way that we can get Ginger out of that hell-hole in a timely fashion. Everything and everyone, who isn't with us with us on this, is against us. We have no reason to wait or care about anyone who is not with us on this. We need to take this situation into our own hands, for Ginger's sake." Jay said.

"If we take the illegals' headlamps and leave them in the dark they will be helpless," Sam noted.

"Exactly, then we can seal them in," Jay replied. "No one will know what happened. Everything and everyone is working against us and no one cared much that we almost died."

"All they give us is poison," Sam said.

"Agreed; the more we drink the more we play into the stereotypes they create about us. Life is hard for all of us. Nowadays without money we are nothing. And even with money we are glared at by those who consider that they are on the upper rung of the ladder. This is what divides us all the time."

"You mean our races?" Sam asked

"No, of course not, I mean our position on the ladder divides us. And we all want to be on a higher rung. And someone who seems to be on a higher rung is always looking over their shoulder at us and you know the look," George replied.

"Yeah, that look," Sam said.

"That accusatory, suspicious, you must be Jack the Ripper look that fills you with fatalistic doubt about yourself and your future," Kevin said.

"Every time someone gives me that look I feel they are only seconds away from pushing their panic button and I will be taken away to a hard-labor camp in the Arctic never to be allowed to climb the ladder again," Sam said.

"Yes, pushed off the ladder for evermore." George said

"The Minese miners are closer to us in rank than we are to James Coaltonstone," George said.

"That is for sure," Sam said.

"Coaltonstone gave us this beer. We should be thankful for something. He hasn't given us anything else yet. I bet he is going to make us beg," Jay said.

"Or at least borrow. I don't like the idea of fighting with the Minese. They are miners just like we are," George Smoothman said.

"No, they are not like us. They are on this Island illegally. They take our jobs," Jay said.

"Are you sure they are not like us? Someone brings them here and they seem to be doing work that would be too unsafe and illegal for us to do, since we are quasi protected by safety regulations," George said.

"Right; we could have all been trapped in the mine explosion on Sunday. And Ginger is just waiting, hoping to be rescued. What else can he do? This is his fourth day down there. You are sounding like Ginger, and look where it got him. When it comes to money, greed takes over. **One side wins and one side loses.** Of course it is war," Jay said.

"Well, sort of. Everything, now, seems to be engineered to be like war. We are all fighting to climb to the next rung of the ladder. The ladder is like the common ground; so people are led to believe that it benefits them to provoke each other into a feud which leads to the one on the lower rung into trouble, then pushed down the ladder. We all see the games being played even in Pitville Grocery. We are stared at as if we are going steal something. We have these negative projections thrown at us when spoken to. If we respond, we appear just like the stereotypes they are projecting onto us, sometimes trapping us in their sum-zero role play. They turn around and stare at us as if we are following them when we walk in in the door. Sometimes the door is let to swing in our face." George said.

"Tell me about it," Sam said

"They check our bags for drugs, knives and weapons as if we actually have those things. And they do it over and over again, until we feel that it is normal for them to treat us this way. If we ask a clerk where something is, they sometimes tell us, and sometimes they don't. Sometimes we say something to them they accuse us of swearing at them and then threaten to ban us from the only grocery store in town. That is manufactured exclusion if I have ever felt it. Then we have no job even our wives may stop speaking to us. If the bots take more of our management jobs, there will be fewer rungs on the ladder to climb, and then there will be more reason to be at each other's throats. If we get treated as if we are the scum of the Earth for too long we start believing that we are. And they treat us like that, so they can feud with us, and push us to an even lower rung of the collective ladder," George said.

"Ginger tried to reason with them. And look where he is now. We do what we are told and now most of us have some form of lung disease and are broke and are treated like the scum of the Earth. And if we are not careful, we start believing that we are. Nothing works in our favor and time is shorter for us than those who were lucky enough to find work up on the surface," Kevin said.

"We can't let the 'doggie eat doggie' culture poison our state of mind. We must see what could have been the way Ginger does." George said.

"Ginger is a visionary because he has the courage to be a visionary; that is why we have to get him out of there. He is one of a kind." Jay said.

"To win, we must think like winners, the way James Coaltonstone does. To find a better way we must see the state of things as visionaries, the way Ginger does." George said.

"You know why nothing works for us?" Jay said.

"Why?" Sam asked.

"We don't make the decisions. People with money and power make the decisions and those decisions turn our lives upside down. I remember how Mathew kept saying, before he was crushed on July 4th, 2021; that one day, one of was going to get crushed by that old continuous mining machine while that horrible boss bot whistles and yells at us," Jay replied.

"And Mathew always prayed that it wouldn't be him," Kevin added.

"I remember Mathew actually kneeling praying," Sam said.

"And in the end it was him that was crushed. Now Christina is getting pushed around by Bots R Us just the way we all get pushed around," Jay said.

"It is not that I don't agree with you all, I do agree with you all, but I think we should wait until we sober up," George said wisely.

"When we sober up we won't be as brave. Did you see Ginger coughing on the com-screen, I don't think he is going to last much longer if he doesn't get out of there soon," Kevin said.

"I agree with Kevin," Jay said.

"Ok, assume that I am in; how are we supposed to get Ginger out of there any faster than those heavy duty outfits waiting for the okay to go in?" George asked.

"Because we are going to try, and all they are doing is waiting for someone from G.O.D. to tell them to go in. Ginger needs us. It is a crime to let a man die on his birthday," Jay said.

"Totally agreeable with Jay," Kevin replied. "All we have to do is take the equipment from the illegals. If they can get into the shafts with their harnesses and cables and battery operated generators, we can too."

"We are healthier and smarter so we have the advantage," Jay said.

Sam started to cough uncontrollably again. He took his green puffer out of his pocket and inhaled his medication.

"We are also bigger than most of the Minese, in many ways tunneling is a lot easier for them," George said.

"So you think the Minese will just hand us their equipment?" Sam asked.

"Of course not. We will have to use force to take it from them," Jay replied.

"How many Minese are there down there?" Sam asked.

"Don't know. We should take this beer with us," Jay replied.

Chapter 10

December 25th 2030, around 11:00 p.m.

Welcome viewers to Black Times. I am Dianne Black on location to report yet another disaster in Pitville. This time the victim is no other than Pitville's very own James Coaltonstone, owner and the Chief Executive Officer of Coaltonstone Mines and associate of the Big Seven Coal Group .

"Welcome to our show Mr. Coaltonstone.

"Thank you Dianne, under other circumstances it would be a pleasure to be here.

"Could you please tell our loyal viewer what actually happened?"

"Well I am not actually sure what happened. I was taking my private train to my home. As you know I have a private train station nearby our administrative building which connects to our mines. It was a terrible feeling when the earth sank beneath my tracks."

"I bet. Mr. Coaltonstone, can you tell our audience how such a terrifying event could happen to the CEO of Coaltonstone Mines.

"There has been a terrible problem in Pitville. We have thieves who routinely steal our Anthracite Coal Pillars since they are so valuable. These pillars are holding mines and part of my railway together. When they are stolen there is often a danger of infrastructure collapsing. My guess is that some evil person, probably an illegal, stole my coal pillars which were holding up my railway track infrastructure. It is lucky no one was hurt. These coal pillar thefts are getting out of hand. One day someone is going to get killed."

"Why do you think there are so many disasters plaguing Pitville and your mining operation? Do you think there is some truth that these events are due to the curse of the Black Diamond or is it just an accumulation of bad management practices over the years?"

"What kind of question is that? Dianne; when a pillar is stolen under a private railway, my conclusion can only be that our society is in terrible decline. I am ordering 24 hour guard duty, effective immediately, to protect what is left of my assets."

"And what will your security team do if they catch the person who is allegedly stealing the pillars."

"Shoot him if necessary. What do you mean alleged? It is obvious the pillars that were under my Railway are missing. I will not allow those illegals to ruin me or endanger the safety of my crew and family. Endangering my private railway is the last straw. And I hope you riff-raff are listening out there, because I am speaking to you."

"Now that we have you in real life, can you tell our viewers when Ginger Goodwin's rescue will begin?

"For security concerns, our current plans cannot be shared with the public at this time. Dianne, if I may, I would like to make a very important announcement. I am seeking nomination to run for president in the coming election so that I can give that A.B. Peel and his Exclusion League cronies a run for their money. And one of my promises will be to expose Deep Coal, whoever he may be, for I am sure he is behind this pillar theft and possibly even the explosion which occurred at Pitville harbor on Christmas day as well as Sunday's early morning Pit Five explosion. Those illegals and their cohorts must be stopped or our way of life will be ruined forever."

"Can you summarize the steps which need to be engineered before rescuing Ginger Goodwin from Mine Five can begin?

"Not really. We are trying our best, which is all that I can promise. Good Day, Dianne."

"Mr. Coaltonstone before you leave, you must tell us whether the rumors are true. Are you Ginger Goodwin's biological father?"

"Preposterous. Mr. Goodwin is my primary suspect in the Deep Coal data theft and I am also wondering if he is involved in this pillar being stolen under my railway. Did you know that Mr. Goodwin calls me a crony capitalist behind my back? I know this because I have heard it with my own ears while he was socializing with that George Smoothman and Jay Paylor. No son of mine would betray me in such a way."

"Are you saying that Lance Diamond is lying and did you just say that you have the Miners' Cafeteria under surveillance?

"You can't possibly believe that I am going to answer such loaded questions? This interview is now over."

Thank you, Mr. Coaltonstone.

"One more thing; as president of Tut Island I will be personally involved in establishing railways to connect the world starting with a railway to connect Eurasia with North America by building a bridge across the Bering Strait. I believe that the railway could connect the whole planet and help bridge the gap between the have nations and the have not nations. As president of Tut Island I will make sure that our nonviolent prisoners are put to work putting out fires, especially the troublesome fire which is threatening Stonely Mountain and when they aren't putting out of fires they will be helping our cadets build our security wall.

"Thank you again for your time Mr. Coaltonstone."

"Hold on Dianne, I would like to announce that if I am elected as president of Tut Island I will not only legalize the hemp industry I will support, facilitate and revitalize the manufacturing sectors of Tut Island. We have external forces which threaten to disrupt our hailing economy, but I will make Tut Island great again."

"I thought tut Island was already great."

"Yes, but not the way it used to be, before the explosion in Mine Five, before Deep Coal betrayed the entire network of

Coaltonstone Mines. And I promise you this if Mina continues to engage in High Altitude Nuclear Explosions which we know for a fact are able to turn off our street lamps, then we will hold back payments on our debt to that country. We must all agree to not test nuclear weapons in outer space. This practice is far too dangerous."

"Thank you again, Mr. Coaltonstone. Now, let us hear a word from our sponsor."

Chapter 11

December 26th 2030, around 8:00 a.m.

NEWS FLASH

The membership of G.O.D., the Tut Island chapter, have declared war on the Minese. Every able bodied man must sign up for service.

Chapter 12

December 26th 2030, around 9:00 a.m.

"Why are we having another back room meeting in my office?" Mayor Stern asked James Coaltonstone.

"Because I called another meeting because we need another meeting. We have to figure out why it is taking so long getting Mine Five back in operation," James Coaltonstone replied.

"I thought the drilling crews would have started their work by now." Mayor Stern said.

"Well they haven't. I owe the Minese and our own authorities tons of money. I am supposed to transform this coal into money, but I can't as long as the mine is closed."

"Well we have to wait until conditions are safe. There are a lot of union people working on this rescue operation and certain safety requirements have to be met," Mayor Ted Stern explained as if he were talking to a small child.

"I pay for results," James Coaltonstone said. "Otherwise I would go broke."

"Times are changing James," Mayor Stern said, almost whispering.

"I know exactly what you mean. Being able to do things fast and independently made me who I am today. I am the one taking the risk. It is my money tied up in that mine."

Ted Stern had never seen James Coaltonstone look so worried and defeated before and it scared him.

"Thank you for joining me this evening." Mayor Stern said as he observed the men who had joined him in his conference room, in the south wing, of Pitville's City Hall. Don and John Bell's glum looks appeared to be contagious for. James Coaltonstone was not looking any happier.

"And thank you Susan for bringing us these refreshments so efficiently. Remember it is still Christmas Day," Mayor Stern said while trying to force a smile

"I thought the drilling crews would be more organized today," James Coaltonstone said before he helped himself to a piece of pizza and a bottle of beer. "I suppose on top of everything else, we are still under a water boil advisory?" James Coaltonstone grumbled as he removed the bottle cap with his teeth.

"That is right James. We just have to go with the flow and roll with the punches," Ted Stern replied a little too cheerfully.

"The mood outside is quite festive, Sir. It could have been a lot worse," Don Bell said.

"There are people clinging to the security fence. Others are decorating it with flowers," John Bell said. "I find this behavior very inappropriate," he added.

Chapter 13

December 26th 2030, around 10:00 a.m.

"Your honor, may I be allowed to use George A. Smoothman's journal and email to summarize the events which occurred early morning on the day of the explosion. Mr. Smoothman is foreman of the morning crew that Mathew Watson was working on. I am asking for this consideration, your honor because Mr. Smoothman is still missing," David Bell, joint council for Boss Bots R Us and Coaltonstone Mines proposed.

"I object," Jack Jones, council for the People said abruptly.

"Overruled; you may use Mr. Smoothman's journal, Mr. Bell," Judge Bell replied.

"Thank you, your honor."

You May proceed Mr. Jones.

"Ginger Goodwin, who is also missing, refused to certify that the mine was safe, on December 22nd, 2030, only moments before the explosion. I have asked for Mr. Goodwin's journal to use as evidence, but have been denied this request because it has been classified as Secret. I am asking once again if I could have access to Mr. Goodwin's journal."

"Permission denied," Judge Bell said.

"Sir, with all respect, Mr. Goodwin's professional opinion, as assistant safety manager, the mine's environmental conditions did not meet the accepted standard for mine safety.

I have a file, full of frantic skype messages praising Ginger's quick thinking which prevented the morning crew from descending into Mine Five at the regular starting time, but doing so left him trapped in the Mine. Due to his own quick thinking he managed to find his way to the safety chamber in Section E, where four on his crew, George Smoothman, Jay Paylor, Sam and Kevin Jones found a way to rescue him, but now all five of them are missing. So none of the men who were working in Mine Five at the time when Mathew Watson was crushed, back in 2021, are available to testify. So again, I request an adjournment until these men are found.

"Denied," Judge Bell retorted. "Just summarize Mr. Jones."

"Certainly, thank you, sir. On the morning of December 22nd, 2030, Ginger Goodwin showed his true colors. He would not allow the crew to descend into Mine Five until his safety inspection was complete. According to the witnesses who are not present at this time, the Whistle-Boss Bot 5C was whistling while hovering around Ginger Goodwin's head for at least twenty minutes. This is the same behavior that Whistle-Boss Bot 5C was acting out only seconds before Mathew Watson's accident, which occurred on July 4th, 2021. Whistle-Boss bots always whistle nonstop whenever there is a conflict of commands between the mine's safety department and the mine's productivity department are also in conflict. Both Mathew and Ginger had little control over the whistle-boss bot's whistling when their lives were put in danger. Often the whistling stops only after the boss bot files a complaint, which permanently degrades Coaltonstone Mines' employees' work record. For workers at this company, it is like being marked by the mechanical beast for life."

James Coaltonstone nudged his lawyer expecting to cue him to object to the submission of documents which did not flatter his operations and implied that Coaltonstone Mines had conspired to avoid legal and environmental safety standards in the pursuit of profit.

"Objection," David Bell said.

"Overruled," Judge Bell replied.

"Sir, this last statement by Mr. Jones is an opinion, not a fact and is inflammatory."

"I have noted your objection. Your objection is overruled because the atmosphere in the mine affects safety all the time."

"Mr. Jones continue and please refrain from the theatrics and drama."

"Thank you sir, I will sir. The people of Coalton Valley are regulated by these whistle-boss bots day and night. The whistle-boss bot whistles once at the end of each shift and whistles twice when the next shift begins. When there is an emergency the whistle-boss bot will whistle four times, if it is able to. If the whistle-boss bot is disabled, then the siren-bot, which belongs to the volunteer fire department, will kick in and do the whistle-bot's job, but only louder."

The audience in the court room couldn't help but laugh.

"Order in the court," Judge Bell demanded. "Please continue Mr. Jones."

"Alex Coaltonstone, Christina Watson's boss, and lead accountant for Mine Five, was very much old man James Coaltonstone's son. Alex Coaltonstone had scheduled recovery related tasks for Christina to do before the financial markets opened Monday morning, December 23rd, the day after the explosion in Mine Five. Christina was instructed to phone suppliers and the bank that day and asked for a ninety-day extension on all accounts payable. Christian Watson was also authorized to buy back COALT stock before the stock price fell the next day.

Don Bell is Ginger Goodwin's boss and lead administrator in Mine Five's Safety Department.

Don Bell's twin brother, John Bell, who is head of mine security, spends most of his time with John working out security issues related to operating Coaltonstone Mines. The day of the disaster, and December 22nd was no different

Mine Five has always under staffed so I find it hard to blame any one individual for this horrible nightmare. Well that is not entirely true. I do blame James Coaltonstone. He seems to have no scruples when cutting back expenses so he can increase his profits for himself and his cronies.

Alex Coaltonstone appeared to more concerned about the fate of Whistle-Boss Bot 5C and the chance that panic selling of COALT stock might spiral out of control tomorrow morning. Alex didn't even mention Ginger, he just told Christina to buy blocks of COALT stock as soon as analysts recommended selling. Sunday the financial market was closed, so panic selling of COALT stock could start as soon as world markets opened Monday morning. Anthracite coal is in high demand so it was possible that any event which threatened supply may drive the price of COALT stock up instead of down.

Christina asked Alex Coaltonstone if anyone was going to issue a press release related to rescuing Ginger Goodwin and salvage plans. Alex replied that he did not know. Christina Watson was shocked and thought that it would be prudent to have some form of communication with the public as soon as possible."

"Objection; Mr. Jones is mixing fact with hearsay."

"I will overrule this objection, but Please Mr. Jones, try to be less colorful."

The audience started to laugh again while Judge Bell demanded silence.

"Please continue Mr. Jones."

"Thank you, sir. Your honor, many of the issues which I am describing are in the missing miners' journals which have been assigned classified status and cannot be disclosed at this time without your permission, therefore I request again, that this case either be remanded until the missing miners are found or allow me to use Mr. Goodwin's journal," Jack Jones requested."

"Request denied. Court is adjourned. I will return to my chambers and once I have determined fault in this case you will all be notified. Good day."

Chapter 14
Email message to Muni Bugden: Confidential

December 26, 2030

Dear Christina:

I wanted to let you know from me. Your case has been decided in favor of Bots R Us. Judge Bell ruled that this case has been going on for way too long, according to the judge; our request to postpone the hearing day appeared to only serve to anger the judge. I am so sorry I can't represent you. This case has taken every penny that I have and I can't finance our Pro Bono arrangement any further. I am so sorry Christina.

With kind regards,

Muni Bugden (Attorney at Law).

****

Email message to Jay T. Paylor (Assistant Foreman for the morning crew)
Confidential

December 26, 2030:

Hi Jay:

Where are you? I saw Chief Cuff drive by in her ghost car. I always know it is her. She has that bumper sticker on her car advertising their 25K reward for reporting gang members. I really wish that I could report the Power Clique as a gang of conspirators.

COALT stock is being sold off in huge blocks. This started Friday, about fifteen minutes before the market closed. Someone seems to have chosen the last day and the last fifteen minutes of so called open market, before Sunday's first explosion. Something is up. We are supposed to be sitting here quietly, while Ginger is down there breathing toxic fumes, someone is buying stock dirt cheap and all I hear is bullshit and stall tactics. Talk about gang bullying, disregarding the legislation which is supposed to keep ordinary people safe.

I lost my case Jay. I am going to be a prisoner forced into involuntary servitude, spending imprisoned in a glass cage with no privacy for the rest of my life. I don't know what to do Jay. Where are you? Where is George? You were missed in court.

Your friend forever, Christina Watson,

(Accounting Assistant to Alex Coaltonstone).

Chapter 15

December 26th 2030, around 1:00 p.m.

In a closed meeting, Judge Bell ruled that the robot manufacturer Bots R Us was not negligent in the design of Boss bots. He also ruled that James Coaltonstone was not negligent. Judge Bell ruled that Bobby Coaltonstone was criminally negligent. After hours of expert opinions and testimony, the judge ruled that there was plenty of evidence showing criminal negligence during the design of the ventilation system and while monitoring coal dust. It was ruled that the gas explosion in Mine Five on December 22nd was Bobby Coaltonstone's fault and James Coaltonstone only benefitted from Bobby's recklessness because he owned the mine, not because he ordered Bobby to be reckless. The judge rules that Bobby had been reckless on his own. Coaltonstone Mines agreed to pay Ginger Goodwin an undisclosed amount for pain and suffering, but James is suing Ginger for intellectual property theft since he still believes that Ginger is Deep Coal.

An email written by an employee and wife Christina Watson of the deceased miner, Mathew Watson, was proof that much of the suffering endured while working in Mine Five at Coaltonstone Mines was preventable.

Chapter 16

December 26th 2030, around 2:00 p.m.

"I have a memo here that Doctor Knight is requesting more information related to the way we are softening the City's water supply. She suspects, that what used to be considered food related obesity is actually water retention to the process which creates added salt to our water. Have you ever heard of anything so radicicolous?" Mayor Stern was not expecting an answer.

"Sooner or later water will be the new gold," Susan Jones said.

"Now Susan what did I say about talking?" Mayor Stern said as he frowned.

"Without water nothing lives and everything turns brown and dies," Susan added.

"We will either have to find more water or dig up more coal, so that we can generate electricity for the next generation," John Bell said.

"Pitville was never designed to be anything more than a temporary mining town," James Coaltonstone remarked.

"Pity," Ted Stern added.

"I suppose no one will notice if Pitville grows darker and smellier and the ash-piles in Buzzard Creek just grow higher," Susan Jones said.

"Now Susan, what did I say about talking?" Mayor Stern scolded Susan on more time.

Chapter 17
December 26th 2030, around 3:00 p.m.

"Good afternoon viewers. I am Dianne Black and welcome to the Black Times show. I am bringing to you another live update from the Pitville Mine Disaster of 2030." Dianne announced as she tried to conceal her disappointment with the verdict.

"Judge Bell has ruled that even though there was a failure to monitor the buildup of gas minutes before the 5:20 AM explosion which occurred December 22^{nd,} in Mine Five owned by Coaltonstone Mines, member of the Big Seven Coal group.

Judge Bell ruled that it could not be proven beyond the benefit of reasonable doubt that the monitor on the shearing machine had been turned off intentionally, therefore Judge Bell ruled that the cause of the explosion was accidental.

Judge Bell did rule against Bobby Coaltonstone, son of James Coaltonstone, CEO of Coaltonstone Mines. Judge Bell ruled that Mr. Bobby Coaltonstone was criminally negligent when operating as lead Ventilation Engineer. Judge Bell has ruled that Bobby Coaltonstone had taken risks with miners' safety to save money. Therefore he was the only one that has been found criminally negligent and has been sentenced to twenty six years of hard labor in the Arctic Mines.

The judge also ruled that it was reasonable to conclude that over the years Mine Five had been operating in a reckless fashion and was partially responsible for the death of Mathew Watson. A settlement between Mr. Watson's estate and Coaltonstone Mines had been agreed upon during the year of Mr. Watson's accident, 2021.

The judge also ruled that during the current war effort, Tut Island's alleys must rely on the region for it coal therefore the mine cannot be closed down, but will be watched very closely.

Alleged illnesses related to breathing coal dust will be addressed at a later date since their testimony is not relevant to the case at hand.

Judge Bell also ruled in favor of Bots R Us, leaving poor Christina Watson to pay, whatever way she can, ten years of legal costs."

"Without us today is Christina Watson, Welcome back to our show."

"Thank you."

"This must be a very hard time for you, Christina; losing your case and all."

"It is devastating. I feel gutted."

"Here in my hand is a leaked email from your lawyer to you and I hope you don't mind if I read this to our audience.

"And don't you worry, dear, you can't let this devastating set back destroy your confidence in yourself or your future," Dianne replied.

Email message to Christina Watson from Muni Bugden (Attorney at Law):
Confidential
December 26th, 2030
Dear Christina:

I wanted to let you know from me. Your case has been decided in favor of Bots R Us. Judge Bell ruled that this case has been going on for way too long, according to the judge; our request to postpone the hearing day appeared to only serve to anger the judge. Settlement hearing is scheduled for July 6th 2031. I am so sorry I can't represent you. This case has taken every penny that I have and I can't finance our Pro Bono arrangement any more. I am so sorry Christina.

With kind regards,

Muni Bugden (Attorney at Law).
Email message to Muni Bugden (Attorney at Law):
Confidential
December 26th, 2030
Dear Muni:
I know you did your best. It went on for ten years. I feel so devastated. I haven't just lost Mathew and the case, my freedom and possibly body organs which are deemed unnecessary to maintain life, I have lost my faith in the system. And that for me is my biggest loss.
Regards Christina Watson
"I was going to say that I rather you didn't read my confidential email and actually I do mind. That email to my lawyer was supposed to be privileged and private."
"Christina, I am sorry, is too late; your most inner thoughts about this case have been broadcasted around the world. Is there anything you would like to add?"
"No."
Thank you loyal viewers for joining us, as we follow moment to moment in related matters concerning Pitville Disaster of 2030.

Chapter 18

December 26th 2030, around 9:00 p.m.

"Jackson," Dianne whispered as she focussed her eyes as carefully as she could while trying to keep her binoculars steady. "Do you see what I see?"

"Well let me see," Jackson said as Dianne placed the binoculars in front of Jackson's eyes.

"You are wiggling."

"Sorry."

"I can't believe it. It looks like pot plants are being burning inside a pretty primitive greenhouse setup. Imagine if all that smoke goes up, wonder what it will be like when that hell-hole Pitville smells and breathes all this?"

Dianne tried not to laugh. "Jackson this is serious, get as many shots as you can. Make some long shots and some zoomed in.

"Yes, boss, we are live."

"Welcome viewers. This is Dianne Black reporting live on location. As you can see, we are broadcasting live from the beautiful, but smoky skies above the Stonely Mountain fire. We at PPZ are asking questions, but we are not getting all the answers that we would like. There is always something we don't know and we at the PPZ, and especially me, believe that the public should know details of public policy. We are on our way to Pitville's Alternative Radio Station and we will cover the Stonely Mountain fire which is growing while we fly by. From what we are able to observe from the smoky sky, there is no visible effort of a fire suppression service that we can see.

   With us today is one of my favorite Pitville personalities, and I know he is also one of yours too; I am pleased to re-introduce to you, Doctor Smith.
   "Welcome Doctor Smith
   "I know this mountain fire is beyond your expertise, but you certainly can tell us how this smoke will be affecting the public's health."
   "First though, just for fun, how do you think this fire started?
   "I really don't know. My guess is as good as anyone's. I am willing to guess that the fire on the mountain though is sharing either the same or interconnected coal seams as the fires we are seeing under the sidewalks in Pitville do," Doctor Smith replied.
   "How could such a thing happen?"
   "If a disaster is going to happen it will happen in Pitville," Jackson said spontaneously.
   "Shh Jackson, I am asking Doctor Smith."
   "As you can see this fire is spreading at an alarming rate. There are theories. I hope that any investigation includes an enquiry to why trash was being burned on top of a coal seam at the Buzzard Creek garbage dump, which has been the main location for burning Coalton Valley's trash, for over a hundred years."
   "The glow of the fire is quite beautiful," Jackson observed as he tried to hold his camera steady while the helicopter was hovering about.
   "Viewers, as we hover above these trees, using our artificial light source, we cannot be amazed at the numerous species of wild life which make their homes in the tree tops covering the lower region on the Eastside of the beautiful Beartut Mountain Range.
   "Let I remind you, that Coalton Valley was once a beautiful place and had plenty of salmon. The Glacier has shrunk over the years, but when I was a boy, that glacier was iconic."

"Could we please get back to the pressing question, how do you think this fire started?"

"I have no idea," Doctor Smith replied. "Technically the coal seam could have been ignited either naturally or through another source. The source could be lighting or something as simple as careless smoking."

"As you can see viewers, below us appears to be extensive damage to a primitive greenhouse which is storing what appears to be thousands of very tall and thick plants. We will let you, the viewer decide what kind of plants they appear to be. According to our map, the greenhouse is on Federal land and it is not clear who owns the greenhouse. My word, I had no idea such an operation could be going on so close to civilization."

"Civilization? Those people on Stonely Mountain are not allowed to benefit from our sophisticated fire suppression services. At the same time, the militia and military are building walls that are antagonizing Ginger Goodwin's supporters. Members of G.O.D. are demonizing those who are climbing the wall, while tens of thousands of people are peacefully standing by the wall. Some of those people might be quietly praying for a miracle, and the life as we know it to return. I fear our way of life might be gone for ever. Ginger Goodwin, is now on the run while suffering from a serious lung condition; still willing to die for what he believes in."

"Well what about Tut Island's security. The draft is used to acquire men to fight the enemy so that Tut Island is protected from illegal miners who are steeling pillars from under the ground and causing infrastructure on the surface to collapse."

"Yes, but the key words here are able bodied men. Ginger is technically very ill which is a fact being ignored by members of G.O.D. With all that said, it is obvious that Ginger does not see the Minese workers as his enemy because they risked their own lives to save his life."

"Does Mr. Goodwin see the authorities as his enemy?"

"I suppose it depends on what the members of G.O.D. do to him next.

Dianne asked while Jackson was shaking his head while Christina was beginning to feel cramps of agony that she had never experienced before."

"I can't speak for Ginger, obviously. From my point of view, the ruling class are not that expert at things. They hire experts. Historically the ruling class hired servants to dress them and feed them. Authority is a subjective word. Expertise on the other hand is measurable."

"Now, to answer your question about the effects this mountain fire will have on public health. Theoretically, when combining the health risks with the coal dust that is usually in the air, and the extra pollution caused by all the recent explosions, I would advise anyone who has chest related issues or weakness to stay indoors, or better yet, find a way out of Pitville."

"Thank You so much Doctor Smith now back to you Steve."

"Thank you Dianne."

"Don't go away viewers. We still have more news to share. Ginger Goodwin is believed to be at Pitville Radio Station at this time and we are taking his beautiful partner to see him, which will be the first since his bizarre rescue which I still find unbelievable. Yes, viewers there were ten illegal immigrant miners and four of Ginger's mates from his morning crew, supported by borrowed emergency equipment, who found Mr. Goodwin in Section E's rescue chamber. He was carried through a maze of tunnels and led to freedom through an undisclosed exit.

Mr. Goodwin's four mates are still missing and are under investigation for unauthorized use of Coaltonstone Mine equipment, which I and my colleagues believe is unfair and very callous indeed.

Understandably, Mr. Goodwin's lung condition has worsened. Our moles tell us that Mr. Goodwin complained the whole time he was being carried to an undisclosed exit of the very complicated and undocumented tunnel system which lies under Coalton Valley that he could walk. Our moles tell us the two secret service bots that were accompanying Mr. Goodwin, and this situation is also under investigation, were left in Section E's safety chamber. Our moles tell us that Mr. Goodwin spent most of his time reading 'The Rights Of Man' to them.

Christina Watson is soldiering on and is sitting behind us as we speak. Christina is not feeling very well, but we can report that she did tell us how excited she is to see Ginger. We at PPZ are more than happy to facilitate this meeting. This will be first meeting since the first terrible explosion which occurred around 5:20 AM Sunday morning. Christina has been waiting for Ginger all that time.

My mole has also told me that Ginger Goodwin's A1 status is now non-negotiable even though only hours before he had been automatically classified as 4F due to his chronic lung condition which is documented in his personal medical records. Back to you Steve."

"Are we off the air now?" Doctor Smith asked.

"Yes we are," Dianne replied.

"Jackson I still need to talk to you about something in private, you know it is very important that…

"Look, I am trying to hear what Steve is saying. Please Doctor Smith, the other thing will have to wait."

"As you can see, Dianne, the cadets from Pitville Military Academy are involved in two jobs. They are helping the militia build the war around the security fence which is around Coaltonstone Mines' Administration building, but they are also monitoring, and sometimes pushing people who are climbing the wall. Some of these people actually appear to have climbing ropes and long spiked shoes, which appears to be serving two purposes. The shoes are facilitating the climbing of the wall, and they are also turning out to be dangerous when used as a weapon. Things are getting nasty around here that is for sure. Hold on, there seems to be a very young man flyking over the walls, wearing a camera, wanting to know his mother, Christina Watson is. He has gotten over the fence and has been allowed into the administration building.

"Oh my God," Christina said."

"Dianne, we need to do something, Christina has gone into shock and she is about to deliver her baby."

"Pilot, fly us to Pitville General Hospital as fast as you can. Christina is going into labor."

Chapter 19

December 26ᵗʰ 2030, around 10:00 p.m.

Welcome to Pitville alternative radio Station. We are located on Stonely Mountain and have a beautiful view. With us today is Ginger Goodwin; that is thee Ginger Goodwin, the one who escaped from Mine Five with the help of four members of his morning crew, and about a dozen illegal immigrant miners.

"First of all I want to say how wonderful it is to see you in person Ginger. And congratulations; children are such a blessing. I really don't know where to start."

"Well, let me start. I am against this war on the Minese on Tut Island. And I am against the Exclusion League. The question here is not borders, the miners who I met were decent men, and risked their lives and freedom to help save my life. They carried me all the way from the safety chamber in section E, through a maze of tunnels that I did not even exist. And they did that not because they were being paid or were receiving in personal gain, they helped me, because I was a man in need. They stood by me, and carried me until I saw daylight. These so called illegal immigrant workers are doing a job no one wants to do."

"Regardless of the ethics behind our economic conditions which I agree is never fair, doing the thing which feels right and natural should be our choice. The mega rich seem to be getting wealthier while the poor get poorer, don't you agree that is just the way things are and you have to accept them, Ginger?"

"Of course I don't agree. I believe there are times sharing ownership of production and working at a safer pace would shape a better world. The problems we are faced with today were created over a hundred years ago. The undocumented mines are hiring undocumented workers, but those undocumented mines were left here as a legacy of those who were here before us. A hundred years ago, when mine owners avoided bureaucracy and filing fees, many mines were left undocumented and abandoned. Today, when undocumented mines are broken into and the anthracite pillars are stolen, whoever is above that area and beyond is placed at serious risk."

"So, Mr. Goodwin, are you in favor of A.B. Peel and the Exclusion League members who back him?"

"Of course not."

"Why not?"

"The question you should be asking is who will be excluded next? Who will be degraded by poverty, homelessness and nuisance fines which only serve to keep track of the most vulnerable? When I was alone in the Pit, I thought I was going to die. I thought they were going to leave me down there to die and I had never felt so excluded in my life. When I came back up, it was like I had been away, and I noticed a negativity that I never noticed before, but now looking back, I know it existed, but I just was not as aware of it, until I, in a way, became an outsider looking in. So the question is, who will be next to be excluded?"

"That is a very good question and will probably never be answered."

"I and my crew have slaved in the pits of Coaltonstone Mines for over fifteen years. We have worked under conditions that were almost as bad as the conditions the illegal immigrant miners face. The difference is, we work in mines which are documented and have a minimal amount of transparency. The Minese work in mines which are invisible. The difference between our conditions is only due to an accident of birth. My Minese miner brothers are being forced to work in mines which are invisible to the general public and when they die, they are left in those mines to rot. Members of G.O.D. and the Exclusion League are forcing the draft onto us as and forcing us to fight for them, as if the ruling class were on our side, instead of our exploiters. They don't care if we are killed or disabled with lung disease while we work in their hell hole mines. If A.B. Peel and his Exclusion League backers have their way, they will inadvertently expand the beggar class, because in the end that is what exclusion does to people."

"So, Ginger, are you saying that you feel closer to the Minese Workers than you do to the members of G.O.D.?"

"I certainly do. I waited for three days, my air was almost gone, I was coughing and I really did think I was going to die. And who did I see coming out of nowhere, Sam, Kevin, Jay and George and ten Minese Miners who risked their lives and what little freedom they have, to rescue me. They rescued me, when the members of G.O.D. refused to let the rescue team go into Mine Five to rescue me, because it was too risky and expensive . And as my grandfather worked himself to death, no one helped him. So why wouldn't feel just as close to these illegal immigrant miners than I do to the members of G.O.D. who have drafted me to kill my miner brothers?

"I always find it strange that my poorest friends are the ones who are called for active service and my richest friends have never been called."

"Why should I turn on my miner brothers after they risked their lives to save my life?

"The authorities are calling you a draft dodger, a dodger of duty? How do you feel about that?"

"Really, they are calling me a dodger of duty. I am suffering from a lung disease since I have been exposed to mine dust since I was fifteen years old, and I was at one time documented as unfit for military duty. Why should someone who has bone spurs in his heels be exempt from military duty, but someone with a lung disease be forced to fight? This is just another example where politics does not make sense and only benefits one side, or one class of people, at the expense of the other side or class. And my point is that I am in the same class as my Minese miner brothers, and the ruling class does not care if I live or die. This was demonstrated during the reckless endangerment me and my morning crew experienced in Mine Five."

"What do you say to those who call you a coward?"

"Try putting the time I put in trapped in the pit. The only thing that saved me from going mad was the literature that I found. The rights of man was inspiring to me, it showed how common sense makes us intelligent. Without being allowed to think we are not just in chains like some of the miners I saw in the tunnels underneath us, we have had our humanity compromised".

"Ginger Goodwin, will you be honest with me. Are you Deep Coal?"

"I sat there for three days in deep coal waiting to be rescued and my grandfather, the only man besides my morning crew and the Minese, died trying to get someone to move. I was totally isolated from the surface, just the way the minese I saw in the tunnels were, how could I possibly have been Deep Coal. It defies common sense."

"So the answer is no."

"Yes the answer is no."

"So, what now?"

"I would rather die than kill my miner brothers, no matter what color their skin happens to be. I would rather die than to have my humanity compromised. The team had to wait for the members of G.O.D. to authorize the mission, and those members were waiting for the perfect time for me to be rescued. They actually let George Coaltonstone seal Mine Five while I was still trapped. Now who would you feel you had a duty to serve and protect; the men who actually rescued me, or the men who were waiting for the perfect time to rescue me. If conditions had been perfect, there would have never been an explosion to start with and then I would have never been trapped. Of course the conditions in Mine Five are dangerous. Then when I reached the surface, I was treated like a criminal. I was not only accused of being Deep Coal, whatever that is, I was also found to be guilty just because I was being accused.

"Oh my God they are banging down the door."
"What?"
"Get out of here. Run, Ginger, run."

Chapter 20

• December 27th 2030, around 7:00 a.m.

"Hello viewers. So much has happened. And it has happened so fast. Ginger Goodwin has been shot. John Bell is accused of shooting him, the city hall is on fire. And the fire is being called suspicious by the volunteer fire department. There isn't any fire repression service on Stonely Mountain. The Stonely Mountain taxpayers voted against having a separate fire suppression service, and Pitville taxpayers do not consider themselves to be part of the mountain community taxpayers association. So Pitville public policy on this matter, transmitted through a press release to us by the members of G.O.D., is to let the mountain fire burn, unless and only unless, human life is in danger.

In other Pitville Mine Disaster news, Christina Watson, Ginger Goodwin's partner, has delivered a very premature baby boy. The policy at Tut General Hospital is to not offer intensive care to premature babies with a gestation of twenty-two weeks and six days or less. The policy is to allow the babies to die of natural causes without interference. James Coaltonstone has been rumored to have taken the baby to an undisclosed location. The walk-in Pitville clinic is now closed until further notice. Both Doctor Smith and Doctor Knight are possibly at an unknown location looking after Christina and Ginger's baby. James Coaltonstone has also paid all debt Christina Watson owes Bots R Us, when she lost her civil case, which was to compensate her for the loss of her husband Mathew Watson. This case has been in the courts for over ten years, and has accumulated a hefty legal bill for Bots R Us. The fact that the case had been in the courts for so long worked in favor of Bots R The time delay certainly did not benefit Christina Watson who is now reported to be in a fragile state.

"We at PPZ draw opinions from many sources, and today we would like to introduce and welcome Doctor Janice Bell.

"Thank you, Dianne."

"I know I have been reporting one tragic event after another, and usually a birth is wonderful news. So what can you tell us about these very premature births? Could you begin telling Black Times' viewers why Pitville General Hospital doesn't treat premature babies with a gestation period of twenty-two weeks and six days or less?"

"Dianne, it is incorrect that we do not treat such undeveloped babies. We want all of our patients to be comfortable, no matter how small they may be."

"My mole informed me that James Coaltonstone bought his own life support mobile unit, and is keeping the baby alive, and he is doing quite well considering the circumstances."

"Please Dianne; you are interrupting my train of thought. I just forgot what I was about to say."

"We, at Black Times must report all the news. In this case, for the wealthiest man on Tut Island to buy such a unit for this little boy, is not only news worthy, it is in my opinion, a wonderful heartwarming story."

"Everyone has a right to their opinion on this emotional issue. You do know that Mr. Coaltonstone actually took our equipment and then gave us payment for it. We did accept the payment and his generous donation to our hospital, but we at Tut General Hospital cannot condone such disruptive behavior."

"Thank you for telling us all the details in regards to how Mr. Coaltonstone acquired the new baby's life support equipment. Without this equipment, the baby would have died, isn't that right, Doctor Bell?"

"We at Tut General Hospital see how these babies struggle. Such premature babies can only survive when given extreme intensive care."

"How can a member of the public get this equipment fast enough to save their baby, if they choose to do so?"

"I don't know if there is a way, unless you take our equipment the way Mr. Coaltonstone did. And if anyone pulls a stunt like that again, we at Pitville General Hospital will certainly be pressing charges."

"And what will you do with the babies? Throw them out on the floor?"

"Certainly not; we have an appropriate place for these preemies to rest."

"You mean to die?"

"We at Pitville General Hospital do not believe it is right to burden families and society as a whole with the complications such premature births present. The expense to offer every premature baby with a gestation period of twenty-two weeks and six days could bankrupt our medical system. Extreme premature babies cannot live without intensive medical intervention, so we have made a policy at Pitville General Hospital to only offer life support to babies who are born after twenty-four weeks of gestation and onwards, but not for babies who are born after only twenty-two weeks and six days or less of gestation. Do I make myself clear Dianne?"

"Certainly, Doctor Bell; back to you Steve."

"Is that it, my interview is over? It is not only Pitville General Hospital which has this policy; the bioethics committee for G.O.D. has given all medical practitioners the very same directive."

"Thank you once again Doctor Bell. I must follow Steve's report, so please excuse me."

"Hello everyone, we have more ground breaking news to report on our show, Black Times. The fire on Stonely Mountain is growing and it is about to engulf the Alternative Radio Station, Volunteers have hiked and flyked up to the mountain, some are ignoring orders to let the radio station burn, and some of the hikers are being arrested. Feelings are also being flamed at this moment due to reports that Pitville's hero Ginger Goodwin has been shot, though his body has been left in a disclosed area. We also have, what is now just a rumor that James Coaltonstone has married Christina Watson possibly around the time Ginger was shot though we do not know for sure. What we do know is that the Justice of the Peace and his wife, and adult son and daughter were woken up at 5:00 AM and performed a civil union, and the debt owing to Bots R Us has been paid in full. Christina Watson is free and she won't be forced to sell any of her unnecessary organs to help pay for her debt in a timely fashion.

"Now for the weather. We have very smoky skies above Pitville, so to all of you holiday flykers, caution is advised. And for those with respiratory issues there is an air advisory still in progress."

Chapter 21

- ## December 28th 2030, around 9:00 a.m.

Welcome viewers Black Times, on location at the Pitville Mine Disaster of 20130.

Jackson, my loyal camera man was filming what appeared to be more smoke coming out of the road. As we were discussing whether it was possible that the smoke was a sign that one or several coal seams underground may be on fire, the road dangerously close to the right side of our car opened up without any warning. I am still shaking as you can see. It is hard to know what to report first. The Pitville Mining disaster is not just one event, as you can see; it is one thing after another. We are also discovering that many of the Pitville miners are suffering from black lung and were never told or treated for it. Apparently the miners were warned that if they sought medical attention for any lung problems they would lose their jobs and their related medical insurance coverage.

Another story we are following is the series of explosions that were detonated fairly close to Eagle Claw beach.

It is not our job at PPZ to speculate actual causes to all of these dangerous events, we usually invite experts to voice their opinions. Unfortunately no one from G.O.D returned our phone calls.

Many of our loyal listeners have voiced concerns that the recent explosions may have been experimental and possibly the actual source of an unexplained Bird-Flu like virus which closed both Coalton Elementary and Pitville High schools for three days, sending after around two hundred students had severe vomiting.

Chapter 22

- ## December 28th 2030, around 10:00 a.m.

"Don't look out of the window Christina," James instructed.
"Why can't I?"
"Because everything looks so poor. Poverty can be mind-numbing and has no future. You see all those gates, all those broken dreams. The force of nature built all this and man's nature always seems divided."
"I want to see all that I am leaving behind and I want to see where I am going." Christina said; disgusted by Coaltonstone's greying facial stubble and stale tobacco smelling breath.
"You mustn't think that way, Christina. Don't feel like you are leaving your life behind, feel like you are moving into a new world. Once we reach the North Lands you will see how wonderful it is. Imagine building a technology to warm and melt some of the Arctic. It will be another one of my great dreams coming to life. Just wait until summer, you will see for yourself how wonderful the White Nights are. I love White Nights. You must remember that we have a life waiting for us, which will be even better than the life we left behind. We have little James…"
"I would rather you call him Ginger," Christina said.
"Ginger lived in his own little world, where love and kindness could overrule weapons of war. So now he is on the grave yard shift…

"Please, call the baby Ginger, and he is not your son, he is your grandson."

"Actually you are wrong. He is legally my son now; you signed the papers which make him legally my son along with the marriage license agreement which makes you my wife. We are all Coaltonstones now. To succeed in life, Christina we must compromise. Ginger is gone. You are now Mrs. Coaltonstone. Wealth is like a wall."

"You mean like that wall you kept building around the security fence of the Administration building, antagonizing peaceful protestors until they grew so angry they climbed it."

"Well not exactly. And that is not how I see it."

"Well it is the way I was forced to see the situation as I waited for three days, watching the crowds grow, waiting for Ginger to be rescued by his own people, who at the end did nothing, but break Ginger's granddaddy heart. No wonder he died so suddenly."

"Christina, you know life has limits and limits are different for different people. Not everyone can live on our side of the wall and if they did there would be far less for us to share. We have left the south behind the wall and the future is in the North. And if we wanted to we could put a no entry sign in every little shop which gets in the way of progress."

"Can you do that?"

"The Question is dear, what can they do? That is always the question. We will build high speed highways which lead to my golf courses, selling my wine, my beef, my beer. My name will be on all the labels. I will build the tallest of towers and I will be remembered for my achievements forever. I will be feared for my power will affect everything. Monuments made by me to feed my wealth will have a place in every major city on this God fearing Earth."

"You only feel this way because you lost the nomination to A.B. Peel. The Exclusion League delegates would have never nominated you. The Exclusion League went on about possible future court proceedings you could be involved in and then stacked all the cards against you. Your chances to be the commander of chief to G.O.D. have been destroyed."

"No, my dear, I don't feel this way; I am this way."

"What about us?"

"I have a beautiful honeymoon planned for us. We will be cruising around the Northern passage and then we will be welcomed by the highest of military officials on the other side of the Bering Strait where only very few are given permission to enter."

"Will we be able to leave there when we want?

"Of course we will be able to leave! Why do people throw out their refrigerators and old trucks anywhere that is convenient? Look at that mess. Everywhere you look, all you see is old and decrepit appliances and cars. It is nice to leave the war zone; despite all this garbage the country side seems more beautiful the further north we go," James said trying to sound pleasant.

"Christina stared out of the window feeling sick to her stomach.

"A bit of Champaign will make you feel better Christina, we are safe now. The crew are on our side, our capital keeps the beast at bay, you understand that don't you Christina."

"I miss my life, this is your life."

"No, this is our life, now."

"I could say that your old life was lost once you lost your case."

"No, my old life was lost when Ginger was shot."

"Are you sure this bridge is safe?"

"You doubt this miracle of modern technology?"

"I am just getting a terrible feeling. The ride feels shaky."

"Well these long bridges often feel that way."

"I feel terrible not being with the baby. And I am surprised we weren't arrested when you took one of their mobile life support systems. That was really something."

"I did convince them to take my money. I always do, you know. He is a cute little guy. All head. We will see him soon. Our doctors tell me he is fighting for life and there is nothing wrong in that. He will grow up to be a fighter that is for sure."

"He is so small and vulnerable. I feel guilty keeping alive and I would feel even guiltier letting him die."

"The doctors are there with him. If kangaroos can survive out of the mother's womb why can't humans?"

Christina stared at James in disbelief.

"The matter has been settled. Your life is always better when you are with me. Baby James cannot live without me. I am providing him with the latest technology and he is going to live because of me. We are going to have a great life and you will learn to love me. That is how arranged marriages work. A room is set up for Baby James and I was able to convince your doctors to meet us there, since they owe me a big favor, they were glad to set things up while I settle a few details with Ono."

"Settle what things?"

"This shipment is very valuable."

"Have you heard anything from the doctors yet?"

"Yes, he is just fine."

"How can he be fine if he is so small?"

"It will take a while, but he will be just fine."

"Keeping a baby that small on life support is purely experimental you know, James."

"Not exactly; they do it all the time in Mina. We have been stuck in Pitville for way too long. Anyway life is always experimental. That is how you move on from life's tumbles. You get up and do what you can to exist and survive. And Baby James is a little fighter. The doctors all agree. Doctor Knight and Doctor Smith will remain with us until Baby James doesn't need such intensive care anymore. Oh please don't look like you hate me, I am giving you a chance to keep your son alive.

"You know I am incredibly grateful for the things you have been able to do for us, but sometimes I wonder if we would have been better off if all these horrible mishaps had been prevented."

"Baby James will grow and learn and see the world in a special way and if he survives, he will be stronger than any of us who have had it softer, will ever be."

"What happens if he is blind, deaf, or has heart problems?"

"He won't be. He will beat the odds. He is a Coaltonstone. Christina, it won't take long to feel at home on our ship. We will work on our second book, which could be just as popular as 'The Blessing: Black Diamonds' and you will learn to be happy with me. This was a similar arrangement I had with the first Mrs. Coaltonstone. Maybe we could help find a cure for cancer. That would be great. We must live the lives fate presents us with and so Baby James will learn to do the same. With everything that you might detest about me, you eat better, you dress better and you couldn't look more beautiful than when you are with me. I will take care of baby James as if he were my own, because he is part of you.

"And part of Ginger. I mean he is your grandson, so of course he is part of you too."

Chapter 23

• December 29th 2030, around 10:00 a.m.

"Isn't this wonderful," James Coaltonstones said as his feet dangled from the ship into the cool water.

"The water is too cold for me," Christina said as she quickly stood up.

While putting on her shoes and socks, James said, baby James is in his special place and Doctor Knight is attending to his every need for the 12 hour day shift and Doctor Smith will be doing a 12 hour night shift."

"How did you manage to persuade them to close their clinic?"

"The same way I persuade everyone to do what I need done. It wasn't that hard to do. I explained to them, we as a crew, will be the first civilians to be allowed into the brand new tunnel connecting North America to Asia and Europe. This will be a similar journey taken by our ancestors two hundred thousand years ago, but only in the opposite direction. This Tunnel could change everything. We will be guests of the small military base on the other side where I will meet Ono. He is with the shipment, of coal, hemp and jade and I forget what else, some electronics I believe."

"Are you joking?"

"About what?"

"Don't look so glum. You are a Coaltonstone now which means positive thinking and a stiff upper lip."

"You are sounding like a member of the Royal Family.

"In a way I am. I have often been referred to as King Coal, but now that hemp and Boss-bots are in such demand, soon I will be referred to as King of Everything. The Jade we are exporting is just icing on our cake."

"You mean smuggling?"

"No, I mean exporting. You always make me sound so despicable. We are surviving and living a lot more than the folks we left behind. We are the winners. We won the race. I am providing everything James will need, and I am certain he will grow into a capable and strong man. He has already beaten some odds against him; just like I do. Baby James will be the son my other sons could never be. I don't know where I went wrong. I tried so hard to provide them with a life balance. Now I have one son in jail, and the other son refusing to speak to me.

"Christina, what is that?" It looks like a boy flyking. I didn't know that those suits had such a range."

"Oh my God it is Mathew."

"Your son Mathew?"

"Tell me son where did you get such a wonderful flyking suit? I just love all those feathers you have sown on to it."

"Actually Grandma helped. I collected the feathers and Grandma sewed them on for me. Then when I made ten thousand dollars selling photographs to a guy called Steve from the PPZ, I bought all these extra things. I sold some photographs and refitted my flyking suit into a new hybrid pipe model which recharges with the wind and sun."

"Isn't that amazing? He looks so much like his father, Christina. I always wanted you to know how sorry I was about the accident, but business is business. You know that. It is the way it must be. You know how members of G.O.D. have decimated the coal and steel industries. I wanted to bring them back to the way they used to be, but I lost. I wish I could bring Mathew back, but you lost. If I could make it all up to you I would, but business is business. Let us have lunch together, like a real family.

"Mom, I found you. I thought I would never see you again."

Mathew landed on the deck, and before he was able to turn off his suit he was being hugged by a tearful Christina.

"Mom, I want to see my new brother, I want to be with you. Grandma said that I had to accept the way things are. Ginger never would do that why should I?

"Hello Son. We were just about to have lunch in Baby James' special room.

"Baby James? His name is Ginger. Right Mom?

"Why are you calling him Baby James? His name is Ginger; right Mom?

"We can talk about this later, Mathew. Now when you see your brother, make sure you are very quiet and careful. And you have to stand behind glass until he gets stronger.

"Why?"

"Your brother is very tiny and very weak. He is the size of a twenty-one week old fetus and he cannot fight germs the way you and I can."

"Why?"

"Because your brother is very tiny and very weak. He is the size of a twenty-two week old fetus."

"I thought he was a baby."

"Well he is a baby. I meant that your brother is at the same developmental age as a twenty-one week old fetus. Now thank your Uncle James for helping us. I would still be in Debtor Prison if it hadn't been for him, and your baby brother would not be alive if it wasn't for your Uncle James. You like Doctors Knight and Smith, right? They are here too. They work separately in twelve hour shifts, so baby James will have 24 hour care.

"What would you like for lunch Mathew?"

"I would like ice cream."

"Ice cream it shall be."

"James, Mathew will be having what we are having. First will be lobster soup. Then we were going to have salmon and rice, then and only then we will have ice cream."

"Okay, you are the boss dear."

"Why did you just call my Mom dear? What is going on?"

"We are married. Your mom and your baby brother James are Coaltonstones."

"Why?"

"Son, not every young man gets to enjoy a luxury cruise owned by his new step dad."

"I won't have to call him Dad, will I Mom?"

"Of course not. You can continue calling me Uncle James, like you always have," James Coaltonstone said as he tried to hug Mathew while he was pulling away.

"Mom, I want to go home."

"Mathew, please. You must act mature now. We are going to a new life. Your old life is gone."

"You mean like Ginger? Are we all going to get shot?"

"Of course not, Mathew," Christina replied.

"It is horrible in Pitville now. I flyked over the wall to see if I could find you; everyone told me you were gone, and Grandma was crying. And all these armed men were either guarding or building a wall around the security fence. And you wouldn't believe what I saw in between the two walls? Then Steve from PPZ came up to me and said that I was the first to flyke over the wall and then he noticed my helmet camcorder. He asked me if it was on. I said yes. And he bought the photographs and my memory card. I have two more memory cards though."

"I know what lies between those two walls; I am the one who authorized John Bell's designs. What you know is classified and we need to talk about this later. Now on to lunch and before you meet your little brother remember that he is very frail, a miracle of my generosity."

"Uncle James is saving your brother's life. The hospital has a rule so we had to take the baby home."

"Damn those G.O.D. members, they write all their rules in stone."

"James, please, they are the Government's Official Directors and they do a lot of good work."

"They are always watching. They don't respect privacy or private property the way we do. They would have watched Baby

James die without ever having a chance to live; while we the taxpayer pay them to write a report."

"Why are we calling the baby James, I thought his name was Ginger?" Mathew asked.

"Well, we can call him both dear, isn't that right, James."

"Certainly. Ginger James sounds grand, doesn't it?" James Coaltonstone said, agreeably.

"Why was he born so fast? Was it so we could share birthdays together for as long as we live?"

"Maybe, dear."

Chapter 24:

- ## December 29th 2030, around 10:00 p.m.

"Christina where are you going? Christina answer me! Christina don't. Oh Christina. Stop the ship. Someone help me please."

"Mom! Someone help my mom please, will someone help my mom.

The crew on hand pulled Christina out of the frigid cold water and she was soon on life support, lying beside her baby Ginger.

Doctor Knight read the quick text Christina had written before she fell from the ship or jumped off. No one knew for sure.

Hi Doctor Knight:

Well here I am in a terrible state. I am Mrs. James Coaltonstone. The Justice of the peace was phoned early in the morning hours after Ginger was shot, and the baby was born and it was also Mathew's fourteenth birthday. The Justice of the Peace was at home, we married at his house, his wife and his two adult sons were witnesses. I told James Coaltonstone that I loved Ginger and he told me only as a family could we save baby Ginger James. I made sure that I kept my poker face on so he couldn't tell how much I hated the whole idea. He said now that I am Mrs. James Coaltonstone I am too rich to harass or hurt in any way.

I know now it is impossible to fight the system and I can hear Ginger calling me.

I want a better life for Mathew Junior and Ginger Junior That is why I allowed James to change their names. We are spending our honeymoon speculating on how James can use dam technology to warm the Arctic Ocean to free the wealth frozen under the virgin north, the New Frontier for him and all of his labels.

THE END

FIRESTONES: The MINER BOOK THREE

Chapter 1
The Aftermath

December 31ˢᵗ 2030, around 10:00 PM: " W hat a horrible New Year's Eve. This whole Christmas has been the worst one in my entire life. Everyone is either dead or almost dead. I am stuck here on a boat in the middle of the Arctic Ocean. It is dark and cold and there is a continual cracking and humming noise," Mathew said.

"Mathew, don't be so glum. Alright as an artist there may be a good argument for feeling glum, but as scientists we must stay objective. Science is a wonderful thing. Science keeps your mother alive; science keeps your brother is alive. And as you can see baby James is growing like a weed. You are much better off here anyway. There are too troubles in Pitville,' James explained.

"I wanted to go to Ginger's funeral but my mom and my little brother might die next so that is why I am here. Everyone seems to go so fast without any goodbye. It is almost like a domino effect first Ginger gets shot and then Jay, George Kevin and Sam just disappear," Mathew Watson Junior said.

"I have been to enough funerals in my day to know how funerals wind people up to tears. Funerals can bring back the diseased and wind people up beyond the comfort zone," James said.

"My grandmother says that funerals are meant to remember and share those life memories of the person who just died," Mathew interjected.

"I can just imagine your grandmother saying that. Though you call me Uncle James, and there is nothing wrong with that, I am really your new step dad, and we are going to have a new beginning here. We are going to see a new world, a new way of life. And to top it off we will be observing how Minese and associates thrive while living under a ten day calendar and a ten hour clock," James explained.

"A ten day calendar? How does that work?"

"It is very complicated. The calculations at the moment are top secret. The folks in Mina have been operating under this revolutionary calendar for some time and it seems to be working for them, so I am sure it will work for Coalton Valley 2. As for Jay, George, Kevin and Sam, I am sure that they are lost on purpose, probably avoiding their wives' scorn for drinking too much on Christmas Eve. And poor Ginger, I feel terrible that he is gone. This horrible year will be over in two hours. Your mother and baby James…" James Coaltonstone said before he was interrupted.

"How can anyone be lost for a week and why do you keep calling him Baby James instead of baby Ginger?

"Most people who go missing are running away from something and Ginger is not a name, it is a nick name. James is a fine name and suits your baby brother to a T. James is a name which commands…"

"What happens if people get his name mixed up with yours and he gets shot when he grows up?"

"Why would anyone want to shoot me? Anyway, I have expanded my body guard crew to include ten of the state of the art guard bots. Where people have failed me my bots will make up for it. I am sure when the time come when needed these bots will surpass all my expectations," James said expecting Mathew not to reply.

"At least your bots don't die. I don't know why it feels like people want to kill you. It just does. Everyone blames you for Ginger's death. But I don't. Who is to blame for Ginger's death, Uncle James?" Mathew said.

"Sometimes there isn't anyone to blame though John Bell is blaming Ginger and says that he shot him in self-defense," James replied.

"Ginger would never hurt anyone even those people who seem to be almost stepping on him all the time," Mathew said louder than he normally spoke.

"This entire week has been unbelievably terrible. Ginger was so young and his whole life is gone. Don's wife is scheduled for surgery on Friday and I won't be there. Christina is getting stronger but she doesn't seem to want to wake up. I have never had a patient as small as this baby but he seems to be making up for his size by being brave." Ashley said without meaning to interrupt.

"Well he is a Coaltonstone, of course he is brave. It has always been the Coaltonstone way.

"I miss Ginger. I miss my mother nd I wish that my brother was a lot bigger. I wish I knew what really happened to Ginger." Mathew said.

"Sometimes we never find out what really happens but over time there will never be a shortage of opinions. We just have to remember all the people who benefitted from Ginger's life and quick thinking right before the explosion in Mine Five. It would be nice if they named the Parkway after him. That would be one way of honoring him for being such a friend. That reminds me, I have your birthday present right here in my right pocket. And your Christmas present in my left. Is it okay if Mathew opens them now Dr. Knight?

"Certainly," Ashley replied.

"Thank you very much Uncle James," Mathew said as he opened up the box. "You gave me a gun for my birthday? Is it real?" Mathew asked.

"It certainly is. And what do I have in my left pocket? Your belated Christmas present which is a pocket full of ammunition. What do you think about that?"

"Did you get baby Ginger a gun too, Uncle James?"

"Not yet. I did get him his fancy life support system which is doing a very good job keeping him alive, with the help of Doctor Knight's gifted hands, may I add."

"I am trying my best Mr. Coaltonstone, but I can't perform miracles?" Ashley replied.

"You certainly can," James interjected.

"So until baby Ginger gets his own gun, how will people not get your name mixed up with his? You are always in the newspaper and baby Ginger looks so innocent and tiny. He sort of looks like an alien," Mathew said.

"First of all, baby James' last name is hyphenated just like your new name is. So you both are going to have Watson-Coaltonstone as a last name, now. A double barrel name if I have ever heard one," James said as he grabbed another bottle of water from the fridge. Anyone need anything to drink?

"Sure I will have a water. Is that your face on the water bottle Uncle James?

"It sure is. It is my label that goes on all of my products," James explained.

"Why doesn't baby Ginger have Goodwin as part of his name?" Mathew asked.

"Because the baby's name has been legally changed but like yours has been. Like I said before you are both Coaltonstones. And I have a feeling you both will be great ones. Your little brother has already defied the odds. He lives, he breathes, and one day he will join the chapter of our special club which is just open to men," James predicted.

"Why don't you let women join?" Mathew asked. "I don't know if I would want to belong to a club that women were not allowed to join."

"It is tradition. We are a man's club. You will soon learn how distracting women can be," James said.

"If the truth be known Mathew, most men are terrified of women," Ashley interjected.

"And with good reason," James said as he sipped his water.

"Are you sure you and baby James won't get shot one day the way Ginger was?" Mathew asked.

"Absolutely sure, all true enemies usually want each other to stay alive. A man in my position may wonder who his friends are, but true enemies give meaning to life and can be blamed for all kinds of things," James said.

"So what do you think happened to Jay, George, Kevin and Sam? Do you think Mr. Bell shot them the way he shot Ginger?" Mathew asked.

"We have no idea what happened to them but my guess is they are hiding from their wives. What happened to Ginger was most a terrible and tragic accident," James Coaltonstone replied.

"What actually happened to Ginger?"

"I don't know yet," James replied.

"Is that true Doctor Knight or is Uncle James lying to me?"

"I am sure Mr. Coaltonstone is saying the truth his way, just like he always does," Ashley said.

"Okay, I will tell you something but it is a secret as in 'inside information', so you must swear that you won't give our secret away to anyone," James explained. "And that means you too, Ashley," James said as he winked.

"You have my word, Uncle James."

"You know everything you say to me in confidence stays here," Ashley replied.

"Okay, the secret is, I belong to a lodge and…"

"Is that the secret?" Mathew asked.

"Yes, partly, we have members all over the world, which means that many of our members are citizens of countries which are in conflict with each other. But brothers don't kill brothers. We have secret handshakes, secret words, secret agendas, and one day Mathew you will be invited to join."

"Why?"

"Because you have what it takes to be a brother of our order. You made $10,000 selling your photos, you have modified your flyke suit so you were able to flyke all the way here to visit us and your new brother. You are staying on our state of the heart ice melting ship. In life, son, what nature does can be devastating, but the power of money and brother can make up for some of it. Not all of it son, but some," James Coaltonstone said.

Mathew continued to look glum. "Uncle James, that gun and those bullets give me a very eerie feeling. Can we put them away?"

"Certainly, I thought it would be fun, to have a little target practice first thing we do at the beginning of the New Year," James suggested.

"How can we see the target, it is dark here all the time, all you can see are things that are lit up like drones and other people on boats," Mathew said.

"Ships, Mathew ships. We are on a ship not a rowboat. Did you notice all the drones flying back and forth? James asked.

"I did, they almost flew into me even though I am lit up just as much as a Christmas tree as all the other flykers," Mathew said.

"So where do you think all those drones are going and what do you think they are carrying?" James asked fighting back a smile which made Ashley smile for this was a side of the King of Coal very few would ever see.

"I bet they are carrying all kinds of Christmas presents," Mathew said.

"I think so too. Those drones are probably carrying all kinds of presents. Presents that were late being shipped, presents that were sent to the wrong address and now have to be returned to be resent. I bet there are all kinds of presents that fell through the cracks of the system, and if we shoot them down, they didn't only fall through the cracks in the system, they will be falling out of the sky into our laps. Even the unwanted presents could fall right into our laps," James replied.

"You think we should shoot down drones, Uncle James?" Mathew asked. "I saw protestors do that but I don't feel right doing that even if they were taking my picture. I think the drones were taking photos of the protestors before the protestors shot them down.

"I am sure your Uncle James would never do that, he is kidding, right Mr. Coaltonstone," Ashley asked James.

"I certainly am not. But if the boy does not feel right shooting down drones, he is a much better man than I," James said as he winked at Mathew.

"Seriously now, if we put your gun and ammo away we must them where we can get hold of them quickly if we have to. We might need your gun and my gun if those riff raff you saw on the way here board our ship without being granted permission," James said as he padded his coat pocket.

"You are kidding again, right, Uncle James?"

"I certainly am not. I follow the law of the sea. If it were up to me I would be following the French Revolutionary Calendar and today would not be New Year's Eve and I would only have to pay my workers for one day of rest every ten days instead of seven." James explained.

"You are joking right. How could anyone work for 10 days without rest. I need to rest on Sunday, at least. I sure miss everyone. I wish they were here. Or maybe I wish that I were with them right now," Mathew said.

"Mathew, you are doing very well, and don't feel guilty for doing so well when others around you are suffering. Sometimes that is one of the hardest things to learn how to do, isn't that right Mr. Coaltonstone."

"Well, that never bothered…"

"Mr. Coaltonstone!" Ashley exclaimed horrified that her humanist approach to life could be hijacked by James Coaltonstone's Machiavellian tendencies.

"My mother might be close to death and the only reason why my brother is alive is because Uncle James forced the hospital to sell him one of their incubators. It is cold and dark here all day long. And once we cross the Bering Strait we will have entered the military zone and everyone will be cross. You know Uncle James, I am hungry, can we eat now?"

"Having our last meal of the year together is grand idea, isn't that right Dr. Knight?"

"Certainly, I am getting hungry myself and I am sure Dr. Smith is even hungrier than I am.

"You see, Mathew. The world is not the happiest of places unless we make it happy. And little James is growing every minute. He is a little fighter. Your mother had an accident but she is going to recover nicely, isn't she Doctor Knight?" Coaltonstone gave Ashley such an intense glare it scared her.

"I am doing my best. That is all we can ever do," Ashley replied.

"No, as long as we best our competitors we win, regardless if it is our best or not," James said with a slight grin on his face. Ashley's make shift office on James' ship was adequate but not comfortable and James was beginning to feel cramping in his long legs..

"Now, Mathew, you have to be a little bit more positive or you will drive yourself insane and I would have failed you as your physician," Ashley added.

"So tell me what is good about my life right now."

"First of all you will be witnessing history. We are building a very new town beside Cold Feet Mountain," James said.

"The protestors have signs saying that you are moving a cemetery and a bunch of dead people to make room for Coalton Valley 2, that you bought the land super cheap and it could even be radioactive. Is that true?"

"Would the protestors prefer that I build our new town right on top of the cemetery?"

"Mr. Coaltonstone!"

"There are lots of things to be thankful for," James Coaltonstone said as he winked at Ashley. "You will be seeing the other side of Bering Strait which is a great privilege. And most important of all, you are now a Coaltonstone; a hyphenated one, but still a Coaltonstone. Your mother is in good hands and is recovering day by day. Isn't that right Doctor Knight?"

"We are doing the best we can sir under the circumstances," Ashley replied.

"I am sure you are. And Doctor Smith is attending to your mother and your little brother as we speak. You have money in the bank that is earning interest. The New Year will be rocky and at the same time very exciting. Just keep moving forward young man," James said.

"Mathew, your Mother needs to see a brave face when she wakes up and she will need to see a smiling face," Ashley said as she patted Mathew's knee.

"Quite right and you will love my castle. All the houses that can be moved from Pitville to Coalton Valley 2 are being moved. So once Coalton Valley 2 is set up, it will remind you of your old home in Pitville. It will just take time to adjust to everything, but Pitville is not what it used to be. That is what happens in life, things change, often for the bad. Only the winners thrive under such circumstance and only one person can win the race.

"What will the people left behind in Pitville do, Uncle James?"

"This will be a very exciting time for the tourist industry. We are arranging tours of the mines including Ginger's escape route, complete with ladders, ropes and special effects."

"What about all the protests? What about the coal seam fire? Have they been able to put it out yet?" Mathew asked.

"No, the coal seam fire is still burning. I am sure it will add to the value of the Pitville economy though. The tourists will soon be flocking to the smoke coming out of the roads and sidewalks," James replied.

"What about the polar bear protestors?" Mathew asked.

"You mean the polar bears are protesting too?"

"Uncle James, you know what I mean. Protestors are out on boats trying to save the polar bears."

"And those protestors know polar bears are meat eaters, right? Anyway, if the bears don't take care of them, I will have John Bell handle them in the same way we handle all of them."

"Isn't he the guy who killed Ginger? I hate him."

"Now, Mathew," Ashley interjected.

"I am sorry, Doctor Knight I just do hate him."

"Well we don't know what happened," James said wishing that he hadn't mentioned John Bell's name, and made a mental note to never mention his name to Mathew again."

"So, is Mr. Bell going to kill the protestors the way he killed Ginger?"

"Mathew, what happened to Ginger was a mistake. And if the protestors don't attack us, we won't have any reason to shoot them. That is the law of the sea," James said.

"What about the ones on the ship I saw when I flyked in? They seemed to be really concerned for the Polar Bears that have been found drowning or cannibalizing each other," Mathew said.

"Well those people need someone to hit them over the head."

"Mr. Coaltonstone, I do not think such comments are very helpful." Ashley intervened.

"Dr. Ashley, why am I being blamed for polar bear cannibalism? Next thing you know I will be blamed for poor Doctor Max's sudden heart attack that he suffered while on vacation, before he was scheduled to speak on how human behavior is effecting climate change," James complained.

"I think the issue here is that the polar bears' ice habitat is melting, which changes how these bears are able to follow their instincts. Bears are drowning, and bears are resorting to each other to ward off hunger."

"And you think we humans would not resort to cannibalism if we could not expand ways to grow food for themselves. If those protestors are so concerned for the polar bears' health why don't they just jump in the ocean and make the world a better place."

"Mr. Coaltonstone, really. This family meeting is losing its focus to say the least," Ashley said.

"Well those protestors are ruining everything. They are interfering with my way of life and encouraging my miners to strike."

"A lot has ruined my life too. My mom is on life support, my brother is on life support, Ginger is dead. Why did Mr. Bell kill Ginger, Uncle James?" Mathew asked.

"We don't know yet. John said Ginger had a gun," James replied.

"Ginger hated guns, he would have been a conscientious objector if they had allowed him to do that," Doctor Smith said as he rushed into the meeting room to defend Ginger's honor. "Where did you come from, Dan?" James Coaltonstone asked.

"I was stretching my legs and couldn't help but over hear your family meeting. I am sorry, James. I guess I got carried away. I delivered Ginger as you know.

"You did?" Mathew asked. "Wow. Was he has small as baby Ginger."

"You mean baby James," James interjected as Ashley threw her hands up in the air in exasperation."

"No Mathew, your baby brother is a preemie and our friend Ginger was full term." Doctor Smith explained.

"Oh," Mathew replied as he looked at Doctor Smith's watch.

"I can't bring Ginger back, but we can celebrate his life while introducing some of my new products. We will be serving Coaltonstone beef and Coaltonstone beer. We will be selling all kinds of souvenirs. Your baby brother will grow, and whatever weakness he has, he will find the strength inside himself to meet the challenge. And you, young man are a very talented photographer; you have sold your photographs. You must have a very handsome account balance as we speak."

"Actually I have around seven thousand and nine-hundred and fifty-seven dollars left. I took rest stops at a couple of Starbucks and MacDonald's in between here and Pitville. I also added some new features to my suit before I left. I had to get a really good head lamp and a down suit. It is so dark and cold all the time here.

"You have a great flyking suit. It is amazing that you flyked all the way here."

"If birds can do it, why can't I?"

"No reason at all. That is exactly what I mean. Bad things happen and good things happen. The work we will be doing up in the Arctic will make that part of the world more habitable to humans and easier to mine. During this decade we will own the weather, Mathew. Bad things will always happen in this world. And we have to find ways to survive and stick it out no matter what. Owning the weather is part of that struggle. The future will is full of promise. The Arctic owns more than a fifth of the world's oil and gas resources, rare earth metals, coal, uranium, gold, diamonds, zinc, platinum; mostly untapped and there for the taking. All we have to do is quicken the melting of the ice caps, tilt Earth's axis a little, and we could turn the Arctic into a warmer and more habitable where the wealth becomes accessible."

"How are you going to do that, Uncle James?"

"We are hoping that our private submarines blasting the ice with nuclear warhead will work otherwise we will have to wait until one of the many countries at war decide to throw nuclear bombs at each other, which could be any day now," James said

"How are we going to survive a nuclear war," Mathew asked.

"We will have to keep our distance son and work on peaceful uses so that one day we can own and control the weather now. Just imagine the world with an ice free Arctic Ocean would mean a huge boom in oceanic shipping between Europe and East Asia. The wastelands in Northern Canada and Siberia would be free for farming, increasing the food production supply for all. An ice Free Arctic would lead to more rain even in desert regions. Imagine the world with more places to grow food. Many people, including myself believe that the prophecy in the bible, turning weapons into ploughshares, meant this type of project. Where we can use nuclear energy for good, and expand shipping roots, free up more farmland while expanding our mining capacity."

"But Uncle James wouldn't melting the ice caps lead to more global warming, tilting of Earth's axis toward Canada and raise sea levels? What about all that radiation. Isn't that why there are so many protestors following us, because they claim that people you know were hiding radioactive materials, and those materials led to people getting cancer who wouldn't have normally gotten it. And how did people in the old days, when the bible was written, know about nuclear energy and nuclear weapons?"

"Just imagine a warmer world, Mathew? Imagine a world without hunger."

"But Uncle James what will happen when the see level rises."

"It won't rise that much. This coming New Year will be grand. I promise."

"But Uncle James what happens if the Arctic Ice comes back."

"It won't."

"How do you know? Weather seems to be getting harder to predict."

"Because this year I am going to own the weather. Don't look so surprised. Think of all the coal I own. It is just logical that I should own the weather too. Besides that, ice will be harder to form when the sun's radiation no longer has ice to reflect upon sending it back into the Arctic Sky. Once the ice is gone, the sun's radiation won't be able to reflect back into the sky the way it does now, so the retained heat will keep the Arctic ice from coming back ," James said.

"And what about the rest of the world?" Mathew asked.

"What about it?" James replied.

"People say that that when the Polar Ice Caps melt, the earth could change its tilt, seasons could be effected, and oceans could rise and drown all kinds of people all over the world," Mathew said.

"The brothers that belong to our lodge will be fine. They are builders and problem solvers and most of them are very good swimmers, may I add."

"What about everyone else?" Mathew asked.

"What about them?" James asked back.

Chapter 2
Waiting for Alex

December 31st 2030, around 10:00 PM: "Where is Alex Coaltonstone? I thought our main focus at this meeting was to focus costs related to moving Coalton Valley, or as much as we can of it, to our new location. I bet you anything he has been delayed by all those protestors taking over the streets."

"Actually sir, they are going to a memorial meeting for Ginger Goodwin. Since the autopsy has delayed the funeral, the public needed to celebrate his life and his death and his senseless shooting," Susan said as she her eyes fixed on her computer screen. "I could phone him, sir," Susan Jones offered.

"Why, haven't you already?"

"I was taking notes, sir," Susan replied beginning to sound as nervous as she felt.

"As you know James is speculating in the Arctic…"

"I thought he was looking for Polar Ice Caps to Nuke," Susan interrupted.

Mayor Stern looked at Susan sternly and continued. "Nevertheless, James has assured me that Alex would be costing the moving to Coalton Valley 2 operation, in real time not his time."

"Excuse me, I think the coffee is here, Susan please get the door," Mayor Stone ordered nicely. As Susan opened the door a drone flew in carrying four cups of from in broad daylight at Starbucks I have been using this service and I love it. As you can see I ordered Alex a cup of latté in its cargo container.

"Ever since my car was stolen I wish I had used this service before my car had been stolen," Mayor Stern said.

"Didn't you get your car back Mr. Stern? I thought I saw it parked in the driveway," Susan said.

"Yes, I got the car back but the schedule with very special calculations, which James had been sourced out, is missing and James is furious with me. Why we had no other copies made is beyond me," Mayor Stern said not even trying to hide the exasperation he was feeling. This was New Year's Eve. His wife was hosting a small get together with Club Leaders.

"Why would a schedule be top secret?" Susan asked.

"Beats me," Mayor Stern replied.

"Sir, shouldn't we also be costing security in Pitville? Jethro and Bill have sent urgent email to John that those protestors hanging out on Cold Feet Mountain are just as furious as the protestors are who are hanging out in Pitville. They are upset that Ginger was shot, upset that the Mine doesn't seem to be opening so men are now out of work. They are upset that the loans James will be granting to unemployed miners will have a 10% interest rate which will be compounding semi-annually attached to them. Now there is intelligence that the schedule that Mr. Stern is talking about is the protestors' hands, and there are thousands of copies being made," Don explained.

"I don't get it, with all that is going on, why would anyone care about a schedule?" Susan asked.

"I don't know but Jethro and Bill are assuming that all this anger will lead to violence. Today's protest has been going on all day and into the night. The situation is very dangerous. You don't need to be an intelligence officer to figure that out," Don said.

"Funeral, Don, it is a funeral. I don't understand. What is the big deal about the schedule?" Susan interjected.

"How can we cost something what we don't know is going to happen? These protestors, as a class of human being, are impossible to predict. We need to talk about the costs related to the moving of our most valuable structures to the Coalton Valley

2 location. Our new location in the cave country is beautiful and will be great, and we need Alex here so can be briefed on costs," Mayor Stern said.

"How are the locals handling the moving of their cemetery?" Susan asked.

"Pretty much as expected; we have air surveillance overseeing operations. Those assets are working beyond our most optimistic expectations. The whistle bots call shift cycles and the deportees are obeying those signals, as if their lives depend on them following the ten day week as if they were still in Mina." Mayor Stern said.

"For how long?" Don asked.

"For as long as they live, and they better obey all orders for as long as we say, if they want their lives to be long," Mayor Stern said.

"You are kidding right?" Susan asked.

"What do you think, Susan? Choosing that flat spot near Cold Feet Mountain as our new base was a stroke of brilliance. The mountain is already proving to be very profitable and is more than making up for the wasteful work stoppage these protestors are causing," Mayor Stern said as he slammed his coffee cup down on his huge Brazilian mahogany desk, unintentionally. "The disruptions to our way of life by these outsiders, is unacceptable. Our most capable deportees are being sent as replacements and will be bunked under Coalton Valley 2," Mayor Stern explained.

"Sir, the work stoppage is in honor of Ginger Goodwin. Everyone has all kinds of emotions. Some are still in shock and still can't believe that Ginger of all people is dead. Others are furious that John shot him and don't believe it was necessary," Susan said as she was still waiting for Alex to answer his phone.

"I just hope that those protestors don't mistake me for him," Don said trying to not sound like he was whining.

"Just keep wearing your name tag," Susan said as she covered the mouth piece of her phone with her hand.

"Where is Alex? Why can't you get him on the phone?" Mayor Stern asked.

"Here he is sir," Susan said and he handed the phone to Mayor Stern.

"Finally," Mayor Stern said.

"Oh my God," Alex yelled out in pain.

"Alex where are you and why are you yelling in my ear? Have you gone mad like everyone else around here?" Mayor Stern demanded to know.

"I am sorry. Mr. Stern, I just spilled my coffee all over my lap when I grabbed my phone," Alex said. "I just stopped for a coffee at Starbucks, Oh no!"

"Oh no? Alex what is wrong"

"Mayor Stern?" Police Chief Cuff asked?

"Yes, who is this? Oh no, it sounds like Police Chief Cuff."

"I don't just sound like her, I am her. Need I remind you and this Coaltonstone boy, tonight of all nights, being New Year's Eve and the never ending Ginger's funeral related events, that I have zero tolerance for talking on phones while driving? In this case I didn't just catch the Coaltonstone boy talking on the phone but drinking coffee too. I have a good mind to arrest him and throw him in the same cell as his brother who is downright miserable right now and we all know how misery loves company. But I am only giving him one warning. Consider the phone hung up."

"What else could go wrong today?" Don Bell asked.

"Don't ask," Susan Jones said. "Don how is your wife?"

"She is okay but there are so many decisions. We never know if we are making the right one. Our family doctors have disappeared so we are getting by with the help of ER docs," Don explained.

"Oh please, we are sorry for your situation, but time is money," Mayor Stern interjected.

"I am sorry. It is all I think about," Don Said.

"I am sorry too," Susan replied.

"So the question is what could possibly go wrong today?"

"As head of Mine Five Safety 'what could possibly go wrong today, is the first question I ask every day," Don Replied.

"Well Mine Five isn't operating anymore and the best houses are being moved to Coalton Valley 2 Where are Jethro and Bill? Weren't they supposed to be helping John with security?" Susan asked.

"I don't know where Jethro and Bill are? I never know where they are. They are technically spies so they are probably spying on the strangers which seem to be everywhere. They could be assisting the cemetery moving-crew. Or they could be assisting in the rounding up of the Undocumented Illegals before they are scattered all over the region. Jethro and Bill are helping with security somewhere and they usual operate under cover and secretly," Don said.

"I certainly hope someone from security is overseeing those two," Mayor Stern said.

"Actually there has been no sighting of Jethro and Bill in Coalton Valley 2. I checked with our people there. I described them. They are not hard to miss. Both of them must be over 6ft 4. There are protestors were camping all around, and even on Cold Feet Mountain chanting and dancing," Susan said.

"I hear that those locals are descendants of Neanderthals," Mayor Stern said.

"We are all descendants of Neanderthals," Susan said.

"Susan, please, silence is golden. Now Don, can you please tell us, one more time, why your brother shot Ginger Goodwin?" Mayor Stern asked without trying to hide his exasperation.

"No, I can't"

"Try!"

"John said it was self defence, sir. I wasn't there, Sir. I have to believe my brother's word but from my own personal experience, I have never known Ginger to be violent or ever owning a gun. I have no idea what happened. I am just as tormented about all this as anyone would be. Ginger was a loyal employee and John is my brother." Don Bell explained.

"Aren't you afraid that you might get mistaken for John, Don, and get shot," Susan asked.

"Susan!" Mayor Stern scolded.

"Of course I am scared. I am terrified. That is why I got my permit to carry a concealed weapon. It was actually John's idea for me to carry one."

"I guess we will just have to wait until John is released from the police station; then he can tell us what actually happened." Susan Jones said.

"John is head of our security, he was just doing his job," Mayor Stern interjected.

"I can't believe my brother would shoot Ginger for no reason, and I can't believe Ginger would have a gun. Ginger hated guns. He should have been given conscientious objector status. This war against the Minese

"G.O.D has declared war on the Minese so every able bodied man was ordered to sign up for service and most of us have, but we also have to differentiate between the Minese Government which we re technically at war with and the actual innocent people who risked their lives to help Ginger out of Mine Five, when our own people could or would not," Don said.

"War always makes everything complicated. And when it is over," Susan said.

"Please, everyone, we need to be focusing on strategy so that the protestors do not get out of hand. This meeting is going to be useless. We don't have our head of security with us, he is in jail. Where is Alex? These protests could get very nasty," Mayor Stern said.

"Actually sir, as I said, the public are participating in Ginger Goodwin's memorial service."

"Susan you mindless fool just shut up. What did I say about talking? I told you to shut up," Mayor Stern screamed as he glared at Susan.

Chapter 3
Lost In A Strange World

December 31ˢᵗ 2030, around 10:00 PM:
Decade II, First Day Of Snowy In The year CCXXXIX of the

Revolution: "Where are we?" Jay asked.

"I wish I knew," Sam said

"Everything I had on me is gone. What are we doing in these striped pajamas?" Kevin asked.

"I still have my father's watch on. It is still working and it lights up amazingly enough. We have two hours left and then this horrible year is over. My headlamp is gone." George replied.

"So we lost a week somewhere? Did we fall into the abys or what?" Jay asked.

"Where ever we are the lighting system is rather cool," Sam said.

"Dangling bulb," George said.

"The light hurts my eyes! Kevin said while the others were glad to see where they were.

"It looks like we fell into a Nazi storage room," George said.

"This stuff looks like a century old," Sam said.

"Yeah, it probably is. Jay said.

"We are obviously somewhere underground," George said.

"Look at all this stuff, what did we fall into?" Sam said as he looked around, feeling miserable.

"I thought all this stuff had been blow up almost a century ago," Sam said.

"Apparently not; it looks like all this stuff has been sitting around waiting until it came back into style," George said.

"We must be in some creepy Nazi cult storage room for. Do you remember anything at all, anyone? Jay asked.

"Last thing I remember is getting hit over the head by something when we were in one of the tunnels trying to help Ginger.

I remember a big Minese guy who said he was going to help us," Kevin said.

"Well where do you think we are?" Jay asked

"Somewhere in a very cold and dark realm," George said

"As in the Reich?" Kevin asked

"Wherever we are it feels like Hell," Jay said.

"I thought Hell was supposed to be hot," Kevin interjected.

"Welcome, to my world, you are in Mina." Ono said as he walked into the room.

"Didn't we meet in one of Mine Five's tunnels? Where are we?" George asked.

"You sloppy men are in one of the many Firestones' storage rooms. You have been sleeping for what you call a week, but we in Mina call a decade. Your friend Ginger Goodwin is dead; shot in cold blood by one of your people, John Bell.

"John shot Ginger? Why would he do that?" George asked.

"John Bell claims self-defense but we say John Bell is a coward and shot a hero, our friend, Ginger Goodwin in cold blood. So in tough times are created by and for tough men. Isn't that right Jethro, Bill any one of you can speak?

Bill and Jethro looked at each other then looked at Ono. Either one of you can answer."

"Yes sir, Sergeant Ono." Jethro and Bill said in unison.

"I remember you two. Weren't you working on John Bell's crowd control team?" George asked.

"We cannot discuss Firestone business with unauthorized personnel," Jethro replied.

"What are you talking about?" Jay said.

"While you drank yourselves silly and jumped into our hemp crate that was being sent with shipment the world has changed drastically in just a mere week, which is why we, in this nation of foresight, have been right all along to call a week a decade.

"What are you talking about? Where are we, really?"

"You are in our underground tunnel system deep underneath the Military Zone. We call our land Mina, but you already must have known that. You have a recall chip in your forehead so that is why you recall nothing."

"What?"

"We discovered you sloppy men in your mess in our hemp crates. We cleaned you up, processed you, under our mandatory recall chip program. This is the way all illegals are processed." Ono said before Jay interrupted him.

"Recall chip? Last thing I remember is being hit over the head with a really hard object. I don't remember anything, and why are we wearing stripped pajamas?"

"You are in the uniform of the illegals. You have no legal identity here. You entered our military zone illegally,"

'Since when did you care about fashion, Jay?" Sam asked.

"Since the word 'fashion' is so close to the word 'fascist', that is when," George retorted back.

"We helped Ginger escape from Safety Chamber E. He refused to fight us in this stupid war you people have raged against us," Ono said.

"Hold on, we are at war?" Kevin asked.

"Yes, and Ginger was shot on the 27th of December, but in our calendar we call December 'Snow' and our New Year is September 22nd, Fall Equinox. Ginger Goodwin refused to sign up to fight us because we were the only ones who actually helped him and because we are all miners," Ono explained.

"That isn't entirely true; before we bumped into you in the tunnel, you were ignoring Ginger's tragic situation just like everyone else was," Jay interjected

"I do not need to argue with you sloppy men. We are not hiding in your world; you are in our hidden world now. Ginger gave a beautiful speech straight from his heart for everyone who would listen. He said it on Pitville's Alternative Radio Station, and was shot minutes later in the heart by heartless men, while he was dying; his son was born and is called James Coaltonstone…"

"What? How could Ginger Goodwin's kid be named after the very man who may have ordered him to be shot?" George asked.

"Boss is a good man. He would not order his son shot and he has adopted his grandson and married Christina. You will be protected here, as long as you obey. Soon Boss will be King of Everything, so we must show respect to him. Baby James was born a few hours after Ginger died. Christina went into labour, and James Coaltonstone woke up the Chief Justice of the Peace so they could marry before baby James was born," Ono explained

"I didn't think Christina was that far along," Jay said.

"No, she was under 22 weeks, actually. James had to coerce the hospital to sell him the life support equipment. Christina was only married to James Coaltonstone for less than a week before she jumped from his ship into icy Arctic waters. Enough gossip.

"Figures, I would do the same if I married James Coaltonstone," Jay said.

"Hold on, is Christina okay, will the baby be okay?" George asked.

"It is not for me to talk about boss's business. I have said too much already. You are now in the militarized zone on my side of the Bering Strait, without a permit. And let me add that you are here very illegally.

"That is terrible English," Jay said.

"So what? It is now you sloppy men who must watch your every step, the tables have been turned.

"I don't understand. What are you talking about? Where are we? Why are we here?" Jay asked

"We need miners. You have been smuggled out of your tunnels into ours," Ono replied.

"But why don't you just keep your miners at home, if you need miners so badly," Sam asked.

"Because the miners want to be paid in American money," Ono explained

"So do we!" Jay interjected.

"Here, you are paid nothing. You work. You live. Pitville chapter of G.O.D. and the Exclusion League, have declared war on the Minese people even though we carried Ginger Goodwin out of the mine, when no one else would. We are good people and before war was declared we were treated like garbage. Now after war is declared we are treated like your enemy even though we are all miners. We find the wealth of the world. Without us, there would be no resources, no fuel nothing. Now you are here, you get to know us. That will be good," Ono said.

"So what else did you bring over to the other side besides us, and how did we lose a week. I find this very hard to believe," Jay asked.

"I told you before what you call a week, we call a decade. To answer your question, which is really none of your business, we brought over anthracite coal of course, hemp, jade and gold. The boss is moving some of the houses in Pitville to Coalton Valley 2 So we will be going back and forth from this base. Boss is also going to melt the Polar Ice Caps a bit so it will be easier to mine up in the Northern Wasteland," Ono explained.

"How is he planning to do that?" Jay asked.

"Knowing Coaltonstone, he is going to nuke them," George said.

"Exactly," Ono replied.

"Wouldn't that melt the ice caps, sooner before later, making the axis tilt and make the climate even more extreme than it already is?" Jay asked.

"We in Mina only look at the positive. We cannot control nature. Climate change happens naturally. Earth changes, we all change. It will be easier to mine everything now. It was too hard to mine what was mineable in that frozen wasteland. We ship out on our new routes. We work under Boss' flag. Once those ice caps are melted we will have a North East Passage to glory, and a new asset to tax," Ono explained.

"Is mineable even a word?" Sam asked.

"Come on Sam," Jay said.

"What about the radiation?" George asked.

"What about it? And why do you mock me, sloppy man in stripped pajamas. One day I will be one of the most powerful generals on this planet, and no one will even remember that you existed at all." Ono responded.

"Well, where we come from radiation is feared just as much as cancer is," George said.

"Radiation? Cancer? We are never told about those things," Jay said.

"It is all natural. Anyway it is Boss' business, not yours. You do as you are told or you will be sorry. And you are now in the Military Zone without a permit," Ono replied. "You will use these tunnels to work and you will be assigned a place to live in the cave district and you must keep it clean. You walk there in these tunnels, you must not litter. These tunnels are your world now. They are black and shiny and have state of the art lighting system. We work a ten hour day and a ten day week."

"You mean you work for ten hours?" Sam asked

"Yes and we have ten hour days. You see our clock; we have ten hours not twelve.

"What?" Jay asked.

"You have a lot to learn about our ways. You can't stay here; we are making very important experiments further north. You will be happy in cave district. You will work. Discover our ways," Ono explained.

"Well what about our wives and kids? We can't just forget them. We need them and they need us," Jay protested.

"You are foolish men. They will soon forget you. They will think you are dead. Christina married Boss the day Ginger was shot. We are at war." Ono said.

"This war is already very stupid and cruel, isn't it?" Jay Paylor added.

"War is stupid when leaders refuse to be reasonable. Now that the ice has thawed enough so that Northern Sea Route is able to change everything, the whole world of power will be turned upside down. No one is going to let that happen without a fight. Of course there will be conflict between haves and not haves," Ono said.

"You mean have nots?" Jay said.

"Yes, 'the have nots'. We are in hidden land of Mina and will prevail. Boss will soon become king of everything. Boss is working with G.O.D. so that we will own the weather and today we own you. We don't pay you but we feed you. If you don't do as we say, exactly, we blow you up. Why are you sloppy men laughing? You, stand by that wall, now." Ono ordered as Sam obeyed. You three stand far away," Ono ordered again as he took out an ancient looking remote control and pushed a button."

"Sam appeared to be burning up in a flame as he disappeared into a pile of dust.

"How did you do that? I mean why did you do that? He did nothing to you." Jay said almost in tears.

"Warning for you, obey. This is a militarized zone. You are lucky that I don't blow you all up. You are nothing but a nuisance to me. Be grateful that I have spared your lives. You owe me your lives. I am your master. These tunnels go to many places, and we will continue digging. You now work for me. You men talk too much. You must be silent to be successful in Mina. You will live in ten hour days and ten day weeks, just like we do. You are in my land. You will live here until you die here."

Ono said as he blew his whistle. Four men in black SS uniforms, complete with swastika armbands and black boots, appeared at the entrance. They kicked their heels and stood to attention while a fifth man wearing a black robe entered the room.

"Sergeant Ono, are you a fool? Your father tells me that you are being trained to replace the Supreme One. Just tell me that you are not a fool," Judge Bell commanded.

"Judge Bell? What are you doing here, are you going to arrest Ono for blowing up Sam?" George asked.

"Actually I should be asking you that question. Judge Bell sounding more irritated than condescending. "You are the ones here illegally in a military zone, you are a fool, only a fool would be here.

"I am not sure how we got here, or where we are, or what happened," George said.

"Why did Ono have to kill Sam? He never hurt anyone," Kevin said.

"Sergeant Ono made a mistake, that will never be repeated," Judge Bell said as he raised his voice.

"Why did Ono have to kill Sam so mindlessly like that, as if he didn't matter to anyone. Sam did matter. He mattered to us and he mattered to his family," George said.

"Ono, did you hear that. You blew someone up who will be missed. You are acting like a fool. Where is your sense of strategy? Your father assures me that you have inherited such a mind. I do not see a strategic mind that is why we admitted you to the Firestones." Judge Bell said.

Chapter 4
Doctor Ashley Knight wonders what to do.
In-Reach Entry, LOG #3, written by Dr. Ashley Knight

December 31st, 2030, Around 10:15 PM: I am not sure what happened to Christina. I am not sure if she tried to commit suicide or if she fell from the ship's deck. One of the ship's staff said that she heard Christina call out Ginger's name and may have seen his projection in the water.

Daniel suspects that it was Jackson, from the PPZ, who stole my patient's InReach files during his and Dianne's visit to my Pitville office. Talking about my Pitville office, I am very concerned that Laura Bell, Don Bell's wife, will feel that I have abandoned her during what could be one of the worst days of her life, because she will be losing her left breast to breast cancer. I am here on this ship just staring at Christina and her little baby who is so small; it is a miracle he is still living. He is quite the fighter. James has shown me medical files where a number of Minese babies who have been born before their time and thriving, a little weaker maybe, but thriving anyway. James swears that the Supreme Being is less rigid with time clocks than we are. First time I saw one of James' ten hour clocks and ten day calendars I thought he was crazy. Now I think he could drive us crazy by disorienting us with this strange way of measuring time. Like everything else, this strange schedule system is self-serving for James. Shorten days by 2 hours, less time to sleep.

Another pressing problem, though it now seems to be a world away, is that the possible misuse of my patient's InReach files by the PPZ cameraman goes against every book of ethics that I can think of. The whole point for my 'InReach Project was to help my clients find their inner strength, their inner diamond, which once found, will enable them to meet any objective or goal of their choosing. I am appalled that anyone would steal my clients' files and then use inside information to create a make believe whistle blower called Deep Coal. And with Ginger Goodwin being Ginger Goodwin, he was assumed to be Deep Coal, which may have been one of the reasons why John Bell shot him. Who knows? I am just devastated so I can imagine what kind of frame of mind Christina was in before she fell from the ship's deck, into that icy Arctic water.

Ginger died too soon on the very day his son was born too soon.

I know my theory works and has the potential to heal. Having the internal strength to face the external world as a stronger and more focused person, is everything. As a humanist psychologist, I do not want to use psychology to dehumanize. I want to use the tools to uplift.

Men create goals and objectives as their birthright and often are given the freedom to do so. But women tend to have their goals cut down before they are obtainable. Especially in Pitville, women are judged, very harshly may I add, by attributes others place on them, not by their accomplishments. And once these unfair judgements get under the skin, I have seen this over and over again, mental distress sometimes leading to chemical changes to their system. Men tend to have it much easier, when it comes to managing their lives by following objectives. Even when a woman has a clear objective, goal and possibly even love for a profession, she is treated as bossy, egotistical, and the busy bodies of Pitville are out in force, pecking her into submission.

To come back to us, Christina needs to feel safe again.

Now baby Ginger, James Coaltonstone has managed to engineer a speedy adoption and has legally called baby Ginger James Coaltonstone Junior. The only reason why they are not referring baby Ginger as Junior, is because Mathew Watson

Junior has been called Junior all of his life. Since Mathew Watson's horrific mining accident, I have advised Christina to rotate the use of the name Junior with Mathew, for obvious reasons.

It is so dark and cold here. We have to dress from head to toe in down suits, parkas and all kinds of layers, especially on our feet and hands, when we go outside. Mathew is actually flyking everywhere. His first photography sale, I believe has helped him to stay on task and move forward with his future, even though he has had terrible tragedies in his life. His father killed in Mine Five, Ginger being shot, both his brother and his mother on life support, and now his name change. James Coaltonstone has managed to defy reason as usual, and for some reason Mathew seems to be still functioning following example's both James and Ginger seem to have taught him. When I left, what I call my patient meeting room, James was showing Mathew a secret handshake he calls the Firestone Shake.
End of In-Reach entry, LOG #3 by Dr. Ashley Knight MD (Coaltonstone Ship).

Chapter 5
Doctor Daniel Smith torn between worlds
In-Reach Entry, LOG #3, written by Dr. Daniel Smith

December 31st, 2030, around 10:15 PM: I don't know where to start. I feel so drained. Baby Ginger is so small, so fragile, and such a little fighter. Ashley fights back tears as she cares for the little guy. Poor Christina; I am still not quite sure what happened. I go from thinking she may have jumped, to she might have fallen. The rumor that she may have been pulled in by Ginger's ghost is totally in bad taste. Anyway Ginger would never do such a thing to a woman he loved so much, and I know she loved him, just as much.

When I delivered Ginger Goodwin, thirty years ago on Christmas day, he was the same way. Anyway the little guy is now legally James Coaltonstone's son and his name is now James Watson-Coaltonstone.

I am certain that Christina Watson suffered from a moment of despair before she jumped into that icy cold Arctic water. James swears that the Supreme Being saved Christina in the same way that he is saving the little baby. I try not to delve into the unexplained since that kind of thing drive me crazy.

What motivates a person to jump from a ship? Christina needs to want to wake up. How can I encourage her to wake up, when all I want to do is sleep away this nightmare too.

That water should be ice. We shouldn't even be this far north on this ship. The ice is being continually zapped by the aerosol guns which are attached to the fleet of ships belonging to the Big Seven Coal Group. This aerosol technology is primitive and barbaric but if that doesn't work, the powers to be are going to nuke the Polar Ice Caps into submission.

Mathew sleeps with his wings on. Everyone around him seems to be dead or almost dead. He has agreed to his name change as long as he could hyphenate Coaltonstone with Watson. Mathew seems to be blocking off his feelings and doing a pretty good job of it. He sold some of his photography to that creepy cameraman from PPZ, Jackson Green. Speaking of Jackson Green, I am certain that he was the one who stole Ashley's project data; leaked it, called the whistleblower 'Deep Coal', and made people think it was Ginger Goodwin.

My guess is that John Bell will be out of jail and about as if nothing happened any moment now, and so will Bobby, which will only motivate the unemployed miners to rebel, maybe even violently.

Talk about violent, I thought it would be serene here, despite the bitter cold and darkness, there are a lot of loud explosions and cracking sounds. Mathew Junior told me that when he was flyking he saw a lot of run down boats that looked like protestors were heading here and that we might be getting tracked. So who knows what the future will bring.

And who can blame them? Rebelling is the preferable option to suicide I suppose.

The new town is going to be even more depressing than the old town and should be called Machiavelli Valley 2 instead of Coalton Valley 2. And this obsession with ten hour clocks and ten day weeks is just beyond belief. I have seen my share of Machiavellian personalities in my day, but James Coaltonstone beats them all. To use ten hour clocks and ten day weeks to manipulate and confuse people will also stretch the work day and work week, leaving little time for much else.

I think Christina and Ginger's baby will be okay. He is a little fighter. And only time I see any softness in James is when he places faces with the baby. I have never seen him like that before. He is both grandfather and father to the little guy which is a very strange situation. I hear rumors that James was glad to see Ginger shot, but I find it hard to believe that any man would want his son dead, even a son he refused to acknowledge, yet he has taken to the baby as if it were his own, technically he is his grandson, he seems to be acknowledging that in a roundabout way.

Poor Christina; I am still not quite sure what happened. I go from thinking she may have jumped, to she might have fallen. The rumor that she may have been pulled in by Ginger's ghost is totally in bad taste. Anyway Ginger would never do such a thing to a woman he loved so much, and I know she loved him, just as much.

I hear that Jackson Green and Dianne Black will be coming aboard soon to celebrate New Year's Eve. I must have a talk with Jackson, but I am not sure how to go about it.

End of In-Reach entry, LOG #3 by Dr. Daniel Smith MD (Coaltonstone Ship).

Chapter 6
Looking For The Coalton Ship

December 31st 2030; around 11:00 PM: "I can see the Coaltonstone Ship on the tracker," Jackson announced.

"Wonderful," Dianne replied. "I wonder what Coaltonstone is planning to do?

"We know that he is moving buildings from Pitville to a flat spot near Cold Feet Mountain and he will be calling his new mining town Coalton Valley 2. We also know that coal mining is already an ongoing concern at that location. No one is on strike there, and the mountain is full of coal. I have heard rumors, but they sound crazy, even for Coaltonstone," Jackson said.

"What rumors?" Dianne asked.

"Coaltonstone is alleged to be involved in the nuking of the polar ice caps, so he can free up the natural resources now stuck under all that ice, and create new shipping lanes." Jackson explained.

"You are right, that is crazy."

"That is one of the rumors," Jackson said.

"Okay, what is the other rumor?" Dianne asked.

"Well if it is true it is a big one. The radioactive waste is buried all over the place, and some of it might be leaking. They just seem to dig holes, making it look like it is a burial, since that location is a cemetery, and bury these containers of radioactive waste.

"Where is the waste come from/"

"I would guess that it is from the polar ice melting project. Now they have to move it all to make room for Coalton Valley 2. If that is not bad enough, he is trying to push the natives from their ancestral land, Frozen Feet Mountain.

"We are already hearing eskimos swearing that the sky is changing. The sun sets and rises slightly differently than the old days. They are attributing the change to jet trails, melting of the Polar Ice Caps, and the tilting of the axis.

"Dianne you are looking ravishing in your down suit, permission to board Ship One is granted. Just come aboard when you are ready." James said then added "Doctor Smith just sent me an email; he wants to talk to Jackson, man to man about some sort of dysfunction that he appears to have,"

"What? I don't have any dysfunction," Jackson said louder than he intended to.

"Oops," James said wondering what the message was really about.

Chapter 7
Mina's cave district

January 1st, 2031, around 1:30 AM Pitville Time:
Decade II, Second day of Snowy in the Year CCXXXIX of
the Revolution: " Well here we are; home away from home.
What are we supposed to do now? Jay asked.

"You sloppy men do what you always do. You make some Mr. Noodles and tea then you should go to sleep.

"That is not what we usually do. We usually have a beer and a dish of Mr. Noodles," Jay said.

"You have two hours less to waste in sleep. You have no Sunday here. You should thank the Supreme Being for the gift of work. Eat, sleep, wake up when the bot whistle whistles, go to work like usual," Ono blared from a loud speaker which was situated in the corner of the small cave room.

"Wow, is this even real?" Jay asked.

"I would think so, Jay. You are never in my dreams," George replied.

"So do we have a plan at all?

"You eat, sleep and go to work on Boss Whistle's command and nothing more. Death is your only escape from here." Ono sounded angrier this time as he blared from the speaker.

Chapter 8
Mathew's Homework Problem

December 31st 2030, around 11:30 PM: "It is half an hour before New Year's Eve and you are doing homework? I am not sure if I should hug you or ostracize you?"

"Maybe you can help me; I am really confused about this history assignment. I don't get it," Mathew complained.

"And you think I should get it? Tell me why?

"Well you were born four years after the Kennedy's assassination so don't you remember why they kept so many files secret and they just opened them up last year?" Mathew asked.

"How would I know? It was all secret and I was busy flittering my youth away playing with super balls, yoyos, toy robots and slinkies.

"So how am I supposed to answer the question?" Mathew asked.

"Well, what is the question?"

"There are a few. Why did JFK get assassinated, why were files only opened last year, and what color of dress was Jackie Kennedy wearing at the time.

"Jackie's dress was pink. You must have known that answer. It is hard to know why JFK was assassinated. Lee Harvey Oswald allegedly shot him, but popular thoughts seem to ride with he had help or he may have been a decoy. It was a terrible thing. He was so young with so much promise and maybe that is why someone wanted him shot. Who knows why people shoot other people. Some people think just because a person owns a gun or two makes them want to shoot it, unstable people anyway, normal people won't feel like that. Normal people like us."

"So why was it so secret? Why did they open the files up last year?" Mathew asked.

"Nobody really knows. Some say it might have been just to cool down speculation but by making files secret only made people more curious in my opinion," James explained.

"What about Pay Of Pigs?"

"Sometimes Presidents have to choose between the least evil, and the decision is almost never a winning choice. At the time, Russia had missiles so close to us, we were terrified. Somethings, especially in politics, have no answer.

Chapter 9
Threats

January 1st 2031, around 10:00 AM: "I am holding this meeting because ever since the Warner report has been declassified, concerning cold war secret technology, the more radical miners have found a way to acquire an electromagnetic bomb which would cause mass destruction to our electronic equipment. The end result to our assets would be comparable to being attacked by bolts of lightning," John Bell said.

"My God, are you sure?" Mayor Stern asked.

"Almost, we always knew declassifying those reports would be a security risk," John Bell replied.

"Well it sounds rather farfetched to me," Mayor Stern said.

"No the threat is real and the weapon is very portable. Electromagnetic Pulse generators are getting easier to build. And considering how much copper wire has gone missing lately, I think we must remain vigilante," John Bell said.

"When does it end? Was it really necessary to shoot Ginger? The miners are really protesting the shooting," Don Bell said.

"Maybe, but many of our best employees are moving their houses as we speak and joining Coalton Valley 2 at the foot of Cold Feet Mountain. And that is what we should be doing with our time. A lot of preparation is going into this move. We have moved the cemetery and the waste piles which have been contained in safe containers."

"We also have to consider the chaos being caused as the ice caps are being nuked. Part of the fall out is ionization, but the effect seems very minimal where we are," Don said.

"Pitville is old and tired and our coal seam is burning. We are much better off leaving this nightmare behind us." John Bell said.

Chapter 10
Cold Feet Mountain

In-Reach Entry, LOG #1, written by Don Bell
Coalton Valley 2, Hut 7

January 5th 2031, around 10:30 PM: I am here.

Coalton Valley 2 is quite amazing. Considering how long it took for Coalton Valley 1 to develop, it is like Coalton Valley 2 sprung up overnight. James has assured us that all the radiation has been cleaned up, though I am not quite sure how that was done. The radiation counts have been tested and all three times they have been found to be safe. There are a lot of protestors sitting by little fires beside little tents.

Mr. Coaltonstone sent my brother to the other side of the Bering Strait so he can learn how they handle the protestors who are going on about dump radioactive materials in the Bering Sea. Actually it is alleged to have happened a long time ago, but it is just recently that so many cases of cancer have come to public attention.

There is a lot of commotion outside. I am always getting mistaken for my brother. I am still not sure what happened or why John shot Ginger, the whole situation is pretty hard to understand. Ginger didn't even own a gun. Ginger was one of the very few people around here who didn't carry a gun.

There are lots of people around my house. I think they are protesting as if I was the one who shot Ginger, and it wasn't me. I still can't figure out how it happened.

End of In-Reach entry, LOG #1 by Don Bell (Coalton Valley 2, Hut 7)

Chapter 11
Warming The Arctic

January 6th 2031, around 10:30 AM: "Hello loyal viewers, this is Dianne Black, up in the very cold and dark Coalton Valley 2.

We are here to report the very sad and senseless shooting of Don Bell, who, we believe had been mistaken for his brother, John Bell who, as head of security for James Coaltonstone's Mine Five, part of the Big Seven Goal Group, is alleged to have shot Ginger Goodwin. John Bell claims self-defense. While working at Mine Five, Don Bell mostly functioned in the capacity of Safety Manager for the mine, though sometimes he did assist his brother in security matter. Ginger Goodwin was Don Bel's assistant and was considered a hero after he prevented the morning crew from descending into Mine Five, only minutes before the December 22nd explosion, which James Coaltonstone's son, Bobby was found negligent and presently serving twenty-six year sentence of hard labor working in one of many Penal Colonies located in the Arctic Mine District.

Don Bell was transferred to the Coalton Valley 2 only days earlier and was to work in a supervisory role while the installation of assets, many of which have been transported from Pitville.

Chapter 12
The weather Is Not ours to change

January 6th 2031, around 12:30 PM: "So here we are Mathew living the dream. All dressed up, with Beautiful Dianne and her cameraman and you need to pay attention, so you can learn as much as you can from Jackson," James said as he looked over Jackson's camera to make that is his hair was combed over correctly.

"Actually Mathew could teach me a lot. He has an amazing eye for photography," Jackson replied.

"Now look at all these incredible ice sculptures, talk about luck. What do you think the chances are that a Supreme Being managed to carve all these pieces?" James asked.

"The Arctic is so vast and these Ice Sculptures are incredible but why are talking about a supreme being. I would have never thought of you being a religious or superstitious man, James," Dianne said.

"I suppose that I am still in shock that someone would actually kill Don Bell. He was a great safety manager," James said.

"Everyone is getting shot. Uncle James, when do you think they will shoot you?"

"Never,'

"They shot JFK, they shot Ginger, they shot Don, who else do you think will they shoot?"

"No one can really know these things. So as you can see we have a route here, and we are not the only ship. We usually dock at the work camp and the shipping containers pick up whatever they happen to be mining," James explained. Just think what is under all this ice, once we get to it, we, I mean me, will be richer than anyone's wildest dreams," James said.

"Are you going to build a new town here Uncle James?"

"Certainly not, we are going to warm things up and then try to build in the ground where it is warmer and less wind, and then we will build tunnels to connect to the harbors. Mina is a land of tunnels. They are safe, they are warm enough in the winter, cool enough in the summer, and they let the miners live right where they work," James explained.

"I guess that makes a lot of sense since Mina is on ten hour days and ten day weeks, they save time by not having to commute," Mathew said.

"Exactly," James said.

"Do families live in these cave like dwellings too?" Dianne asked.

"Yes, some do, some prefer to live on the surface. But out here you don't find many families, mostly just work crews," James explained.

"What happens if Earth's Axis changes tilt, will it affect us in a drastic way?"

"It might help us warm things up," James said. "If the change does affect the seasons we will just have to adjust. If the change affects the sky you will just have more interesting things to take pictures of, right? There are a lot of positive things which could come out of this melting of ice. That is why I am helping it along a bit, and I am sure that I am not the only one. We will just have to monitor everything very carefully from a distance. Dianne did you know that I will be donating a few wind mills and solar energy panels to those tiny settlements that are scattered about," Coaltonstone revealed.

"No I didn't know that. Such a thoughtful gift would make those people's lives a bit easier, I would think," Dianne replied.

"That is what I thought. I am not that concerned about the axis changing tilt. If it added to the extremeness of the weather patterns I would just have to get the authorities to round up more deportees and prisoners to work the mines that are located in hostile locations or may have a bit of radioactivity leaking," James explained.

Chapter 13
Flying around

"As you can see Dianne, while Pitville is going bust, there is a boom going on big time in Arctic Coal mining. As the Polar Ice Caps melt there will be more shipping lanes, more prosperity and most importantly, more happiness," James said.

"So when is the next nuclear explosion so you can melt more of the Polar Ice Cap?" Jackson asked.

"What are you talking about?" James said as he winked.

"Don't you think it is rather pathological to be nuking the Polar Ice Caps for material gain?" Jackson asked.

"And you think using this technology to blow up cities is less pathological?" James shot back.

"You are evading Jackson's point," Dianne interjected.

"You better believe I am," James replied. "Now, Dianne, I am sure it is obvious by now I am giving you an incredible opportunity to see the vastness of the Arctic. The best way to see the Arctic and my little oil wells, is to fly over them. The Arctic is the last frontier to explore, besides space, I suppose. As you can see... Hold on, there is a polar bear, quick get my rifle Mathew."

"You are not going to shoot it are you? Polar bears are pretty much endangered and that one isn't hurting anyone," Mathew said.

"What do you think Dianne, do you think I should shoot

the polar bear?"

"Absolutely not, James, please don't," Dianne begged.

"You are kidding, right Uncle James. You would never shoot a polar bear, unless it was in self-defense, right?"

"Jackson are you getting good shots? If it is a female she probably has cubs nearby," Dianne said.

"I am getting great shots."

"How did I find myself in a plane with a bunch of protesting environmentalists? It is the story of my life," James complained.

"You are having a good life; why not let the polar bear just live his or her life.

Chapter 14
Melting Ice Cap opens shipping lanes

"So what do you see when you look around, Mathew?" James asked

"I guess I see all kinds of oil drilling rigs and shipping containers," Mathew replied.

"And what else?" James asked.

"Fishing boats; I see lots and lots of fishing boats. I don't see many people on some of those boats." Mathew replied.

"Well people running fishing boats and oil rigs are pretty passé," James explained.

"I know what I see," Dianne interjected. "I see flags, lots and lots of flags. And all those flags are waving in the wind representing all the countries who want to break this all up. And the weird thing is all these rigs are so close to each other, yet they never seem to collide as if they all belong in parallel universes.

"Not yet anyway," James said.

"What do you mean not yet anyway?" Mathew asked.

"All these rigs and ships and flags haven't collided yet. I suppose right now they are satisfied with colluding with each other. I guess it is just a matter of time when all these interests conflict. The million dollar question is when.

"So is it true that a fifth of the earth's oil may be under all this and the Arctic is as big as Africa? Mathew asked.

"Pretty much; if all the countries that claim a stake in all this try to carve it up they may make it even more chaotic than it is right now," James said.

"Well it doesn't seem chaotic at all right now," Mathew said.

"Exactly, wait until the regulators takeover. Mathew you are witnessing history. One day all this ice on this ocean could be gone. And then it might seem to us more of an estuary than an actually ocean so that the most powerful will gain control of the expanding shipping routes and the least powerful may feel scorned and act like saboteurs," James explained.

"And that is why I hate politics," Jackson said.

"Well, the beauty of this situation right now is that there isn't any regulation. Soon this wild crazy place will be micromanaged to death, and anyone doing anything will be intimidated by the slippery arms of bureaucracy, ready to grab whatever it can in fees and taxes," George grumbled.

"How much tax do you pay, Mr. Coaltonstone?" Dianne asked.

"As little as I can dear, and you know why? Because I am smart. Why should I pay into a system which only grows more slippery arms to grab whatever it can from me and people like me, so they can just give it to unemployed bums. The system is set up just to intimidate and get its mob rule policies in place, then everything you try to do is stopped in its tracks accept the slippery arm that charges exuberant fees to let you apply to something that you are eligible for but don't qualify for. One is either forced to give before one even starts or one has to find a way to get around the entire aggravating mess." James snorted while he took a breath.

"I totally disagree with you," Jackson said.

"You would," James retorted. "You are working because you are funded by public money. All those bums that are getting in my way whenever and wherever I turn live only because they get public money. If it was up to me, I would have every single one of them shot the way that general in the south does. We don't need all those people ruining everything. My bots serve mankind politely and don't ever demand anything back when I ask them to do simple things. Coalton Valley 2 is going to be as automated as possible. We are going to have most of our coal transported by driverless trucks, and you will see how fast and efficient my town will be compared to Coalton Valley 1. And will all these new shipping lanes being opened up between North America and Eurasia, there will be an infinite demand for my coal,"

"But what happens to all those people who lose their jobs when they are replaced by your bots," Mathew asked.

"Shoot them if they can't adapt to the modern world. Shoot them before they breed even more malcontents," James retorted.

"

Chapter 15
Using Disputed Arctic Routes

"Why would anyone call my technology pathological? James asked looking hurt. "Mina has a right to use these new shipping routes just like any other country has that right. We are in a new era and we should be enjoying it. The Arctic is just a remnant of an old Ice Age, and who wants to go back to that?" James said defenselessly.

"Uncle James, it is just an article," Mathew said feeling guilty for his unintentional betrayal of his new step father.

"No it is not just an article. The Pitville Times rag is using my favorite step son's photographs. That is not what I was expecting from you."

"Well I actually sold the photos to Jackson and he sold them to different places. Jackson gives me royalties and then I send most of the money back to Grandma Watson," Mathew explained.

"How is your grandmother doing?"

"Not good and not bad. She is renting out the backyard to a couple who are expecting a baby."

"Are those people protestors, and are they planning to have the baby delivered in the backyard?

"I don't know. Grandma refuses to rent out my room t and she wants me to come back home as soon as I can. My guess is that the couple camping outside may rent my room if they decide to stay, and I will have a good reason to build the tree house that I have always wanted," Mathew said looking for a clue to how James really was feeling.

"That plan makes sense. You love flyking why wouldn't you want to nest in a tree like a bird,"

"Uncle James!"

"I don't see why your grandma doesn't move in with us," James said. "Does she still blame me for Mathew's death? The way she goes on about it you would think I set deliberately set up that boss bot to cause the accident. And the key word here is accident. It was all an accident," James said.

"I think Grandma understands that it was an accident but I think she wishes that you would have apologized more, instead of just offering everyone money and then disappearing," Mathew said.

"We can't keep looking backwards, Mathew or we will be not further ahead than all those losers we left behind in Pitville," James said.

Chapter 16
Melting Polar Ice Caps

"More pictures, more insults," James complained.

"You can't blame me for the article. Jackson says that if articles were positive they would never sell newspapers, Mathew protested.

"But you took the money didn't you?" James said accusingly.

"And you wouldn't have if you had been me?"

"You took credit for picture and I see you just use Watson in your byline not Watson Coaltonstone," Mathew said feeling even more guilty than he had before.

"I have been using Watson as my last name all my life, I just feel funny using Coaltonstone as part of my last name," Mathew said feeling very guilty.

"When I was fifteen I was making my own decisions too. That is what men do. You don't need to be apologizing to me for any decision you make, Mathew. You are the one who will have to live with the consequences," James said.

"Well it was the bot that calls himself IQ who made the decision," Mathew interjected.

"You are making that bot sound human. First of all how can a bot call himself anything at all? It is impossible for any bot to just make a decision like climbing up a tree to make friends with the one and only Mathew Watson-Coaltonstone. The bot gets the order somehow and then acts upon it, James asked.

"I don't know, he just introduced himself to me as IQ and asked me if I would like to be his friend," Mathew explained.

You were using my state of the art bot to lift you in the air to click a button on your camera to take that photo even though the explosion was supposed to be kept totally secret,"

"I didn't ask the bot to help me. He just climbed up into my tree house and we started talking and that is when we both saw the little mushroom cloud in the distance."

"I am not saying that I don't believe you Mathew, since you have never lied to me, so I don't have any cause to think that you would like to me, but your story is unbelievable," James said.

"I don't know why you say this is unbelievable; you are the one who goes on about artificial intelligence more than anyone else I have ever known," Mathew replied.

"But it is a theory. I always mean in theory," James retorted.

"Can't I just tell you what happened?" Mathew begged.

"I thought that was what you were doing, with or without my permission. And as I said before, when I was your age, I was my happiest when I did things my way," James said hoping that his tone was sounding a little more pleasant than it had been.

"I didn't take do this my way, the bot did. IQ just picked me up and I just clicked and I got this picture. And then he put he jumped out of the tree holding on to me, and then I got an email from Jackson asking me if I had any new photographs, and I sent him that one. It was almost like Jackson could see me or something," Mathew said feeling a little embarrassed that his story sounded so crazy.

"I believe what you are saying is what you believe to be true. And let us leave it at that. Who knows what happened to that bot when it was with Goodwin trapped in the Safety Chamber. When it comes to Ginger and technology, anything could happen," James said.

"You are not saying that you think Ginger is living in IQ," Mathew said.

"Of course I am not saying that," James retorted.

"Anyway the bot is really friendly and loves reciting passages out of the Rights Of Man to me when he visits me in my tree house," Mathew said.

"Those are guard bots, not data bots or photograph taking bots. I guess you know I know Ginger found a copy of Rights of Man in Safety Chamber E and read it to the bot, foolish thing to do," James said wishing that Ginger was still around so he could scold him for his foolishness.

"The bot just stood out on the ground and took the photo during the blast; you have to admit it is pretty amazing. You can see that explosion in space on the ground. This darkness is good for something. We see everything in the night sky but not much on the ground unless we have fires, flares, electric lights.

Chapter 17
James Is Being Criticized

"Good morning James," IQ said as he moved pieces on a chess board. Mathew forced himself out of bed.

"Good morning sleepy head, that was quite a climb up into your little fort in a tree. I brought you a housewarming present," James said as he placed the scales beside the chess board.

"You didn't need to bring me a present but it is really nice that you did," Mathew said.

"I really think that you needed these scales more than I do. These scales of balance will remind you, whenever you look at them, what it means to be a Coaltonstone and a Firestone," James explained.

"Is something wrong?" Mathew wondered out loud.

"There certainly is, as James placed a very thin newspaper on the table. Another article criticizing me, and what should be above the article, a photograph that you took of a polar bear which appears to be drowning, and in the background, hundreds of minese walking to work, wearing helmets with flashlights duct taped to them, complete with lunch pails in hand. Yes something is very wrong. I do not think these criticisms are fair. These failing newspapers are using me to sell newspapers and I resent this exploitation very much," James complained.

"But Uncle James you brought all those deported Minese out here. You set them up in houses that used to belong to people living in Pitville," Mathew protested.

"That is wrong. Those houses belong to me, the miners only live in those houses while they are employed. When they are no longer employed by my mine, for whatever reason, then I have a right to evict them. That is the law and the nature of the world. Those people will find somewhere to stay," James said as he tried to reassure Mathew, that things have always been this way.

"Jackson told me that a lot of the miners are living in the campgrounds near town," Mathew said.

"Not that horrible place that floods all the time, where we send out of towners," James asked.

"Yes that is the one. It floods all the time," Mathew said.

"That is why I offered to build a wall. A security wall could keep some of the water out, and people who might boat by won't have to feel offended when they see poor people.

Chapter 18
Pitville Times compares
James Coaltonstone to Hitler

"How could anyone compare me to Hitler," James said looking hurt.

"I don't know, the papers do it all the time."

"Mathew, you are not helping," James retorted.

"I meant they are calling people Hitler all the time. Not just you, that guy in the south is being referred to as Hitler too, all the time. That is what I meant," Mathew said.

" I don't think it is fair either Uncle James. I mean those people who are working for you are not complaining, so whose business is it of anyone's what you pay those people? They are not supposed to be in this country. They came here to mine. So that is what they are doing," Mathew said.

"Exactly, there is a war on, we need resources, the Minese can't be let go right now, because they could use information and other secrets against us but I am not institutionalized a holocaust. It will cost billions to move millions of illegals; so if illegals are in this country they need to pay their way. And those people don't have anything to lose the way I do. If I lost everything, I would be worse off than them, because I would be in debt for at least $10 billion dollars. You know what this like son. Having that clock ticking overhead, compound minute by minute, what does anyone know about that.

I may be one of the richest men on the planet, but I am also one of the most indebted. I am King of Coal, but imagine if they started to call me King of debt. Can you just imagine those robo calls coming in every second, tying up all my phones, demanding money now, or else. What do those people know about that?"

"Uncle James it is okay," Mathew said as he gave James a hug. "I understand a lot more than people think I do. Just because I am a kid, flyking around as if I didn't have a care in the world, like a bird, doesn't mean I have a bird-brain. Now that we are staying in Coalton Valley 2, do you think I could build a tree house in that big tree in the back yard," Mathew asked.

"I don't know. You are flyking around a lot; you hang out in trees a lot. Are you sure if I let you build a tree house you will still socialize with us who live on the ground," James said.

"Uncle James, if I get a tree house, you would be always welcome," Mathew said.

Chapter 19
G.O.D Shuts Down Coaltonstones' Disposal Wells.

" T hey just came here, without an appointment, they handed me this piece of paper ordering me to close down over two thousand disposal wells that I own," James said as he slammed his coffee cup down on the table, making some of the chess piece roll onto the floor with such force they bounced and then fell out of Mathew's tree house.

"Uncle James, you have to calm down," Mathew said as he motioned for IQ to get their check pieces.

"Your blood pressure must be through the roof Mr. Coaltonstone," IQ said.

"IQ get those check pieces, please," Mathew begged.

"Do you know what I could lose now?" James asked.

"I don't know, I suppose a lot," Mathew said.

"No, more than a lot. I could lose everything," James whimpered. "Everything, while the interest on the interest compounds second by second.

"I know how you feel, Uncle James," Mathew said.

"No you don't. How could you possibly know how I feel," As he pushed the table, Mathew was pushed into IQ who was just climbing up the ladder with the chess pieces,"

"Oh My God, Mathew, I am so sorry," James said.

"It is okay, IQ caught me," Mathew said.

"Sir, Mathew has lost his father when he was a child, his mother has been in a coma since the evening of December 29th.

Mathew's baby brother was only 2 days old at the time when his mother became comatose. That little baby has lost more than he or anyone will ever know. He will try thing as he gets older and everything will be much harder for him than mostly everyone else he knows. He might face a life of rejection and daily challenge. The only saving grace that protects that tiny guy is that he doesn't know yet how fragile his life really is. He doesn't know that he is defying death with every breath he takes. He doesn't know what it means to be what he is; an extreme preemie with less than 22 weeks in gestation. And while in gestation, before that state was rudely interrupted, he lost his father, and that little baby is now having to learn to lie in a fetal position, and does he cry? No. It is Doctor Knight who cries. The day Ginger was shot, Mathew lost a man who was partly his best friend and partly a surrogate father. Sir I think you owe both Mathew and his little brother a sincere apology," IQ said.

"No, it is Okay. Really," Mathew said.

"I am sorry Mathew. I really am. I know you have lost a great deal too and so has your little brother,"

"Yes, but Uncle James you saved his life. You have to see both sides of everything or you will drive us and everyone else nut," Mathew said as he tried to hug James.

"You just don't understand how serious this will be. I could lose everything, I mean everything. Everything is tied into everything. What I could lose could be huge. I just don't think those G.O.D. members have a clue. They said that they think that my wells contributed to some obscure earthquake in some God forsaken place that no one will ever care about. They said they suspect. They don't even know for sure. What I could lose is huge. And when I mean huge I do mean huge. All my assets are interconnected and intertwined with each other, because they are all used as collateral for all my projects. When one of my assets is taken out of my stack of assets, it could be like a whole house of cards falling down, not just on me, but on everyone who depends on me," James said as he was trying not to panic. "And besides that it is embarrassing. Those numbskulls from G.O.D. don't have anything close to what I have to lose. Do they know what it will cost me to have all my wells shut down? The domino effect will be huge, just huge. And just because an earthquake has upset some Eskimos living in igloos or whatever they live in these days," James said as he pouted his face was turning red.

"It will just take a minute, roll up your sleeve and I will make sure that your blood pressure is in the normal range," IQ said.

"What kind of bot are you? Stop ordering me about! I am the one who is supposed to be ordering you about," James said. "What is wrong with everyone? I am the one who is supposed to be giving out orders, and today all I am getting is orders from faceless bureaucrats and now from a stupid bot."

While James was yelling Mathew was sure he just saw a tear drop falling down his cheek.

Chapter 20
Cold Feet Mountain Walks

March 15th 2031, around 4:00 AM: "Deep Coal is angry. Cold Feet Mountain is about to roll. Run everyone run," IQ said as loud as his hardware allowed.

"Jackson, can you hear me," Dianne yelled through the door.

"Of course I can hear you. You are yelling at me through the door. Is it time to get up already? I thought I just fell asleep."

"Something awful is happening. I think it is an earthquake or something. Can't you feel it. It sounds like the mountain is roaring but that is impossible. Get up Jackson. Can you hear me? Get up; we got to get out of here."

"Wait, I have my earphones on."

"Can you hear me? Hurry!"

"I am not sure if I am hearing what you were hearing. I am hearing a lot of screaming.

"Hurry, Jackson. We have to get out of here, something is happening to the mountain,"

"What? Why are you bitching at me so early in the morning. It is 4:10 AM,"

Jackson grabbed his huge duffel bag that was already full with towels belonging to the hotel, his camera, phone and wallet. He grabbed the van keys from the table and left everything else behind. Dianne had already grabbed her purse and house coat. They ran through the empty hotel hallway hand in hand. They ran down the stairs and through the glass doors as fast they could. They jumped into the van and were thankful that the road was as empty as the hotel's hallways. How they managed to drive away in the nick of time, they would never know. The mountain came tumbling down and buried the west side of Coalton Valley 2 which included the bank, the hotel and twenty-five huts. The roar of the mountain was deafening.

"Don't look back Di."

"We are journalists."

"Yes, but we aren't heroes. We can look back later."

"All those people buried. It was lucky you were awake, what were you doing?"

"I was having a bit of an argument with Coaltonstone on Twitter. Then I heard a voice coming from somewhere yelling that Deep Coal was angry. We were both deleting our tweets while laughing at each other. We started around 3:00 AM. It started with a comment from him about my past loves in war zones. Then I could feel the earth shaking, and right after we escaped from there that awful noise. And seconds later everything there seems to be gone. The bank, the hotel and those little cottages, they are all gone.

"You know Di, I would have still been in there, it happened all so fast,"

"Yeah, you lucked out, I was about to leave you there, after you accused me of bitching. I am the boss you know. If I were a man would you call me a bitch? Of course not.

"I am sorry."

"Where are your clothes besides those disgusting underwear?" Dianne asked.

"I suppose they are all under the rubble. I put all the important stuff in the duffle bag. Everything is gone. It happened so fast. We need to get out of this dust. Where should we go, Di?"

"Drive East I suppose until you see something open. A donut shop or something. You will have to put on my spare wardrobe until we get you some clothes."

Chapter 21
Coaltonstone Visits Cold Feet Mountain

March 15th 2031, around 5:45 AM: "W hat do you mean Cold Feet Mountain just fell on the west side of Coalton Valley 2 and the men trapped in the mountain are probably dead?" James asked.

"Sir, it was the most massive rock slide in Tut Island's history. The wedge that was hanging broke away and an estimated 90 million tons of liquid rock came down in seconds and crushed the west side of Coalton 2," David Bell said.

"And there was no warning?"

"Just the usual tremors we feel in the cave every day. Hold on there was a report that some of the survivors heard a voice screaming around 4:00 in the morning, that Deep Coal was angry and everyone needed to evacuate. That was ten minutes before the actual slide which happened in seconds,"

"Who was it?" James asked.

"We don't know. I suppose people thought he was a drunk," Dave said.

"There is an estimated ninety people buried in the rubble and maybe another twenty men buried in the mine. The railway track is gone but the train was saved. A young man was able to run around the rock and flag down the train before it crashed into the slide, sir. Our mining operation's entrance is buried in rock and we must assume that the men trapped inside are dead, or for all managerial purposes, will be dead soon. Most of those men were just deportees, sir. The area has been yellow ribboned," Dave said.

"So your train still has a human driver?" Dianne and Jackson asked at the same time.

"Of course it does."

"Can your driverless technology respond to random human hand signals, in a situation like this?"

"Obviously not in the same way humans can communicate to each other. . The boss bots usually are the ones who control and communicate to our trains," James replied.

"What would have happened if the train had been driverless and a human tried to stop the train with nothing more than just hand signals?" Dianne asked.

"Now, Dianne you know how I hate to speculate when I am speaking to the press."

Chapter 22
Coalton Valley 2 Disaster

March 15th 2031; around 5:55 AM: "This is Dianne Black, with the PPZ, reporting live from the Coalton Valley 2 Disaster at the very foot of Cold Feet Mountain. Good morning and thank you for joining me. I just had the shock of my life. I heard a voice ordering us to run, and I woke up Jackson who was sleeping in another room, in the same hotel. I mean we were sleeping separately but close by.

"It is okay, Dianne, we understand and thank God you are okay and may I say that you both look stunning in your housecoats, but you must be cold." Steve said. "Please carry on."

"Thank you Steve If it weren't for Jackson, I could have been under the rubble. Steve, I owe you my life."

"Hold on Di, you were the one that woke me up. So I think it is I, who owe you my life."

"Look you two, you are both sounding incredibly traumatized and look incredibly cold. I feel cold just looking at you. At least Di has her slippers and house coat on but you Jackson you are wearing a super tiny house coat and it looks very girlish,"

"Obviously it is Di's spare housecoat, I don't waste space carrying housecoats or pajamas when I am on assignment, Steve," Jackson replied.

"Can you go on?

"Certainly, as you know I am a war correspondent, and have had many near misses during my career. I have been to many war and death zones over the years, but today was supposed to be a celebration so as you can see we were not prepared for such a disaster. But no one ever is, unless they are called to one. Let us see if we can get a closer look. Sir, thank you so much. A kind man has just handed Jackson a beautiful parka and matching boots and even a pair of socks.

"Di, take a break come back in five," Steve ordered from the PPZ office thousands of miles away.

"Dear viewers, after these important messages from our sponsors we will be back with a closer look at this tremendous rock slide which some experts believe could be close to 90 million tons of liquid rock which has buried the Western Edge of Coalton Valley 2, including the only bank."

"Quick Jackson; we have five minutes for you to put on those boots and coat and walk to the edge of the rock slide,"

"Di, what is that?"

"Where?"

"Up there, in all that dust?"

"It looks like a giant eagle taking photographs. No, only person that I know who would be taking photographs in a flyke suit is Mathew Watson."

"Mathew? What is he doing here, I thought he told me that he was going to stay with his grandmother for a while," Dianne said.

"He always tells me that too, but something tells me that his grandmother would not be allowing him to flyke around taking photographs as he pleases, dropping in on classes through his computer as he pleases, and making money selling some pretty incredible photos. That part his grandmother probably would be happy with but never would admit it. He was probably here for the same reason that we were all here; to celebrate the opening of Coalton Valley 2, and now look, so much has been lost," Jackson said. Feeling more numb than cold.

"Let's get closer."

"Phone him," Dianne ordered. "Tell him to get down here on the double. What would his mother think?" Dianne said.

"His mother is fighting her own battle," Jackson said.

393

"We are live," Steve said. "Why aren't you dressed, Jackson."

"Thank God," Jackson said.

"I mean we are on the air," Steve clarified.

"The Watson boy is up there flyking, taking photos. We are zooming in on him," Jackson replied.

"Let me look," Dianne ordered. "Oh my God, I can see people's hands, and heads. Everything is so horrible; I just want to close my eyes to make it all go away."

"I really need to take a break Steve. It is all getting to me now," Dianne said before she collapsed.

Chapter 23
Mystery Around Rock Slide

March 15th 2031, around 6:15 AM: "Hello Dianne," James Coaltonstone said as he stepped from behind the rock slide. "This is just terrible. Horrific. But you look ravishing and I want to let you know I deleted all of the tweets from our early morning spat,"

"Well I feel awful, so don't remind me about that silly twitter thing, can't you see what it really matters. Ninety people are estimated to be dead, twenty men are presumed dead in the mine, and I just fainted in front of the whole planet watching our broadcast.

"I don't think the whole planet is watching your broadcast, I am sure they are waiting for my next tweet," James said.

"You are the most aggravating…" Dianne blurted out.

You are the same old Dianne Black. No one would ever know that you just fainted, and Jackson you need to put on some clothes on before you get frost bitten in places that matter.

"Are we still live?" Dianne asked as she picked herself up from the ground. "Are you saying those things while we are on air?"

"We certainly are and yes I am." James said.

"Is that Mathew I see flyking in all that dust. A boy should not see what I just saw."

"Well that boy appears to be a natural photo journalist," Jackson said.

"That boy is going to be an accountant, just like his mother. It is a much safer job," James interjected.

"So how is Christina?" Dianne asked.

"The same," James said. "She doesn't seem to want to wake up," James explained.

"Which means?" Dianne asked.

"She will be okay. It will take time. We have all been through a lot. This is terrible. I have never seen anything so awful. We might have to leave this as it is because it is all so unstable. That is what the experts from G.O.D are telling me. They are saying that this slide is just huge, really huge. A terrible tragedy to always remember; I am going to build something very special here. That is what I will do," James said.

"So what are you going to do? Start printing out tickets stamped with your brand," Dianne asked.

"Christina, there is no need to be unkind. We will rebuild. There is nothing wrong with the mine, it just needs another entrance. We will have to bring in some track and rebuild the railway. Luckily a young man, I have yet to thank and promote, saved the train from colliding in all this rock and death. It is all so terrible, but at least we managed to save the train, the cargo and 92 passengers and one classified pot that we managed to salvage from Mine Five. The other classified bot seems to be running amok, and if Goodwin were still alive I would blaming him."

"James, whenever you speak I just have more questions. I don't know where to start," Dianne said.

"How about staying focus on this awful rockslide. And think about all the people who have just lost their lives or who were injured," Jackson said. "For once let us think of the victims of all this."

"But those people are just deportees; just illegals," James said.

"Just take one question at a time, and remember here, like in Mina, we work on a ten hour clock and a ten day week." James recommended.

"First question, who were the passengers on your train," Dianne asked.

"Replacements," James replied.

"Replacements? That was fast," Dianne said as she took notes.

"That is not what I meant and why are you taking notes? I did not give you permission to take notes. The Minese were not safe in Pitville even though we are not at war with the Minese people just with the Minese government, like usual the civilians are always the first casualties in these conflicts," James explained.

"Actually we are at war with the Minese. The Minese are mostly here illegally, and are taking jobs from the hard working people of Pitville," Jackson said as both James and Dianne stared at him in disbelief. "I think that is how the Pitville Chapter of G.O.D worded it," Jackson added.

"Anyway, the Minese are now officially deportees, which is a shame. They are better trained and are more experienced in Long Walling than every single one of our local people. My guard bots are networking with my drone watchers and of course my whistle bots. Our boss bots will be performing a supervisory role over the deportees while they remain under our jurisdiction," James explained

"Where will they live?" Dianne asked.

"In the vacant houses that we managed to salvage from the Pitville District housing project, James explained."

"But aren't those buildings occupied?" Dianne asked as she continued writing notes.

"Of course not. How can those houses be occupied while they are being transferred to my new town. Anyway I own those structures. It is up to me to decide when they are vacant," James replied.

"I thought the Pitville Miners dissembled their homes there and reassembled them here, so that they could live and work here," Dianne said, looking troubled.

"Yes, well the Pitville Miners were eligible for these new jobs in Coalton Valley 2, but most of them did not qualify; they did not speak Minese. They may feel those homes are theirs but I actually own them. Many of the minese miners enjoy living in caves and are from the cave district in their homeland. As you know this land is home to many caves which could be fabricated into homes to the best of our ability." James explained.

"I don't understand. The official language spoken on Tut Island is English; Pitville Miners have had experience long walling in Mine Five. How do you justify working with the Minese when we are at war with Mina?" Dianne asked.

"We are not at war with the Minese people, I certainly am not. Our government and their government are at war with each other, I must go, lovely chatting."

"And what about all that anthracite coal that you have been exporting to Mina, a country we are technically at war with?"

"As I said the coal is to help the Minese people and I have nothing against the Minese people," James Coaltonstone said.

"So, dear viewers you heard this straight from the famous King of Coal; James Coaltonstone."

"You, mean this was live?" James asked feeling vulnerable and violated.

"Yes it certainly is."

"How do you justify all this?" Dianne asked.

"Why do you keep making me repeat myself? We are at war with the Minese government not the people, and as I said before, Dianne, my new guard bots function at their best when they speak minese. Dianne we are in the middle of the worst rock slide in Tut Island history, and we should really be discussing these side issues at a later date," James said.

"Just one more question, please. Aren't tut island tax payers who are paying for these roads that your driverless trucks use to transport your coal and what have you to Mina?"

"I suppose so. Dianne look! My Minese are helping to remove the rock.. They just got here and are already helping with the rescue. I think I see some of those awful protestors helping to take rocks away and they have thrown their signs into a pile. Maybe we should set them alight for warmth. I have no idea where our rescue staff are? Some of them were refusing to come here because of the little radiation problem we are rumored to have, as if the waste wasn't in indestructible containers.

"Hold on the phone is ringing, It better be important, It is Mathew.

"Mathew what is wrong?"

"Look out the rubble, can you see a little toddler sitting on the rubble. She is crying her eyes out, can you guys help her?

Dianne, is that a little baby I see on the rubble?" James Coaltonstone asked as he took his binoculars out of his jacket pocket.

Dianne grabbed them from him. "Mathew just phoned us to report that he could see her from the sky,"

"I thought Mathew said that he was flyking to his grandmothers and help her out a bit," James said.

Mathew saw the baby too and decided to take a few photographs

"My God, we have to get to her. She must be terrified. Where are her parents, I wonder?

"Where do you think they might be Di?" Jackson asked then immediately regretted his outburst. "We have to get to her."

"Dianne be careful, I have got her," Jackson said.

"How would you like to come with us, until all this gets sorted out?" Dianne asked.

"The little girl cried hysterically as she called out "Mommy, Daddy".

"Isn't it amazing that all these people are now working together to get people out of the rock slide. The same people who were at each other's throats only a few days ago. Are your parents lost in that rubble?"

The little girl nodded and continued to cry.

"Now for a message from our sponsors," Steve interjected as he stared at his screen oblivious to the growing number of PPZ colleagues who had been crowding into his small office.

THE END

Produced by S.E. McKenzie Productions
First Print Edition September 2016

Enquiries: 1(778)992-2453
Mailing Address:
S. E. McKenzie Productions
168 B 5th St.
Courtenay, BC
V9N 1J4

Email Address:
messidartha@aol.com

http://www.amazon.com/SarahMcKenzie/e/B00H9RWX48/

ABOUT THE AUTHOR

Sarah McKenzie lives on Vancouver Island and is a graduate from Thompson Rivers University: School of Business and Economics. Areas of study (Management studies 2007) (Accounting Technician 2012).